Kamikaze Boys

Jay Bell Books
www.jaybellbooks.com

Acknowledgements

Writing is said to be lonely work, and it sure can look that way from the outside. But if I could teleport into my office all the people that help my books come to life, you'd see that it isn't lonely at all. Linda Anderson would be there the most, surrounded by red pens drained of ink and a good number of empty M&M wrappers. Andreas would be in the corner, painting covers for books I haven't dreamed up yet, while Katherine Coolon and Kira Miles occasionally pop in to lift me up or smack me down, depending on how my ego is fairing that day. Zate Lockard would be there as well, waiting patiently by the door, since my books never see the light of day without his say. Occasionally my mom would barge in, hopefully with a vacuum cleaner to take care of the mess around me. (And no, I don't live at home anymore, but a guy can fantasize, right?) Add in all the wonderful readers and reviewers, and you'd end up with a workspace that is more crowded and much happier than any corporate cubical farm. In short, thank you one and all for making my long hours of toil feel like one big picnic.

For Kati, who once saved me from three very nasty bullies, and who has had my back ever since.

Kamikaze Boys

by Jay Bell

Chapter One

A concrete field stretched out before David Henry, a herd of secondhand cars idle in the afternoon sun. Among them was one shiny and new—the bull among cows—standing next to it the person determined to kick his ass. David supposed he could still turn around, flee back into the school and choose a different exit like he had the day before. The problem was, there was no avoiding the ten-minute walk between school and home, and so much could go wrong along the way.

One way or another, he had to pass by the school parking lot to get home. Yesterday he had thought the busy street traffic would hide him. He had almost made it too. But before reaching his neighborhood, a car had zoomed up behind him, engine roaring and horn blaring, voices howling in amusement as he raced off down the street. David had run across a perfectly manicured yard and hid behind its two-story house for nearly an hour, but even that humiliation was better than a bloody nose.

Today was another chance for the bullies to catch up to him, or if he was lucky, for him to get away. David stood in the school doorway, uncertain what action to take if any, until one of the students swarming around him hissed at him to move and shoved him from behind. David stumbled out into a mild Kansas afternoon, the kind he used to love when he was a kid. Too distracted to notice who had pushed him, he glanced over the slowly departing cars to see if Chuck Bryl had spotted him. Beady black eyes locked onto his. Chuck had seen him, all right. Now, even if David reentered the school, they would know they had him on the run. And they would find him.

Chuck wasn't the most popular guy in school, but he had more status than David did. For one thing, Chuck had friends; a couple of them were flanking him now, eyes hungry for a show. Their lanky frames only made Chuck look more toadish, like a frog squatting between two tall flowers.

Or like a fat troll, which was exactly the description that had landed David in this mess. These foolishly courageous words had escaped his lips in the middle of fourth period math. David's head had been bowed—as always—while he covertly read a fantasy novel hidden behind his precalculus book. He was just reaching the end of a chapter when Chuck had reached over and grabbed the novel, taking one look at the cover before tossing it to the floor.

"Faggot," Chuck had muttered, and not for the first time.

David's face had burned as he reached down to pick up the book. On the cover was a picture of a longhaired man clutching at a white horse. David had known the stupid cover with all its lavender swirls would attract attention. He liked the book anyway, but felt angry that he couldn't even read without people recognizing him for what he was. So angry, in fact, that he didn't think about the consequences of the words he said next.

"Fat troll."

David's bravery had swiftly fled to be replaced by fear, because he knew Chuck would be waiting for him outside after school. And Chuck was glaring at David now, or squinting, as he always seemed to be. Maybe he needed glasses. Maybe he was just a big nerd inside that was terrified of being discovered. One thing was for sure: As Chuck leaned against his shiny new sports car, he appeared more stocky than fat. David had never noticed how broad his shoulders were or considered how hard toppling Chuck's heavy frame would be.

Not that he was going to fight. God only knew what David was going to do besides whimper as they pummeled him.

He could run. They would laugh and they would chase, but David could run. He glanced to his left, toward the street, to see another of Chuck's friends, the one with the long grungy hair. That escape route was blocked. The right led toward the sports field behind the school, dangerously deserted by now, so David kept moving forward, hoping to duck between parked cars and escape.

But Chuck was through playing games and stepped into the center of the lane. "Hey faggot. I think you and I need to talk."

"What?" David's voice came out as a squeak.

Chuck pushed the dry, thin hair from his forehead and smiled, already knowing the battle was won. "You owe me an apology."

The other guys chuckled.

A car honked from behind. David jumped and moved out of the lane, bringing him closer to Chuck's car. Cursing his stupidity, he fought the urge to cry. He should have gone back into the school and pleaded with a teacher to drive him home. That would have made him feel even more pathetic than yesterday, but he would have been safe.

Chuck and his friends circled around him, blocking David in. He turned, Chuck's car at his back, not daring to take his eyes off any of them. Maybe David could still talk his way out of this. "Listen, I shouldn't have called you a troll. I was just—"

Chuck shoved him. David had been right: Someone who weighed that much had a lot of force at their disposal. David stumbled backward, arms pinwheeling, but his backpack threw him further off balance and he fell. He landed ass first on the hood of Chuck's car, then slipped onto his hands and elbows.

The guys surrounding him sucked in air between their teeth. They knew what was coming. David did too.

"Get the fuck off my car, faggot!"

"Sorry, I—"

"I said get off!"

Chuck was moving forward, fists balled as David braced himself for the inevitable.

"Hey, Chucky!"

An arm wrapped around Chuck's neck, pulling him down as if he weighed nothing before subjecting him to a good-natured noogie. "What's up, Chuck? Causing trouble again?"

"Get off me!" Chuck pulled away and turned, scowling, to see who he was facing.

Connor Williams. If their school had a bigger monster than Chuck, it was Connor. Big was the right word too, not necessarily in regards to height, but Connor had the mature build of a college guy. In fact, Connor might be college age, if the rumors were true, but for now he was still a high school senior. His green eyes were amused as he playfully shoved Chuck, and for a moment the sun reflected off his buzzed blonde hair, making Connor appear like a deranged sun god.

David didn't remember seeing Chuck hanging out with Connor before, but this meant his situation had gone from bad to a freaking disaster.

"Fuck off, Williams," Chuck mumbled, keeping his eyes down and glaring at the asphalt. His friends, whom Connor hadn't even acknowledged, shifted uncomfortably. David didn't blame them. Everyone knew what a psychopath Connor Williams was.

"What's going on?"

David realized that Connor was addressing him and felt the blood drain from his face. He opened his mouth to speak, but nothing came out.

"This asshole," Chuck said, having recovered, "just threw himself on my car."

Connor raised an eyebrow. "Weird. To me it looked like you pushed him."

As if to demonstrate, Connor shoved Chuck again. This time he didn't seem to be playing.

Chuck stumbled but managed to stay standing. "He's a faggot!" he said, as if this made a difference.

There was a good chance it would. If one word could turn others against him, David knew that word was faggot. He had worn the label for most of his teenage life. By junior high, everyone seemed to have figured it out, even before David did.

Connor looked at David. "Yeah?" Then he cocked his head, gave a crazy smile, and turned back to Chuck. "Funny, 'cause I'm a faggot too."

Chuck swallowed. "Shut up."

"No, seriously," Connor insisted. "Push me too." He moved to the front of Chuck's car, his back to the hood and his arms spread wide. "Go on. Push me. Push the faggot."

Chuck shook his head and fumbled in his pocket for the keys while mumbling something about having to go. His friends, following his lead, piled into the car. David moved out of the way, but Connor stayed where he was, turning to stare at Chuck through the windshield. The engine came to life, but still Connor stood his ground, as if daring Chuck to run him over. Just when the situation was about to reach critical mass, Connor stepped aside, and Chuck sped out of the parking lot.

David wished his adrenaline would let up. His heart was still thudding, his body drenched in sweat. Connor turned toward him, increasing the temptation to run.

"Do you have a car?" Connor said.

"No," David croaked.

"Want a ride?"

David stared at him, waiting for some bizarre twist to this offer, but Connor no longer looked as insane as he had a minute ago. His expression was serious, which only made it more intimidating. The hint of stubble on his chin and the scar running from his jaw to his Adam's apple reminded David of the legends that followed Connor. If he got in that car, Connor would probably drive him to the edge of town to play some hellish game with him. David imagined himself running through the woods, fleeing from Connor's maddened laughter and crazy green eyes.

"No. Thanks. Thank you."

David turned and walked away while keeping his head down, certain that Connor would call out or follow him in his car. The tension lasted until he reached the edge of the parking lot. Only when he crossed to the other side of the street did David dare glance back. Connor Williams was nowhere to be seen.

The condos where David lived weren't far from school, the walk just long enough for him to gain control of his nerves. What a mess he had gotten himself into! If he could travel back in time, he'd keep his mouth shut in math class. Or maybe he would go even further back and leave that book at home. Then again, seeing someone push Chuck around was almost worth it.

He remembered the first time he had seen Connor. David's ninth grade history class was in the library doing a project on ancient civilizations. The girl David had been partnered with had pointed across the worn desks to the old card catalog that no one used anymore. Standing there, flipping through the index cards with his back to them, was Connor.

"He used to go to the same junior high as me," the girl had said. "That was before we moved to this side of town. He's psycho. They sent him to juvenile hall for a whole year."

"Why was he in juvie?" David had asked.

He still remembered the girl's excited expression, as if she had been hoping David would ask. "He tried to kill his dad!" she whispered. "Almost did, too. The guy survived, but he's a cripple now."

"Nuh-uh!"

"Wait until he turns around. He's got this scar on this throat. A couple of guys tried to kill him while he was in juvie. Connor nearly beat them to death."

Ignoring his assignment, David had sat and waited for Connor to turn around. When he finally did, David was surprised at how human he appeared—handsome, even. Then David had noticed the scar and knew the stories were true.

He shook away the memories and hoped that, like most people in school, Connor would forget he existed. Besides, Connor had seemed more interested in messing with Chuck. Maybe Chuck had opened his mouth at the wrong time, attracting the anger of a bigger fish in their little pond. High school was vicious, as David—the lowest on the food chain—knew all too well.

Lowest except for Gordon, maybe. And there he was, sitting on the front steps of the condo and waiting for David to come home, just as he always did. Gordon was like a kid brother to him. Only a year's difference in age separated them, but the chubby cheeks and goofy bowl haircut made Gordon seem younger than he was. He was homeschooled too, which added to his naïveté. Gordon was bright, but so socially awkward that David felt cool by comparison.

David never figured out why Gordon's parents kept him home. They weren't overly religious and seemed like fairly normal people. Maybe their school days had been rough too, and they wanted to spare their son the same pain. Sometimes David felt a little sorry for Gordon, but on days like today, he was envious. At least it was May. David just had to make it a little longer until summer break.

"I think I understand why we can't steal the dragon armor from the orcs," Gordon said, standing up and unselfconsciously tugging the wedgie from his cargo shorts. He held up a video game strategy guide. "We haven't completed the quest for the crystal chalice yet."

"I thought it was optional," David said.

"It is, but not if you want to get the dragon armor."

David unlocked the condo's front door and held it open. So what if Gordon was a little weird? At least David could be comfortable around him. Much of that comfort came from knowing what to expect. He and Gordon had their daily rituals, tried and true. They would grab a juice box from the fridge, go down to his room, and David would play video games while Gordon poured over his most recent strategy guide. He treated these guides like bibles, reacting with shock if David ever went against their advice. David suspected that Gordon enjoyed the guides more than the actual games.

This routine was rarely broken. Only occasionally would the fantasy games and books inspire them to go out for a hike. On these rare outings they would walk through the woods, discussing plots or pretending they were on the verge of crossing over to a magical realm. But usually they just stuck to their familiar habits.

David opened the door to his room and breathed out a sigh of relief. This was his sanctuary, the place where the madness of the world receded and he could relax. The blinds were pulled, as usual, to create the illusion of night outside. The walls were dark too, every square inch covered with posters and pages torn from magazines. Some had to do with David's hobbies, others were pictures of remote locations he wished to visit someday: Egypt, Greece, China—anywhere but here. Then there were the images of male models, barely noticeable among all the rest. Not that David had anything to hide.

David plugged in the bar lights—strings of Christmas lights with plastic jalapeños covering every bulb that cast a mellow glow over the room. Gordon pushed past him and took his usual seat on the edge of the bed. Although he sat in the same spot every day, no butt-shaped indent had formed in the mattress quite yet.

Gordon had been the first person David came out to. He had paused the game they were playing and blurted:

"I'm gay."

Gordon had scrunched up his face and replied, "Well, I'm not."

And that had been that. They had kept playing games, and the topic had never come up again. Of course Gordon had loaned him the fantasy novel with the lavender cover. The main character of that book was gay, by no coincidence. They didn't discuss this, but David took it as a supportive gesture.

"I'm looking forward to playing today," David said. He meant he was glad that Gordon was his friend, but saying it this way was easier.

"I'm excited too." Gordon flipped through the pages of his guide. "There's a couple of good treasures on the chalice quest that I think will help us later on."

The game console hummed and purred as it booted up.

"You're lucky you don't have to go to school, you know."

"I know," Gordon replied, even though he didn't.

"Any plans for the weekend?"

Gordon sat up straight, a rare event. "I got a birthday card in the mail from my aunt. I haven't opened it yet, but she always sends me a couple hundred dollars."

"Sweet!"

"Yeah. I thought we could go to the mall on Sunday. The new Final Fantasy just came out, and we can hit the used bookstore across the way. Think you can get the car?"

David nodded. He hadn't figured out what to get Gordon for his birthday, but maybe he would find something while they were out.

They spent the next hour gaming, David working the controller while Gordon split his attention between the screen and the book in his lap. Usually this was enough to let David forget his troubles, but today his mind kept wandering back to the confrontation in the parking lot. Chuck was likely to be twice as pissed tomorrow.

"Let's call it a day," David said at the next save point.

Gordon looked at the clock, knowing they had another half hour before David's father came home, but he didn't say anything. He loitered another ten minutes, discussing what they would do tomorrow, before he finally left.

David closed the door to his room and counted under his breath until he heard the front door close. Then he turned on his stereo, set his MP3 player to shuffle, and cranked up the speakers. He loved to dance. The music didn't matter as much as the rhythm, as long as the beat was strong and he could move to it. Hip hop, metal, pop, anything. On the really bad days, dancing was his ultimate cure, a surefire way to exercise and exorcise his demons. David loved to freak out when he danced, not doubting for a second that bullies would line up around the corner if they could see the way he flailed his arms and spun around, but he didn't care. He was home. David unplugged the bar lights and moved his body, lost in a world devoid of light but filled with sound.

"Did you set the table?"

David nodded at his father and finished filling his glass with tap water. Then he took his seat at the small, narrow table. For a piece of furniture, it wasn't very optimistic. The table could only sit two comfortably, implying the owner wasn't planning on guests or a larger family.

When David's parents had divorced, he had pictured a lazy bachelor's life with his father. Richard Henry would finally loosen his tie and sit with his son in front of the TV every night as they picked at their microwave dinners. David had assumed his mother's nagging and constantly pursed lips had made his dad a starchy person, but his dad had only gotten worse since she left.

His father set a plate in front of him before taking his seat. Pasta with tomato sauce, as usual. On the weekend, his father cooked a big pot of pasta sauce, divvying it into freezer bags. When he came home on weekdays, he would boil a pot of water for the pasta and toss the sauce bag in the microwave. If his dad was feeling energetic, he would make a chopped salad. David would prefer having pizza delivered or going out for a greasy bag of fast food, but neither was as cost-effective as the endless parade of pasta.

"How was school?"

"The usual," David answered between bites. Despite his lack of enthusiasm for the cuisine, all that dancing had made him hungry.

"Only a few weeks until summer break. Any sign of your grades?"

"I don't know. Straight A's? Isn't that what I always get?"

His fathered peered at him from over his glasses, chewing carefully before dabbing his carefully trimmed mustache with a napkin. "Last semester you got a ninety-one in math. That's two points away from being a B."

"Well, math isn't my best subject. Especially this year."

"Do you find precalculus challenging?"

"Boring is more like it."

Of course having his desk next to the biggest asshole in school didn't help. If only his dad knew what he went through every day, but David couldn't imagine them discussing it. Then again, why not? That's what parents were for, and it sure beat talking about grades.

David set down his fork. "Did anyone pick on you in school?"

"Are you having trouble?"

David shook his head. "I was just wondering what it was like for you."

"Is that why your grades are slipping?"

He sighed. Why couldn't his father just talk to him instead of treating him like a problem that needed to be solved? "My grades are as good as they're going to get. But yeah, there are guys at school who make my life hell. I don't want to go back."

His father wiped his mouth again and shook his head. "You can't be homeschooled with Gordon. I know you think that sounds like fun, but his education isn't as rounded. He certainly won't be getting into a decent university."

"I don't want to be homeschooled," David said, his voice starting to rise. "I just want people to leave me the fuck alone!"

As starchy as his dad was, he never had been bothered by what his mother used to call "foul language." David used it sparingly enough that when he did, his father took him seriously. "I can talk to your teachers if you want," he said. "No one has the right to pick on you."

"It won't help," David said.

"Why not?"

"Because you can't change who people are. It's human nature to hate anything that's different."

His father tossed his napkin on his empty plate and sighed. "Is this about your sexuality?"

"I don't know. Maybe." David hated it when he called it that. Sexuality sounded so clinical. But he was grateful that his father didn't have a problem with it, being too logical and pragmatic to have any objections. The truth was, David didn't know why people hated him. Faggot and gay were fairly general insults, but with him, people seemed to mean it. He wasn't particularly feminine, hadn't been caught doing something with another guy, but people assumed he was gay anyway. And it was true, which meant he was alone. He didn't know any other students that were gay, at least not openly. And what Connor Williams had said today was just to pick a fight with Chuck. David was sure of that. People said a lot of things about Connor, but not that he was into guys.

"Listen, son. There are a lot of ignorant people in the world who make life unpleasant for the rest of us. If you want revenge, keep your head down and study. Make something of your life.

Then, when they're hauling away the garbage from the curb of your house every week, you'll be glad you didn't sink to their level."

For his dad, the advice wasn't terrible, but what his father didn't understand is that turning the other cheek was likely to get David hit on that side as well. He just didn't get it, but he was in for a rude awakening. When they sat at this table to eat dinner tomorrow, his father would see the bruises and cuts, and David would at least have the satisfaction of proving him wrong. Maybe tomorrow things would finally change.

Chapter Two

Connor lit another cigarette, considering the ghostly wisps of smoke surrounding him before reaching over to roll down the passenger-side window. Sitting in the car for the better part of an hour—having cut sixth period class—had left the oxygen level dangerously low. In the corner of his eye the school doors opened, the students pouring out. Connor turned down the radio, the knob coming off like it always did, before he turned his attention to the oncoming crowd.

Before long Chuck came out surrounded by more minions than usual. Connor allowed himself a cocky smile. Chuck could bring all the reinforcements he wanted. It wouldn't make a difference. When the leader was scared, the troops were terrified, and Connor knew just how afraid Chuck was. Regardless, he leaned his seat almost all the way back, Chuck and his lackeys passing without noticing him. They headed for the silver Mazda RX-8 that David Henry had taken a spill over yesterday. Chuck even wiped the hood with his sleeve as if the handprints were still there, before he turned his attention to the school.

Connor followed his gaze, shifting his seat back up and searching for the same person. Out the door David came, walking down the lane without making an attempt to hide or run. Except he wasn't feeling brave or planning to make a stand—that was clear from his body language. His lanky frame was tense with fear, his shoulders hunched. David had a decent build. Standing up straight would make him taller than Chuck, a good advantage in a fight. Instead he played the quintessential victim. Connor supposed David's short curly hair didn't help, nor did the full lips that somehow made him appear sensitive, like they had become pink and swollen from reading too much poetry aloud.

Why was David doing this? He wasn't going to fight, probably wouldn't even find brave words, but still he was marching on as if meeting his fate. Connor looked back at Chuck and saw his little rat eyes glimmering with excitement. He had probably stayed up all night jerking off over the idea of taking out yesterday's humiliation on David today. And David was willing to make all his fantasies come true. How could he be so stupid?

Just as David was passing by, Connor stepped out of his

car. When David turned to face him, one of his shoes pivoted on a piece of gravel with a sound like a needle dragging across a record.

"Get in the car."

Connor hadn't meant to say it like that, with irritation and maybe a little hostility. All his anger was directed at Chuck, and he was having a hard time controlling it.

David glanced between Chuck and Connor, clearly weighing his options. Connor knew then that David had heard everything about his past. Not surprising since there wasn't a soul in this godforsaken shithole who didn't whisper the stories as he walked by.

"Get in," he tried again, but knew he would have to give David just a little more. "I have to pick up my little brother. He's in grade school."

David's brow furrowed as he tried to reconcile this information with the monster in his mind. One wary look toward the group of bullies sealed the deal. David headed for the passenger-side door while Connor kept his eyes on Chuck, making sure he stayed put. And he did, looking like an angry child on the verge of a temper tantrum. Once David was seated, Connor flashed Chuck his biggest smile and got back in the car.

Turning the ignition, he let the engine growl a few times before blasting out of the parking lot. In the rearview mirror he saw Chuck flip him off and smirked. Chuck would never have the balls to do that to his face.

"Actually, I don't live far from here," David said, clutching the door handle with white knuckles.

Connor slowed to the speed limit.

"Just a couple of blocks, really," David tried again, still appearing afraid.

"I can't keep my brother waiting. Just one detour."

In truth, he still had plenty of time, but he was desperate to prove that he was more than what the rumors claimed. If only he could think of something to say. He drummed on the steering wheel, willing his mind to start working.

"Sit tight. We'll be there soon." Smooth!

"So," David said, looking resigned to his fate. "What kind of car is this?"

"1968 Chevy Chevelle."

The car was a piece of crap, the paint stripped away to the gunmetal gray below. His uncle had been planning to paint it before marrying a woman with three kids. With his new minivan life, he sold the Chevelle to Connor. Considering all the rust and engine problems, the car should have been free, but it was all Connor could afford. At least with an old muscle car, people assumed you were an enthusiast and in the process of restoring it.

"So are you fixing it up or something?"

Right on cue! "Yup. Some paint and a little work, and she'll be as good as new."

Or in the junkyard by the end of the year, but so far the car had held together. The conversation lulled again, so he reached for the radio, only to notice he hadn't picked the knob off the floor yet. Why was this so hard?

"Uh, I'd offer you a cigarette, but we're almost there. I don't smoke with my little brother in the car."

"I can't stand the smell of them anyway."

Great.

"Not that I mind," David added quickly.

"No, you're right. Nasty habit."

Connor rubbed his chin, wishing he had shaved that morning. Instead he had eaten his bowl of cereal slowly, imagining a situation similar to this one where he and David ended up hanging out, talking the night away. Everything would have been perfect. Except now Connor couldn't muster a single damn word.

The blinking school zone sign came into view, which meant they were close to picking up Tommy. Two minutes to be charming, Connor. Now or never!

"Fuck," Connor muttered. He glanced in the rearview mirror, not surprised to see that his expression looked just as hopeless as David's. He hit the turn signal and pulled in behind the other cars already waiting, Tommy running down the sidewalk even though he was supposed to stay by the door. They shared the same green eyes and blonde hair, except Tommy's—flopping behind him—was still the platinum blond of youth where Connor's had darkened to gold years ago. Tommy sprinted to the car, a doofy grin on his face that turned to puzzlement when he noticed the passenger.

"Two door car, right," David said, stepping out. "You can sit up front, if you want."

But Tommy scrambled in the back anyway. "Who are you?" he asked as the car pulled away from the curb.

"David. And you?"

"Tommy. Are you my brother's friend?"

David looked at Connor, appearing amused. "Sure."

Tommy was far from finished. "Do you like comics?"

"No. Well, I like to read, so kind of."

"What about movies?"

"Yeah, especially black and white stuff with a lot of murder."

David's description failed to impress Tommy. The kid had grown up on dubbed Japanese cartoons, but Connor knew a little about film noir.

"Ever see that one with the two sisters? One used to be a child star, except now she's old and taking care of her handicapped sister."

David grinned. "*Whatever Happened to Baby Jane.* That one is crazy."

Connor chuckled. "Doesn't she make her sister eat a bird or something? She's completely psycho." He hesitated, not wanting the conversation to turn to such subjects. "Or *Casablanca.* I know that one doesn't have much murder in it, but it's not bad."

"Yeah," David nodded. "I like that one too."

Silence reigned supreme for half a second before Tommy conquered it. "What about music? Do you like rap?"

David started rattling off the names of the bands he liked, and in that moment Connor decided to get a tattoo on his forehead that read "I love my kid brother." Tommy kept pestering David with questions as they headed back toward the high school, giving Connor a couple more chances to interject.

"Turn here," David said.

The sign on the subdivision read "Bonita Vista Condominiums." Connor never understood what differentiated a condo from an apartment. He pictured condos as little boxy units stacked on top of each other, probably near a beach. The condos here appeared more like townhomes, row after row of two-story buildings, all connected to each other. Maybe some marketing department had decided that "condo" sounded wealthy, whereas "townhome" sounded quaint. Regardless, Connor was relieved that David didn't live in a big house. Not that the condos were likely to be cheap, but at least this put them both in the same financial solar system.

"Right there." David said. "Where that guy is sitting."

Sitting on the front steps of one condo was a chubby-faced kid with glasses just as round as his face. The kid stared with an expression of confusion so intense it neared revulsion.

"Is that your little brother?" Connor asked.

"No, just a friend." David grabbed his backpack from the floorboard. "Listen, thanks for the ride, but none of this is going to make a difference."

"You mean with Chuck?"

David nodded. "He's just going to beat me up tomorrow. Or the day after."

"Not if I give you a ride home every day."

The words slipped from Connor's mouth before he had a chance to consider them, and he blessed their careless speed.

David just stared in open surprise.

"Okay?"

David nodded and fumbled for the door handle.

"Byeeeee!" Tommy said, clambering through the gap between seats to get to the front.

As soon as they were out of the subdivision, he gunned it toward the west side of town.

"I don't think he likes you," Tommy said after a moment.

Connor laughed. "That's because your big brother is a scary guy."

"I don't think you're scary."

Connor grabbed Tommy's stomach, causing him to shriek and giggle, but even this didn't silence his questions.

"Do you like him?"

Connor thought about it a moment. "I don't know. We'll see."

Florescent light poured through the windshield, bathing Connor's bare chest as he considered the shirt in his hand. He leaned back against the car's leather seat, the creaking noise strangely comforting before he gave in and pulled the shirt over his head. Working at McDonald's was bad enough without the crappy uniform. Why did anyone care what he wore? It's not like the patrons had discerning taste, or at least they abandoned it when deciding to eat here. So what if the employees wore jeans and T-shirts?

The ugly maroon shirt with its gray and yellow horizontal

stripes always smelled like grease, even after Connor washed it, which wasn't often anymore. Even more annoying were the black slacks that went with it. Connor unbuttoned his jeans and pulled them down, kicking off his shoes. He was groping around in the backseat for his work pants when someone knocked on the door, causing him to jump and bang his head on the roof.

"Fuck," he said when he saw it was Riley. "Don't do that!"

Riley smiled through multiple lip piercings.

"What are you doing in there?" she asked after Connor rolled down the window. "Jerking off or something?"

The idea was definitely more appealing than flipping burgers. Connor barked a humorless laugh and got his pants on as quickly as possible. Not that he was shy, but Riley was sneaking glances at his package and not bothering to hide her interest.

"Is Mike here already?" he asked as he fumbled with the annoyingly small zipper.

"Of course." Riley brought her eyes back up to his face. "I don't think he's noticed you're late yet."

"Good."

Connor got out of the car, wishing Riley would step back a little. She had only been working here a week and had taken to Connor immediately. Well, not right away, but shortly after being warned by the other workers what a psychopath he was. That was his main appeal for Riley. She was a freak, or at least desperately wanted to be. Her long hair was dyed black, except for a single streak of blue, her heavy makeup echoing these hues.

Of course this was all a charade. Underneath her Halloween appearance was a normal girl screaming for attention. Not that Connor couldn't relate, but others had chosen his mask for him. But Riley was okay. At least she was someone he could talk to on breaks.

Together they trudged into McDonald's. Connor was heading for the grill when his manager appeared from around it and pointed at his watch. Mike's appearance matched his insides—tidy, blond, and unforgiving. He would have been handsome if he wasn't such an asshole. Mike was only a year or two older than Connor, but he acted like he was fifty.

"Fourth time this month," Mike said, still pointing at his watch.

"I didn't know you were keeping count." Connor winked. "How sweet!"

Mike glared at him. "I expect a written explanation as to why you were late. And an apology. You can write it on your next break."

He wasn't kidding. Mike had asked him to do this before, and Connor had complied, because as much as he hated it, he needed this stupid job.

Mike stood there, staring at Connor and daring him to talk back, until one of the cashiers came over and asked for his help. Mike turned away, leaving Connor to face an industrial-size grill and a cardboard box full of frozen patties. He barely glanced at the order screen. After one year, he knew how many burgers were needed for each hour of the evening. That was a depressing thought, but at least it meant his body could run on automatic while his mind was free to think.

Those thoughts took the form of David, and his surprise when Connor offered to drive him home every day. Or was he afraid? Maybe tomorrow he wouldn't be in the parking lot—or if he was, he would walk right past him. Hell, if it wasn't for Chuck, David probably would have run away to avoid speaking to him. Maybe Connor should send Chuck a thank-you letter and buy him a bouquet of flowers.

"Are there pickles on a Filet-O Fish?" Riley shouted over the kitchen's din.

Connor glanced over at her. "Nope. Just cheese and tartar sauce."

"Thanks." She smiled like Connor had just saved her from a burning building.

He didn't return the gesture, turning his attention back to his station. The last couple of days had been the worst. Riley, realizing that Connor wasn't likely to strangle her or anything equally insane, had been flirting shamelessly. She had absolutely no idea. No one did. Connor could walk right up to someone and announce he was gay, like he had done with Chuck, and no one would believe him. But when someone like David walked down the hall, thoughtful and quiet instead of being a macho asshole, everyone assumed he was gay.

People were clueless. All they ever went by was appearance and rumor. Riley wasn't stupid for dressing the way she did. She wanted to be something she wasn't and understood that all it took was the right costume. She should give David lessons, dress him up in some Satanic gear to scare away the bullies. Hell, maybe Connor should hook them up. It would probably be love at first sight.

"Number three, Williams!" Mike boomed at him.

Connor nodded. One of the perks of working at McDonald's was getting free meals. Smelling the greasy food for hours made the prospect repulsive, but Connor's treacherous stomach demanded he eat something. Mike always ordered the quarter-pounder meal. Even if plenty of those burgers were on the rack and ready to go, Mike insisted that Connor make his fresh.

"I got this one," Connor said, bringing the burger patty to the dressing station.

Riley moved aside as he threw on all the usual ingredients— ketchup, mustard, diced onions, pickles, cheese. Connor glanced around to make sure they weren't being watched.

"Can't forget the secret sauce," he said, before quietly hocking the biggest, slimiest loogie he could muster right onto the burger. He added a bit of extra ketchup to help disguise it before smooshing the bun on top.

Riley covered her mouth, laughing but also looking green beneath her white makeup.

"Funny," Connor said. "I've been reprimanded four times this month, and Mike's eaten the secret sauce four times this month. Go figure."

When Connor's shift was over, he pocketed the month's new Happy Meal toys and headed home, not bothering to change his clothes. When he pulled into the trailer park and parked outside his family's home, all the windows were dark except for one, flickering with blue light as it always did. Once inside, he found his father sitting in front of the TV, watching some syndicated sitcom he had probably seen before. Connor murmured a greeting, left the Happy Meal toys on the kitchen table where Tommy would find them the next morning, and headed to the bathroom.

Leaving the light off, he stripped out of his clothes and felt his way to the shower. Once the hot water was coursing over his body, the smell of McDonald's washing down the drain, he pressed his forehead against the cool tile and sighed. Maybe tomorrow things would finally change.

Chapter Three

David spent most of math class watching Chuck from the corner of his eye. He pretended to take notes when the teacher was talking, scrawling doodles instead and waiting for Chuck to make a move. David always felt like he was in a lion's cage during math (or maybe a gorilla's cage was more apt), but now the ante had been upped.

And yet, David felt more relaxed today than he had in a long time. Seeing Connor stand up to Chuck had much to do with that, although David hoped Connor was serious about driving him home. Better the devil you barely knew than the one you knew all too well. Or something like that.

The bell rang, startling David. Chuck, perhaps sensing his renewed fear, chose then to address him.

"You're dead, fag."

Really? I don't feel dead. Or maybe, *Yeah, dead sexy!*

Not the best comebacks, but any response would have been better than just standing there. David gathered up his things, delaying just long enough for the teacher to move toward the door.

Last year a student had brought a gun into school and flipped out after class, waving it around while screaming incoherently. The gun wasn't loaded, so he only managed to scare everyone, but since then the school had adopted a new policy: Between classes, teachers were to stand outside their classrooms and monitor all activity in the hallway. David didn't see what use they would be against a loaded gun, but this meant he was mostly safe inside the building.

Of course people could still push or trip him, and they sometimes did, but no one could beat him up. Once Chuck was out of sight, David wandered to his computer science class. No one bothered him this period, but he often spent it worrying about what would happen after school—stomach churning in fear, wishing he could teleport to the safety of home.

Today he thought about Connor instead.

Sometimes he wondered if he had been suckered into some intricate plan to break him down. Maybe Connor and Chuck were in cahoots. As soon as David let down his guard, they would spring their trap. Or maybe Connor's past had made him an outcast, and he was desperate for a friend. They would make an odd pair—the guy who had done terrible things, and the guy who hadn't done much of anything.

By the time computer science was over, David found himself eager to see how the afternoon would play out. He even forgot his fear until he saw Chuck standing by the front door, surrounded by his goons. David stopped, but then forced himself to keep walking. Maybe he could slip outside unnoticed and make a break for Connor's beat-up old car.

David had just reached the glass doors when Connor sidled up to Chuck and threw an arm around his neck. For a moment, David thought they really were on the same side, but Chuck's nervous flinch told him otherwise. Taking a deep drag off his cigarette, Connor blew the smoke in Chuck's face.

"There's my man," Connor said when he noticed David. His eyes had that crazy, slightly unfocused quality again. "Ready to go for a ride?"

"What the hell?" Chuck snarled. "Is he paying you or something?"

The smile fell from Connor's face, replaced by a nightmare. "Are you calling me a whore?"

"No." Chuck pulled away from him. "That's not what I meant."

"Good." Connor gave him a friendly punch to the arm, making Chuck wince, before holding out his half-smoked cigarette. "Here. Hang on to this for me."

Chuck took it with hesitation, Connor motioning to David that they should leave. About five seconds later, a teacher noticed Chuck holding the cigarette and came over to lecture him.

"Thank you," David said. Had he said that yet? Until now, he hadn't been sure if Connor was honestly doing him a favor.

"My pleasure," Connor said with a grin. He had a very slight underbite, making his chin jut out the tiniest bit. It made him look as cocky as a pit bull, especially when he smiled. "You all right?" he asked when he noticed David staring.

"Yeah!" David forced himself to look away. "I was just thinking, maybe I should pay you."

"Now *you're* calling me a whore!"

David risked a laugh, hoping he had understood right, and was relieved when Connor joined in. "Not a whore, no. More like a bodyguard."

"Yeah, maybe. I could wear a pair of shades and always have my finger pressed to my ear, like I'm Secret Service."

If only that were possible. David would love to have someone he could call on whenever he was in trouble. "Are we picking up Tommy again?"

"Yup. Door's unlocked. Nobody wants to steal this thing, believe me."

What David wanted to know, more than anything, was why. Why him? Why now? The only explanation he could think of was that Connor was trying to atone for past sins. Maybe he was born-again or something like that.

"What do you usually do on weekends?" David asked as they pulled out of the parking lot. If Connor was ultra-religious, he would start talking about church soon enough.

"When I'm not working? Just hang out. Same stuff everyone else does. You?"

"Play video games with my friend or sit around reading. Sometimes Dad tries to get to me to do thrilling things around the house, like dusting shelves or scrubbing the toilets. I keep telling him I have a weak heart and can't stand such excitement."

Connor chuckled but didn't offer any more information about himself. As they pulled into the grade school parking lot, David wished Tommy would turn his endless questions on his brother. Then he could just sit back and enjoy the interview.

Tommy came pounding down the sidewalk, looking happy to see David again. He practically climbed over David to get to the back, but soon had his body pressed between the front seats so he could talk to them.

"See my new Transformer?"

He held it up for David to examine. Small and cheap like a fast food toy, it resembled the yellow car from the movie.

"You can try it," Tommy said, shoving it toward him.

David took it, switching it back and forth between robot and car in a few easy steps.

"I used to have some of these," he said, handing the toy back. "Might still have them around somewhere."

Tommy's mouth became an "O," which made David laugh. He would have to dig through his boxes to see if he could find them.

"My brother gave me this one," Tommy said. "I have a huge

collection of Happy Meal toys. I think I have every single one."

"They've been making them since the Stone Age," Connor said, "so I don't think you have them all."

"Do you eat there a lot?" David asked.

Connor scoffed. "Are you crazy? No, I just work there."

"Oh."

"I really do have most of them," Tommy insisted. "You should come see all my toys."

Connor turned to David, his green eyes intense in a different way now. "Yeah, why not?"

"You mean now?"

"Yeah. I don't have to work tonight."

"Okay."

Tommy cheered and David forced a smile, having no idea what to expect. He had wanted to learn more about Connor, and for better or worse, that wish was about to come true.

The trailer park was on the west side of town. David hadn't known there was such a thing in Olathe and had never been in a mobile home before. The strange thing was, Connor didn't live near the high school he attended. The city of Olathe had four high schools, two of them much closer to Connor's home.

"I'm surprised you don't go to Olathe North," David said. "Isn't it just down the road?"

"Yeah." Connor cleared his throat and slowed down for one of the trailer park's speed bumps. "Mom thought Olathe South was a better school. Plus I was having a hard time up here, and she thought that would help."

In other words, he was trying to escape his reputation, but that obviously hadn't worked.

David looked out the window at the rows and rows of trailers, each one different. Some were wide and looked fairly cozy, while others appeared to be hammered together out of old siding. The one Connor pulled up to was somewhere in between. It wasn't a double-wide, but someone cared for the trailer's appearance and its tiny strip of yard.

Tommy leapt out of the car after David and dashed inside, the door slamming behind him.

Connor shook his head. "At least that will wake up Dad."

The same dad Connor had attempted to kill? David was

having an increasingly hard time believing these legends. Inside the trailer was dark, which was probably nice on a hot summer day. The front door led to the living room, which spread out to the right. To the left was a small kitchen and dining area. The way the kitchen was decorated, with little feminine touches his father would never consider, made David yearn to have his mom around again.

From the television an audience booed at a woman's loud-mouthed rant on stage. Facing the daytime talk show was a pair of recliners. One was occupied, the table next to it cluttered with prescription medicine bottles.

Connor led him in front of the recliner where an overweight, balding man sat.

"Dad, this is my friend David. David, this is my dad."

"Hi, nice to meet you," David said.

Connor's father smiled and nodded but didn't seem compelled to make conversation. Instead he turned back to the talk show.

Making an agitated noise, Connor shook his head. "Let's go in my room before Tommy has a heart attack."

Down a short hallway were two doors, only one open. Tommy was inside, slowly scooping the contents of a toy box on the floor. The décor was schizophrenic. On one side were the trappings of a child: toys, Pixar posters, and a little drawing desk covered in crayons and an old laptop. The other side of the room was much less childish. A dresser nearly exploded with clothes, on it a stereo that still took cassettes as well as CDs. Above them both a battered acoustic guitar hung on the wall. Twin-sized beds rested against opposite walls, confirming that Tommy and Connor shared this room.

"Told you I had a lot!" Tommy said.

"You're making a mess!" Connor complained, stuffing some of the clothes back into the dresser drawers. "Sorry. It's always like this."

"Look at this one!" A plastic dinosaur with light-up eyes was shoved in David's face. For the next ten minutes, he was subjected to a year's worth of show-and-tell presentations.

"Tommy," Connor said finally, "why don't you show Greg the new Transformers you got. Most of those aren't supposed to be given away until later this month."

Mercifully, Tommy agreed. He gathered up the toys in question and left the room, the trailer's front door slamming shut after him.

"Let the neighbors deal with him," Connor said as he bent to put the toys away.

David was soon on his knees, helping shovel countless fast-food premiums back into the toy chest. He was close enough to Connor that their shoulders bumped a couple of times. The faint aroma of cigarettes came from him, a scent David normally didn't enjoy. But somehow it smelled masculine on Connor, almost like musky cologne.

Once they were finished, Connor sat on his bed and gestured for David to take a seat on Tommy's.

"Not the most luxurious accommodations," he said.

David smiled. "It's fine, really."

"So you're a junior, right?"

"Yeah." Could Connor tell just by looking at him, or did he ask around? Then again, David knew Connor was a senior without really remembering how. He asked anyway, just to appear casual.

"Yeah, I'm a senior. Just a couple more weeks to freedom. I'm long overdue, since I was held back a year."

David's eyes dropped to the scar on Connor's neck. He averted them immediately, but Connor had noticed.

"Look, if you want to know, just ask. It's not a secret."

"Sorry," David said, but Connor didn't reply, waiting for him to say more. "Is any of it true?"

"What they say about me?" Connor shook his head. "My dad used to work in a factory, really early shifts, which meant he would drink sooner than most people. Noon was like night for him, so a lot of the time when I came home from school, he would already be drunk. He handled it well. Dad wasn't one of those loud or abusive assholes. He just liked to unwind. Anyway, we were out of everything one day, and I was starving, so I talked him into bringing me to the store."

"He drove you when he was drunk?"

Connor nodded, his expression defensive. "We all make mistakes. We were going through a four-way stop on Ridgeview Road, up where it's pretty narrow and hilly, when some guy goes barreling through without stopping. Dad hit the breaks, but a couple seconds too late, and the other car hit us so hard that we spun into a ditch and flipped."

"The whole car flipped?"

"Yeah." Connor absentmindedly rubbed the scar on his neck. "The other car smashed into Dad's side and messed him up pretty bad. Our car was an old Plymouth Roadrunner, and I guess the plastic dashboard got pretty brittle over the years since part of it shattered on impact. A shard went through my neck, but by some miracle it didn't sever an artery. I got some other nicks too."

Connor stood and pulled up his shirt. David's eyes moved over the muscles first, then the lightly haired chest, before he noticed more pink scars by the left shoulder. He tried to focus on these, feeling guilty for finding Connor's body attractive when he was telling such a painful story.

"Must have hurt," David said when Connor dropped his shirt again.

"Most of it's a blur. I was in the hospital for a week, Dad for way longer than that. He came out with a couple of pins in his arms and a jacked-up back. He never really recovered from it, so I'm lucky."

Connor sighed and started digging through a nightstand drawer while he talked. "Mom flipped out, of course, and didn't send me back to school right away. She still had to work, and Tommy was really little then, so everything was a mess. I think she was scared that something else might happen to me." Connor found a small box, set it on the nightstand, and closed the drawer. "Long story short, I missed too much school and had to repeat eighth grade."

"That sucks." These words, the only ones David could think to say, felt wholly inadequate. "So I guess you know all the stuff people say about you."

"Yeah."

"Where did all that come from? Who would make up a story like that?"

Connor shrugged. "Why do people say things about you that aren't true?"

Except in David's case the rumors *were* true. He was gay, although people probably thought they were insulting him by implying he was. He didn't like the hate behind the slurs, but in essence, they were right.

"People just believe whatever they want to," Connor said. "You can't let it get to you." He opened the little wooden box and pulled something out. "Want to smoke a joint?"

David's eyes widened. "And here you had me believing you're a saint."

Connor shrugged. "I've always done whatever I wanted. And yeah, maybe I've always been a little nuts, even when I was thirteen, but everything I told you is true."

Connor handed him the joint and a lighter. David pinched it by one of the little twisted ends and held it away from him, as if it were a firecracker about to go off. "I have no idea what to do with this. I've never even smoked a cigarette."

"Seriously? Well, all right. Give it back and I'll get us started. I mean, if you want to."

David nodded. All those anti-drug commercials had done one thing: They had made him curious. "What about your dad?"

"He doesn't care. Did you see the mountain of pills they have him on? He's higher than we'll ever be. Still, I don't want Tommy seeing this."

Connor stood, locked the door, and cracked a window, the joint hanging from his lips the whole time. Then he sparked it up and winked at David as he took a deep drag, holding it in before exhaling a thick cloud of smoke. "See? Nothing to it."

He offered the joint to David, who took it and put it to his lips. The paper was wet where Connor's lips had been. This thought was still on his mind when David pulled on the joint. One second later he was coughing and desperately trying to get fresh air into his lungs.

"Don't worry." Connor forced away a smile. "Totally normal for your first time. Did you get any in?"

"I have no idea," David wheezed.

Connor took another drag while David recovered, then handed it to him again. "Take it slow this time."

David did, but still ended up coughing.

"You have to inhale or all your suffering will be for nothing."

Connor left to get him a Coke from the fridge. The cold liquid felt heavenly on David's throat, but he didn't think he could smoke anymore.

"Let's try this." Connor sat on the bed next to him. "Know what shotgunning is? No? I'll take a drag, then I'll blow it into your mouth. Just breathe in like you always do. You'll get a good mix of air with it, and it'll be easier."

The idea sounded silly, but as Connor took a drag and leaned closer to David, he found he liked the suggestion after all. Connor's lips were just inches away when he started to blow. David inhaled, glancing into those emerald eyes for only a second before breaking contact, afraid of what his own gaze might reveal.

"Good." Connor said. "Hold it in as long as you can."

David did, and when he exhaled, smoke floated on his breath. Connor grinned at him and repeated the process twice. David was sure that Connor's lips were coming closer each time, that something big was about to happen—if only by accident—and he realized just how much he wanted that.

Then Connor leaned away and took a couple of drags for himself before stubbing out the remainder in an ashtray. When he turned on the stereo, David felt like he was hearing music for the first time. The difference was like living in a monochrome world and one day stumbling out into a kingdom of color. Dorothy, eat your heart out!

Then they talked. The subjects didn't matter because everything they said felt so important. Every thought carried a tremendous amount of weight, and no matter what David said or how odd it was, Connor seemed to be right there with him, understanding exactly what he meant.

David hoped this wasn't just the drugs, that they really did have such an empathic connection. As Humphrey Bogart was famously misquoted as saying, "This could be the beginning of a beautiful friendship." Except for one little issue. Connor had told him the truth, and it was time David did the same. Connor knew how it felt to be an outsider. Surely that would make him tolerant of David being gay.

"Connor—"

"Hey!" The doorknob rattled, then Tommy knocked on the door. "Aren't you going to get dinner?"

Dinner! The electric digits of the nightstand clock were burning toward seven. His dad would already be home and putting dinner on the table. And what about Gordon? David pictured him still waiting on the front steps, morosely flipping through a strategy guide.

"I need to go home."

Connor nodded. "I have to pick up something for the brat to eat anyway."

David found he didn't enjoy the world outside the trailer. As mellow as his buzz had been inside, suddenly he felt awkward, like everyone they passed, even in traffic, was staring at him, aware that he was high. He didn't make good conversation, and when it came time to say goodbye, he struggled to find words that sounded normal.

"Doing okay?" Connor asked.

"I think I'm freaking out," David admitted.

Connor nodded as if concerned before laughing. "You'll be fine. Just get inside and eat something. That'll give your head something to sing about. I'll see you tomorrow."

He was right. Being inside did help, but being high around his father was another level of weirdness entirely. When he got the first bite of pasta in his mouth, all was forgotten. How could he have ever tired of this meal? It was pure bliss!

"This is really, *really* good, Dad."

"It's just the same as it always is, although I think I did use more basil than usual." His father had waited for him, already enjoying a glass of wine. "So tell me about this new friend of yours. Does he do well in school?"

"I don't know, Dad. I don't compare report cards on a first date."

"Is that what this was? You were on a date?"

David instantly felt uncomfortable. He meant it as a joke, but now it had been twisted into another prying question, one that could lead to more academic advice if David didn't answer correctly. His father knew he was gay, and had reacted to that news with about as much interest as David reporting a sore throat. David could probably claim to be a serial killer and his dad wouldn't care, as long as he got good grades.

"He's straight," David said. "We're just friends."

When dinner was finished and the dishes were clean, he went to his room and turned on some music. It didn't sound quite as mind-blowing as it had a few hours ago. The high was fading, but when David thought of Connor, he found the feelings were just as strong if not stronger. Those hadn't been drug-induced. David thought back on the afternoon and smiled. He would happily shotgun carbon monoxide just to get near those lips again.

Chapter Four

Connor fumbled with the cardboard lid of his cigarette box, flipping it open and shut over and over. He had made it almost a day without smoking so far. Maybe he was being stupid. David didn't like the smell of cigarettes, but so what? He usually wasn't around when Connor was smoking, so it shouldn't matter. And yet, it did.

Mr. Wesley, his English teacher, was giving him the eye, so Connor pocketed the cigarettes and stared at the clock until the bell rang. Then the entire class came to life, shuffling their belongings and getting ready to leave. Mr. Wesley cleared his throat, a chorus of groans coming in response.

He always did this. Be it a power play or just plain cruelty, Mr. Wesley would often make them stay behind an extra minute or two, just to reiterate their assignment or remind them of a test. Here it was, Friday, sixth period, and he was trying to hold them back. They should riot, trampling the old geezer as they made a desperate break for freedom.

Finally Mr. Wesley gave a benevolent wave, signifying they could leave. Connor did some mental calculation as he pushed his way through the halls, hoping he could still get to the parking lot ahead of David.

Summer had made an early debut outside, the sun bright in the faded blue sky. People chatted happily to each other, the weekend vibe already working its magic and putting everyone in a forgiving mood. Perhaps this cheerful environment had prompted Chuck to park right next to Connor's car. Or maybe it was another ploy to get at David. Chuck hadn't had the guts to stand up to Connor before, so why now?

As Connor came nearer, he heard the Mazda's engine rev, saw Chuck peering out at him from a barely lowered window. Then Connor noticed his car, and as trained as he was at keeping his cool, he broke into a run. Beige paint ran down the windshield, dribbling off to each side and splattering on the parking lot. A streak stained the car's top, having slopped up and over the windshield when the paint bucket was tossed—the very bucket that was now sitting upside-down on the hood.

Connor was ready to make all the rumors come true. They

wanted to see a murdering psychopath? Fine. Connor ran toward the silver Mazda, but Chuck was already gunning it out of the parking lot. He only braked once, just long enough to yell out his window.

"Hey, Williams! About time you painted your car!"

Then Chuck hit the accelerator, the rear of the Mazda swinging dangerously and almost hitting a row of cars on the way out. Connor grabbed the empty bucket, throwing it after him in a futile act of fury.

Shit! When had Chuck gotten so brave? Not that pouring paint on someone's car and fleeing for your life was courageous, but for Chuck this was something new. At least he would avoid Connor now, which meant a free pass for David. Chuck would be too busy laying low to give him any trouble.

"What happened?"

Even David's arrival did little to ease Connor's anger. "Chuck grew a pair, that's what."

"I'm sorry."

He turned to David, saw the look of guilt there, and some of Connor's anger melted away. "It's not your fault. Chuck was an asshole before either of us came along." Besides, one ruined car was easier to bear than David's face being bloody and bruised.

Connor sighed, dug the keys from his pocket, and went to the trunk. He found some old towels from the last time he changed the oil. If he was quick, he could get the windshield clean enough to see through so he could drive. As it turned out, all the towels did was smear the paint around.

"What about windshield wiper fluid?" Already David had paint on his fingers and a couple of stains on his green hoody.

Connor felt his anger growing but tried to keep it suppressed. For now. "I guess it's worth a shot."

David sat in the driver's seat and pushed the button to spray fluid. The wipers sent paint flying, but the fluid helped dilute it somewhat. Connor wiped between every spray, eventually clearing a milky spot on the driver's side.

"There's no way I'm going to make it to work tonight." Connor took the phone from his pocket, the edges wrapped in tape where the casing had broken, and dialed McDonald's. A dayshift manager he barely knew took his message. At least he wouldn't have to deal with Mike.

"Maybe we should hit a car wash," David said. "There's a do-it-yourself place up on Sante Fe. Think we can make it that far?"

Connor imagined the last ten bucks he had in his wallet disappearing in a puff of smoke. At least payday was tomorrow.

"Okay. Let's get Tommy first. He'll think this is funny."

Hilarious was more like it. Tommy howled halfway to the car wash. Once there he made a nuisance of himself, begging to use the pistol that shot streams of high-pressured water as Connor blasted off as much of the paint as possible. Then he fed his last two dollars into the machine and let Tommy have his fun.

"I want to kill him."

The words took Connor by surprise since they came from David. His expression was indignant, as it should have been every time Chuck called him a name. Maybe there was hope for him yet. David *could* get angry and show his claws. Just not for himself.

"We'll get back at him." Connor looked at his car. It was a piece of shit, but it was his. "Yeah, we'll definitely make him cry."

David kicked at a pancake of chewed gum that had hardened in the sun. "If you want out, I won't hold it against you. My whole life has been like this. People give me shit all the time. I'm used to it, but I don't like seeing it happen to you."

Connor snorted. "Hey, I'm the psycho who tried killing his own father, remember? People have always given me hell too. They call me names behind my back, and instead of messing with me, they avoid me completely. That might not be worse than what you go through, but it sure as hell doesn't feel good. So don't worry about it. These are the cards we've been dealt. Simple as that."

Tommy shouted as the water pressure nearly knocked him backward, and they laughed.

"You guys can hang out at my place," David said quickly, as if he had been rehearsing the words and wanted to get them out. "If you want to, I mean."

"Sure."

When they got there, the weird kid was sitting on the front steps again, making Connor wonder if he ever moved. He scowled at them from behind his thick glasses, except this time he appeared to be genuinely angry rather than confused.

David groaned. "Oh man! I forgot to tell Gordon where I was yesterday."

"And he's going to make you sleep on the couch tonight?"

"Well, he's going to be mad."

As it turned out, Gordon's anger was soon replaced by curiosity. Connor wasn't assuming this. The kid wore everything on his face, as if he had never learned to keep all his conflicting thoughts and emotions secret. In a way, this put Connor at ease, since he knew Gordon was more likely to say something rude to his face rather than behind his back. For instance:

"Your car is a piece of junk," Gordon said after David introduced them.

"Yeah." Connor nodded. "It is."

Gordon stared at him before he turned to David. "Where were you yesterday? I thought we were going to fight the brotherhood of dark clerics together."

"Hey, is that a Dragon Death game?" Tommy grabbed the strategy guide from Gordon's hand.

Connor was about to yell at him for being rude, but Gordon seemed thrilled by his enthusiasm. Soon they were both speaking in a language that Connor could barely understand, while David unlocked the front door and ushered them all inside.

The condo was nice enough. A stairwell in the entry led up to another floor, but they stayed on the ground level, entering a dining area that bled into a living room. A kitchen was set off to one side, separated by a breakfast bar and a row of counters. Everything was much newer than what they had at home. No surprise there. With Dad's medical bills, they were lucky to get by. But while the furniture was in better condition, the place also lacked personality. Sherlock Holmes could spend an hour in here and not deduce anything about the occupants.

Past the living room, a stairwell twisted once on its way down, leading to a small rec room that was empty except for boxes in one corner. David led them to a door here, opening it to a welcome burst of color and personality. The walls were covered in posters and magazine ads. A large bed dominated most of the room, but there was still space around it for a canvas chair and an entertainment center.

Gordon took a seat on the bed, and Tommy plopped down next to him.

"That's usually where David sits," Gordon said.

"Maybe he can take over for me today," David suggested, handing Tommy a controller. "You just have to do what Gordon says. He won't steer you wrong."

"Okay!"

Tommy was thrilled with the idea, Gordon less so as he adjusted his glasses. But soon his attention was on the strategy guide, and he and Tommy were chattering about dragons and magic cups or something.

David sat next to them, his attention on making sure this new partnership was going to work. Connor watched them for a while, glancing only occasionally at the screen. Then he grew bored and turned his attention to the magazine pages on the wall. He had barely perused them when David was up and at his side.

"Wanna help me grab some drinks?"

"Only if I get a grand tour of the house as well."

"All right."

Connor followed him back up to the kitchen, checking out David's buns as he rummaged in the fridge. He pulled out three Cokes and a Diet Dr Pepper, squinching up his nose at the diet soda. "Someone's going to have to drink this."

"Give it to Tommy. He doesn't need any more sugar."

"Okay." David held out two of the cans for Connor to carry.

He took them, then set them back on the counter. "You promised me a tour."

"Seriously? Okay, but there's not much to see."

Connor tried not to laugh as David led them through the living room, pointing out the obvious. "This is the big TV. That's the sofa. This is the dining room table … where we eat." Then he led them upstairs to a short hallway with two rooms. "This is my dad's office."

Most of the room was dedicated to book-laden shelves, all nonfiction judging from the subdued spines. A medium-sized desk bearing a computer sat against one wall. On the other side of the room waited a lush leather chair, the trashcan next to it filled with empty wine bottles.

"What's your dad do?"

"He's a professor at the University of Missouri. The branch in downtown Kansas City, I mean."

"So he's a smart guy then."

"Yeah."

Connor nodded to the trashcan. "And he likes to party."

David looked uncomfortable, making Connor regret his joke. "At night he comes up here and puts on classical music and just sits there drinking. I guess it's the one thing we have in common. The music, I mean. Sometimes that's all I do at night."

While lying in bed? Connor pictured David on his back, staring at the ceiling, the green hoody pulled away from the line of his jeans, revealing a hint of flat, smooth stomach.

"So, yeah," David said, almost causing Connor to jump. "One room to go."

The final room was the most telling. The unmade bed, the lack of decoration—aside from the family portrait on the wall—and dressers clear of anything remotely feminine. Mom didn't live here anymore. Despite the three smiling faces on the wall, Connor didn't think she had for quite some time.

He considered the photo. David was in the center, embarrassingly juvenile. His face was chubby and his curly hair a miniature afro. Connor had to glance over at him, just to verify how much had changed. Height had stretched the chubbiness out of David's face; the curly hair now short on top and the sides cut close. While his hair was still a little bouffant, Connor found it alluring. Would his fingers get tangled up if he tried running them through it?

"I look horrible, I know," David said. "I never want to be twelve again."

Connor returned his attention to the portrait. David had improved in every way, except one. The brown eyes of his twelve-year-old self were glassy with joy. The David of today had eyes that appeared sad when not guarded.

The two adults at either side were an odd couple. The father shared David's thin but broad-shouldered build. The rest of his features were hidden behind glasses and a beard. His appearance was stern, but Connor almost found this appealing compared to what his own father had become. The mother had an open face and long curly hair. Her smile was open-mouthed, giving her a slightly surprised appearance.

"She left him the year this was taken," David said.

"What happened?"

David took a deep breath. "Well, she said that she needed to find herself and a lot of other stuff that never made sense to me. She remarried less than a year later. I think she was seeing the new guy while she was still with my dad, but I've never asked."

"And you decided to stay with your dad?"

David nodded. "I didn't understand it all like I do now, but even then I knew my dad was the loser in the situation. I felt like someone should stay with him. Worked out well for me since Jeff, my mom's new husband, is an asshole."

Connor hoped he never had to deal with that. His dad might be a drugged up blob, but the idea of a stranger taking his place was disturbing. As they left the room, Connor glanced back at the family portrait once more, at the cherub face in the center, and wished he could see David's eyes light up like that again.

The atmosphere in David's bedroom was thick when they returned. The television was blasting out a heavy bass rhythm, and Gordon was on his feet, head whipping between his book and the screen as he read and reread paragraphs to Tommy.

"Holy shit, is that the Dragon Lord?" David said, rushing to join them.

Gordon nodded grimly. "I didn't expect to fight him this early in the game."

"Don't worry," Tommy said. "I'm kicking his butt."

Connor shook his head ruefully, feeling like the only adult in the room as he nursed his Coke. David stared slack-jawed at the screen, his full attention absorbed by the game, so Connor took the chance to stare at him.

This wasn't good. His intentions had been noble enough at the beginning. He didn't want to see the underdog beaten down, especially not by an asshole like Chuck, so he had stood up for David. But those protective feelings were quickly turning into something more.

Not that Connor minded. He welcomed such emotions, felt high on them, even though he knew they would turn to frustration and pain. Eventually the price of protecting David would be getting hurt himself. But Connor wouldn't let that stop him.

The battle with the Dragon Lord raged on, so Connor examined the images on David's walls. Most were of far-away locations—beaches, mountains, deserts, even underwater oceanscapes. Mixed among these were advertisements for different bands, a handful of fashion models strutting down catwalks, and two shirtless guys with their arms around each other.

Connor stared. The black and white image was the typical homoerotic advertisement Abercrombie and Fitch liked to use, but here it stood out. He took a step back and looked at the collective images—far away places, music, and guys. No female fashion models, no tanned women on the beaches. The only women on David's walls were band members.

A victorious roar came from the gamers; Connor spun around. David was grinning and patting Tommy on the back, but when he saw Connor at his wall, he was on his feet in seconds.

"I have way too much stuff up there," he said, as if explaining it all away.

Connor fought back a grin. No doubt about it, David was nervous. "I like it." Connor turned back to the images. "Have you been to any of these places?"

"Huh? No. I wish." David considered the pictures, still tense. "I'd love to get out of Kansas. Go anywhere, see anything—just get away from here."

"Yeah, you and me both. Hey, we like a lot of the same bands. I didn't peg you for an Outkast fan."

David nodded. "I like anything weird, and André 3000 is a freak."

"And these?" Connor pointed to a pouty runway model with long blonde hair. "You want to be a model? Or maybe a fashion designer?"

Connor kept his eyes on David, who was shaking his head as if at a loss for words. Then Connor moved his finger down from the blonde model to the guys with their arms around each other. David's nervous expression ceased, replaced by one of stubborn pride, a refusal to feel ashamed. Connor wanted to kiss him right then and there. He might keep it buried deep inside, but David had strength.

A knock on the door made them both jump. When it swung open, the man Connor had seen in the family portrait upstairs was revealed, except now his beard had more grey and his hair was thinner.

"You're home early," David said.

"I told you yesterday that I would be," Mr. Henry said.

"Who's this?"

David made the introductions, Mr. Henry appearing more puzzled by Tommy's presence than anything else. Connor stood up straight and made sure his handshake was firm, hoping to make a good impression.

Mr. Henry eyed him a moment before turning to his son. "I have some errands to run. I'd like you to come with me."

"Oh. Okay. I'll be up in just a few minutes."

There was some fuss over saving a game that Connor ignored. Instead he furtively wished he could turn back time and continue the interrupted moment. He was sure he hadn't imagined it, positive he hadn't misunderstood.

David walked them outside, Gordon heading next door to his home.

"Sorry about your car," David said, scowling at the remnants of paint.

Even his angry face wasn't any good. He appeared more frustrated or concerned than anything else. Connor wanted to wipe away the creases on his forehead, kiss his pert little nose, and tell David to stop trying to be what he wasn't.

"Don't worry about it," he said instead. "Chuck has a much nicer car, so getting back at him will be ridiculously easy. Do you know where he lives?"

"Huh-uh. I know his dad has an office over on 151st Street. He's a dentist."

"Well, maybe I'll tail him home one day, like in a Hitchcock film."

David grinned appreciatively. "See you around."

Soon, Connor hoped. Those old movies were good at maintaining suspense, but Connor needed to find out if he had a chance, and needed to know now.

Chapter Five

David tossed the paperback aside and sighed. His concentration was failing him and he was tired of reading the same lines over and over again. Jacking off sounded good, but didn't own a single porn magazine, and the office upstairs was no doubt occupied by his father. Sometimes he surfed porn on his phone, but another idea occurred to him.

David pushed off the bed and went to his bookshelf. At the end of a row of worn paperbacks were a handful of yearbooks. He selected the most recent and returned to bed, sitting cross-legged with the book in his lap as he flipped through the pages. David was a sophomore last year, so most faces in the junior section weren't familiar to him. But one was now—Connor Williams, third to the last photo in that section. His hair was a little longer, not the buzz cut he had now, but he still looked older than everyone else in his class.

Connor wasn't smiling, eyes cold. Even the crazed energy that had been evident when he first stepped in to save David was absent. Only days had passed since that event, but already Connor seemed a different person. The Connor from that day, like the Connor in this photo, were complete strangers. Fakes, even.

A tapping on the window made David stiffen. He sat perfectly still, thinking he had just imagined it when it came again. *Tap tap tap!* A number of scenarios raced through his mind. —Chuck having tracked him down, Gordon desperate to talk about Dragon Death some more, or Connor come to hear the confession that had been on David's lips earlier. That last thought put him in motion. He went to the window and peeked through the blinds.

The first things he saw were a wide grin and a glint of madness in green eyes. Okay, so maybe Connor *was* a little crazy. David pulled up the blinds and opened the window.

"What are you doing here?" he asked, sounding more put off than he meant to.

Connor beamed at him. "I just wanted to see what you're up to."

"You could have called."

"I don't have your number."

David's cheeks flushed. "Oh. Right."

Connor pushed at the screen. "Help me get this off. Do you see little tabs on your side?"

They worked together on the screen like some sort of trust-building exercise, Connor describing what David should do and David trying to make sense of it, until the screen finally popped off. Connor set it aside and waited, still crouched on the ground.

"Aren't you coming in?" David asked.

"Nope. You're coming out. Let's go for a walk."

Coming out? David blanched at his choice of words, wondering if it was a slight or a light-hearted jab. Or much more likely, Connor was still clueless. He probably thought David really did want to design wacky clothing that would never make it to the shops.

David pulled himself up and out, Connor grabbing him under the pits to help him. Then they stood, cramped together in the narrow space between the building's wall and a row of bushes and brush. David slid the window mostly shut behind him, then let Connor lead him around an air conditioning unit that had been waiting since last summer to have purpose again. Pushing through a section of brush that was thinner than the rest, they tumbled out into the street.

"Bad news and good news," Connor said, picking up a plastic bag on the ground. "The bad news is that Chuck only lives about ten blocks from here. The good news—" He dug in the plastic bag and pulled out a bottle of water. "—is that we're going to have some fun."

"Yippie," David said as he accepted the bottle. "Please tell me this is actually vodka."

"You drink?"

"No. Well, at least not yet. I didn't do drugs until just the other day."

Connor smirked. "Well, drink up. It's just water, but I need you to chug it."

After digging out another bottle from the bag, Connor opened and downed half of it. David did the same as they began walking.

"How did you find out where Chuck lives?"

"Internet," Connor answered. "I looked up the site for his dad's dentist office and got his first name. There aren't many people named Bryl in the phonebook and only one with the right initials, so that gave me the address. I cruised by on my way here to make sure."

"Why aren't we driving now?"

"Because we need stealth." Connor winked at him. "My car isn't exactly quiet. Now drink up."

Excitement stirred in David. What were they going to do? Toilet paper his house? Leave a bag of burning dog poop on the front porch? The plastic bag Connor had been carrying was now empty and stuffed into a back pocket, so whatever their plans were, they didn't involve any supplies.

The condos behind them now, they crossed a busy street to a community of houses that weren't exactly luxurious, but many had three-car garages, or the occasional boat parked on a trailer outside. David glanced up at the moon, half-obscured by clouds, and felt heady. Here he was, sneaking out of the house in the middle of the night. Hell, he could probably have walked out the front door with his father's permission. He was almost seventeen and it was Friday night, but doing it this way gave him complete freedom.

"There it is," Connor said as they rounded a corner.

The house wasn't as impressive as its neighbors, only having a two-car garage, but a hint of blue light between the planks of the privacy fence suggested a pool. Parked out front was Chuck's silver Mazda RX-8. Despite it being alone and unoccupied, David shivered at its sinister presence, an extension of its owner's malevolence.

"What are we going to do?" David whispered as they strolled toward it.

"Nothing much. At least not tonight. I just want to give us something to smile about when we see him Monday. You take the driver's side."

Connor walked up the driveway as if he owned the place. The street lights were spaced far enough apart that the driveway was in shadow, but David still felt exposed. Not understanding the plan, he waited by the driver-side door while Connor stood by the passenger's side. He fumbled with something, glancing down once, before he looked up and grinned at David. Then came the sound of trickling water.

"Are you pissing on his car?" David hissed, trying not to laugh.

Connor gave a crooked grin and nodded. "Next time one of Chuck's friends opens the door, their hands will end up sticky. How about the driver?"

David glanced at the door handle. Why the hell not? After double-checking the street, he unzipped his pants, pulled out his dick, and went to town. He had to step back to avoid splashing, and his aim wasn't perfect because he was laughing, but Chuck was guaranteed to get a handful of stale, sticky piss.

Connor came around the car when David was done. "Feel better?"

He did. And next time he sat next to Chuck in math class and had to listen to his insults, he could take solace in having indirectly pissed on him. Except it wasn't enough to make up for what had been done to Connor's car. Even if he got the windshield clean, other parts of the car would still be stained. At the very least, Chuck's car deserved to be equally marred.

Acting on impulse, David kicked the car. He was hoping to dent it, but the exterior was tougher than he expected. What *did* happen was that the alarm went off, an annoying looping siren that filled the empty street.

"Shit!"

They both blurted it at the same time and raced off in the direction they had come from. Once they made it around the corner, Connor started laughing. David was too scared they would get caught, pumping his legs as fast as he could to get away, almost yelping in fright when a hand grabbed his arm. It was Connor, pulling them to the side of one house that wasn't lit.

Connor was still laughing. "Can't breathe!" he wheezed before he doubled over again.

The alarm wailed for a second longer before it beeped and turned off. David strained to hear if anything was happening the next street over, but there was nothing. Like most car owners, Chuck probably glanced out the window while turning off the alarm and nothing more.

"And people say I'm crazy!"

David chuckled nervously. "Sorry. Seemed like a good idea at the time."

"No harm done."

They stood together with their backs pressed against the house, making sure trouble wasn't following. When it seemed they were safe, they made their way back toward David's home.

"What are you doing this weekend?" Connor asked.

"Nothing tomorrow. Sunday is Gordon's birthday, and I promised to take him shopping. He'll probably want to do a video game marathon the rest of the day."

Connor kicked a pinecone off the sidewalk. "Well, I have to work Saturday, but only during the day. Maybe we can get together afterwards. Go for a drive or hang out at my place. Tommy usually stays at a friend's house on the weekends."

Would that mean a sleepover? Or would they just hang out and go their separate ways later? It had been so long since David had a friend other than Gordon that he barely knew what to expect.

"Yeah, okay. Just give me a call when you're off work."

Connor pulled out his cell phone, which looked almost as beat-up as his car. "What's your number?"

"Wait until we're back to my room. I left my phone there, and that way I can punch in yours at the same time." Not to mention that David didn't have his own number memorized. There wasn't anyone to give it to, except for his parents and Gordon.

Climbing back into his room through the window felt oddly like breaking into his own home, but everything was where he left it, so he didn't think his absence had been noticed. Unplugging his phone from the charger, David casually navigated to the menu that displayed his number and read it to Connor. Then he had Connor repeat his number twice as he keyed it in. He turned to plug the phone back in, and his heart started thudding.

Connor needed to know. David liked him and wanted to be friends, but they couldn't be until the air was cleared. Being gay didn't define who David was, but it was still a part of his life, and he couldn't be friends with anyone who didn't accept that aspect of him. Hopefully Connor's experience of being treated differently would make him more receptive. If not, well … it would hurt, but that was a risk he would have to take.

"Connor, I need to tell you something." David spun around.

Connor was holding the yearbook, still open to where David had left it, and staring at the tiny thumbnail image of himself. Thank god he was distracted, because David could feel his face burning. The yearbook was carefully shut and set back down on the bed. Connor looked up, eyes intense. At first David thought they were crazy again because they practically hummed with energy, but no, this was something different.

Then Connor stepped toward him, reached out, and placed his hand on the back of David's neck. That was it. He just stood there, staring into David's eyes. At first David couldn't concentrate—too many worries muddling his thoughts, too many explanations desperate to burble forth as his body buzzed with panic.

But David's heart was brave. He stepped forward, bridging the gap, and pressed his lips against Connor's. His eyes were squeezed shut against the explosion of anger that would come if he was wrong. Arms tense at his sides, he shook from fear, excitement, hormones—everything! Connor's body came closer, an arm wrapping around David's waist, the hand still warm on his neck. David relaxed. He was about to place his hand on Connor's chest when the contact between them broke.

When Connor stepped back, only the hand on David's neck remained, their eyes searching each other's faces.

Connor grinned wildly. "That's what we both wanted, right?"

David struggled to find his voice. "Yeah."

Connor nodded before he let go of David. "Good. I'll see you tomorrow."

"Why are you leaving?" David blurted out. "I don't want you to go."

Connor licked his lips, and for a moment he looked ready to pounce. "I want to do this right. I'm not going anywhere and neither are you, right? We're both stuck in Kansas."

David's laugh was almost a sigh. "That's for sure."

Connor winked. "Tomorrow then."

Like a thief, Connor slipped out through the window and was gone. David listened until he heard the sound of an old engine grumble into life and fade away. Then he sat on the bed and waited, just in case Connor changed his mind. Head spinning, he tried to imagine what life was going to be like now. He had always wanted this, but figured college would be his earliest chance, and that was still more than a year away.

Half an hour later, David decided that Connor wasn't coming back. He closed the window, shut the blinds, and opened the yearbook again. Tomorrow couldn't come quickly enough, and as David unbuttoned his jeans, he decided that he couldn't either.

* * * * *

Connor shifted uncomfortably in the driver's seat on the way home, wishing his stupid erection would go away. He was half-tempted to whip it out and deal with it as he drove, but seeing through a paint-blurred windshield made driving dangerous enough. Besides, he wouldn't be surprised to get pulled over, considering how terrible his car looked, so he turned his mind to a subject guaranteed to turn him off—his first time.

He had been sixteen, David's age probably, when he had started using gay chat rooms. At first Connor would just sit there, reading the lewd comments or over-the-top jokes but not contributing. His user name, MrNobody92, didn't exactly inspire people to private message him, but eventually someone did.

Chatting openly about being gay and finding other guys attractive had been exhilarating at first. Connor never had that before. His sexuality wasn't a secret, but he didn't have any friends to confide in, and talking about it with his family sounded gross. Besides, his mother had enough to deal with, and his father never came down from his opiate-induced high. So Connor had poured his heart out to this stranger and felt, quite stupidly in retrospect, that he was in love before ever having met the man.

This was remedied less than a week later. He met Victor at McDonald's—the very same one he would end up working at—trying to be smart by keeping their encounter public so nothing could go wrong. By the end of the meal, he agreed to go to a movie with Victor.

The guy wasn't really his type. Victor was twenty-three, which seemed pretty old to Connor at the time. He had a light beard Connor didn't like, but he did have a nice lanky frame. Connor couldn't remember a thing about the movie. Victor had held his hand, later stroking his arm and rubbing his thigh. To Connor the experience had been life-changing—another man, touching him and allowing himself to be touched in return.

After the film, Victor suggested they go back to his apartment. His caution abandoned, Connor eagerly agreed. They had a couple of beers, but this wasn't Connor's first time with alcohol, and his head was clear enough to know what he wanted. The beer simply made it easier to admit.

Soon Victor was undressing him, eyeing him in a way that made Connor feel attractive. The sex wasn't great. Connor felt like he was doing everything wrong, and once Victor came, he was no longer interested. But Connor figured it was just their first time, that they would have other chances.

The next morning, Victor was distant and defensive. He obsessed over Connor's age, saying that the beer had impaired his judgment. Connor reassured him that everything was fine, that he wouldn't tell anyone and had enjoyed himself. Victor thanked him, and Connor thought everything was going to be okay. That was the last he ever heard from Victor.

Connor wasn't heartbroken, not exactly, but knowing his first time had been with someone unimportant, someone he had known for all of six hours, took the shine off the memories. Now Connor looked back on the experience with disgust.

He tried a few more times after that, meeting other guys online and being more cautious with his emotions. He soon realized that these men were also just looking for a hookup. Connor began lying about his age and experience, and for some reason this made them more honest about what they wanted. Connor only slept with a few other guys, simply because they were hot and Connor was horny, and that had been it.

Still, he remembered that feeling in the movie theater, as if the fantasy world he had always dreamed of had suddenly become real. Everything had been possible in that moment, even if nothing had come of it. David had probably felt that tonight. Connor was sure that the kiss, clumsy and uncertain, had been David's first. Not that Connor hadn't enjoyed every second of it. Right now David was probably floating on blissful cloud of limitless potential, and Connor intended to keep him there as long as possible. He wouldn't let David rush in and do anything he regretted. If Connor was lucky, maybe David could help him get back to a place he thought lost forever.

Chapter Six

When Connor entered his bedroom the next morning, towel wrapped around his waist and a trail of wet footprints behind him, the phone on his dresser buzzed with a text message. He had a good idea who that might be. After all, he had just been thinking of David while in the shower. The goofy grin slipped off his face when he saw it was from Riley. Since when did she have his number?

Mike pissed u missed work. Sez u have 2 work a dbl. -Riley

Connor swore, loudly. Luckily Tommy wasn't in the room. No way was he working a double shift. He would go in, do his eight hours, and meet David once he was cleaned up again. His message to Riley was short and sweet.

WTF?

Her response came shortly after.

M says dbl or fired. So gay!

Mike had been looking for an excuse to fire him for months now. Connor was clueless as to why. Maybe Mike had heard the rumors and taken it upon himself to punish Connor. Or maybe he was just an asshole.

Fine.

Connor tossed the phone on the bed, trying not to punch something. Then he got dressed. An extra shift would bring Connor right up to midnight, and no doubt he would be expected to close. So no date with David, all because Mike wanted to make his life hell.

Connor sat on the bed and tried to get his emotions under control. Once he was as calm as he was going to get, he picked up the phone and called David.

"Connor! Hi!"

David sounded ridiculously excited, which made the news all the harder to deliver.

"Bad news. I have to work a double shift today."

"Oh. That's okay. What time do you get off?"

"Probably about one in the morning."

"Oh." David's tone remained upbeat. "You could still come by. I'll stay up. Or I could come visit you."

Connor grimaced. "Please don't. Working there is bad enough

without you seeing me in a McDonald's uniform." He tried to laugh, but it sounded hollow. "Afterwards I'm going to be tired." And smell, and feel anything but sexy and confident.

"Okay." There was a pregnant pause. "I understand."

Shit. Now David thought he was getting the brush-off, that their kiss last night had been a fluke. Forget his pride or how self-conscious he might feel. David needed to know that Connor was for real.

"If you're still going to be up," Connor said, "I'll come by, just for a little while."

"Really?"

"Yeah. I have to get my goodnight kiss, right? Just don't fall asleep on me."

David laughed nervously. "I'll stay awake."

Connor said goodbye and hung up. Screw Mike. He could make Connor work, but he couldn't take away how David made him feel.

"A double shift!" his mother said as she shoveled more pancakes onto his plate. "I think you're the only person in the world who has a job worse than mine."

"What can you do?" Connor grabbed the syrup and poured a small lake. He loved having his mom home. She brought everything together, even forcing Dad to wake up at a decent time and sit at the table instead of in front of the television. Sure, he was dozing off, but at least he was there. Tommy was too, playing a Game Boy he had found at a garage sale that was probably ten years his senior.

"I'm back on the early shift," his mom said as she sat. She looked tired, as she always did, but still good for her age. Her figure was well maintained, mostly from not having time to eat, and her hair still had natural blonde highlights. Connor wondered if his would get that dark when he was older.

"Does this mean you'll be picking up Tommy from school again?"

She nodded. "There's a new nurse on the nightshift I trained last week, and as long as he doesn't turn out to be another pill thief, things should be back to normal."

Back to normal meant his mother breaking her back running a nursing home while making the same amount as the new nurse they hired. The former manager of the nursing home had quit more than a year ago, Connor's mother named acting manager. She had been promised this designation was temporary, that the position would be given to her permanently, but all corporate had done since was make excuses. Obviously upper management had realized they could pay a nurse to do a manager's job and get away with it.

His mother tisked. "Stop clenching your jaw or you'll break a tooth." She patted his arm. "If they don't give me the position by summer, I'll start looking."

She had said the same about spring. Connor glanced at his father, who was poking at his pancakes without interest. Didn't he have any opinions about this? Or had his feelings for them been permanently numbed by pills? Sometimes Connor wanted to freak out, shake his father and yell at him to get his shit together. But then Connor often felt pissed off lately. The older he got, the more injustice he saw. So much of it was on a small scale, affecting the little people who were too tired, poor, or uneducated to fight back.

His mood stayed foul through most of his first shift. Riley tried making small talk, Connor only grunting in reply. Mike came in when the second shift began, which didn't help improve his mood, the thought that he should be out with David infuriating him. Connor nearly quit, leaving it all behind just to reclaim that time with David, but he couldn't. Graduation was coming, the end of high school, which would have been a huge relief if Connor had solid plans for the future. College was too expensive, so he needed a real job. McDonald's wasn't it, and he had no idea what would be. What he did know was that he needed money and had started saving up a year ago. Anything that wasn't spent on gas, his car, or helping mom pay the bills went into savings. That didn't leave much, but it was better than nothing.

"Williams, number three!"

"Yes, sir!" Time to make Mike's burger, complete with secret sauce.

"Two shifts, two loogies," he whispered to Riley at the dressing station.

She squeezed her eyes shut, refusing to watch. Connor didn't blame her. The food here was enough to turn his stomach, even without his added ingredient.

The evening was surprisingly slow for a Saturday, Connor doing everything he could to clean in advance so closing would go quickly.

"Dish duty," Riley said, sidling up to him. "How fun."

"Yeah." Connor finished rinsing the trays with the industrial strength sprayer. "Hey, shouldn't you have been off hours ago?"

Riley pulled the edge of her shirt coyly, stretching the fabric tight over her breasts before answering. "Just working some overtime, earning extra cash."

"Cool." Connor busied himself with straightening up the sink. He could feel what was coming, like the pressure before a thunderstorm.

"So what are you doing with the rest of the night? Not that there's much left of it." Riley laughed awkwardly before clearing her throat.

"I have a date," Connor said. Time to nip this in the bud, but he wanted to minimize the damage and let Riley know there wasn't another woman. "Well, not a real date because it's too late for that, but I promised him I'd drop by anyway."

"Him?" Riley's laugh was short lived. "Wait, seriously?"

Connor gave her a friendly smile. "Yeah. I dig guys."

"Oh. Okay. Just guys?"

"Yeah."

"That's cool."

But she didn't sound like she thought it was cool and soon wandered away. Connor figured she needed time to adjust to the idea. Only when he had finished the dishes did he realize that she had clocked out and left.

Connor busted his ass the rest of the night. At half-past twelve, he and Mike were the last ones out. He was sure it was a record. Maybe that's why Mike didn't have some smart-ass comment as they closed up for the night. The doors were already locked, meaning he had to wait for Mike to let him out. He watched with disinterest as Mike punched in the alarm code--hiding the keypad as if this secret could launch nuclear warheads—before they both left. Mike pulled the door closed behind him. He did it wrong, as he always did. The latch didn't click into place if you didn't yank up on the doorknob, but Connor didn't care.

He jogged to his car, waited until Mike pulled out of the parking lot, and changed clothes inside his car. While he was shirtless he sprayed on some cologne he had swiped from his dad. He thought about smoking a cigarette, just to help cover up the grease smell, but resisted. Instead he chewed a piece of gum, wishing it had nicotine in it.

By the time he arrived at David's place, all was forgotten. Riley, Mike, his mother's crappy job, and the endless patties he had grilled—all gone. The only thoughts that remained were of David. Connor parked his car close to the back of the building and made his way down the narrow path to David's window.

The light was on, his breath quickening. He crouched down and saw David on his back, sprawled out on the bed. Connor could hear music, but couldn't tell if David was listening with his eyes closed or sleeping. When he tapped on the window, David didn't respond. Connor knew what he would do—he would push open the window, crawl into the room, and lay down next to David. Then Connor would wake him with a kiss, but this time he wouldn't hold back. He would take all the frustration he felt and transform it into passion, making David's first time something he would never forget.

Connor placed his fingers on the window and slid it to the right, trying to be quiet, but the glass juddered noisily in the frame. David started and sat up, looking confused and then embarrassed before rushing to open the window the rest of the way.

"Sorry," he whispered. "Dozed off. Can we go for a quick walk? I'm worried my dad will hear us talking."

Connor's fantasy disappeared, but he didn't mind. He was with David, and that's all he really wanted. He helped David climb out the window, and once they were both on their feet, there was an awkward moment of expectation. Connor knew the cure for that. He leaned forward and kissed David, lightly and teasingly, before he took his hand and led him down the path.

"Where do you want to go?" Connor said.

Leaves crunched beneath their feet as David considered. "There's a playground not far away."

Connor grinned. "Okay."

David took the lead once they were out in the street, guiding them to the subdivision entrance and continuing past it. There, next to a community pool, was a swing set and a small jungle gym. Connor sat on one of the swings, the kind with the floppy rubber seat, and lazily twisted back and forth. David took the other, leaning his head against one of the chains while watching him.

"How long have you known?" he asked.

Connor considered the question. "About me or about you?"

"Both."

"Well, I wasn't completely sure you were gay until you kissed me."

David laughed, his expression a strange combination of embarrassment and pride. "I didn't have a clue about you until afterwards."

"The kiss wasn't convincing enough?"

"Not as much as you not punching me."

Connor smiled. "I almost tackled you, but for different reasons." They both paused and considered what this might have led to. "I figured it out when I was twelve," Connor continued. "There was a kid in our neighborhood who stole a porn magazine from his parents. He offered to loan it to anyone for five bucks, so I paid him and was completely disappointed. It was just a *Playboy*-type magazine, so no guys were involved, just women, and they did nothing for me. There were some ads in the back though, and some had tiny pictures of guys. I stayed up all night squinting at those rather than looking at the centerfold."

David grinned. "Are you out?"

"Yeah. I've got nothing to hide. My mom figured it out even earlier than I did, but for the wrong reasons. She came home when I was eight and found me dressed up in my older sister's clothes. Since then she just assumed I was gay and didn't blink an eye when I told her. Cross-dressing has nothing to do with it. I'm not a drag queen or anything. I just thought it would be funny. I looked damn good, though."

Now David laughed, and Connor focused on those pillowy lips and the teeth they framed. He wanted to be close to him. Pumping the swing a few times to gain height, Connor jumped, feet thudding in the sand. Then he walked around the jungle gym to one of the benches, glancing back to make sure David was following. He was, just like a puppy.

As soon as they were both seated, Connor groaned and rolled to the side, pulling up his legs on the bench and resting his head in David's lap. "Long day," he murmured.

David touched Connor's hair, tentatively at first, before moving the tips of his fingers back and forth along the buzzed hair. It had been much longer just two weeks ago, before Connor asked his mom to trim it with the electric clippers. David stroking the short hairs sent tingles of pleasure along his scalp.

"Does that feel good?"

"Yeah." Connor closed his eyes. "Tell me about when you came out."

"I never really had to," David said. "Enough people called me gay that everyone just assumed it was true. I didn't know they were right until a couple of years ago. My dad had this field trip sort of thing planned for his students. He teaches urban planning and wanted to show them different parts of Kansas City that related to the lessons. Naturally he dragged me along. The people walking around downtown were way more interesting than my dad's lesson, so I started checking them out. I was staring at this guy on a street corner who kept checking his watch as if he were waiting for someone.

"The class had already moved down the sidewalk, but I pretended to tie my shoe, just because I wanted to see who he was waiting for, or if they wouldn't come. Then this other guy comes up behind him and does the whole covering your eyes and 'guess who' thing. It was so cheesy, but then the waiting guy turned around and kissed him."

Connor rolled over onto his back and opened his eyes to watch David tell the rest. David's fingers were still moving, even though he probably wasn't aware of them, and they felt good as they brushed along the skin of his neck.

"When I saw them kiss it was like my heart stopped. The whole world, which had always been confusing and weird to me, suddenly made sense. I knew then what love looked like and where I fit in. I hadn't felt anything like that before or since. Until last night."

David looked down, noticing Connor and giving his fingers direction, moving them over Connor's eyebrows, down the bridge of his nose, and across his lips to his chin. Then he traced the line of his jaw. Connor became self-conscious of the stubble there, the sound like sandpaper.

"How old are you?" David asked.

"Thirty-seven," Connor said with a straight face.

"No, really."

"I'm nineteen, but I started shaving when I was fourteen." Connor considered David's baby-smooth face. "How old are you?"

"Sixteen."

Connor grinned. "Sweet sixteen. I had no idea I was robbing the cradle."

David looked offended. "I turn seventeen later this year."

"Yeah, well, until then you're sweet sixteen."

Connor rolled onto his side again. The warmth from David's lap, his gentle touches, and the long day behind him made sleep almost irresistible. He didn't want to make a fool of himself by drooling all over David's crotch, at least not like this, so he forced himself to sit up.

"I have to drive home while I can still keep my eyes open."

"Sorry."

"Don't be. Seeing you was the only good thing about today."

Oh, what the hell. Connor could manage a little longer. He leaned over and kissed David—kept kissing him until he felt on the verge of doing too much, even if they were in a public place. A passing car made them both stop. They laughed nervously, stood, and walked back to David's home.

"I guess this is it until Monday," Connor said.

"Yeah. If tomorrow wasn't Gordon's birthday—"

"I know. Have fun together anyway." They were at the window now. If David asked him to stay, Connor would. Even though his mind said to take it slow, his hormones and heart had his brain outnumbered.

"Goodbye," David said, kissing him once more before climbing through the window.

Connor sighed. Karma. It had to be karma for leaving David hanging last night, but when next the opportunity arose, Connor wouldn't say no.

Chapter Seven

If David were cruel enough, he could record Gordon eating, upload it to the Internet, and the video would go viral in seconds. Like everything in his life, Gordon ate without a shred of self-awareness. He ripped into his mall pizza with reckless abandon, sometimes taking two or three bites before he started chewing. Sauce smeared his left cheek. The great thing about Gordon was that he never minded if you stared.

The food court felt like a step up in maturity after last year, when Gordon insisted they go to Chuck E. Cheese for his birthday. David had protested just enough to prove how grown up he was before happily giving in. Who didn't love arcade games and creepy singing robots? But maybe Gordon was feeling the looming pressure of adulthood, now that he was sixteen.

Not that their activities today had been especially mature. They had bounced back and forth between the mall's two video game stores, pricing titles and considering their options. Then they hit the bookstores so Gordon could find the brand of strategy guides he liked that neither of the game stores carried. David had bought two of those for him as a present. Now they were just finishing eating and about to leave for the used book store.

David considered texting their destination to Connor so they could "accidentally" meet. Maybe they could sneak a desperate kiss or two in an empty aisle before parting again. As he finished his pizza, David wondered how Gordon would react if they were caught. Would he stop and stare at them kissing, fall over dead, or simply ask what they were doing? Love and sex were two topics they never broached. David tended to keep quiet since he didn't want the gay thing to make Gordon uncomfortable. That, and until recently, he had nothing to report. Gordon wasn't exactly forthcoming with any details either.

"Have you ever been in love?"

In a rare display of manners, Gordon chewed and swallowed before answering. "Mrs. Fridley."

David stared. "The woman who lives at the end of the block?"

Gordon nodded. "Yeah, the one who has me feed her cats when she visits her family in Poland."

"But she's like a hundred and two!"

"She's forty-six," Gordon said, before noisily sucking up the last drops of soda. "And she's a good kisser."

David's world fell apart, breaking into a million tiny pieces, before being put back together by a rusty staple gun and rolls of yellowing adhesive tape. He tried to picture Mrs. Fridley, the woman with the weird accent and a penchant for cat sweaters, locking lips with Gordon. "So, are you guys an item?"

"Not right now. She was into me, but said that I was too young. I looked up the age of consent, and in Kansas it's sixteen years old unless your parents object."

"Are you going to tell them?"

Gordon pushed his glasses back up his nose. "Do you think I should?"

"No! Definitely not." David gave a mad chuckle. "Definitely keep this one to yourself. So now that you're sixteen—"

Gordon adopted his best cool guy expression. "Let's just say I'm considering my options. I don't know if I want to get tied down just yet."

David still felt like he was floating through a bizarre dream as they walked toward the department store closest to the parked car. Gordon and Mrs. Fridley. Love was a crazy beast! Then again, how would the people at school react if they knew about Connor and him? The nerdy loser and the alleged psychopath. They would never believe it.

David's dreamlike state soon turned into a nightmare. Ahead, on the other side of the hallway near a music store, stood Chuck and a couple of his friends. David tried to stay calm. They hadn't been seen yet, so they could still duck into a store. As he was about to ask Gordon to do just that, one of Chuck's friends noticed him, eyebrows raising for a second before he nudged Chuck.

David didn't hesitate. He grabbed Gordon's arm, yanking him down one of the side halls that led toward the open parking lot. The car wasn't anywhere nearby, and being outside would leave them exposed, so David whipped his head back and forth as he dragged Gordon along, searching for a place to hide.

"What are we running from?" Gordon huffed.

A gruff male voice shouted from behind, so David ducked into the nearest store. A women's store. For large ladies. Not the best place to make a final stand, but the back of the store provided booth-shaped sanctuary—if they weren't all occupied. David dodged the saleswoman and practically dived into one of the dressing rooms, pulling the slatted door shut behind Gordon.

"Were those guys after you?" Gordon asked, clutching shopping bags to his chest as if thieves wanted his loot. "Who are they?"

"Just some guys desperate to kick my ass. Did they see where we went?"

"I'm not sure."

They listened for signs of a commotion, but the store was quiet aside from elevator music and murmured comments about fashion. Of course. What could Chuck do, hold the saleswoman hostage unless they came out?

"Does this happen a lot?" Gordon whispered.

David thought about how many close calls there had been lately. "Pretty much every day, yeah."

Gordon's eyes grew wide. "I'm so glad I don't have to go to school."

They listened for a moment longer, then David nodded toward a clothes hook where a giant leopard-spotted bra hung. They burst out laughing until someone knocked on the door.

"Yeah?" David said, heart in his throat.

"Do you need any help in there?"

The voice was female, no doubt one of the sales clerks.

"No," David said. "Just trying on a few things."

They held their breath until she moved away before snorting and sniggering. They felt much more somber when they decided to leave, embarrassed when a number of women watched them go. Luckily they saw no sign of Chuck and his friends.

"Move with the stealth of a ninja!" Gordon whispered as they made their way down the mall hallways again.

David had no idea how that was done, but kept his eyes peeled for any sign of trouble. Maybe the patron saint of birthdays was watching out for them, because they escaped the mall and reached the car with no trouble.

The used bookstore felt like a safe place, since David couldn't imagine Chuck being there in a million years. Gordon could spend hours shopping for books, so after David was finished browsing, he sat in one of the reading chairs and pulled out his phone.

I miss you.

He typed the text message but didn't hit send, even though it was the truth. He missed Connor, even if he barely knew him. When he thought back, he realized they had known each other less than a week, and yet David felt like he couldn't live without him ever again. The thought was unreasonable and unsound, but he didn't care. He hit the send button and sat waiting, feeling both stupid and relieved. Then the answer came.

Don't cry Sweet 16. 2morrow is ours.

And a few seconds later, another one.

I miss you too.

David dug through his closet the next morning, trying to find the right outfit. He never worried much about his appearance and usually dressed for comfort. Now, with Connor in the picture, he wanted to try harder. He put on a dress shirt he had worn to a family reunion last fall, but once he checked himself in the mirror, he decided he looked ridiculous. He undid the first few buttons and pulled it off over his head, opting instead for a T-shirt and his favorite brown hoody.

Just when he was putting on his jeans, his phone buzzed, David hopping toward it as he pulled them up.

Play sick.

He reread the message a few times, as if the two simple words held greater meaning. Then again, Connor could have texted *invest in rice* and David probably would have done so without question. School was by far his least favorite place on Earth, so of course David had played sick before. He always had to call his dad, who left early to beat the northbound commuter traffic. The only problem was that David preferred to fake a few symptoms the day before. Last night he and Gordon had stayed up late playing video games, which made feigning sudden illness more suspect.

David debated between puking and diarrhea. The former was reliable, but the latter less expected. Puking was as generic as faking a fever by holding the thermometer against a light bulb. Then again, maybe it being so expected is what made it unexpected. Or something. David coughed and cleared his throat to make his voice sound more hoarse before calling his dad.

"I threw up," he said, skipping the formalities. David could hear voices in the background. This could either be good or bad. His dad might be too preoccupied to question him or too busy to call into school. "I think it was food poisoning," he added.

His father sighed. "Do you still feel nauseous? Maybe you got it out of your system."

"My stomach hurts," he said, dodging the question. He wouldn't ask to stay home. That was too obvious.

"Well, do you need me to come home? I'm very busy."

"No." David made a throaty noise as if more was on its way up. "I just need to get back to bed."

"Very well, I'll call your school."

"Thanks. Love you."

"I love you, too."

David hung up the phone, feeling genuinely ill for a moment before he remembered he was faking. Then he miraculously cured himself and texted Connor.

Done.

Whens the old man go 2 work?

David grinned as he texted back. *Already gone.*

On my way.

And then what? David didn't care about the consequences. He wanted an entire day alone with Connor. But what if his father came home at lunch to check on him? Or Gordon noticed Connor's car parked outside and decided to visit? Gordon's presence wouldn't be very conducive to a romantic mood. Unless you were Mrs. Fridley, apparently. Of course there was one place they could go to be alone, at least for a little while.

David quadruple-checked his appearance in the mirror and began pacing between the living room and the front door. Finally he saw more than an empty street when he peeked outside. He was out the door before Connor could turn off the engine and practically slid across the hood Dukes of Hazard-style to get to the passenger-side door.

"Somebody's had their cornflakes this morning," Connor said as David hopped in the car.

David responded by kissing him.

"So where to?"

"Shawnee."

Connor looked puzzled. "Why there?"

David grinned. "That's where my safe house is. The cops

won't find us there."

Connor shook his head but said, "You're the boss."

Eastern Kansas didn't have a lot to offer. People often thought of Kansas City before they realized that most of that city was on the Missouri side. But from there began a massive urban sprawl. Interstate 35 wound southwest through cities whose borders had long ago merged, forming one beast with many names. The urban sprawl became suburban before reaching Olathe, the last sentinel against the rural world beyond. Leaving Olathe almost always meant going north, at least if the destination was more than just farmland and small towns.

As they drove past the high school, David imagined the teachers and bullies spilling from the brick building and filling the street to halt their progress. Soon the school was behind them, the wild freedom making David feel high. The sun was out and everyone else was locked away at work or school, all but Connor and him. He watched Connor switch gears as he turned onto the highway, grateful when they reached a steady speed and his hand was free for David to hold.

"Up to 87th Street," David said. "Then take it toward Shawnee Mission Park."

The house there belonged to David's mother and her second husband, but David had never called it home. She had given him a key ages ago—mostly out of guilt, he suspected—but today would be the first time he had used it. The couple both worked days, his mother as a technical writer and Jeff as a pharmacist, meaning their lovely suburban home would be unoccupied.

The neighborhood was soulless, every two-story house some variation of beige and gray. The only saving grace was a state park nestled up against the homes, its thick forests contrasting with the spindly trees on each front lawn.

As they pulled into the driveway, David wished he had X-ray vision and could see if the garage was empty. How would he explain his presence if someone was home?

"Wait, don't tell me," Connor said as he killed the engine. "You're actually a millionaire who's been slumming it until he could find someone that loves him for more than his money."

"Exactly," David said, "but I let it look like my asshole stepfather is the one with all the cash."

"What's he do?"

"Drug dealer at a pharmacy. Bible thumper on his days off."

They left the car, David leading them to the front door where he rang the doorbell, just to be safe. He stared at the wooden custom sign hanging on the door, painted butterflies surrounding colorful letters that spelled out "Sharon and Jeff Perkins welcome you!" David wondered, had he chosen to live with his mother all those years ago, if his name would be up there as well.

When no movement came from inside, he unlocked the door. He and Connor entered quietly. Walking through the entryway, they passed a dining room on the right and a family room on the left to reach an open, two-story living room. Most of it bore his mother's mark, from the fake floral arrangement on the fireplace mantel to the couch covered in small delicate pillows with sayings stitched on them. The large screen television was all Jeff, though.

"Nice," Connor said.

"Is it?" David recognized that everything in the room cost money, but none of it had ever felt comfortable. The condo where he lived with his dad was simple, but at least it was paid off and small enough to be energy-efficient. At least, that's what his dad always said when the subject of this house came up, but now David felt like agreeing with him.

"Not a bad movie collection."

Connor was browsing a shelf full of films that David's mother had tried to hide behind painted flower pots with fake birds perched on their edges. As cheesy as he found her decorating style, such frilly items reminded him of what was missing from home.

"After we look around, we can watch something if you want," David said. Still a little nervous, he felt the need to make sure no one was home. He and Connor toured the house, but he didn't have much to say about it. David felt like a stranger here. He visited only on the occasional holiday. Normally, to avoid Jeff, he asked his mother to pick him up and take him out somewhere.

"The way you described your stepdad," Connor said as they headed back to the living room, "I expected to find a painting of Jesus in every room."

David frowned. "Jesus is probably too progressive for Jeff. He's definitely an Old Testament guy."

"You don't get along?"

David shook his head. "It's the whole gay thing."

"Ah." Connor plopped down on the couch, spreading his arms wide. David hurried to put in a movie so he could feel one of those arms around him. "And your mother? Is she okay with you?"

"She doesn't tell me it's wrong, but she doesn't argue the point with Jeff either. I try not to care. He's not my dad, and I'm lucky my real parents don't have a problem with it. So are you."

"Absolutely." Connor cocked his head. "Of course, my sister helped pave the way. She's a dyke."

David blanched. "Are you supposed to say that?"

Connor shrugged. "That's what she calls herself. She's pretty intense. Too bad you can't meet her. She moved to Florida last year to be with her girlfriend. Anyway, being second to come out in the family is easier, although I think Mom is secretly desperate for Tommy to be straight, if only for the grandkids."

David returned to the couch, sitting further away from Connor than he intended. He wanted to be cuddled up against him, but still wasn't sure how to make the move. Instead he fiddled with the remotes until the movie started.

The movie was *Rear Window*, his favorite from Hitchcock. As they watched it together, he thought he understood why. James Stewart plays a photographer with a broken leg, cooped up inside his apartment. Out of boredom, he starts spying on his neighbors and sees strange events that make him believe he witnessed a murder. In a way, it was the perfect metaphor for David's life. He felt trapped in Kansas, unable to move freely, while convinced life was more exciting outside the state. Maybe, like Jimmy Stewart's character, David should find an excuse to leave. Anything, no matter how dangerous, just to get away from here.

Feeling brave with this realization, he leaned into Connor, rewarded when the arm came off the couch's back to wrap around him. David barely paid attention to the rest of the movie, focusing instead on the warmth where their bodies met or the feeling of Connor's strong hand on his shoulder. When the movie ended, David didn't want to move, but his stomach grumbled loudly.

"Me too," Connor said. "Think we can raid the fridge?"

"Yeah."

Of course this would leave evidence of someone having been

here, but David wanted to make Connor happy. The kitchen seemed much larger than two people needed. Maybe his mom and Jeff used every inch of available counter space for huge dinner parties. He wasn't even sure which of them cooked. He felt a surge of guilt for knowing so little about his mom's new life, but she wasn't particularly involved with his, either.

David went straight for the freezer, searching for frozen burritos or pizzas. Connor, looking over his shoulder, reached in and grabbed some ground beef.

"This has potential."

"It does?"

"Yeah. You're not a vegetarian, are you?" Connor bared his teeth. "I'm a rabid carnivore."

David closed the freezer. "I eat meat, but I don't know how to cook it."

"Leave it to me." Connor popped the meat in the microwave to defrost. David expected they would grill burgers in the backyard, but Connor started pulling other ingredients out of the pantry and refrigerator: macaroni, a can of tomatoes, a bell pepper, onions, cheese. He waited for Connor to make a face, like he was kidding around, but instead he started hunting for pots and pans.

"You know how to cook?" David asked.

Connor lowered his brow. "Either that, or I'm about to start juggling."

David stared in awe as Connor diced an onion. He wasn't quite as good as the TV chefs, but David couldn't even peel an onion. At least, he had never tried.

"Did you learn this working at McDonald's?"

Connor snorted. "Trust me. Everything at McDonald's comes out of cardboard boxes. My sister taught me most of this. She had to take care of me and Tommy when we were younger and is a health nut, so she hates prepackaged food. She used to put on a show while she cooked, I guess to keep us occupied while she did what she needed to, but after awhile she figured out we could be helpers."

"So Tommy can cook too?"

"Ha! No, but if you need something stirred, he's your man. Are you sure these things won't be missed?"

David thought they probably would, but he didn't think his

mom would call the police over ground beef, or suspect David of whipping up a meal. "It's fine. Anything I can do?"

"Just stand there looking pretty. It motivates me. Oh, maybe grab some drinks and set the table."

He should film this—Connor the psychopath tossing macaroni into boiling water with one hand while shaking a pan of frying onions with the other. Then everybody would see how wrong they had been about him.

"Goulash," Connor said later when he placed two plates on the table. "I have no idea what that is or if this is it, but goulash is what my sister calls it."

It looked like beef and macaroni in tomato sauce, and after years of eating his father's generic pasta creations, David thought it tasted exquisite.

"You should work in a real kitchen," David said. "I'd pay money for this. If I had any."

"I think you have to go to culinary school for something like that."

"Why don't you?"

Connor looked surprised. "Honestly, I've never thought about it. I just cook occasionally for my family when the mood strikes. I guess it'd be better than flipping burgers. What about you? Any big career plans?"

David shrugged. "Travelling salesman, Greyhound bus driver, cruise ship janitor, border drug runner, anything like that."

Connor chewed in silence for a moment before he understood. "Travel?"

"Yeah. I have no idea what I want to do, but whatever it is, it won't be in Kansas."

"People are people," Connor said.

"You mean it won't be better anywhere else? Maybe. I'd like a chance to find out."

Once they finished eating, David jumped up to wash the dishes, eager to show Connor he wasn't completely helpless in the kitchen. He did his best to put everything back where it belonged, chuckling over the thought of wiping down the pots to eliminate fingerprints. He even did the dishes by hand so they wouldn't be in the dishwasher. When the kitchen was restored, he turned around and glimpsed the trees beyond the backyard.

David yearned to be out there. This house, with its quiet established style of living, wasn't what he and Connor were about. They didn't belong here. He would rather be outside, running through the woods like the lost boys that they were.

He turned to Connor, who was watching him as if waiting for David to speak his thoughts.

"Let's go for a walk."

Chapter Eight

Shawnee Mission Park functioned as an oasis of nature in a land of strip malls and highways. David and Gordon ventured there occasionally, most recently after watching YouTube videos of people live action role-playing while dressed up Renaissance style. This looked like good nerdy fun, so they had given it a shot. Gordon had been serious about it, but David hadn't been able to stop laughing, so the expedition hadn't exactly been a success.

The park spread out around Shawnee Mission Lake, a body of water large enough for sailing that took about twenty minutes to circle around at the speed limit. David asked Connor to drive to the mountain bike trails at the northern part of the lake. Paved paths for pedestrians existed elsewhere, but David preferred the more natural dirt trails.

"Last time I was here was with Tommy," Connor said as he parked the car. "I let him run all over the paths until he wore himself out. Of course by the time we drove home, he was hyper again."

The parking lot was mostly empty, which meant they would have privacy. David breathed in the fresh air once out of the car, wishing the entire world consisted only of him and Connor. As if reading his thoughts, Connor took his hand, and when they reached the shelter of the trees, he stopped David to kiss him.

Suddenly David wished they hadn't left his mom's house. As unappealing as that environment had been, at least the house provided enough privacy for something more to happen. The idea intimidated him. He didn't know if Connor had slept with other guys, but David's experience began and ended with kissing Connor. Regardless, he wanted more to happen between them, but wished he could take a training course first—Gay Sex 101 or something.

In the green light of the woods, David found himself relaxing, feeling like he had escaped into a fairytale where all the troubles of the real world faded away. The sound of cars receded the farther they walked, replaced by the bird chatter and creatures foraging through the underbrush.

"You like it here," Connor said.

"Yeah. How'd you know?"

"Because you're usually tense, like you're waiting for something to explode."

David shrugged, embarrassed. "I don't mean to look that way."

"There's nothing wrong with it. It's just weird since you're strong."

David glanced over at Connor in disbelief. "I'm not strong."

"Really? Are you ashamed of being gay?"

David increased his grip on Connor's hand. "Not at all!"

"There you go. People are always giving you shit for being gay, but you're not in the closet, and you don't let them make you feel ashamed."

"They still make me miserable," David said. "If I pretended to be straight, I'd be even more unhappy. Believe me, people like Chuck get to me. Sometimes I can barely sleep at night."

Connor wasn't willing to give up. "Taking all that abuse though, not letting it break you. That's strength."

"Maybe. Sounds more like endurance to me. This is strength." David's hand slipped away from Connor's and moved up his bicep. Connor flexed it, and they both laughed, although David was impressed as well.

Their hike continued north, the occasional bicycle rider passing them. They would step aside to let the rider pass, but never let go of each other. One biker kept his head forward but strained to see out of the corner of his eye as he passed. An hour later and the paths ended, leaving them to slowly pick their way through the trees. They went far enough into the woods that David wondered if they would find their way back again. Finally, the trees gave way to water and they could go no farther.

A creek wound through the land, filling the air with burbles. On the other side was a line of trees, beyond which a large open field was barely visible. They walked along the creek until they found a patch of bare earth where they could sit, David's feet hot and sore from the hike. He kicked off his shoes before sitting cross-legged on the ground. As soon as he did, Connor leaned over and plopped his head in his lap, an expectant grin on his face. He closed his eyes when David began stroking his face, sighing contentedly.

David moved his fingers over Connor's cheek bones, toyed

with his ears, and then moved his fingers down to his neck. The scar was flat, a pinkish-white line running from below his ear to just above his Adam's apple. Now that David knew the reasons behind it weren't sinister, he thought it looked kind of cool.

"Can I touch it?"

Connor's eyes shot open, searching David's for a moment. "Go ahead. It doesn't hurt."

David brushed his finger up and down the scar, stroking it as if he could erase it with his touch. The skin was smooth, stubble unable to grow there.

They sat together for some time, listening to the water flow and the light breeze that tickled the trees. David eyed Connor's chest, wanting to touch it but worried about leaning forward. What if Connor noticed how hard he was? If Connor moved his head, even an inch, his erection would be obvious. But the temptation was too great, so David very carefully leaned forward, running his hands over the strong pecs and leaving one hand there with fingers splayed. He wanted to keep moving that hand, to slide it below Connor's shirt to touch skin against skin, but was already too turned on.

"I wish I was more like you," David murmured.

This puzzled Connor. "You can start doing pushups if you want, but I like you the way you are."

"No, not that. I wish I was brave like you. You never seem afraid."

"Then start now."

"What do you mean?"

David started to move his hand away, but Connor grabbed his wrist to keep his hand where it was. "Being brave is just doing whatever the hell you want, no matter how bad it scares you. What do you want to do now?" Connor moved his other hand to touch David's lips with the back of his fingers. "Whatever it is, do it instead of just saying it."

That was all the encouragement he needed. David grabbed Connor's T-shirt and tugged upwards.

Connor grinned. "You want me to take this off?"

David nodded and smiled, not speaking a word. This could be fun! Connor sat up on his knees and stripped off his shirt before turning around to face him. David stared at the light dusting of blonde chest hair, the half-dozen small scars on his left shoulder, and the muscles that made him look like a man where David still felt like a boy. He wanted to press himself against that body, to feel its strength directly, but that would reveal the hard-on straining against his jeans. He glanced down to see that Connor was in the same condition.

Be brave. David rose up on his knees, and Connor met him halfway, their lips crashing together. Connor's fingers slipped into David's hair, and he pressed his mouth even closer, their tongues dancing. Moving his hands over Connor's chest, David almost whimpered in bliss. This is what he had fantasized about so often. Always it had seemed like an impossible dream, but here he was with another guy, touching and tasting—and it was better than he imagined.

He pulled away to kiss the scar on Connor's neck, then those on his left shoulder, but he wanted something desperately more. His hands moved to Connor's hips, gripped tightly, and pulled upward.

Connor understood the signal. He stood, not moving away from David and leaving him eye level with his crotch. David glanced up at Connor, who held both his hands up in surrender. Then David tore at the zipper of his jeans, barely glancing at the tighty-whiteys before yanking them down. Freed, Connor's cock flexed, already awe-inspiring as it swelled further. David could have sat and stared at it all day. Sure, he had one of his own, but that didn't decrease the fascination of seeing the subtle differences in thickness and length.

Then David's fantasies came roaring back and he took it in his mouth. Too carelessly at first because he gagged, but he did his best to adjust. He was doing well enough to make Connor moan when he accidentally nicked him with his teeth, Connor flinching. David pulled it out of his mouth to mumble an apology, but Connor only smiled and helped him to his feet.

"Take it easy," he said. "There's no rush."

"Sorry," David said again.

Connor kissed him and started lifting his shirt, but David pulled away, suddenly uncomfortable. Connor's build was incredible, exactly the kind he wished he had. David's body was just skinny. He couldn't imagine that Connor would like what he saw, so he grasped for an excuse.

"We could be seen," he said.

"Oh, I understand!" Connor laughed. "You've got me nearly naked in the woods, and that's fine, but I can't do the same to you!"

"You said to do whatever I want," David teased.

"And I plan to do the same." Connor kissed him once more before pulling David's shirt up and off, this time without any resistance. Then Connor stepped back and looked David over. By some miracle, his eyes filled with even more lust. He pulled David close, kissing his neck, arms, nipples, and stomach. David's back arched with pleasure, and Connor hadn't even touched his dick yet. He soon rectified this, working at getting David's jeans open while kissing his neck. As soon as it was out in the open, Connor fell to his knees, and David's world became a blur of pleasure. He tried his best to hold back his moans but failed, feeling everything building to a peak much too quickly.

"Stop, I'm close!"

Connor deflected David's attempts at stopping him and kept working, relentless until David had ceased bucking and began whimpering. Then Connor pressed his cheek against David's abdomen and started pumping his own cock. David wanted to help him somehow, but he could barely breathe. Connor growled, the shoulders beneath David's hands tensing before he huffed a few times.

After catching his breath, Connor stood, pulling David's jeans up before his own. Taking his hand, Connor guided him down to the ground, first sitting and then laying on his back. David had fantasized about this almost as often as he did sex. Cuddling with another guy—holding him or being held. Of course he had never pictured this happening in the middle of the woods, but he wasn't complaining. Putting his head in the nook of Connor's arm, David lay next to him, scooting closer so their bare torsos touched. Feeling complete, David closed his eyes, listening to the drum of Connor's heart and the gentle song of his breathing.

Shadows danced across the curve of Connor's back, distorted leaf shapes that made his skin appear camouflaged. Connor stood facing a row of trees, answering a call of nature, which made David feel weird for being turned on. But hey, he looked good in nothing but a pair of beat-up old jeans. They could live out here forever, escaping the wishes of their parents and making a home in the wilderness, like a gay version of Robinson Crusoe. When Connor came back, digging in his front pocket for his cell phone, David knew he was about to make the opposite suggestion.

"It's getting late," Connor said, squinting at the display. "If I don't get you home soon, your dad's going to find out you've gone AWOL."

David shrugged. "I don't care." He was willing to face any punishment to spend more time with Connor. Especially now that they'd had sex. What was supposed to be a physical act had somehow intensified his emotions to the brink of being overwhelming.

"*I* care," Connor said. "You getting grounded means me seeing less of you. I have to work tonight anyway."

"Play sick," David said. "You can tell them you caught it from me."

Connor laughed, but David knew he wouldn't call in.

As they made their way back to the car, hand in hand, they didn't talk much. Instead they exchanged stupid grins or sometimes looks of such passion that David was sure they were going to do it again, right there on the bike path. The world seemed to have changed as they rode home, windows down even on the highway, the wind whipping through their hair and clothes. Smoking a joint had made music sound multidimensional, but having sex with Connor made David feel alive as never before. Everything he had known seemed smaller, including the school as they passed by. For once, seeing it didn't fill him with dread.

He worried that returning home would break this spell, but kissing Connor before he got out of the car was a reminder of their first kiss in his bedroom. They had left their mark here as well, and when the beat-up old Chevy rumbled away around the corner, the strange spell over David's world remained.

Gordon wasn't waiting on the doorstep, which meant David was late. He felt bad about that and made a note to call him from now on if he wasn't going to be home. Hopefully he would understand.

The house was silent when David entered. His father wasn't home yet, but they had cut it close. He just managed to get to his bedroom and take off his shoes when he heard the car pull into the garage. There wasn't time to check his appearance, to see if he had dirt on his face or leaves in his hair, but he managed to get under the covers before his father knocked on the door and opened it.

"How are you feeling?"

"A little better."

"You look like you're running a fever."

David touched his face, feeling the sun there. "I'm a little hot, I guess."

"Maybe you should stay home tomorrow."

And miss seeing Connor? "No, I think I'll be okay. Don't want my grades to slip."

His father smiled and left to get dinner ready. David went into the bathroom to search his face in the mirror, checking for any telltale signs his father might not have seen. Maybe he was crazy, but he could swear that he looked different, like the day's events had changed him. The real test would come tomorrow when he was in school, facing everything that made his life difficult.

When David stumbled out the front door the next morning, Connor's car was waiting at the curb, almost as if it had circled around and spent the night there. But Connor was wearing a different shirt—maroon with a tie-dye pattern—and his skin, when David got in and came close for a kiss, smelled of soap.

"What are you doing here?" David asked. "Are we skipping again?"

"Nope. Just figured it didn't make sense dropping you off but not picking you up." Connor put the car in gear. "Everything go okay with your dad?"

"Yeah. How about work?"

Connor frowned, reaching up to toy with a cigarette behind his ear. "My manager's a real asshole, which is nothing new. Then there's this girl, Riley, who has the hots for me."

David felt strangely jealous. Connor didn't like girls, did he? "Doesn't she realize there's no chance?"

"Yeah. Not at first, but I told her a couple of shifts ago. Thing is, I thought she would get over it, but she's still distant. Last night Mike, the manager, was flirting with her, and she didn't seem to mind."

David shrugged. "Seems like a good thing to me. Maybe if

she hooks up with Mike she'll get over you and things will go back to normal."

"Maybe."

"Do you have to work tonight?"

"Nope."

David grinned until Connor looked over at him and chuckled.

"Yeah, I'm happy about it too," Connor said.

"So we're hanging out after school?"

"Yeah. Oh, hey! I whipped something up last night." Connor kept his eyes on the road while popping open the glove box. Inside, along with the usual insurance cards and paperwork, were two little chunks of wood with nails hammered through them. Connor held one of them up. "These are for our friend Chuck."

David knew exactly what they were for. They were his happy thought throughout the day. That, and the way people looked at him and Connor when they walked into school together. They didn't hold hands or anything as ostentatious as that, or kiss goodbye when they parted in the hallway, but David watched Connor go with reluctance.

Not that he was entirely alone. There were other people like David in school, outcasts and weirdoes, who in times of need would keep each other company. This was most common in PE, since the warlike playing field of sports encouraged the idea of safety in numbers. A fat kid might sidle up to David, or David to a guy so awkward he made Gordon look cool, and they would converse in low voices while warily watching their surroundings. Such friendships of convenience could be nice, even if born from desperation, and David had one such contact in almost every class.

These friendships were also crucial in the cafeteria. No one wanted to eat alone, focusing on the food and hoping the surrounding laughter wasn't directed at them. David had been unlucky this year. All of the outcasts he knew were assigned to different lunch schedules. His next best option was to sit in the hallway nearest the cafeteria, which was still close enough that teachers never gave him trouble about it. Others sat there, too—a couple of goth girls and an emo boy in their senior year, as well as two freshmen dressed as if they had time traveled from the seventies.

Like them, David sat with his back to the wall as he ate

lunch—sandwich in one hand, a book in the other. He didn't mind, really. He loved reading and didn't have to carry on a stilted conversation with someone he barely knew. The half hour always passed quite pleasantly. Usually.

"You're David, right?"

He glanced up to find one of the school's generically pretty girls staring down at him. Any other guy might fantasize about her noticing him, but David didn't. He turned his attention back to the book.

"I heard that you're paying Connor Williams to be your bodyguard."

David tried not to smile but failed. This obviously wasn't the reaction the girl hoped for, because she made a disgusted noise before adding:

"I also hear you pay him to suck your dick."

That bothered him. He didn't want it to, but it did. Maybe if she had reversed it, if David was the one paying for the privilege of sucking off Connor, he wouldn't have been upset. He was used to people insulting him, but he couldn't stand Connor's name being tarnished further.

"If you're worried about competition," David said, "don't be. There are still plenty of guys you can suck off for lunch money."

The girl's eyes grew wide and incredulous, as if a peasant had dared talk back to royalty. David smirked and looked back at his book, staring at it without reading.

"You're such an asshole," the girl said as she stomped off.

As soon as she was gone, David sighed. Some angry boyfriend would probably be after him next. Tomorrow he would sit somewhere else, just in case. All he had to do was survive the next couple of weeks and the school year would be over.

Putting up with Chuck in fifth period was easier than usual. Chuck kept staring at him, hoping to intimidate, but David risked smiling back, thinking of what Connor had planned after school. When the bell finally rang, David rushed down the hall so fast that he was one of the first people in the parking lot. His early arrival brought the usual feeling of vulnerability. Without Connor there, anything could happen, but David kept his head held high until a familiar arm wrapped around his shoulders.

"Hurry," Connor stage-whispered as he guided them toward his Chevy. He had parked a few rows over from Chuck's gleaming sports car, but when they sat on the trunk, they had a decent view. Chuck and his friends strutted to the Mazda, hanging out around it and making snide comments at students passing by. They noticed Connor and David, but only laughed, no doubt thinking of the paint they had dumped across the Chevy's windshield.

"I should have just slashed the damn tires!" Connor said with an exasperated sigh.

When Chuck finally got in his car, he revved the engine before shifting into drive. David thought they would hear the tires pop as they rolled over the nails, but the squealing rubber was much louder. Connor must have placed the nails under the back tires, because Chuck's car swung forward as it always did, but the rear lost traction and continued to swing. That is, until it hit the car on the other side of the parking lot aisle with a nasty crunch.

"Oh shit!" Connor choked back a laugh.

David joined him, both trying to stifle their laughter until they were in the car. Already they could hear Chuck swearing and shouting.

Connor grinned. "Someone's daddy is getting a call from the insurance company."

David beamed back at him. "Let's get out of here!"

He glanced over at the wreck as they pulled out and caught a glimpse of Chuck, pale faced and slack-jawed.

"You know they're going to retaliate," David said. "They'll know it was us when they find the wood and nails and probably slash your tires tomorrow." And Connor couldn't afford to replace them so easily. No doubt all Chuck had to do was go crying to his parents.

"You used to walk," Connor said. "How about tomorrow, I come to your place and leave my car there. Then we can just walk the rest of the way."

Walk back and forth to school every day with Connor? Like David was going to say no to that. He wished they could also share lunch and classes. Hell, then David would probably start loving school. He would go all mental, expressing his school spirit at the pep rallies, screaming out the stupid chants until his head exploded with confetti.

Gordon waited on the doorstep, looking relieved that David

was there today. Without Tommy, David tried to entertain them both at once. Connor was a good sport about it, sitting next to him and watching them play video games for a while. Then David gave Connor the controller. The game was an RPG with timed battles, which couldn't be easier, but somehow Connor managed to kill everyone in their party except one knight who was both poisoned and turned into a frog. Gordon laughed so hard, snorting desperately for air, that David feared he would need CPR.

When his father was due to return home from work, and after Gordon had left, David had an idea. "Stay for dinner," he said. "Your mom is home tonight so Tommy is okay, right?"

"Yeah." Connor looked uncomfortable. "You sure your dad wouldn't mind?"

"Of course."

In reality, David didn't have a clue. He never had anyone over except for Gordon, who usually went home to eat. David strained to hear the garage door, running up the stairs when he did so he could talk to his father alone.

"I'm studying with a friend," he said. "It's late and he's still here, so I thought he could have dinner with us."

His father slowed in hanging up his suit jacket as he considered.

"I have a big test this Friday in history," David pressed. "Okay?"

"I suppose so. I'll call you when it's ready."

"Thanks!"

As David returned downstairs, he began to have doubts. He had been thinking only of spending more time with Connor. Now he couldn't imagine all three of them sitting at the tiny table.

"You're in my history class," David told Connor. "I only mention this because my dad is school-obsessed."

"Whatever you say." Connor was on the bed, pushed up on his elbows. "Gordon's a great guy, but I couldn't wait for him to leave."

David knew the reason for the change of topic. "We can't do it now! What if my dad comes down here?"

"I wasn't talking about sex, horn dog!" He looked so offended that David almost apologized. Then Connor grinned. "Okay, so I was. Come kiss me at least. Be my little appetizer."

David shook his head. "What does that even mean?"

Connor sat up and reached out, grabbing him by the wrists and pulling David down on top of him and trapping David in his arms.

"Let go!" David howled in protest before remembering they were supposed to be studying. He muted his laughs against Connor's neck, kissing the soft skin there once he had calmed down. "You smell good," he murmured. Then he pulled back in shock.

"Why do you look so surprised? Do I normally stink?"

"No! Well, not in a bad way. But you don't smell like cigarettes anymore."

Connor's smile was sly. "I wondered when you'd notice."

"You quit?"

"Mm-hm." Connor came in for a kiss, but David dodged.

"Why?"

"So I could kiss you without tasting like an ashtray, but since you refuse to put out, I'm starting up again."

"No!"

"Yup. I'll start smoking cigars too. Then I'll really stink."

David ignored the teasing. "I can't believe you quit for me."

"Then make it worth my while." Connor brought his lips close to David's. "Shut up and kiss me."

Chapter Nine

Mr. Henry was intimidating. Connor had nearly forgotten how authoritative normal fathers could be. His own dad had turned to mush long ago, not just because of the pills, but also from the confidence-destroying guilt surrounding the accident. Mr. Henry wasn't like that at all, his mind unnervingly sharp.

"Are you a junior too, Connor?"

He finished chewing before he answered. The pasta was just okay, the side salad better, but he was grateful for the meal anyway. "No, I'm a senior."

"And you share the same history class?"

Sharp as a tack.

"There was a scheduling error," Connor lied. "They didn't give me a social studies course last year, so now I'm taking both U.S. history and economics."

Mr. Henry's attention was on his plate. He had a strange habit of asking a question while appearing uninterested in the answer. Connor almost thought he wasn't listening, but little escaped his notice. He also wiped his mouth each time before speaking, which made Connor wonder if he should do the same. He glanced at David, who appeared sympathetic.

"So you'll be graduating in a couple of weeks," Mr. Henry said. "That must be very exciting. What are your plans?"

"Getting a full-time job for the summer. Beyond that, I don't know."

"He has a part-time job already," David said proudly.

Mr. Henry appeared impressed. "And your plans for college?"

Connor gave a long mental sigh. He should have known a professor would be most concerned with education. No doubt he thought college was the ultimate and final goal, since his adult life was still centered there. Connor wouldn't lie about this. He had nothing to be ashamed of.

"I've been saving up to get my own place. If I budget right and get a roommate, I might be able to afford community classes at night."

"Aha." Mr. Henry, finished with his plate, pushed it away. "So you didn't have any luck with scholarships? How did you do on your SATs?"

David groaned. "That's enough, Dad. He'll make an appointment with the school counselor if he wants a lecture."

"I'm just trying to learn more about your friend. Am I allowed to ask what kind of career he'll be pursuing?"

"Ballet dancer," Connor said without missing a beat. Then he grinned, David laughed, and Mr. Henry smiled after a moment of surprise. "Actually, I'll probably keep working in the food industry. Your son thinks I'm a good cook, so maybe I have potential there."

"Then you'll have to cook for us sometime," Mr. Henry said. "You know, the Art Institute in Lenexa has a culinary arts program."

"I'll keep that in mind." After that, Connor tried to steer conversation to other topics. Mr. Henry wasn't exactly fun to be around, but he wasn't terrible either. At least he gave David direction. When the meal was over, Connor thanked him, shook his hand, and walked with David to the front porch.

"Half an hour?" David said.

"What?"

"I need to do dishes, and Dad will soon be upstairs with his wine and music. I figured you could sneak back in."

"For dessert?"

David nodded. "See you then."

Connor drove a street over and parked, checking his watch occasionally as he waited. Mr. Henry's questions weighed heavily on his mind. The truth was, Connor didn't like thinking about his future. There weren't many options. He had never bothered to take his SATs because he knew complete scholarships were rare, and he couldn't expect his family to support him. Loans were out of the question and a part-time job at McDonald's wouldn't cut it. David's idea of a career in the food industry was all he had, and realistically, that probably meant more fast food.

The thought was depressing. With his father supporting him, David would probably be off to college in a year and meet someone with more potential. Having a high school boyfriend who flipped burgers was one thing, but David wouldn't feel so proud of Connor's job when they were older.

He checked his watch again and saw more than enough time had passed. Connor left his car where it was and walked around the block, still distracted by his thoughts when he reached the bedroom window. He almost expected to see David looking disappointed already, but instead he had that same vulnerable smile that always made Connor melt.

"You did really good!" David said once Connor was in his room. "My dad's a pain with all his education stuff, but you handled it well."

"Thanks, but I doubt he'll give me your hand in marriage any time soon."

David laughed, and somehow that made everything easier. Connor pulled him close, wrapping an arm around his waist and leaning back just enough to look into his eyes. He didn't want to lose David, no matter what he had to do.

"Are you okay?"

"Yeah." Worried he looked pathetic, Connor put on a fake smile. "Is the door locked?"

David grinned. "Yup!"

Connor didn't waste any time. No matter what the future held, he would enjoy these moments to the fullest. He kissed David a few times, but they had done plenty of that earlier and he wanted more. He ran his hands up David's back, pulling his shirt over his head along the way. Then he placed his forehead against David's and looked down. David's body was defined, the muscles more of an outline than actual mass. Connor ran his fingers down David's side, feeling his ribs and envying how his torso narrowed as it reached the tight waist and stomach—every inch smooth and perfect. Somehow the people at school didn't see how beautiful David was, but Connor wasn't about to make that mistake.

He slid a hand down into David's jeans.

"Wait." David pulled away from him. "This time I get to have all the fun."

He turned Connor's back to the bed and pushed. Connor flopped down on the mattress and put his hands behind his head. If David wanted to be in control, that was fine by him. Crawling onto the bed beside him, David tugged up Connor's T-shirt, kissing his belly button and his hips, but he was obviously impatient. He barely had Connor's jeans open before he tugged them down. Then he lay sideways across Connor's waist, propped up on one elbow. This was good, since it meant David wasn't too far away to touch. Connor reached for him, David's excited breath on his cock before warmth engulfed it.

Connor moved his hands down, one playing with David's curly hair, the other stroking his back. There was so much he wanted to do, but he enjoyed how assertive David was being. Connor closed his eyes and let himself be selfish, whispering a warning just before he came, but David didn't pull his mouth away.

"Okay, okay!" he said a minute later when it was clear David didn't intend to stop. "At least give me a break."

"Sorry."

Connor pulled David upward and close, holding him so tightly that he worried he might be hurting him, but he couldn't help it. "Promise you'll always stay with me." God, he probably sounded desperate or crazy, but he didn't care. He needed to hear David say it. "No matter what happens, just stay with me."

"I will." David made a little noise, as if he wanted to say more, but then he just squeezed Connor back.

As they held each other tight, Connor committed every detail of this moment to memory—the dim light in the room, the feel of David's hair tickling his cheek, even the cool drying saliva where David's mouth had been. He never wanted to forget how good it felt to be near him, just in case one day he wasn't so lucky.

"I promise," David added, and Connor was glad, because he needed to hear it once more. "This means I'm your boyfriend, right?"

Connor did his best not to chuckle. "Nah, I'm *your* boyfriend."

David smiled, his cheek shifting against Connor's shoulder.

"All right," Connor said. "Your turn. Then mine again. Then yours, mine, yours, mine."

David laughed, and they did their best to make this crazy idea a reality.

When Connor got home that night, a light was on in the kitchen window. He thought his father had left it on again, but once inside, he found his mother sitting at the table, a can of beer next to the almost-empty glass in her hand.

"You're up late," Connor said, easing into the seat across from her.

"Just enjoying the quiet," his mother said. "How was work?"

"No work tonight. I was out with a friend. Well, more than a friend. I met somebody."

"That's nice."

His mother considered the back of her hand, then the ring on her finger. He hated it when she did this. She wouldn't ask, in the same way she didn't enjoy discussing Tracy's girlfriends. Connor told her anyway, because it was part of his life, and he couldn't talk to Dad or Tommy about such things.

"I have a boyfriend now. His name is David."

She made eye contact again. "Does he make you happy?"

Connor grinned. "Yeah."

"That's important. You deserve to be happy."

She became distracted again, and Connor realized it wasn't the topic making her distant, but something else.

"Are you all right?"

She nodded and waved a hand dismissively. "I'm fine."

"You can talk to me," Connor said. "I'm not a kid anymore."

She looked him over, as if assessing this truth. "No, you're not. It's just— Well, I've met someone too."

Connor glanced toward the recliner his father always occupied and could tell by the tilt of his head that he was asleep. "You're having an affair?" he whispered.

"No. Well, one of the heart, maybe, but nothing has happened. Yet."

"With who?"

"The new maintenance man at the home." His mother put a hand on her cheek. "Isn't that terrible? I could lose my marriage and my job. But he's handsome. And interested. I'm sorry. I shouldn't be telling my own child these things!"

"No, it's fine," Connor said, not sure if it really was.

"It's just that your father hasn't been much of anything to us for such a long time, and I get lonely."

Connor could imagine why. What if David started doping up, just sitting around all day and staring at the TV? How many years had his father been like this now? He wanted his mother to have more, but the idea of his parents divorcing made his stomach clench. They had so little—only each other, really, and his dad had been great once. Tommy was too young to remember that, but Connor still did, and he wasn't ready to give up on him.

"We should talk to the doctor or maybe find a different one," he said. "Talk to Dad too. He needs to be told that he's on the verge of losing us. Just give him one more chance before you take this further, okay? I mean, you still love him, right?"

His mother was silent for a moment, which told Connor how long she had been struggling with this. In the end, she nodded. There was still hope, no matter how small.

"We can wake him up now," he said. "If you want."

"No! Let him sleep! I'll talk to him. Just promise that you'll let me tell him."

Connor nodded. "I promise. You're a good mom, you know that?"

She smiled. "And you're a good son."

Connor said goodnight and kissed her on the forehead before quietly entering his room. Tommy was asleep, his mouth open and his breathing loud. Connor was glad his mother had confided in him. He wasn't going to be around forever, and Tommy had already gone too long without a father. As he crawled into bed, he tried to imagine what having a normal family again would feel like, picturing a perfect Christmas—his mother and father toasting each other with champagne glasses, Tommy tearing through presents, and David at Connor's side, their fingers intertwined.

Connor stared at the grill and yawned. Lately he felt like he had two jobs, one he hated and one he loved. The one he hated involved hot greasy air, vats of fried oil beeping when the fries were done, and squawking drive-thru speakers. Connor let these things recede into the background as much as he could, thinking about his other job.

It wasn't real employment, but looking out for David felt like a serious responsibility—especially after what had happened with Chuck's car. The prank had gone further than they intended, enough that Connor worried he had made David into a bigger target. So, during the past week, he had walked David to and from all his classes. This meant sometimes running down the halls or asking to use the restroom five minutes before the bell rang. The teachers hadn't minded much because school—for the seniors, at least—had been more or less over.

And now it was. Friday had been the last day, and the graduation ceremony that Connor fully intended to skip was next weekend. Poor David still had another week of school, which meant that Connor could only pick him up and drop him off. The rest of his safety was the responsibility of the school system.

And Connor's future was in the hands of someone he couldn't stand. He glanced at the clock. Mike should be here now. He always spent the first half hour of his shift in his office, acting as if he had crucial business to attend to.

"Shane. Take the grill. I'm going on break."

Once free from the burger station, Connor walked toward Mike's office, asking himself again if he really wanted to do this. Of course he didn't, but now that school was over, he needed full-time work. Eventually he would find something better, but for now the pay from forty hours a week at Mickey D's would go a long way toward getting his own place.

Connor leaned against the doorway, glancing around at Mike's toll booth-sized office. Half the tiny space was cramped with boxes of leaflets and other advertising material. The rest was for the small desk, its surface always cluttered with mail, reports, and employee schedules.

Mike was seated at this desk, scowling at a report. Connor swallowed his pride so thoroughly he doubted he would ever see it again and knocked on the doorframe.

"Hello, Williams."

Connor stared. No "what do you want?" or even a direct "fuck off"? Mike actually looked happy to see him.

"I wanted to talk to you about my schedule," Connor began.

"Good. So do I. You're working a double shift today."

"What? Why?"

"Because you missed work on Monday."

Connor felt relieved. This was just a misunderstanding. His plans with David tonight wouldn't be ruined. "I wasn't scheduled on Monday."

Mike held up a calendar. "This says you were."

Connor barely glanced at it. No doubt it said so now, freshly inked by Mike's hand. "It's Saturday," he said, hoping for a shred of sympathy.

"It sure is, which means it's one of our busiest days. Now, what did you want to talk to me about?"

"Nothing." Connor turned to leave and almost ran into Riley. She met his eyes for a second, enough for him to see the guilt there. Good. Maybe she was feeling sorry for giving him the cold shoulder, not that it mattered. She was soon forgotten as Connor thought of his ruined plans with David. Connor wanted to drive him outside the city to Lake Olathe and find somewhere nice and dark to sit by the water. There they would chill together and maybe smoke a joint.

"Fucking asshole!" Connor shouted as he stumbled out into the parking lot. He wanted to punch something, but the only thing around was the building's brick wall. Gritting his teeth, he took out his cell phone and considered his options. He couldn't take Mike's crap anymore. Maybe he could get transferred to a different McDonald's. Mike would probably be glad to see him go, but until then, Connor had to play along.

Sighing, Connor texted David, unwilling to call and hear the disappointment in his voice.

Double shift. Cant play 2nite. Sorry Sweet16.

Connor leaned against the wall and stared at the orange glow of the city lights until his phone buzzed.

Still coming by?

He thought about the late hour, the greasy smell, and the foul mood he was in.

2morrow. OK?

Yeah. :(

Connor hated Mike, even hated himself a little for not being in a better position, but shoved it all aside and went back to work. Today he would do more than just spit in Mike's burger. He deserved something worse, maybe a pubic hair from the toilets or one of the dead flies that were always by the windows.

Except as the afternoon faded into evening, Mike never asked him to make his food. Come to think of it, he hadn't all week. Then Connor realized where Riley's guilt came from and why he was working a double shift. When Riley started giggling at her station, he glanced over just long enough to see Mike there, leaning against the counter and flirting. From Riley's body language, Mike's advances were more than welcome.

Connor had the rest of the shift to wonder what this meant for him. Worst case scenario, Mike knew that Connor had been spitting in his burgers. He could lose his job, but most likely Mike would just make his life as miserable as possible.

This seemed to be his manager's intention when closing time came. Mike sent everyone else home early except Connor, leaving him with four times as much to do. Usually Mike helped out, since he had pride in the place, but this time he only stood and watched Connor work from a distance.

With the front doors locked and the restaurant eerily quiet, they were left alone. Connor wondered if Mike planned to jump him. For whatever reason, Mike had never seemed frightened of him. The thought put Connor on edge as he hurried to get the placed cleaned up. Maybe this was his penance, and he could still get transferred out of here.

At nearly two in the morning, he was finally finished and went to clock out. His punch card stood out among the others—white and clean like it had never been used. When he took it, he saw it never had been. Even the timestamp from this morning was gone. Only his name was there, written in Mike's stupid loopy handwriting. He turned to find the very person watching him.

"What the hell is this?"

"What?" Mike plucked the card from him. "Uh oh. It looks like you didn't clock in today. Or for the whole week. What a shame. You know I can't pay you for hours you can't prove you worked."

Connor knew debating this further was pointless. Instead he waited for Mike to unlock the back door and set the alarm, watching his self-satisfied face glow green in the keypad's light. Once they were outside, Mike had something more to say. Connor didn't find it at all surprising.

"Considering that you haven't been in all week, I have no choice but to terminate your employment."

Even though part of him had expected this, Connor still seethed inside. "Just because I fucked Riley before you could?"

It wasn't true, but it was a well-placed blow. Mike's face registered shock, then anger. Riley would deny it, of course, but Mike wouldn't forget and would be thinking of Connor if he ever made it that far with her.

"She says you're a fag."

Connor grinned. "Well, you know how pissed women get when you don't call them the next day."

Mike's face showed hurt, which was a bonus, but not quite enough. Connor stepped close, almost near enough to kiss him. And there it was. Outside his tiny kingdom, and with Connor no longer under his control, Mike's eyes betrayed fear.

Connor smiled, patted him on the shoulder, and turned away. He stripped off the uniform shirt as he walked, tossing it behind him. Connor swaggered all the way to his car and drove twelve blocks before he pulled over and let his shoulders slump.

He hated money, hated the way life revolved around needing it. Now he would have to find a new job and wouldn't even have references he could use because Mike sure as hell wouldn't put in a good word for him. Connor glanced at his phone, thought of David, and pulled the car back into the road. At the next intersection he did an illegal U-turn and headed toward the south side of town.

David's window was dark when Connor got there, but hadn't been shut completely. Connor smiled at this invitation and quietly pushed the window open the rest of the way. He dropped into the room like a cat burglar and stood, listening to David's breathing and the gentle rustle of sheets as he moved in his sleep. Then Connor got undressed and slipped into bed next to him.

David stirred as Connor wrapped an arm around him, but Connor whispered for him to go back to sleep. He was just tired enough to obey. Connor moved his head near David's shoulder, breathing him in and drifting off with the welcome realization that they now had more time to spend together.

"What an asshole!" David swore.

Connor watched him pace back and forth in front of the bed. He still found it ridiculously cute when David got angry. Or maybe he was just happy with how good the morning had been. The events of the previous night—working the long shift, getting fired, and probably not getting paid—all seemed a lot less serious now. Of course David had awakened him with some nookie, which helped, and shortly afterwards had snuck upstairs for a couple bowls of cereal. Probably not a traditional breakfast in bed, but Connor had enjoyed it. As they ate, he told David what had happened, which was why Connor was still cozy in bed while David stomped the length of the room like an angry general.

"We have to do something," David said. "You can't let him get away with this."

"I guess I could call McDonald's corporate headquarters or something like that, but I don't see why they'd listen to me over a manager."

David stopped and faced him. "I meant more like what we did to Chuck. A little covert revenge."

Connor shook his head. "Let's not make a habit of that."

"But don't you want to? I do, and I've never even met the guy."

Connor considered it, but not very seriously. "Well, he never locks the door right at night, and I think I know the alarm code. We could break in and steal all the Happy Meal toys. Ruin Christmas for everyone."

David glowered at him, and Connor felt oddly touched that he felt so much sympathetic rage when David struggled to get angry at his own injustices. Maybe they were complete in this way, each more willing to stand up for the other.

"Tell you what," Connor said. "If you happened to think of a good plan, one that won't get us in trouble, then we'll do it. For now I just want to put the whole thing behind me. Want to head out to Lake Olathe?"

David glanced at the clock. "Gordon's coming over later, but we still have time."

"Then it's a date."

David smiled. "Mind if I take a shower first?"

"Not if I can join you."

"I think my dad might be a little surprised to see you upstairs."

Connor threw off the sheets so he was fully exposed. "Why's that?"

David laughed before his gaze became longing. Sex this morning had been strictly one-sided, so David still had a lot of pent-up hormones that needed releasing.

"All right," he agreed, "but as Gordon would say, you have to move with the stealth of a ninja!"

Connor leapt out of bed. "A naked ninja!"

As it turned out, stealth wasn't needed. Whatever Mr. Henry was doing, he wasn't on the ground floor. Keeping quiet in the shower was a bit harder, especially for David, but they made it back downstairs clean, undetected, and in very high spirits. Connor borrowed a T-shirt from David before sneaking out the window. Then he brought the car around front and rang the bell, just so it appeared that he hadn't spent the night.

Lake Olathe, set in the far west of the city, felt surprisingly tranquil despite the ever-encroaching housing developments. Connor was surprised that this peaceful location wasn't heavily frequented. Finding a place of solitude was always easy. Soon the car was parked, and they were sitting side by side under a tree, staring out across the water.

"I'm going to miss you in school next week," David said. "It's so stupid that seniors get out early."

"Hey, speak for yourself!"

"You know what I mean. I just have a couple of tests on Monday and Tuesday. After that, maybe I should play sick."

"Or tough it out another three days." Connor plucked at the grass. "Besides, I'm still going to be dropping you off and picking you up."

David's mouth fell open as if Connor had just popped the question. "I can't expect you to wake up early every morning just because of me."

"And yet you want me to."

"Well, yeah."

Connor smiled. "Then it's settled. As for waking up early, this morning wasn't so bad. Maybe I'll be slipping through your window more often."

David laughed and playfully bumped his shoulder against Connor's. "Seriously though, are you excited about graduating?"

"I guess I'm happy it's all over, but I wish something else had already begun. The future is looking pretty damn aimless."

"Well, I envy you. I wish I was the one getting my diploma next week."

"Feel free to show up for mine because I'm not going."

"What? You have to!"

Connor rolled his eyes. "Like the yearbook and prom tickets, it's just another excuse to charge students money. The cap and gown alone cost sixty bucks. If anything, schools should hand each graduate a couple hundred bucks and say 'Best of luck, kiddo, because you're on your own now.'"

David shook his head. "You'll do fine. One day, we'll both look back and realize that you getting fired was the best thing that could happen."

"How far in the future are we talking here?"

David pursed his lips. "Twenty years."

"And how do I look?" Connor asked.

"Balding and excruciatingly fat. No one will want you but me."

"Not so different from now, then."

"Except in twenty years, you're rich."

"Well, that explains how I can get away with being so repulsive."

David was silent for a moment. "I still want to see you graduate."

Connor snorted. "Why?"

"Because of the gowns. They're kind of sexy. Like kilts. I always imagine the guy not wearing anything underneath."

Connor stared at him. "You're sort of a pervert, you know that?"

David shrugged. "I was virginal and pure before we met."

Connor's laughter echoed across the lake's calm water, a declaration of joy sent out into the empty air. As uncertain as the future was, Connor felt like the very best was possible when he was with David, that he could do anything to tame the wild world into a place they could call their own.

When Connor got home, the blinds in the trailer were shut and every air conditioner window unit was running, a sure sign that his mom had been called in to work. The trailer was always bright and friendly when she was there, but his father preferred it dark and cold. Connor didn't mind on hot summer days, but today was the perfect combination of cool weather and sunny skies.

His father, as always, was sitting in the living room watching TV. Connor was about to say something when he noticed Tommy at the kitchen table, a cardboard box and a pile of discarded plastic wrappers in front of him.

Walking over, he grabbed the nearly empty box of brownies. "What are you doing?"

"Eating lunch," Tommy said.

"This is all chocolate and sugar!"

Tommy shrugged. "Dad said I could make whatever I wanted."

Connor glared at the darkened living room. "Do you know what he's eating over here?"

His father didn't respond. Connor marched into the living room and ripped at the cords that opened the blinds. Sunlight flooded the room, Connor almost expecting his father to burst into flames like some sort of pathetic vampire. Instead he just winced against the light, but at least he looked up from the television.

"Where's Mom?"

"She got called in," his father said. "Shut the blinds. I can't see the screen."

Instead, Connor went to the TV and switched it off. His father raised the remote, but Connor stood in the way.

"Tommy is over there eating brownies for lunch. Did you know that?"

"So? You punish him."

For a moment, Connor was thirteen years old again, buckled into his dad's old Dodge Charger as it careened off the road. The memory was painful and confusing, but he still remembered his father's strained voice telling him everything was going to be okay. He had been so comforted, knowing they were both still alive and that his dad was there, but now Connor wished the outcome had been different, that his father had died that day. They would have grieved, but Mom would have moved on and found someone new. Connor didn't blame her for wanting an affair because the man rotting away in the mottled old recliner was worse than dead. Had his father died in that accident, at least Connor could still cherish the memory of a strong man.

His father angled the remote just right so the television clicked on behind Connor. He turned, tempted to put his foot through the screen, but instead reached around and yanked the power cord from the wall.

"What the hell is wrong with you?"

The words should have been Connor's, but they were spoken by his father. He stared, shocked that his dad—as screwed up as he was—had the gall to ask such a thing. When Connor didn't move, his father finally shoved out of his chair. Had he come after Connor, threatened to hit him, or even just yelled, that would have been progress. Instead he just muttered that he needed a nap and shuffled away to the master bedroom. Connor waited until he was gone and went back to the kitchen.

Tommy sat at the table, his mouth just as wide as his eyes. "That was messed up!"

"Yeah. It was." Connor started digging through the counters, pulling out everything he needed to make a grilled cheese sandwich and tomato soup.

"I'm not hungry anymore," Tommy said.

"You're eating. You need something more than Little Debbie brownies. Besides, I'm hungry."

Connor's blood boiled along with the soup and refused to simmer back down, even after they had finished eating. It pissed him off that his mother was breaking her back to make ends meet while his father just sat around doing nothing. Even Connor helped pay the bills, but soon he wouldn't be able to, not if he wanted to live on his own. And yeah, that made him feel guilty, which was also wrong. He should be able to leave home knowing that his parents were going to take care of Tommy and each other.

He scowled at his father's chair, the side table full of prescription pill bottles. He only noticed that Tommy had cleared the kitchen table when his little brother spoke to him.

"Can I go out and play now?"

"No." Connor stood. "I want you to see something. You might not understand it, but you will one day."

With his little brother in tow, Connor went to his father's recliner and started grabbing pill bottles. He told Tommy to pick up the few he couldn't fit into the load he was already carrying. Then they went to the bathroom and dumped the bottles in the sink where they clattered against each other. Connor took one of them and read the label.

Alprazolam - 0.5 mg - Take one tablet every four to six hours as needed for anxiety.

Connor snorted. What did his father have to be anxious about? Dozing off and missing Judge Judy? Connor popped the cap off the pill bottle and dumped the contents into the toilet.

"Ummmm!" Tommy covered his mouth. "You're in so much trouble!"

"Yeah, maybe, but it's worth it."

Connor grabbed a couple more bottles, both containing medications for pain. Shouldn't one prescription be enough for that? He dumped those too, then all the others. He knew his father wasn't fighting off a fatal disease and didn't need any of these to live. Tommy wanted to dump some pills in the toilet too, but Connor didn't want him getting in trouble, so he only let him watch. When he was done, he took the empty prescription bottles and tossed them carelessly onto the recliner's seat.

"*Now* can I go out and play?"

"Yeah, Tommy. Go play."

Connor winced as the front door slammed and waited long enough to be sure the noise wasn't going to lure his father back to watch TV. Then Connor went to his own room. He plopped onto his bed and stared at the ceiling, feeling a little better but not much. He knew his father would just call the pharmacy for refills and Mom would pay for them. Connor stewed in anger before he let his thoughts turn to other matters—losing his job, not knowing where to go next, and figuring out what to do about David. Eventually, his body remembered how little sleep he'd gotten last night and coaxed him into a dreamless state.

When he awoke, the light in the room was dim, voices in the other room fighting to be heard over each other.

"Why do you think he did it, Steven? He's trying to tell you something!"

"I wish you would shut up so I can call these in!"

Connor raised his eyebrows. His father hadn't sounded this animated in years.

"And then what? You can't drive without a license, and I'm not going to pick them up. Or pay for them. Tommy needs summer clothes, and he's not going without just so you can get high."

"It's medicine, Pam! I need them!"

"More than you need us?"

Nice one, Mom! Connor strained to hear his father's response, but instead he heard the jangle of keys, the front door slamming, and the electronic beep of the phone as it was turned off. Connor silently counted to ten before he got out of bed and went to the living room.

His father noticed him, but he looked like a beaten man. "I hope you're happy," he mumbled.

Connor crossed his arms over his chest. "She's going to leave you. She doesn't want to, but it gets harder for her every day. And she has offers, because she's still pretty. Do you even notice that anymore?"

His father slumped down into his chair. "You don't know what you're talking about."

"Yeah, I do. She's going to leave you and take Tommy with her. I'm already on the way out. Then it's just going to be you, your pills, and some old reruns on TV. What are you going to do then? Anything? Are you *ever* going to do anything with your life? Because if not, you might as well fucking quit now!"

Connor's voice was getting louder, but he couldn't help himself. The only thing that kept him grounded was his fear that Tommy was inside and listening to all of this. He glanced around but didn't see his brother, so he looked back at his father. He was staring at the TV as he always did, but now it was off. In the screen's reflection was his father's face, distorted but still revealing how greatly he had changed. Even his strong jaw was turning to flab.

"I miss you, Dad," Connor said. "We all do."

He waited for a response that didn't come. When he stepped outside, his mother was standing next to her car looking lost, Tommy at her side.

"Come on," Connor said. "Let's go grab some dinner and ice cream. My treat."

His mother looked up, eyes questioning, but Connor only shook his head. He didn't know what would come of this.

Chapter Ten

The last week of school dragged by for David, as it did every year. Just knowing Connor was free the whole day made it worse. Connor would sneak in the window to spend some nights with him, then leave in the morning only to pick him up a few minutes later. He was always there when David got out of school, pulled right up to the doors like a getaway car.

Today was Friday, the last trial. That left six classes and a lunch period to slog through, but David faced it with confidence. Even math class with Chuck was no longer a big deal. David had told the teacher his new contact lenses—not that he actually wore any—made his vision a little blurry and that he needed to sit closer to the front. Of course Chuck had a few choice insults in the hallway, but none of them bothered David anymore. When anyone called him a faggot or a cock sucker, he just smiled and said: "Yup!"

Sixth period on the last day of school was the worst. Even the teacher seemed eager for the bell to finally ring. When it did, students nearly stampeded to the door. In the hall the situation was far crazier. No one wanted to stay in the building, even to hang out or wait for friends. Instead everybody fled out the doors as if the building was on fire. When David reached the main hall, he couldn't see through the glass doors. Usually he saw Connor's car parked there, but the mass of bodies was too thick today. He soon realized why.

Only one of the four double doors was in use. The rest were blocked by students staring out at the scene beyond. David slipped through the crowd, first relieved to see the old Chevy parked there, then worried when he saw the cop car behind it, lights flashing. Connor leaned against his car, nodding or shaking his head in response to the officer's words. Worried by this, David pressed forward. Just as he reached the doors, a hand grabbed his shoulder and swung him around.

"Looks like your white trash boyfriend got himself in trouble," Chuck sneered.

Not now! Not when Connor needed him! David tried to turn away, but Chuck spun him around again.

"Where do you think you're going?"

The crowd shifted around them, the word "fight" already echoing down the hallway.

"You messed up my car, faggot. And now I'm going to do the same to your face."

"I didn't mess up anything," David said. "You driving like a dick is what wrecked your car."

Okay, that felt good. Terrifying, but good. David glanced around, hoping to see a teacher. He thought he heard an adult voice further down the hall, coming toward them.

Chuck heard it too. "You keep running," he said. "It doesn't matter. One day your psycho boyfriend won't be there, but I will, and then I'm going to hurt you."

"Sounds great," David said. "I'm really looking forward to that." He could feel the bar on the door pressing into his lower back, so instead of trying to turn around, he pushed his weight against it and felt the door open. Chuck moved forward just as David looked outside and met Connor's eye. He immediately knew he had made a mistake. Connor became alert, pushing himself away from the car and the cop as well. He actually moved the officer aside with his arm to get to David, the officer's expression changing from bored to furious.

"I'm fine!" David said at the same time the officer shouted.

The cop grabbed Connor's forearm to stop him, and for one terrifying moment David was sure Connor was going to swing around and deck him, but David hurried forward to intervene.

"I'm good," he said. "Nothing happened."

Connor relaxed, but the officer did not.

"Tell me again what you're doing here!" he demanded.

"Picking him up," Connor said, nodding toward David. "I told you that."

"Well we've had reports of vandalism in the parking lot. Your name has been mentioned."

"His car was vandalized too," David said. "You can still see the paint on it."

Among the voices buzzing around them, David was sure he could hear Chuck squealing with laughter.

The officer barely glanced at Connor's car. "You've also been reported for dealing drugs."

Connor glared at him. "Yeah, that would explain the expensive clothes I'm wearing and the money falling out of my pockets."

"I'm going to need to search your car."

"Go for it."

Connor turned his back on him as the officer began his search. He looked David up and down, making sure he was okay, before he glared at the crowd. David felt bad. All the stupid rumors about Connor would be cemented in these people's minds today. Connor shouldn't have to face this anymore, shouldn't have to come back to this godforsaken place. It was David's fault he was suffering their groundless judgment again.

"Kiss me."

"What?" David spluttered, certain he had misheard.

"You heard me. Let's give these losers something to stare at."

The idea was even more frightening than standing up to Chuck, which is why David felt he had to do it. If there was one thing he wouldn't let the world make him afraid of, it was his feelings for Connor. He stepped forward, wrapped his arms around Connor's neck, and kissed him.

The crowd reacted with shrieks of shock, laughter, and of course, ugly words, but David and Connor ignored them and continued to kiss, at least until the officer cleared his throat.

"What's in the box?"

David pulled away and saw a flat, plain white box like the kind from a department store.

"Nothing," Connor said. "Look, you can open it, but just do so on the seat, all right? I don't want anything getting lost."

"What is it?" David asked.

Connor shook his head. "Nothing."

He blocked David's view until the policeman was done. Afterwards Connor opened the trunk for the officer and was subjected to a patting down. When it was clear there wasn't going to be an arrest or another show of homosexual lust, most of the students remembered they were free and began leaving.

The policeman lectured Connor about the dangers of walking away from an officer and laying a hand on one, but mostly he looked as though he wanted to be in his car and back on patrol. He let them leave with a verbal warning. As David got into the car, he saw Chuck watching from a distance. He didn't look happy, obviously hoping worse would have happened. David gave him a satisfied smirk and let Connor drive him away.

"Good thing we smoked the last joint yesterday," Connor

said. "And you wanted to save it for tonight."

"To celebrate," David said, "but yeah, that was a lucky break."

"Anyway, screw them all. We're free!"

And they were. David exhaled in relief. The last day of school always made him feel like he was coming up for air after nearly drowning. The world was full of potential now, every day another slice of summer. He wished Connor would keep driving—out of the city, onto the highway, and away—so that this intoxicating freedom would never ever end.

David turned in his seat, meaning to ask Connor to do just that when he noticed the oblong box again. It still lay on the back seat, long and mysterious, making him think of an old gangster movie where a gun had been hidden in a box of roses.

"So, what's in there?" David said.

Connor shook his head. "Just wait two whole minutes until we're at your place."

As soon as Connor parked the car, David reached into the backseat for the box. It was light. "Now can I open it?"

"Yeah, but it's not a big deal or anything. Or a present, so don't get your hopes up."

David rolled his eyes and took off the lid. Inside was a navy blue graduation gown and tasseled cap. "You're going to graduation for me?"

"Well, for you and my mom. I kept telling her this stuff's a waste of money, but she wanted to surprise me and keeps going on and on about how proud she is." Connor looked moderately embarrassed. "There should be some tickets in there. Yeah, those. I have one extra if you want to come along."

"Of course!" David tried to picture Connor dressed up and walking on stage for his diploma and couldn't. "You want to try the gown on for me?"

Connor gave him a knowing look. "Nice try, pervert. You'll have to wait until Sunday night."

David was still laughing while he fumbled with the front door keys. He almost dropped them when Gordon appeared from between the hedges.

"I have a plan," he whispered before adding in a hiss, "for revenge!"

"What's he talking about?" Connor asked.

"No idea." David ushered them inside. Soon they were standing in the kitchen, nursing juice boxes.

"David told me how you got fired from your job," Gordon whispered in conspiring tones. "It just so happens that I was wronged by McDonald's as well."

"Oh god." David pinched the bridge of his nose. "Not the birthday story."

"Yes, the birthday story!" Gordon said before launching into his tale. "I was eight years old, and my parents asked me what I wanted more than anything else. Besides a magician's kit—you know, the deluxe ones that teach how to do more than hide foam balls and make coins disappear—there was only one desire in my heart. I wanted a birthday at McDonald's. With Grimace."

"You mean the big purple gumdrop guy?" Connor asked.

"He's not a gumdrop," Gordon said testily. "He's … well, I don't know what the hell he is, but he's amazing!"

"So anyway," David prompted.

"Anyway, my parents booked me a party at McDonald's, and the manager swore they could have Grimace there. They promised! And do you know what happened?"

Connor, kind soul that he was, shook his head as if the rest of the story wasn't painfully obvious.

"Grimace wasn't there." Gordon leaned back, having delivered the shocking blow. "David saw it all. Go ahead, tell him."

"It's true," David said. As silly as it was, he couldn't resist egging Gordon on. "They did have that nice clown there. What's his name?"

"Ronald McDonald," Gordon said slowly, "made my birthday a living hell! He hounded me the entire party, harassing me with his banal humor and humiliating me in front of the entire town."

"It was only me and one other kid there," David said. "The guy was just doing his job."

"He wasn't even invited! Besides, I'm pretty sure he tried to molest me at one point."

"You mean the birthday spanking?"

Gordon nodded. "I swear I felt something move in his lap. So as you can see, I have just as much reason to hate McDonald's as you do."

Connor nodded. "Well, it's good to know I'm not alone. Uh,

anyone up for some video games?"

Even this couldn't dissuade Gordon. "I haven't told you my plan yet. Last night I was watching Dateline. They had this undercover investigation about health violations in fast-food restaurants. It was like the hand of God reached down and switched my TV to the right channel!" Gordon held up a scrawled-on piece of notebook paper. "I took notes and figured out what we could do to get the place shut down."

David looked at Connor, who was doing such a good job of faking interest that even David was fooled. Wait, he *was* faking it, wasn't he?

"So what's the plan?" Connor asked.

Oh god! This couldn't be good.

Curled up in bed together, alternating between having sex or cuddling up for some pillow talk, or maybe just going for a drive, finding somewhere quiet to park and staring at the stars together … David had pictured his last day of school being redeemed by any of these activities, but instead, here he was at two in the morning, staring at a darkened McDonald's through the dirty windshield of the Chevy Chevelle.

"I think it's safe to go in now," Connor said, starting the engine.

"Are you sure we shouldn't leave the car here?" Gordon asked. That was another unexpected surprise: Gordon, in the world after midnight, treating this mad adventure as if it were just another quest in his strategy guides. "What if the police notice your car?"

"They won't simply because they've seen it parked there countless times. We'll stand out more if we're creeping across an open parking lot."

Connor parked behind the McDonald's, a moment of hesitation following the engine's silence.

"Okay," David said. "Let's do this."

Between them, they had come up with a really good plan, providing they didn't get caught. His worst fear involved them actually breaking in, or rather, what followed once they did. As Connor had promised, the door was locked but not shut properly. He placed his palm on the handle, which was already covered with his fingerprints from working there, and rammed the door with his shoulder. It swung open, the lingering scent of fast food drifting out and making David's stomach growl. Maybe he could get Connor to whip him up a burger while they were here.

A high-pitched whine chased away thoughts of food. The alarm! This was David's greatest concern. Connor felt he knew the code. *Felt.* The alarm could care less about what any of them felt. It needed four numbers, and fast, before the whine exploded into a full-blown wail.

"It was always two sets of two numbers, top row," Connor said to himself, punching at the key pad with his knuckles to avoid prints. "Two two. Three three."

The keypad flashed, but the whine continued. That wasn't right.

"One one, two two."

The backlit digits flashed again.

Connor hesitated. "Think it's two two, three three?"

"You already did that one," David said. "Try three three, two two."

"Or one one, three three." Gordon said.

Connor stared at them both a moment before knuckling in three three, one one. The alarm chirped happily and the whining ceased. "Figured it would be the last one we thought of," Connor said.

They turned to face the interior, which suddenly felt like it belonged to them. Connor closed the outside door, and everything became much darker. Dim lights in the seating area were on for security, but they were enough to create silhouettes of objects they should avoid. David pulled out the mini-flashlight he had gotten in his stocking last year, and Gordon used his phone to illuminate their path.

"This is the pantry," Connor said like a tour guide as they entered a room full of shelves. "This is where all the condiments and dry goods like paper towels, plastic spoons, and cookies are kept. And of course, gloves for safe handling—or hiding fingerprints. Here, put these on."

David felt like they were preparing for surgery as they pulled on the gloves. They were too cheap to be latex, more like plastic baggies with fingers, but they would do.

"Oh my god!" Gordon breathed. "Are those the new Pokémon Happy Meal toys?"

Kamikaze Boys

He nearly dropped his phone as he started shifting through the plastic-wrapped premiums.

"You might as well take what you want," Connor said. "You're already guilty of breaking and entering."

"I just need Pikachu," Gordon said. "Oh, and Oshawott. Can I have him too?"

Connor laughed. "Sure. Grab a couple extra for my brother."

Once Gordon had his loot, they moved through the hall to a thick metal door. "This," Connor said, yanking a metal handle, "is the freezer."

The inside was—well, freezing. David rubbed his arms, trying to get the goose bumps to go away, as Connor dragged a couple of cardboard boxes into the hallway. The plan hadn't started out this complicated. Gordon had simply suggested that they smuggle some raw meat into the restaurant, hide it somewhere, and call the health department. Then Connor had added his own spin, and David contributed a few ideas of his own. And here they were.

"Frozen patties," Connor said, handing a stack to each of them. "Just pretend it's Easter and start hiding."

Together they ventured into the dark but surprisingly tidy kitchen and began looking for small nooks and crannies to shove frozen patties into. Beneath the grill, in the toaster rack for the buns, on top of the monitors that displayed orders, between the paper wrappers—the possibilities were endless! Connor had to go back for another box of patties before they even got to Mike's office.

"Is that for the security camera?" Gordon asked, pointing to a box next to the computer.

Connor nodded. "Yeah. They're off, don't worry. They only run during the day."

Gordon checked them regardless before getting out of the way. This was what Connor was looking forward to most. He filled every drawer in Mike's office with frozen patties, inserted meat into the folders stored in the filing cabinet, and even crammed a few into a trophy awarded for exceptional service in 1998. As a final touch, the office chair had a flat pillow on it. Connor deposited another red meat patty beneath it.

"Dining room next?" Connor asked.

"Maybe we should get out of here," David said.

Connor put on his best pouty face. "Let's dump a box of chicken nuggets into each toilet first."

David laughed. "All right."

An employee entrance led directly to the restrooms, which weren't visible from the front windows. Connor dumped his nuggets in the toilet bowls, and David, practically blinded by tears from laughter, unloaded some sausage links in the urinals. Then he really felt like they had pressed their luck and insisted they go.

On their way to the back door, they stopped to implement David's little stroke of genius. Connor cranked up the heating unit to the max. By morning the restaurant would be sweltering hot, the meat thawed and goopy. Gordon had already used a pay phone to call the heath inspector earlier in the evening, insisting he had seen employees tossing raw meat around as a game. Their vandalism would be obvious, but they had caused enough chaos to make Mike's weekend extremely unpleasant.

David was sure they would find the back parking lot filled with police cruisers, but when he opened the door, all was quiet. Connor set the alarm and in silence they got in his car and drove the speed limit all the way to David's. En route they saw a police car pulling out of a gas station, Connor's car briefly illuminated in the cruiser's headlights as they passed by. Casually as possible, David turned to see if they were being followed, but the cruiser pulled onto the street and headed in the opposite direction.

He breathed out in relief once they were back at his window. Gordon crawled in first, tripping over something in the dark as he hunted for the light switch.

"I have to go home," Connor murmured.

David turned to face him, disappointed. "Why?"

"Mike's going to suspect me, and I don't want any links back to you or Gordon. Officially, I've been home all night. I'll even wake up Tommy and tell him to quit snoring, just so he sees me."

"Do you have to go now?"

Connor smirked. "The bed is going to be awfully full if I don't."

Of course. Gordon was spending the night so they could execute their little crime. That eliminated any romantic possibilities, so David kissed Connor goodnight.

"Am I going to see you tomorrow?"

"No job, no school. You can have me every day of the summer. I'll even take you for a burger tomorrow."

David laughed. "Better make it Burger King."

"Good idea!" Connor stole another kiss before he turned away. David just barely heard his parting words as he walked away: "Sleep well, Sweet Sixteen."

Chapter Eleven

When David woke up the next day, his father was thumping on his door and saying something about noon. Gordon grumbled and shoved a pillow over his head while David reached for his cell phone and blinked until his eyes were clear enough to see. It was past noon, actually. He and Gordon had been too hyped up on adrenaline to sleep last night. The phone rumbled once, telling David he had a text message.

Looks like trouble.

He read and reread the simple message, his eyes darting between it and Connor's name. It could only mean one thing.

"Gordon, get up."

David shoved him a few times, telling him what time it was. The nice thing about living next door to each other was how easy it was to leave. Both of them preferred heading home for breakfast and other morning rituals.

He didn't mention the text message to Gordon, who might panic at the news. David wanted time to figure out everything. Really big thoughts always required solitude, as if the mind needed the extra physical space to stretch out. As soon as Gordon was gone, David's imagination began flashing red lights to a symphony of sirens.

He checked the text message and saw it was only twenty minutes old. Connor was surely waiting for a response.

What's going on?

He waited, biting his lip, pacing the floor, and finally taking a shower with the phone on the closed toilet seat, the curtain partially open so he could keep checking on it. He was dried and dressed an hour later and still hadn't received a response. *Looks like trouble.* Did that mean the police? Jail? Or had Mike shown up with a couple of friends—large friends—to get back at Connor directly?

David raced upstairs to the kitchen and asked for the car keys, telling his dad that he wanted fast food for lunch. He was in the car and about to drive to Connor's when he second-guessed himself. What if the cops were there? Showing up looking worried would only make him a suspect or make Connor appear guilty. If Mike was there, maybe he could do something, even if it was just calling the cops, but surely they would have gone by now, regardless of their intentions.

Instead David drove by the McDonald's, pulling into a parking lot across the street. At this point he was so frantic that he imagined Gordon might have accidentally turned on the surveillance cameras, which could mean being recognized. He watched as cars pulled up to the drive-thru speaker. Shortly afterwards they would drive away again, empty-handed. No doubt about it. McDonald's was not open for business.

David sat and stared at his cell phone for a while longer before driving home. His father asked where the food was, David mumbling something about not being hungry as he tossed the keys on the counter and went back down to his room. He put on some music to calm himself, but that didn't work. Even dancing didn't make him feel better as he waited for another message. He wanted to send more texts, hundreds of them, but didn't know if Connor still had his phone.

Just when he thought he would drive to Connor's, no matter the consequences, his phone vibrated. David snatched it up.

You alone?

Yes.

The phone rang a second later. When David answered it, Connor spoke in a low voice.

"Just a sec."

David heard the trailer door slam. Then gravel crunching as Connor walked a short distance. The sound of a rusty car door opening and closing came before Connor spoke again.

"You there?"

"Yeah," David said, not hiding the panic in his voice. "Are you all right?"

"I'm okay. I ditched the phone once the cops showed up. I didn't want them scrolling through my numbers."

"Cops?"

"Yup. Mike didn't waste any time in calling them. They brought me down to the station and asked a bunch of questions."

David's breath was so short he could barely speak. "They arrested you?"

"No. I don't think so. I mean, I'm home. I think they were just trying to scare me. I played dumb the whole time, don't worry."

Easier said than done. David was very worried. "Can I come over?"

Connor hesitated. Then the sound of wind filled the receiver as Connor sighed. "No. We better lay low today. Just in case anything else happens. I think we're okay, though. I really do."

Okay or not, David would prefer they were together to face whatever was coming. "When can I see you again?"

"Well, kiddo, graduation is tomorrow night. You going to be there?"

"Yeah."

"Okay. I better go put in an appearance for the family. See you tomorrow."

Thirty-six hours or so? The minutes might as well have been days as slowly as they passed. David zombied his way through a sandwich and some conversation with his dad, the topic his soon-to-arrive SAT scores. Then he invited Gordon over, because the best way to send time hurtling into a void was by playing video games. Besides, letting Gordon tell him what to do was relaxing.

Of course he told Gordon what had happened. David needed someone to confide in, and who could you trust if not your partner in crime? Gordon's response wasn't what he expected.

"We'll be okay," he said with self-assurance. "I checked those cameras, and they were off. The only weak link is Connor. As long as he doesn't crack under pressure, we'll be fine. Unless he's a stool pigeon and sells us out. Do you think he's a stool pigeon?"

David shook his head and laughed. Leave it to Gordon to come up with the weirdest thing to say. His face was dead serious too, his expression scrunched-up as he puzzled over what David found funny.

That night David sent Connor another text.

Still OK?

Yeah. Nervous about grad. Can I skip?

LOL Nope.

Maybe things *were* going to be okay. The police weren't knocking down their doors, and Connor was doing fine. They exchanged a few more texts, most of them about David wanting Connor to be naked under his graduation gown. By the time David crawled into bed, he was smiling.

David felt nervous enough for both of them. He waited in the school parking lot near the doors, but the normally sinister setting was transformed by the large number of families swarming toward the entrance, all of them in high spirits and dressy clothing. David had opted for a sky-blue dress shirt and jeans, and embarrassingly, his father had insisted on adding one of his ties to the outfit. It was maroon, and David was pretty sure it clashed with his shirt, but he left it on anyway.

Looking for Connor wasn't easy since every graduate was wearing the same navy blue gown. As it turned out, Tommy found him instead, running up and taking David's hand to drag him back to the family. Connor's mother was pretty, in a tired sort of way. She reminded David of a female politician, Hillary Clinton maybe, but with more burden than power. She smiled at David and shook his hand, her words lost to him because of the surrounding noise, but he told her how good it was to meet her.

The real shocker was Connor's father. David wasn't sure he was the same man at first, since he had never seen him outside his recliner. Standing up, he had the same build as Connor except with a belly that suggested the baby was long overdue. His face was clean-shaven, and he seemed to wince at the hustle and bustle surrounding them, but he managed a smile and a few polite words.

"You look really good," David said, hoping he didn't sound like he was hitting on his boyfriend's father.

"Feeling good too," Mr. Williams said, but David had his doubts.

Connor's eyes were guardedly proud, as if he thought David might tease him about the cap and gown. They gestured at each other awkwardly, the idea of their usual greeting kiss uncomfortable with his family so near, especially since Tommy was still holding David's hand and chattering about some cartoon he had seen.

Then they went inside together and waited for the families ahead of them to find their places. David did his best to make small talk, but felt impatient to get to wherever they were supposed to be. As usual, Tommy filled any silence. David soon found himself talking to Connor's parents through him.

"Is there going to be cake?" Tommy asked.

"It would have to be the size of the school to feed all these people," David said.

"And you just had ice cream on the way here," Mrs. Williams added.

Tommy moved on to his next fantasy. "Does Connor get a trophy?"

"Only if he beats everyone here at basketball," Mr. Williams said.

"Which is why graduation takes place in the gym," David contributed.

By the time they took their seats, he found himself completely relaxed around Connor's parents. They were crammed into a corner far from the stage, which they didn't mind because some families had to watch on a screen from the auditorium. Connor had taken his seat with the other graduates in the center of the gym, lost beneath a sea of navy blue caps.

Tommy was bored by the time the ceremony began. David couldn't blame him. First came a series of stiff speeches about education and the graduates' futures, all of which sounded like things his dad would say, before the valedictorian gave a cringe-worthy speech about her transformation to adulthood. David watched with a rapt sort of horror, knowing that he would be going through the same process next year. Finally they started calling out names.

As each student moved to the front to collect his or her diploma, cheering would erupt from different parts of the audience. For the popular kids, of course, this meant a huge roar from all sides. Did this mean they were popular with the families here as well? David's revulsion was compounded when a girl's name was greeted with complete silence. He didn't recognize her. She was probably just another lonely soul who had found somewhere quiet to eat lunch. He didn't know why her family wasn't here, or maybe they were too reserved to cheer, but David felt for her. The next name was called out—a girl slathered in makeup and covered in jewelry—and the cheering resumed, which only punctuated the previous silence.

David imagined how quiet the response to his name might be. Jeff would probably talk his mom into not coming to the ceremony, and his father might clap politely, but no one else would cheer for him. And that would feel shitty. No matter how little his classmates meant to him, he wouldn't like how that felt.

"Hey, Tommy. We need to practice cheering!"

Tommy perked up.

"That way we do a really good job for your brother."

The next name was called, and a heavy-set guy with glasses stood up. Only an elderly couple on the other side of the auditorium cheered, but Tommy and David leapt up to clap and shout. They did this for every name called out, and there were hundreds. The people around them glanced at them like they were crazy at first, but David didn't care. Sometimes their cheers joined those for the popular kids, but other times turned moments of silence into celebration. Mrs. Williams began clapping with them, and by the time Connor's name was near, other people in the audience had taken up the cause and were applauding everyone.

"Connor Williams."

His voice hoarse now, David gave it his all, and Tommy positively shrieked. Even Mr. Williams let out a satisfied "Yeeeesssss!" As loud as their little corner of the gym was, anyone might have thought Connor was one of the more popular kids. Not too many names followed Williams, and after a much shorter and looser speech from the principal, some of the graduates tossed their caps into the air. Others seemed too concerned about losing them and kept them on. Then chaos erupted, and families went to greet their graduates.

Tommy ran into the crowd to find Connor, returning on his shoulders. Then they joined the slow-moving exodus to the parking lot. There they stopped outside at an older but well cared-for minivan.

"Do you boys want to go out to eat to celebrate?" Mr. Williams asked.

David held his breath, exhaling gently when Connor said:

"Actually we're heading back to David's place. Going to make a night of it there."

Mr. Williams nodded and extended a hand, pulling Connor in for a manly hug and a hearty pat on the back while muttering something about being proud. Mrs. Williams had hugs for them both, and Tommy begged to go with them, but eventually the minivan was packed full of family and driving away.

"Let's get out of here," Connor said, shouldering a backpack he had retrieved from the minivan's backseat.

David had walked to the school for the graduation ceremony

and felt awkward walking with Connor, even a few blocks, while he was still decked out in his graduation regalia.

"You don't have to wear the gown for my benefit," David said.

Connor's expression was strange. "You want me to take it off? I don't think you do. Not here."

David shot a sidelong glance at him and snorted. "Whatever. You're not nude under there. Nice try!"

The fabric bunching up in his fists, Connor grabbed the robe and pulled upward. There were tennis shoes and bare knees, but David wasn't convinced. He was just wearing shorts. Wasn't he?

"So I guess we part ways here," Connor said when they entered the subdivision.

"No servant's entrance for you tonight," David said. "I asked my dad if you could spend the night, and he said yes."

"But I like climbing through the window," Connor joked, and after a pause added, "He knows about us, right?"

"Dad? Yeah. I told him you were my boyfriend, and he took it in stride. Hey, speaking of fathers, someone brought yours back to life!"

"Yeah." Connor looked proud. "He's doing better. After I blew up at him, I guess he went back to the doctor and asked to get off the opiates and tranquilizers. Now he acts like he's sick all the time, which I almost feel bad about. I don't know. Part of me doesn't want to get my hopes up, but tonight was nice. We felt like a family again, you know?"

David did know. The memories grew fuzzier by the day, but at one time his parents had been together and had taken him places. Maybe if they had stayed together, he would have a little brother or sister as well. He hadn't realized it until recently, but he missed that feeling of family. He wanted that for his kids, if he ever had them.

David could easily picture Connor as a father because of how good he was with Tommy. Maybe someday they could start a family together. If so, he wouldn't let anything tear them apart. Their kids would never have to go through a divorce, not if he could help it.

To his surprise, David's own little family opened the front door when they came up the walk. Rather than being in the office listening to music and drinking wine, his father was downstairs and nearly bouncing with excitement.

"The graduate arrives!" he said, extending a hand to Connor. David could smell from his breath that he had begun tackling his nightly bottle, but he seemed happy rather than drunk. "Congratulations are in order," he added once they were inside. "I know graduation feels like a final step to you now, but believe me when I say that it's only the first. There are many opportunities for you to consider."

"Dad," David said in pleading tones.

"Oh fine. I understand. But if you ever want to discuss your options, Connor, please feel free to come speak to me. Hold on a moment." His father went to the kitchen, took an envelope off the counter and handed it to Connor. "This is for you."

David stared. The envelope had the same proportions as a greeting card.

"Thanks," Connor said, sheepishly scratching the back of his head.

"What were your SAT scores, if you don't mind me asking? Okay, okay, I'm leaving," he said after David glared at him.

They grabbed a couple of cold drinks and headed downstairs to David's sanctuary.

"Sorry. When it comes to education, my dad is like a bridezilla planning a wedding. He's been talking about my graduation since I was in junior high."

"I don't mind," Connor said, sitting on the edge of the bed and opening the envelope.

It was a card, simple and formal. David could see the word "Graduation!" emblazoned on the front. As Connor opened it, a green bill parachuted into his lap.

"A hundred bucks!" Connor said, holding it up. "That's crazy!"

"That's awesome," David corrected. "Next year he better give me cash too!"

They laughed, Connor because he was embarrassed, David because he felt embarrassed for him, but the gesture was nice. As single-minded as his father could be, he wasn't all that bad.

"So what are we going to do tonight?" Connor asked. "Video games? Finally beat that troublesome Demon Master?"

"Dragon Lord," David corrected. "I don't know. I didn't really make any plans."

Except he had. He had given a lot of thought to Connor's graduation present and had come up with something he thought was perfect. But now he felt unsure about broaching the subject.

"We could break into another fast-food joint tonight," Connor said. "We haven't done that for a few days."

David smiled and put on some music. Connor stood as he did so, sweeping around the room in his robes like he was a duke or something. David selected M83's latest album, turning it up just loud enough to be heard but quiet enough that they could still talk. When he turned around, Connor was right behind him.

"You know," he said. "I'd thought you'd be way more into this gown."

"Maybe I'm just jealous." David put a hand on Connor's chest, stroking the fabric, and surprised it was thin enough to feel Connor's chest hair underneath. "No!" he said in disbelief. "You really are crazy!"

David ran his hands down the robe, finding no resistance where a shirt usually ended and jeans began. All he felt was smooth imitation silk and the flesh below.

"A little lower," Connor prompted.

"I can't believe you're not wearing anything underneath!"

Connor winked. "I felt naked in front of the whole school. If I could turn back time, I would go commando every day."

David laughed, grabbing the graduation gown and slowly pulling it upward. Connor stood still and let him reveal his thick thighs, his balls, and the impressive girth standing at full attention. The rest of Connor turned David on just as much as his cock did. His stomach's slightly rounded shape, which reminded him of Greek sculpture, the hair around his belly button, the proud chest, and the strong neck on either side of his Adam's apple. Connor helped him the rest of the way, pulling off the gown and tossing it to the side before their mouths met.

David let Connor undress him, skin tingling everywhere that Connor kissed him. Then they stood back and looked at each other. David had felt so shy in the beginning, self-conscious when Connor's hungry eyes moved over his body, but not any more. He trusted Connor, and they had already done this a surprising number of times since they had first met. Tonight would challenge that comfort level, but David wanted to try.

Connor spun him around, play-biting David's shoulders and

neck, threatening to eat him and making him laugh. Then he tossed David onto the bed, leaping after him and kissing him more as their hands explored each other. When Connor went down on David, he barely noticed. Okay, so he *was* getting nervous, even more than their first time together. He reached casually for the small bottle of lube near the headboard of his bed. Buying it had been embarrassing. He was sure the checkout girl at the pharmacy was going to comment on it, but instead she didn't make eye contact after scanning the container, even when he handed her cash. That was almost worse, but he couldn't worry about that. He knew he would need it.

Connor came back up, bracing himself above David and kissing him. This was the position that Connor always hinted in. He'd rub his crotch against David's, sometimes reaching down to spread his legs. Like now. Connor never tried to force the issue. Sometimes he would let his cock slide along David's ass, and once last week, he had pressed himself against David's hole, eyes seeking permission, but David shook his head. And Connor hadn't blinked an eye, hadn't looked disappointed. He simply moved on to other options, but David knew that Connor wanted this.

"Here." He opened his hand, revealing the bottle, and Connor's eyebrows shot up. "Just— you know."

Connor's expression was cool with a hint of smug. He rolled over on one side and squeezed some lube onto his fingers, kissing David as he moved his hand down. David was used to this. He had practiced all week, trying to get used to the sensation, and he honestly did enjoy it. For some reason—and maybe bad porn was to blame—he thought Connor would simply lube up and shove it in. Instead he took his time and played, sending waves of pleasure through David and relaxing him. By the time Connor rolled back on top again, David was more than willing to take things further.

Connor was too. They both held their breath as Connor pressed against him, and then he was in, but just a little bit. They locked eyes, Connor's entire focus on David's well being. David nodded encouragingly, and Connor slid deeper inside him, just a little more, before he moved back again. Gently, like a sex scene in slow motion, he began to pump his hips. David was in pure ecstasy. He had expected pain, but instead felt only pleasure.

Sure, it was a little strange, but this was eclipsed by the realization that they had become one. Connor was inside him, a part of him, and David never wanted it to end.

He grabbed Connor and pulled him near so that their chests were touching, pulled him down more so that he bore his full weight, almost feeling crushed but wanting to be as close as possible. Slowly Connor moved in deeper, picking up the pace when David breathed encouragement into his ear. David played with himself, often having to stop because he felt too close too soon. He wanted to be wrapped in Connor's arms like this for an eternity. Then the words that had come to mind so often in recent days slipped out.

"I love you."

Connor pushed himself up enough to search David's face. David tried to use his expression to show that he meant it, that these weren't just words of passion. Then Connor was kissing him, his hips slapping against David as they both huffed in pleasure. Connor's huffs turned to groans, and David knew he didn't have to hold back anymore. Together they moaned, mouths against each other's skin, not wanting the sound to leave the room as their bodies shuddered. When Connor carefully pulled out, David was surprised to find the feeling of being connected didn't fade. Somehow they had worked magic together.

Connor's weight shifted to the side, but he stayed facing David. His thick fingers stroked David's face before he leaned forward to kiss his forehead. "I love you, David. I always will. Always."

He said it with such intensity that David knew they felt the same. The world could split in the middle, all the way down to Hell, and if Connor was trapped on the other side, David would pull the globe together again just to get back to him. Nothing was going to get in their way, and if anything tried, they would destroy those walls together.

Chapter Twelve

The newspaper trembled in the breeze from the window air conditioner unit, as if the thin pages were chilled. If so, the paper was the only thing in the trailer that was cold. Summer was in full effect outside, and despite Connor pulling the curtains closed, the trailer walls seemed to soak up the heat. If it got any hotter, Connor felt he would be cooked like a microwave dinner.

Shaking the paper to straighten it, he tried to find where he left off. A classified ad about driving trucks sounded promising, if a special license wasn't required.

An eight-bit version of "Eye of the Tiger" blared from his cell phone. Connor folded the paper and grabbed the phone, happy the boring job search had been interrupted. Gordon's name flashed on the display. The night they had broken into McDonald's, Gordon had insisted they exchange numbers in case they were separated while "running from the law." Connor had figured it was just an excuse to swap digits, but thus far, Gordon hadn't taken advantage.

Connor jabbed the green phone icon. "What's up?"

"There's something I need to tell you," Gordon said without ceremony. "A secret. About David."

He knew Gordon was partial to drama, but still Connor's stomach grew tight. "Tell me."

He listened to the secret and the reason why it was kept so, and soon he was smiling. Nothing he couldn't handle. In fact, he already had a plan he had been toying with for a while.

"Do you have the number of David's dad? I want to talk to him about this."

"I can get it," Gordon said.

Connor was sure he was going to add "for a price," but when he didn't they said goodbye and hung up.

Over the next few days, Connor called David's father and talked with members of his own family as well. He didn't have much time to prepare, but it was enough. He smiled a lot, which was odd since he was about to lose his Sweet Sixteen. Connor supposed that some things in life were inevitable. Change was one of them, so he quickly made his peace with what was about to happen.

The fifth morning of June, Connor drove to David's house and let himself in through the window David always kept open for him. The room was empty, which meant that David was either upstairs eating or taking a shower, so he waited on the bed. Ten minutes later, David entered the room, dressed but with his hair dripping wet.

"What are you doing here?" he asked defensively.

"Oh, that's right," Connor said. "You can't see me today. You were vague about why. Too busy doing something. What was it again?"

David swallowed guiltily.

Connor stood and mussed his hair, sending droplets flying, and said with faux sorrow, "Sweet Seventeen just doesn't have the same ring to it."

"Damn it! Who told you?"

Connor laughed and dodged the question. "Who doesn't like their own birthday? It's not like you're turning forty!"

"It's embarrassing." David scowled. "There's all this pressure to feel happy when it's just another stupid day. Not only that, but I have to go through the whole ordeal twice, first with my dad and then with Mom and Jeff."

"No you don't," Connor said.

"How do you figure?"

Connor nodded toward the closet. "I need you to pack a bag with a week's worth of clothes."

David just stared.

"Swimming trunks too. Or do you not want to see the Atlantic Ocean?"

David's expression turned to wonder. "Are you serious? We're going on a trip?"

"Yup! I have a sister in Florida, down in Daytona Beach, and she said we can crash there for a couple of weeks. Not exactly a four-star hotel—" He glanced at the magazine pages on David's wall. "—but I figured you always wanted to travel. This is the best I can do."

Connor was nearly knocked off his feet when David slammed into him for a hug.

"I already talked to your parents," Connor said, gasping for breath. "They're cool with it, so all you need to worry about is what you want to wear." He gently pried David off. "Of course,

I don't want you to pretend you're happy just because it's your birthday, so we can call the whole thing off."

"Shut up!" David grinned. Then he dove into his closet. Almost an hour later, a duffel bag had been stuffed full of clothes, and they made their way upstairs. Mr. Henry gave David a few presents and some words of caution regarding their trip before they were finally free.

Connor had done his best to spruce up the car, taking it to a car wash and vacuuming it out. In the back seat he had a twelve-pack of Coke and some snacks for their road trip. A new tree-shaped air freshener hung from the rearview mirror. Of course the exterior was still a mix of gunmetal grey and beige house paint, but at least the windows had been scraped clean.

"We're flying first-class today," Connor said as he held open the passenger door. "Please note the emergency exits, because it will be a small miracle if this old hunk of junk makes it all the way to Florida without breaking down."

Once David was seated, Connor hurried around to the driver's side and hopped in.

"All set?"

"Yeah. What's this?" David asked, holding up a present wrapped in Power Rangers paper.

"That's from Gordon." Connor revved the engine once before pulling away. "He made me swear not to say that he tipped me off about your birthday."

"Nice." David chuckled. "I think I can forgive him this time."

He unwrapped a current road atlas, a number of Post-it notes sticking out of the top.

"Looks like he planned our entire route," David said as he thumbed through the pages. "Just like him, really—a strategy guide for the real world."

David flipped the pages of the atlas back and forth as they reached the highway, studying the route and making little puzzled or surprised noises, depending on what he found. "Man, we get to go through so many states: Illinois, Kentucky, Tennessee."

He made it sound like an adventure, when really they had a grueling twenty-hour drive ahead of them. They were crossing the state line over into Missouri when David tired of the maps and set the atlas aside.

"Have you travelled much before?" Connor asked.

"Just a few family vacations. The furthest we ever went was to Mount Rushmore, back when my parents were still together. I think I was eight or so. I mostly remember the drive, sitting in the back seat with a pile of comics. Every gas station we hit, I'd beg for another comic book. I remember more about the stories I read than the actual trip." David toyed with the air freshener, twirling the tree around until the string was tight before releasing it again. "I can't actually remember seeing Mount Rushmore. There's this photo of me with the four giant president heads in the background, but I don't remember being there. Sometimes I wish I could talk to the kid in that photo and tell him to turn around and pay attention."

Connor nodded. "It's strange all the things our parents do for us that we don't remember. When I was a kid, my dad used to drive us out to Branson every year. I had an uncle there who would take us to Silver Dollar City. I've probably been a dozen times, and despite all the roller coasters and everything, all I can remember is some weird tree house thing with a room full of lights. Poor guy should have saved his cash."

"Probably. But maybe it's all still in our heads somewhere. Like our subconscious knows everything our parents did for us, every trip and bandaged knee, and even though we forgot most of it, part of us remembers feeling loved anyway."

They considered this solemnly before they snorted and laughed. Once in Missouri, the car rumbled over highways at least ten years overdue for repairs. David fiddled with the radio, trying to find a clear station with music he liked. Connor let him play DJ as they flew past countless billboards advertising flea markets, cheap hotels, or gas stations.

The music cranked up, David bounced in his seat like a basketball strapped to a kangaroo. The potential for impressive motion was there, but something was holding him back. When Empire of the Sun's "We Are the People" came on, he started moving his upper body until Connor looked over. Then he grinned bashfully and stopped.

"You like to dance?" Connor asked when commercials came on and the radio was silenced.

"Love it," David said, "but only by myself. You know that trite saying about dancing like nobody's watching? Well, that's easiest to do when there really is no one around."

Connor laughed. "You want me to close my eyes?" He did so for the briefest of moments, jiggling the steering wheel as if they were careening out of control.

"Don't!"

"Then dance for me!"

"Okay, but not on my birthday." David crossed his arms over his chest. "I'm supposed to get whatever I want today, it's a rule. If anything, I should be making you dance for me."

"Yeah, well, you'll have to shoot at my feet like they do in Westerns. I don't dance."

Crossing Missouri took almost four hours. As soon as they skimmed by St. Louis, David sat upright, staring out the window like everything he saw was new. He gave a little cheer when they passed into Illinois, pretending to wipe tears from his eyes.

"Somewhere new," he said dramatically. "Finally!"

Connor was glad he was excited, especially since Illinois didn't look so different from Kansas. Just fields, highways, and a lot of sky. He peered at the dashboard gauges. "We need gas."

They pulled over at a truck stop that boasted everything from showers to a chapel. Connor pumped the gas—wondering if lovestruck truckers ever tied the knot here—while David ran to the minimart for food. When he returned, he was carrying two trays of nachos.

"Look! I cooked!" David's smile slipped when he saw the total on the gas meter. "I can pay," he said quickly, but Connor had already swiped his debit card.

"You're getting cheese on your shoes," Connor said to distract him, but this ruse didn't last long. When they were back on the road, David raised the issue again.

"My dad gave me money. Let me chip in for gas."

"No need. I robbed a bank before we left." Connor winked at him. "Seriously though, this is my birthday present to you. I'm paying."

"But it's expensive, and that was just one tank."

"So reward me by not worrying about it." The truth was, the trip was going to be a huge drain on Connor's finances. Over the last year he had managed to save up enough for a deposit and two months rent on a place of his own—if he could find one cheap enough. This trip would probably take away at least one of those months, but he would soon make up for it when he found full-time work. "Chin up, birthday boy, and feed your sugar daddy while he drives you to Florida."

David shoved a chip soggy with cheese into Connor's mouth.

The sun set as they drove, the highway transformed into a dark sky full of red, orange, and white stars that zoomed by as they travelled down the never-ending road ahead. They were in the middle of Tennessee and edging toward Georgia when Connor started fighting the temptation to rest his eyes. David had already dozed off next to him, but some survival instinct must have caused him to stir at that moment.

"Want me to drive?" he murmured.

"Maybe tomorrow. Let's get a room."

If Connor had been on his own, he would have pulled off onto a country road, parked the car, and slept in the backseat. David would probably be up for such an idea, but Connor wanted better for him. Soon he saw a no-name motel advertising a low price and took the next exit.

"You're old enough to get a hotel room!" David said once Connor had returned from the lobby with a key. "That's so cool!"

Wow, that didn't make Connor feel old or like he was dating a kid. "Come on, jail bait. Let's get you to your room."

Their energy returned once they were inside the room. Too bad it hadn't manifested when they were still driving, because Connor would have liked making it a little farther down the road. At least they had covered enough distance that the trip tomorrow would be easy.

"I think my mind is more tired than my body," Connor commented as he stretched.

"Well, gosh," David said with bedroom—or in this case—hotel room eyes. "It just so happens I have a cure for that."

The motel where they stayed wasn't a bed and breakfast by any stretch of the imagination. There wasn't even a breakfast buffet, so the next morning they stopped at a local doughnut joint before hitting the road again. Connor let David drive his car for the first time, which for some reason made him more nervous than he expected. Maybe it was because the Chevy was the only thing he owned except for a little cash and half a bedroom of furniture back home.

As he did his best to kick back and watch the scenery zoom by, Connor mused that the car had renewed value. The Chevy was the key to giving David what he wanted most. Connor didn't have much—no great career plans or promising education—but for now, during this one summer, he could give David his freedom.

"Why can't it always be like this?" David said, beaming at the world through the windshield.

"What? You mean driving?"

"Not just that. It's like we're untouchable when we're on the road. If you go fast enough, life can't catch up with you. Nothing can."

"Except the police," Connor said, noticing the speedometer. "Ease off the gas a little."

"Sorry." David watched the meter sink before continuing his train of thought. "I'm eager to see Florida, but it feels so free out here on the road with you. We've got music, snacks in the back, and anything else we need is just a short stop away. It's perfect. Let's just keep driving forever."

"Well, we can make it down to the tip of Florida. Then we'll splash into the Atlantic, but if we hold our breath long enough, we'll reach Cuba eventually."

David laughed. "Sounds good to me!"

Shortly before they reached Athens, Georgia, they pulled over for gas and Connor took the wheel. The city's traffic was fierce, and there was a lot of street swapping, but they made it through with only a few angry honks and rude gestures. Four more hours of cruising through lush green forests and they left Georgia behind.

Connor wished crossing into Florida meant instant beaches, ocean waves, and Mickey Mouse on a surfboard, but instead the landscape was identical to Georgia. The divisions between states were mostly imaginary, except where rivers created natural lines. Three hours later, in the dwindling daylight, they finally had their first ocean sighting. Connor left I-95 about an hour away from their destination so they could cruise down U.S. 1, which ran as close to the coast as possible. By the time they reached Daytona Beach, the moon was high enough to reflect off white crests rushing toward sandy shores.

"Can we pull over and check it out?" David pleaded.

"We will," Connor promised. "Let's get to my sister's place first."

Now Gordon's atlas really came in handy. Connor had helped his sister move to Florida last summer, but she had since moved into a house he had never visited. David squinted at the Post-it note directions from Gordon, guiding them to a sparsely lit neighborhood of old houses.

"I've seen photos," Connor said, ducking his head and peering out the windshield. "I think it's that one on the corner there. Yeah."

The two-story house, probably once the gem of the neighborhood, was now dilapidated. The combination of salt in the air, the fierce Florida sun, and one too many hurricanes made it look so worn that even a new roof and fresh coat of paint wouldn't help much. The driveway they pulled into was more gravel than pavement.

"Wow! Your sister lives here?"

David sounded impressed, and Connor loved him all the more for it. "The house is owned by two old ladies. Lesbians, of course. Tracy rents a couple of rooms on the top floor. I think her girlfriend lives with her as well." Connor put the car in park and killed the engine. Already it clinked as it tried to cool. "Hey, don't let on that we're together, okay?"

"What? Why?"

"Because my sister always pulls the same shit when I bring a friend around. Trust me, you won't have to play closet-case for long."

He could tell this suggestion made David uncomfortable, but it would be worth getting back at his sister. They grabbed their bags from the backseat and stepped out into an evening warm enough to be day, but with stars above rather than the blinding sun. Connor couldn't wait to hit the beach and feel the sand beneath his feet. He imagined a quick "hello" to his sister before dragging David back out into the night.

He stabbed at the doorbell a few times, no corresponding chime or buzz inside the house, so Connor knocked. Half a minute later the door swung open, warm light spilling out onto the dark patio.

"What's up, Con-man?"

Connor's older sister could have been his plucky younger

brother and had been mistaken for such on more than one occasion. She was built like a sixteen-year-old boy. Well, one a little more athletic than David, at least. She kept her blond hair buzzed short, the longer hair on top gelled and spiked forward like a rooster in reverse. None of the women in Connor's family had much in the chest department, and Tracy used this to her advantage. A loose gray tank top and a pair of baggy jeans helped confuse her gender.

Tracy sprang out of the doorway, locking Connor in a hug that threatened to crack one of his ribs before she turned to look at David.

"So he's finally got a new friend!" she said. "After Sanchez moved out of the trailer park, I thought he'd be spending every Saturday night with Mom."

David, confused by her humor, smiled and clumsily introduced himself. Oh man, Tracy was going to love teasing him! Connor probably should have given David a crash course on his sister's personality, but he'd learn soon enough.

"Well, come in!" Tracy grabbed the duffle bag from Connor's hand.

They followed her in, barely able to take in the details of the house as she tromped upstairs. The banister and stairs were made from real wood, the surrounding walls painted a deep burgundy. The women who owned the house obviously gave all their attention to the interior—not that it wasn't shabby as well, but here the wear and tear was caused by decades of living. Each wooden step was worn down in the front where countless people had walked, different tenants dragging furniture up and down as they came and went. The wood of the handrail was a darker shade, naturally oiled by the touch of many hands.

The upper floor was simple. Directly ahead was a bathroom; to each side one of Tracy's rooms. She brought them into the largest. Most of it was full of living room furniture, except for a corner sectioned off by a decorative dressing screen that failed to hide a bed.

Tracy tossed Connor's bag aside and hopped onto the couch, spreading her arms wide. "Are you hungry?"

"No, we grabbed some fast food just outside town."

"That's good because I didn't cook anything."

She grinned at them both before patting the cushions on either side of her. Naturally she was sitting in the middle, which would be awkward for them. She thought she was being funny. Connor shoved her aside, Tracy doing her best to resist and wrestle him back, howling with laughter all the while. Connor grabbed her by the ankles and was about to pull her off the couch when she finally submitted.

When he turned around, he found David staring at them both with a puzzled expression. All right, so maybe most guys didn't wrestle with their older sister, but Tracy was the exception to rules that hadn't been invented yet.

"Can I use the restroom?" David asked quietly.

"Depends on what you want to use it for," Tracy responded.

"It's fine," Connor said. "Just go."

"He's cute," Tracy said as soon as David had gone. "You didn't bring him down here to try and get in his pants, did you?"

And that was the best part. She didn't have a clue about their relationship. "Straight as an arrow, I'm afraid. If this dry spell keeps up, I'll probably go back to women."

Tracy slapped his arm. "Oh god! Well, I hope you have better taste now than in junior high. Remember Mary Jacobs? She was all metal and antennas."

"Hey, she didn't have the head gear when we started dating," Connor said.

"Did her parents take her to a dentist from the seventies? I've never seen so much steel crammed into one mouth. Tell me you didn't kiss her!"

"If I had, would I still have lips?" Connor missed this—the strange banter of siblings that was so superficial, yet so comfortingly familiar. He didn't have this with Tommy yet, since he was still so young, but someday Tommy would be bringing girlfriends around and Connor would be teasing him about his awkward years.

"You know you guys are crashing on the couch, right?"

"This one?" Connor asked.

"No, not with Daniela staying here. You're sleeping downstairs."

"I thought your girlfriend's name was Sarah?"

Tracy scoffed. "Her? Ancient history. I forgot she even existed."

"You moved down here to be with her."

"Did I? I thought I moved down here for the Cuban *bonitas*." Tracy's grin was shameless.

"Seriously, you have a spare room, right? We can make a bed on the floor or something."

Tracy shook her head. "That room is crammed to the brim with junk. The grannies have been promising to clear it out since I moved in, but I don't think they ever will."

Well, that put a damper on their lodgings. "Do you get cheaper rent at least?"

"That's just it. The room was supposed to be a 'bonus' to renting here. If they could make more money off me, they'd have it cleared out in record time."

When David returned, he wasn't alone. Behind him was one of the Cuban beauties. Her long, dark hair fell in curled tangles around her creamy mocha skin. She was every bit as feminine as Tracy wasn't, her nails and makeup done to perfection.

David held the door open for her, like they were at a restaurant or something.

"David, Connor, this is Daniela." Tracy stood and walked over to her, making sure David was looking. She was *so* predictable. "Daniela is my girlfriend."

Tracy wrapped an arm around Daniela and pulled her close before engaging in a kiss that was anything but subtle. Connor couldn't count the number of times she had pulled this stunt, either in front of the few friends he brought home or out in public. He supposed he had taken inspiration from her when the cop was giving him and David a hard time outside of school, but she still needed to be taught a lesson.

David stared for a second, then moved around them to join Connor on the couch. As soon as Tracy came up for air, she turned a self-satisfied smirk on them. David looked uncomfortable, but only because he was naturally shy.

"I wish you wouldn't do that," Connor said. "You're going to scare away my buddy here." He moved like he was going to give David a comforting pat on the back, but then he went further, bringing his face close to David's. Their kiss was much more dignified. He gave David a gentle peck on the lips before nuzzling their noses together and kissing him again.

His sister squealed, proving just how girly she could be. "Oh my god, I can't believe it! My little brother has a boyfriend!"

"That was good," Daniela said with a smoky chuckle. "Now maybe she'll stop shoving her tongue down my throat at the most embarrassing times."

Tracy ignored her, hopping up and down like she had just won the Showcase Showdown. "How did you meet? How long have you been together? You have to tell me everything!"

"No, I don't," Connor said, taking David's hand and standing. "I'm bringing my boyfriend to the beach before you terrify him any further."

"You can't! You have to stay. I'll even cook, I swear!"

Connor rushed David out of the house like a celebrity being hounded by a mob of fans, represented here by one crazy lesbian. To her credit, Tracy only followed them to the front door before she gave up.

"She's not always that wired," Connor said as soon as they were in the car. "Give her time and she'll calm down. A little bit."

"She's a little overwhelming," David admitted. "It's probably just weird for me because I don't have a brother or sister."

Connor tried to imagine a female version of David, the curly hair grown out past his shoulders and bright red lipstick smeared across his lips. She would probably be just as bookish and shy as her brother. Rather than wrestling, they would probably sit side by side playing video games all night. No doubt Gordon would have a hopeless crush on her.

Connor shook this image from his mind and put the car in gear. They had an ocean to see!

The beach, it turned out, was walled away from the world by hotels, resorts, and high-priced condos. These institutions had long ago staked their claim on the coast, offering their patrons exclusive access to the beach. Connor drove up and down searching for a way in. He had pictured them driving onto the sand just like in the movies, but in the end they had to settle for parking at a restaurant with a deck jutting out over the sand. They snuck around the side of the restaurant, hopping a low fence and slinking past windows that were venting steam and kitchen noise into the night.

Tracy worked here, if Connor had the right place, so if they were caught he could at least mention her name. The pavement ended and the ground descended, steadily blending from earth to sand. By the time they passed the deck, they were already below its height. The restaurant was having an eighties night, judging by the cheesy music blaring both inside and from deck speakers, but even over the music and chatting diners, they could hear the roar of the waves.

David slipped in the sand, but Connor caught him by the arm and took his hand. Then they ran together toward the water, laughing like two madmen broken free from the asylum.

"Let's take off our shoes," David said, plopping down on the sand and ripping at his shoelaces.

Connor watched him, happy to be the one showing David more of the world. Then he lifted his foot to get his own shoes off, hopping around on one leg until he toppled over, causing David to laugh again.

As soon as they were barefoot they ran down the beach, leaving footprints in the sand that wound back and forth across each other before being washed away. They stomped into the water, waves soaking the bottoms of their shorts, but they didn't care. Connor would have gladly stripped off the rest of his clothes and dragged David into the water if he hadn't felt the pull of the undertow during his last visit. David was the first to scoop up water and toss it at Connor, and soon they were splashing each other, dodging and leaping to avoid being hit.

When they tired, they began a leisurely stroll back toward the restaurant.

"Two weeks of this?" David asked as if he still couldn't believe it.

Connor nodded. "Yup. Just you and me. Well, and four lesbians. I told you we're crashing on the couch, right?"

David shrugged. "Sounds like paradise."

Eighties night was still going strong when they reached the beach outside the restaurant. Turning their backs to the building, they held hands and faced the great empty expanse ahead. Moonlight glittered off the nearest waves, beyond this a comforting darkness, as if they could step into the empty space and make of it anything they desired. Connor couldn't imagine anything he wanted more than this moment, being together with David and away from the bosses and bullies of the world.

Behind them, the synth-fueled pop gave way to a slower song that began with a simple guitar riff before bass and drums joined in. Crowded House serenaded them, telling them they shouldn't dream it was over, even if the world came between them. Connor had heard the song countless times, but now it spoke to him directly, like a message from the universe.

"I still owe you that birthday dance," he said, turning to David and putting an arm around his waist. David wrapped his arms around him in return, pulling him closer. Then their bodies moved as one, swaying to the music. Connor bowed his head, let his lips brush against David's neck before breathing in the smell of salt water on his skin.

David was right. This was paradise.

Chapter Thirteen

"Rise and shine, lovelies! I made you some yummy breakfast!"

David groaned and pulled a pillow over his head, but he knew it was hopeless. The last three mornings had begun like this, with one of the grannies waking them up for breakfast at the crack of dawn. He could feel someone watching him, so he shoved the pillow away and found a face close to his. This one was Glasses, as he had come to think of her.

The two old ladies who owned the house were nearly identical. Both were short, pleasantly plump women with a bob of white-grey hair. David could only distinguish them by the reading glasses one always had perched at the end of her nose and by the overalls the other wore. As far as he knew, the grannies didn't have grandkids and seemed to be making up for lost time with Connor and him.

Granted, the breakfasts were phenomenal. He could smell it already, which was enough encouragement for him to mutter he was coming, sending the old woman away. As good as the food was, what David really wanted was to sleep late with Connor. A little privacy once they woke up would also be welcome.

"Is she gone?" Connor grumbled from behind him. They could only rest on their sides, which meant being wrapped in Connor's arms all night, so it wasn't all bad.

"Yeah, she's gone."

They enjoyed a brief moment of quiet before rising and trudging into the kitchen. Both grannies were seated there, Overalls reading the morning paper while Glasses beamed and waited for them to be seated. Omelettes with a side of pancakes were on the menu today, a breakfast hearty enough that they could probably skip lunch.

"Someone didn't sleep well," Glasses said when Connor's first few bites didn't chase away the crease in his brow. She always watched them eat like it was the most thrilling thing in the world.

"It's a little early is all," David said, hoping the hint would be enough.

"Well, our news program comes on at half eight," Overalls grumped, "so we'd wake you then anyway."

"Shame about the extra room upstairs," Connor said. "We'd

be out of your way if it was cleared out."

Glasses nodded sympathetically. "There's even a bed in there."

"Is not," Overalls said, rustling the newspaper as if to banish the topic.

David knew why: The room upstairs was stuffed with her belongings.

"There is too a bed," Glasses scolded. "The last time someone slept in there, it was half-covered with your boxes. I remember being so embarrassed!"

"When was this?" David said.

"Gosh." Glasses put a hand to her cheek. "Let's see. Nineteen— No. Was Reagan or Carter in office?"

"She's being dramatic," Overalls said.

"No, I'm not! We went to all the trouble of drywalling the basement to move your things there, and that was back in the nineties. I think we celebrated by going to a Color Me Badd concert. That should tell you something!"

Overalls lowered the newspaper. "It was a Sarah McLachlan concert."

"Well, has she done anything since the nineties?"

Overalls shrugged, and Glasses resumed eating, the topic fleeing their minds as it always did, but David wasn't giving up.

"You know, if you have a place in the basement where we could put the stuff, Connor and I could clear out the room. We'd be glad to do it."

"That would be wonderful!"

"It's fine how it is."

"But Margie, if they're willing to do the work ... You always say it's your back."

"It is my back, *and* everything is fine where it is."

As the two old ladies argued back and forth, David kept his attention on his food. By the time he cleaned his plate, the battle was over and Glasses had won.

After he and Connor showered, they went to the extra room and opened the door. It looked like someone had walled in a prisoner with cardboard boxes instead of bricks. Connor gave David a hopeless look, but David wasn't dissuaded. With a little bit of work, they should ... could ... might have their own room tonight.

Except the task wasn't quite that easy. David was carrying the first box down the basement stairs when Overalls stopped him and asked to check the contents. She flipped back the cardboard flaps revealing dusty old newspapers inside. As she examined a few with careful fingers, David caught a date of 1983, meaning Glasses wasn't kidding about how long it had been.

"No, I think I need to keep these upstairs where it's dry," the old woman said.

"Do they have articles that you wrote or something?"

"No." Overalls turned to check Connor's box next, which was full of old T-shirts with even older political slogans on them. She held up one with the words "Out of the Closets and into the Streets" that was about five sizes too small for her.

"I can still wear this," she said. "Maybe we should keep it upstairs."

Connor glared at her from behind, his eyes starting to get that crazy look, so David promised to take the boxes back upstairs. Instead he went straight to the living room where Glasses was working on a crossword puzzle. One desperate look from him, and she understood.

After a heated conversation, the grannies left to go shopping and have lunch. Once they were safely out of the way, David sprang into action. He hauled boxes down to the basement so fast that he never stopped sweating. Even when Connor took a break, David kept going.

In a way, David felt like he was building them a home. The last few days had been full of beach trips or short drives to check out how different everything was compared to Kansas. David had spent nearly two hours in a grocery store, marveling at the Cuban foods that he had never seen before. Everything was new and exciting, and the idea of having their own space would make it easier to pretend that this was their life.

Connor was downstairs raiding the fridge when David discovered the bed. The sheets and pillows were still on it after all these decades. By the time Connor finished lunch, David had cleared the entire bed and could see a crack of daylight through a few more layers of boxes.

"That's good enough, don't you think?" Connor leaned against the doorway with an amorous look that suggested he wanted to give the bed a test run.

"I guess those muscles are just for show," David taunted, picking up another box and pushing past him.

Connor took the bait. After another couple of hours, the room was cleared, the sheets stripped off the bed, the washing machine running, and the window open.

"You'd make a phenomenal housewife," Connor said.

David smirked. "Does that count as a proposal?"

When the grannies returned home in the late afternoon, Glasses was positively thrilled with the changes, but Overalls looked faint. The color returned to her cheeks when she saw the basement. Not only had David stacked the boxes for easy access, but they were also labeled. He had been tempted to write "junk" on each one and be done with it, but instead he had given each box its due. Glasses was pleased enough that she slipped some cash in his hand.

"What should we do with it?" David asked Connor when they were alone in the laundry room putting the sheets in the dryer. David could hardly wait to crawl into a real bed again.

"It's your money. You worked your—" Connor grabbed him. "—cute little ass off."

"Hey!" David wiggled free. "I didn't spend all day unearthing a bed just to be sexually harassed in the laundry room!"

"Since when have we ever needed a bed?" Connor tried to grab him again, but David dodged. "Have you forgotten our first time?"

"I haven't, which is why we're doing it the right and proper way tonight." Not that David wasn't ready to go, but a fantasy was playing out in his imagination. "Dinner tonight—your choice, my treat—and maybe a movie. Afterwards, if you're gentlemanly enough, I might let you kiss me goodnight."

"Sounds good," Connor said, backing off. "Depending on where I'm allowed to kiss you."

The restaurant they went to was the same one they snuck past on their first night in Florida. David praised Connor's choice as romantic, but soon learned there was an ulterior motive. The sun was setting as they were seated out on the deck, their waiter rattling off the specials, when he was knocked aside by a waitress with short blonde hair.

"I'll take this table, Charlie," Tracy said, order pad in hand like a reporter trying to get the big scoop. Charlie rubbed his injured shoulder but retreated, leaving Tracy grinning at them. "How sweet of you to come see your big sister."

"That's not the only reason we're here," Connor said, telling her how David cleaned out the extra room.

Tracy reacted as if Christmas had come early and brought Birthday along as a date. "Well, dinner's on me then!"

"No, it's okay," David said. "Dinner is on Glasses tonight."

"Glasses?"

"Sorry. That's just what I call your landlady."

Tracy barked laughter. "Oh, you mean Anna. What do you call Margie?"

"Overalls."

"That's funny. They do look alike, but I just call them the grannies. Anyway, they never would have cleared out that room on their own, so I owe you. If not dinner, then something."

"Careful," Connor said, "or David will be asking to move in."

"Hey, I'd love that," Tracy said. "I miss my little brother. Why don't you move down here? You're both out of high school, right? I'm sure Simon would give you a job."

"I still have another year of school," David said, hating to admit it. Tracy's offer might not have been completely serious, but David loved the thought of moving to Florida. Sand plagued his shoes from all the time spent at the beach, his nose was perpetually red with sunburn, and they had spent way too much money on museums and food, but he couldn't be happier.

"Tough break," Tracy said. "That last year will go quicker than you think."

"Who's Simon?" Connor interjected.

"My boss. He's so light in the loafers that we use a ladder to get him down from the ceiling. One look at you and he'd probably make you head chef. Want to meet him?"

Connor rolled his eyes. "No. This is supposed to be a romantic meal."

"Hint taken. Give me your orders, and I'll try not to kill the mood when I bring your food."

"It's not the worst idea in the world," David said when she had gone.

At first Connor didn't understand what he meant, but then shook his head. "There's no way we can move down here. You still have to finish school."

"There are high schools in Florida. Do I really need my parent's permission to enroll?"

"No idea, but my sister is right. Your senior year will fly by. If you want to apply to a college down here, that would be fine."

David stared at him. "Well, I'm glad I have your permission."

"I didn't mean it like that. I just don't want you wasting your potential."

"What does that even mean?" David's voice sounded loud, even to his own ears. "People keep saying that to me, like I'm some ugly plant that they keep expecting to flower. Well, what if I don't? What if people are wrong, and all that potential they think they see is me being not good enough?"

Connor's face was flushed, from anger or from embarrassment, David couldn't tell, but the couple at the next table was eyeing them. "That's not what I mean at all," Connor said, voice low. "You're smart, and I don't want to see it going to waste."

"Are you on my dad's payroll or something?"

"No, and I wish you'd stop complaining about him because you're lucky! Even now my dad doesn't have a thing to say about my future. I doubt he's ever thought of it. Maybe that's why I feel like I don't have one, I don't know. But you have a future, and you're going to be amazing."

"How do you know?" David insisted. "How can anyone know that?"

Connor's eyes met his. "Because, for the little it may be worth, I love you."

And just like that, the fight went out of David.

"You're not even out of high school," Connor continued, "and you're about the best person I've ever met."

"There's someone better?" David said, a sheepish attempt at humor. To his relief, Connor responded well.

"Well, there's my mom. She's incredible, so you've got tough competition."

David was happy to concede that point. "You do have a future," he said. "We have one together, right?"

"Yup." Connor crossed his arms over his chest. "But only if you go to college."

David's temper was starting to rise again when Connor guffawed and they both relaxed. Maybe Connor meant it as a compliment, but David didn't like Connor telling him what to do with his life. He didn't want this to ruin the evening, so he decided to change topics. "Do you think we could drive to Kennedy Space Center tomorrow? It's not too far away, and I want to check it out before the shuttle is retired and it gets all depressing."

Connor nodded, but still watched him carefully, as if David would sneak away from the table, drop out of high school, and sign a lease for an apartment in Florida. David ignored these looks and kept droning on about the space program. Before long, Connor's posture relaxed, but David's determination didn't. He couldn't picture returning to the world he had known. Not for long, anyway.

A small jungle thrived behind the grannies' house. When David had first seen the overgrown backyard on their first night in Florida, he had thought it abandoned. But during the day the sun beat down on wildflowers, bringing out their vibrant colors. Leafy vines crawled up everything from an old rain barrel to a worn bench in one corner of the yard. The spiky palm bushes so common to Florida were here too, as were a number of quickly ripening tomatoes. David sat near the tomato vines and watched as Anna, formerly known as Glasses, fussed over the vegetables.

As she worked, she wore the same serene smile that she always did. David hoped he would be half as happy when he was old. He supposed living in a house with the love of your life had a lot to do with that.

"How long have you and Margie been together?" he asked.

"Oh, goodness, don't make me count. I met her not long after my thirty-third birthday."

"So late in life?"

Anna tugged the brim of her floppy hat up to scrunch her nose at him. "It only seems late in life to someone your age. Believe me, thirty-three is ancient history for me. I was practically a kid."

"I'm just surprised you didn't meet sooner. You two seem so …" He couldn't find the right word, because honestly, they were an odd couple. Margie was as crotchety and grim as Anna was pleasant. "Did you know right away that you would spend the rest of your life with her?"

Anna tittered as she grabbed a spade and started turning soil. "Well, I remember thinking she was arrogant and self-assured. We went out to dinner and spent most of the meal arguing about the bill before it even came. Margie insisted on going Dutch, saying that either of us paying for the other would be buying into heterosexual stereotypes." Anna sighed as if this were romantic.

"And you agreed to see each other again?"

"Are you kidding? I loved her passion so much that I went home with her that night. We didn't part company until almost a week later. I lost my job for not showing up, not that it was a good one. Margie hated the idea of me being a secretary anyway and was much more pleased when I took a job at a truck stop."

David was tempted to judge, but realized his relationship with Connor probably seemed just as weird to other people.

"Besides," Anna said, "a couple who don't argue don't love each other. Margie and I just got an early start. Do you and Connor argue often?"

David thought of the heated discussion during dinner. Did that count? The weird thing was, he hadn't been upset because Connor had lied or been mean. That was the sort of thing people argued about, he thought. Instead, tension had been triggered by Connor wanting the best for David … in a way that annoyed him.

"We've never really argued," David fibbed.

"Oh you will," Anna said. "Just give it a little more time, and when it does happen, remember it's not the end of the world. You probably won't convince him that you're right anymore than he'll believe that he's wrong, and that's fine, because in his eyes it's the other way around. Here, help me get this loose."

David took the spade and started prying a large stone out of the ground. "So what's the point in arguing if you don't change the other person's mind?"

"Usually it's to blow off steam, something better left to the bedroom. But that isn't always an option, so if you're in a car you argue about the quickest route to the highway or where to park. Now the serious issues, the things that can make or break a relationship, that's when you don't want to argue."

"So what do you do?"

"Discuss." Anna wiped the sweat off her forehead with the back of her arm. "When it gets too heated, you back off and only come back to the table when you think you can be civilized."

David hoped he would never need any of this advice. He couldn't imagine really arguing with Connor about anything, but he knew how complicated a relationship could become. His parents both seemed so reasonable and calm, but when together they never stopped bickering and blaming each other, or worse, engaging in long chilly silences.

"You two seem happy," David said. "I mean, even if you argue, you seem like a good team."

Anna nodded and placed a small plant in the hole they had dug. "We're complete opposites, but we're loyal to each other. That's important, but even more so is being loyal to yourself. I only worked at the truck stop for a few months before I found a job at JC Penny's makeup counter. Margie was still adamant that gender roles would bring about Armageddon and gave me no end of hell for working such a girly job, but it's what I wanted to do. I love all of those feminine things: lace, perfume, summer dresses. I no longer tried to be someone I wasn't for her, and Lord knows she's never been anyone but Margie, and that's why we're happy. You can be yourself and be a mess, and you can do it together." Anna tweaked David's nose with her garden-gloved hand. "Isn't love wonderful?"

He glanced toward the house where Connor was taking an afternoon nap.

"Yeah, it is."

"Whatever you do, *don't* be yourself! There's no quicker way to end a relationship than that."

Connor grumbled and pulled the sheets over his head. This earned him a few seconds respite before the sheets were ripped back.

"Are you even listening to me?" Tracy demanded.

"No," Connor said. "I'm taking a nap."

His sister didn't seem to hear, or maybe she didn't care. "It's not like she was so concerned about my future when she was chasing me all over the club that night. She was so pathetic, like a small dog trying to impress a wolf, but I thought she was cute so I gave her a chance. Now? Now I'm not good enough for her!"

Connor cracked open an eye and peered at his sister. Her cheeks were flushed, her eyes red and wet. Had she been crying? "What a minute," he said, sitting up. "Did Daniela break up with you?"

Tracy opened her mouth to say something smart, but closed it again, shoulders slumping as she nodded. "She kept going on about how we didn't have a future together. I didn't have a clue what she meant at first. Why wouldn't we have a future? The Mayan calendar thing? But eventually it came out. We don't have a future together because I'm a waitress."

Connor frowned. "All she has is a freshly printed degree and a pile of student loans."

"I know! She certainly didn't mind mooching off my waitress salary for the last nine months. But apparently her daddy has found her a job at a law firm, and I'm not good enough for her new caviar-and-champagne lifestyle."

"That's fucked up," Connor said.

Tracy nodded, tears spilling over.

He hated seeing his sister like this. In fact, Connor had *never* seen her like this. "You really liked her, didn't you?"

"Well, she's beautiful and smart and going places. When I was with her, I could pretend that I was too."

"Hey, stop it! You're gorgeous! How many broken hearts have you left behind?"

Tracy wiped her eyes and managed a smile. "A few. Maybe this is just bad karma."

"Or maybe Daniela is a superficial bitch. She's the one who's messed up, not you."

"I guess so. I'm screwed up too, because I still love her. Even now." Tracy shook her head. "You know what I should have done? I should have kept her distant. I shouldn't have told her where I work, and as for this place, I should have told her I owned the house and rented the downstairs to the grannies."

"Then she wouldn't have loved you at all," Connor said. "She would have loved a lie, not the real you."

Tracy sniffed and shot him a surprised look. "Check you out, baby brother! When did you get all wise?"

Connor grinned. "I've always been wise. You just never listened to me before."

"That must be it." Tracy looked toward the window. "I could have made her happy, you know. If she had given me a chance, I could have made her dreams come true. I don't know how, but I would have."

Connor thought of David and for a moment he felt his sister's pain. She was living his worst fear. David would move on to bigger and brighter pastures. Connor wanted him to. He didn't want to see David's potential wasted, but he also wanted to be at his side. His greatest worry was that he would be left behind, that life would continue dealing him a losing hand.

Tracy nudged his shoulder. "Remember when Mom and Dad were happy? Dirt poor and both working terrible jobs, but remember how much they would laugh every night? They were like a couple of kids. And then—"

Connor nodded. He didn't need to be reminded. "They're doing better. If Dad stays off the pills, maybe they can get back to that."

"I hope so. I could use a positive role model about now." She straightened up. "What am I talking about? My brother landed himself a boyfriend, and you two seem okay."

For now. Who knew for how long? The thought put a lump in his throat, so he just nodded.

"Hey! Speaking of which—" Tracy hopped off the bed. "I'll be right back."

When she came back, she was carrying two flat shapes, both brightly colored. She shoved them into Connor's arms.

"Bodyboards?" he asked.

"Yup! I wanted to buy David a 'thank you' present for clearing out this room and thought they might be fun. Do you think he'll like them?"

"Yeah!" Connor said, but he wasn't sure. David wasn't the athletic type, but how hard could laying down on a piece of laminated foam be?

"They're just the cheap kind," Tracy said. "They'll probably break within a week, but there aren't any waves in Kansas anyway."

"They're cool." Connor examined them. "We'll try them out tomorrow."

His hair had grown out just enough to be ruffled, which his sister did. She stood and headed for the door, but hesitated there. "You really think I'm gorgeous?"

"I do."

"Gross!" Tracy said in mock repulsion. "Wait until I tell Mom. Yuck!"

Then she laughed and left the room, shutting the door behind her and leaving Connor shaking his head. Why did family have to be so crazy?

In the waters of the Atlantic Ocean, not far from Florida's sandy coast, a solitary form clung to a cheap bodyboard, bobbing with the water and paddling occasionally until a big enough wave came along to lift both board and passenger. Sometimes. More often the wave would crash down over David's head. Each time this happened, Connor sat up from his towel and strained his vision, willing himself to see beneath the water from his position on the beach. He would hold his breath, as if it were him out there under the waves, until David's curly locks popped out of the water. Usually he managed to wave in Connor's direction before coughing up water.

Connor knew the sensation. He had swallowed enough salt water today to open an aquarium in his stomach. Despite this, getting pummeled by the ocean had been fun, and the rare times he managed to ride a wave had been breathtaking. Now he was done taking the ocean's abuse, but David was still enjoying himself. As he watched, David caught a small wave that brought him close to shore.

David grinned as he clumsily got to his feet and started toward Connor. The two weeks in Florida had been good to him. David tanned much nicer than Connor's lobster-prone skin, and his hair had grown out just enough that he looked like a beach bum in training. More than his appearance, David's demeanor had changed dramatically. Oh sure, he was still socially awkward and had the nerdiest hobbies, but his smiles came easier and his body language was relaxed, no longer braced for the worst to happen. This small boost in confidence was enough to make him stand up straight. Connor had seen plenty of girls noticing David—and a couple of guys as well.

"Aaaaand I'm done," David said as he flopped onto his towel.

Connor eyed the beads of water on his skin, each dancing with light, before he responded. "I thought I'd have to go in there and drag you out."

"It was so fun! Besides, today's the last chance to do stuff like this."

For one second, an expression of dread crossed David's features. Connor hated to see it resurface. He had hoped, even if they were returning home tomorrow, that David's newly gained strength would be carried back to Kansas.

"I talked to Simon," Connor blurted out.

David's forehead crinkled. "Who?"

"Simon. My sister's boss. He owns the deck restaurant."

"Oh?"

This tiny sound of hope spurred Connor on. "I told him how I like to cook, but that I don't have any real experience. I said I could start as a waiter and maybe help out in the kitchen a few hours a day. He said he had enough waiters, but that few people could handle working under his chef. I guess he's a real bastard, so I told him I was used to that. I mean, how much worse can he be than Mike?"

A smile slowly spread over David's face. "What are you saying?"

Connor took a deep breath. "That maybe we'll stay an extra day tomorrow and check out the local high school. If we can enroll you, and I have a job, my sister already said—"

The words were smothered beneath a kiss.

"You're not doing this just for me?" David asked.

The answer used to be 'Yes, of course I am!' But after talking to Simon, Connor felt as if he had finally found direction. He might never be more than a vegetable chopper instead of a real chef, but it was better than flipping burgers back home.

"I figure it's worth a shot," Connor said. "Nothing will probably come of it, but—"

"But nothing! You'll probably have your own cooking show before Christmas."

Connor let himself smile before becoming serious again. "Just don't think that things will be completely different here, okay? I don't want to be depressing, but everything seems perfect when you're on vacation. Your new school will have assholes like Chuck. Money will be tight too, so we might not be able to go out much."

Connor listed more concerns. David listened patiently, as if Connor were an anxious parent. He supposed David would learn soon enough that nowhere was perfect. Assholes bred like cockroaches, but maybe the Florida sun meant they wouldn't come out as often.

"My sister said we can live with her rent-free until we get on our feet, but I want to start looking for an apartment right away. As much as I love you, I don't want to stay cramped up in that room together. And before you get your hopes up, all of this hinges on you being able to enroll."

"Yes sir!" David said, giving a military salute. "Anything else?"

"Yeah," Connor said after a moment's thought. "Your dad is going to kill me."

Chapter Fourteen

Driving nonstop to Kansas had seemed like such a good idea. They would save on hotel costs—a plus considering the expenses of their planned move—and make up for the extra days spent in Florida. Not only had they gotten David enrolled in a local high school, but they had taken a day trip to Gainesville so David could get information on the University of Florida. Connor was determined that David's father would see that the academic plans were still on track.

Now Connor wanted to get David home as soon as possible. They had already stayed away longer than planned, and driving straight through would make up for one of those days. Connor drove the first ten hours and was close to exhausted, but David was eager to prove himself and took the wheel for the next five. When their butts became too numb for comfort, they stopped for fast food and stood in the parking lot, eating over the hood of the car. They had made other stops before this—some to grab snacks or fuel up the car and once to let the engine cool down. All of this added up, and as Connor took the wheel for the final stretch, he realized a twenty-hour drive in theory had become twenty-four hours with the stops factored in.

Now the car was limping into Olathe at six in the morning, David's head on Connor's lap as he drooled his way through dreamland. Connor let him sleep until they pulled into David's neighborhood and parked. Then he reached down and wove his fingers into David's hair, tempted to join him in sleep, but David stirred, sat up, and looked around.

"Don't make that miserable face," Connor said. "It's just for a few weeks."

"Yeah, I know. Do you want to crash here?"

Of course he did, but Connor's family was probably worried, so he shook his head, got out of the car, and carried David's bag to the door.

"Text me when you're home safe, okay?"

"Of course," Connor said, leaning in for a kiss.

Once he was out of the neighborhood, Connor cranked up the radio, glad even for annoying "morning madness" radio. How anyone could regularly tolerate hyperactive DJs and suffer their banal humor was beyond him, but today they were more effective than caffeine at keeping him awake.

The trailer park seemed simple and plain compared to the palm trees and waves they had left behind, but part of him was happy to be home. Even happier when he saw that his father wasn't zonked out in front of the TV. He tiptoed into his room and got his shoes off before Tommy roused from sleep.

Like all kids his age, Tommy could never keep his voice down for long. "I thought you weren't ever coming back!" he complained.

Fortunately Connor had been prepared for this, tossing Tommy a bag of sand dollars, shells, and other tourist fodder. "You know how Tracy is. She barely let me go."

"Why didn't she come back with you?" Tommy asked, but his eyes were locked on the ocean treasures. Bribe accepted.

Connor hesitated. Of all the people he was going to leave behind, Tommy would be the one he missed most. But he had to go. Although he hadn't been as young as Tommy when Tracy had gotten her first Olathe apartment, Connor had still felt torn up inside. Once he was older, he understood. As much as he loved his parents, their life wasn't his. Truth be told, he still felt clueless as to what his life was about, but staying here wouldn't help.

"The place she moved to is really nice," Connor said. "You know they have alligators down there? Disney World isn't far away either."

"Did you go?" Tommy asked, taking the bait.

Connor felt a little bad for manipulating him, but a spoonful of sugar— "No, but I want to move down with Tracy soon. That way you can come visit us, and we can take you there."

Tommy's brow dropped. "You're leaving."

Okay, so he wasn't stupid. "I have to. I know you don't get it now, but you'll want to move out one day. No one stays at home forever." Well, some people did, but parents weren't immortal. One way or another, everyone ended up on their own.

Tommy mulled this over while arranging the souvenirs on his bed. "Are you taking all your stuff with you?"

"Why, is there something you want?"

"If you take your stuff, I can have the whole room to myself."

Ah, they grew up so quickly! "You can have the whole room, but you have to promise to take care of Mom while I'm gone.

Hey, how's Dad doing?"

Tommy shrugged, not understanding the question, but giving an informative answer anyway. "We went for ice cream, and Dad drove."

"Really? Did he get his license again?"

Another shrug, but if Dad was still jacked up on pills, Mom never would have let him get behind the wheel. Comforted that the world hadn't fallen apart while he was gone, Connor stripped down to his underwear and crawled in bed. Tommy chattered about kids in the neighborhood, cartoon heroes on TV, and other breaking news, but even this couldn't keep Connor awake as he sank into a much-needed slumber.

"Florida?"

From his tone of voice, David's father might as well have said "sex change." In fact, had David said he was becoming a woman, his father might have been less shocked.

"I found a great high school down there," David said. Seabreeze High, home of the Fighting Sandcrabs. It all sounded too ridiculous to be true. God, how he couldn't wait to get back there! "They're red-ribbon certified, and were awarded a blue ribbon too." Which made the school sound like a show horse, but David knew what would impress his dad—so he hoped.

His father crossed his arms over his chest. Just moments ago, he had been on the couch, leisurely thumbing through a *National Geographic*, but now that was forgotten as he stared up at his son. "I'm less concerned about the quality of the school than you not having any supervision. What if something happened to you?"

"I'd be living with two nice old ladies." At first, anyway. David sat on the couch next to his father and pulled out his secret weapon—pamphlets from the University of Florida. He handed the biggest brochure to his father. Like an alcoholic being plied with beer, his father appeared reluctant only for a moment. He flipped through the pages in silence, and David was sure he had won, but only for a moment.

"The University of Florida isn't even on the map."

"What?" David was innocently puzzled. "Of course it is."

"You know what I mean." He tossed the brochure aside. "It isn't a top-ranking institution. Did you know that Stanford is interested in you? A letter came while you were gone."

David didn't care, but he had to play this carefully. "The University of Missouri isn't top-ranking either, but you work there, so it must be good. Besides, we can't afford Stanford."

"Scholarships and student loans, David. You know this."

"One year at Stanford would cost as much as four years in Florida. That's in-state tuition, which is why I need to live there for a year before I go. I checked it out, Dad. It's a beautiful school. I was really impressed."

"Well, you haven't seen Stanford yet or any of the other colleges you could go to. Your test scores came while you were gone."

David held back a sigh. His father began going over his test results, line by line. The scores were good—great really—which put his father in a positive mood. But also made him more determined that David make something of himself. Unfortunately, David still didn't know what that something should be. Being smart didn't mean he knew what he wanted in life. His only certainty was that he wanted to be with Connor. Wasn't that enough?

At the end of the conversation, David promised to consider all of his options. Not that he would. The idea of him moving to Florida had been planted in his father's mind. David hoped it would take root. If not, he would give his father an ultimatum: Either he would attend the University of Florida, or he wouldn't go to college at all.

"Prepare to do battle!"

A sword was shoved into David's face, leaving him just enough time to dodge backward. When the weapon was withdrawn, Gordon was grinning madly at him.

"Do come in," David said cordially, as if his eye hadn't nearly been poked out. Luckily, the tip didn't look very sharp or even made of metal.

"I got them!" Gordon declared, apparently happy to stay on the front porch. "One for each of us."

Sure enough, he had two swords. David had nearly forgotten, but before going to Florida, Gordon made him browse a website that sold foam weapons. Aside from the padded blades Gordon was wielding, the site sold axes, maces, flails, and even shields. Naturally this had reinvigorated Gordon's interest in role-playing, although David had hoped his enthusiasm would be fleeting.

Gordon crouched and bared his teeth. "Let's go to the park and cross blades. I demand satisfaction!"

David fought back a smile. Why not? The last couple of days at home had been miserable —the college discussions with his father often escalating into arguments—and Connor wasn't due over for another couple of hours.

"All right, but let's go to the woods instead. I don't want people staring at us."

Gordon shrugged. "Aren't you going to get dressed first?"

David was wearing a T-shirt and shorts, but Gordon wasn't referring to normal clothing. A chainmail shirt that Gordon had bought at the Renaissance Festival last year was draped over his chubby chest. The only thing David owned that was remotely similar was a Harry Potter robe, and he wasn't about to wear that in public.

"It's too hot out. Let's just go."

The woods, about eight blocks away, were in reality an overgrown lot marked by a rotting "For Sale" sign. The asking price must have been too high, because the land had been available for purchase for ages. Enough trees covered the property to provide shadow and shelter, and until a pharmacy chain became desperate for yet another location, this lot would always be "the woods" to David and Gordon.

Once beneath the trees, Gordon launched into character as an evil duke who drove his peasants so hard that most of them dropped dead by age twenty. Gordon loved playing the villain. David, the sole surviving member of the royal family the duke had deposed, became these peasants' only hope. The peasants had hidden him when he was a child, giving up some of their food rations to nourish him until he was strong and old enough to challenge the evil duke.

Foam clashed against foam, their initial laughter fading as they lost themselves in the story. Their role-playing wasn't just sword fighting, but also included dramatic scenes filled with lengthy speeches and grand posturing. David loved it. This was exactly the sort of nerdy fun he could have only with Gordon. As close as he and Connor had become, he couldn't imagine doing something like this with him. Of all the people David would leave behind, Gordon was the one he would miss most.

"I'm moving to Florida."

Gordon, in the middle of whipping some imaginary peasants, stopped and frowned. "I thought this was a fantasy world, not Earth. Or are we doing some weird alternate reality?"

"I mean it. I'm moving to Florida with Connor."

Gordon's arm fell to his side. "When?"

"In about a week. Connor's hoping my dad will agree, which he won't. We're getting a moving truck and heading back there anyway."

Open emotions played across Gordon's face, as they always did, except this time it hurt David to see them.

"That sucks," Gordon said.

And for the first time, it did. He wished he could take Gordon with him, but the idea of tearing him away from his sheltered life seemed unthinkable. Then again, in another couple of years, Gordon would be an adult too and need a life of his own. Maybe David could tempt him into moving to Florida, starting with a vacation down there. "You'll come visit, right?"

"If you win the next battle."

They fought, and even though they still did so in fun and friendship, David knew they were working out their frustrations. The playful banter was gone as their weapons smacked each other with renewed force. In the end, Gordon won, but only because David let him. David was on the ground with a sword pointed at his throat, but the evil duke granted him mercy. And while the peasants wouldn't be emancipated today, Gordon promised he would come visit.

Sweaty and satisfied, they shed their roles and began the walk home, Gordon twirling both swords as they went. With the confession out of his system, David felt free to talk about Florida, doing his best to sell the idea to Gordon by raving about the space program. He had Gordon hooked, the resentment in his eyes replaced by curiosity, when a car pulled off the road so fast the tires scraped the curb.

David took one look at the silver Mazda and all thoughts of Florida disappeared. The car was in immaculate condition, even though last month its rear had sideswiped another car in the school parking lot. Chuck's parents must have spent a small fortune getting it repaired.

Like the evil duke come to life and worse than any Dragon Lord, Chuck got out of his car, a wretched smile on his face as he shut the door. He walked around the car, his movements deliberate, like a wolf waiting for his prey to try fleeing. Not that David would. His body reacted like he was already a stiffening corpse—frozen in fear. Chuck had only one friend backing him this time, but even if he had been alone, David wouldn't have valued his chances.

"Hey, faggot!" Chuck's breath was stale, but David only got one whiff before Chuck shoved him. David tottered backward, barely managing to keep his feet. Chuck sneered, his friend laughing, before beady eyes turned to Gordon. "Who's this? Your girlfriend? Looks like we'll be killing two queers with one stone."

"Watch your mouth!" Gordon swung one of the swords at Chuck, striking his neck from the side, and David wished with all his being that it was made of metal and not foam. After a moment of shock, Chuck stepped forward and thwacked Gordon on the side of the head. It was barely more than a slap, but the effect on Gordon was immediate. The blood left his face, and maybe realizing just how serious this was, Gordon turned and raced off, not once looking back.

David didn't blame him. Gordon had never dealt with anything like this—not grade school scrapes on the playground or even tug of war in kindergarten. For Gordon, coming face-to-face with Chuck must have been like dropping a hermit in front of a press conference—he simply didn't have the faculties to cope with the situation.

And David did? God knows this had happened many times before, but with Chuck, it had become a daily event. David didn't know if life was planned by some less than benevolent god, but he obviously would keep running into Chuck. The fates seemed to shove them together at every opportunity, and David knew he couldn't avoid it. Even if he did move to Florida, he would probably run into a college-aged Chuck on spring break. Maybe he should just finally get it over with.

David's shoulders loosened, and the rest of his muscles followed. What's the worst they could do? Kill him? He doubted Chuck had the balls. Right now the jerk was huffing with adrenaline and rage, but he wasn't doing a damn thing besides leering at him. Screw the fates. David hadn't done anything to deserve this, and he wasn't going to take it any more. He turned to walk away. Then Chuck grabbed him by the arm.

"Where do you think you're going?"

"Home." David marveled at how calm his voice sounded. "I'm going home."

"The fuck you are!"

David yanked his arm free and faced him. "What do you want, Chuck? To admit that I'm a fag? Fine. That's what I am. You want me to apologize? I'll do that too. I'm sorry I ever said a single word to you. Is that enough? Or are you going to keep chasing me around like a crush-obsessed girl!"

He saw it then, the vulnerability on Chuck's face that was forced away with practiced perfection. David's mouth dropped open with the truth: Chuck was gay. And was afraid to admit it. He was just a big, stupid, self-hating homosexual. Like a boy pulling a girl's pigtails, he had taken every opportunity to interact with David, even if bullying was the best his addled brain could come up with.

"It's okay—" David started to say, but the hate on Chuck's face turned to fear and he swung.

It happened so quickly that David wasn't sure where he'd been hit, only that his head had rocked back. When he brought it forward again, he felt liquid filling his nose and tasted blood at the back of his throat. Another fat fist came at him like a blur, light glinting off a class ring before his cheek seared with pain. David was falling, but the pain was so intense that he brought his arms up protectively instead of catching himself. He hit the ground and curled into a ball. Then the kicking started, but David let neither a whimper nor a groan escape his lips. He wouldn't give Chuck the satisfaction, even if they kicked him until he died, which David was starting to believe they would.

Then the assault stopped. He could hear Chuck panting, muttering for him to get up and face him like a man, but there was no honor to be saved here. David had nothing to prove, had never done anything wrong—unlike a coward who didn't have the guts to accept who he was.

"Chuck, man, we gotta go!"

A car door shut across the street.

"What are you boys doing? What's wrong with him?"

The voice sounded old, but thankfully, adult. After one final kick, the two boys' feet pounded across concrete and two car doors slammed. David stayed in the fetal position, sure that Chuck would back over him and finish the job, but the car roared away.

"Are you okay?"

David uncurled and let himself be helped up by an old man with shaking hands. "I'm fine." David's voice had an edge of fear, but at least Chuck wouldn't hear it.

"Your nose is really bleeding! Here, I have some tissues in the car."

David focused on breathing until the old man returned, taking the tissues and dabbing at his nose. He wanted to go home.

"Do you need a ride somewhere? Should I call the police?"

He shook his head. "I'm all right. My house is just over there."

The old man looked worried, but also relieved not to be involved any further. He returned to his car and sat down in the driver's seat, but before he closed the door he said: "Why didn't you fight back?"

David stared at him silently until the old man shrugged, shut the car door, and drove away. Why didn't he fight back? What would be the point? That wouldn't stop Chuck from hating himself, and by extension, David or anyone else who was gay. Connor was right. Countless Chucks existed in the world. David could pump himself up and make it his life mission to pummel homophobic assholes, and he would die old and gray before he got through half of them. Chuck was obsessed with hate. David didn't want to be that way.

When David reached the condo, Gordon was waiting on the front step, pale and trembling, spluttering apologies. David had to reassure him a few times before asking if he had called the police or, even worse, his dad. He hadn't, which triggered new apologies. Gordon rambled on as they went inside and down to the bedroom. David grabbed the box of tissues next to his bed. They weren't usually for a runny nose, but today they were.

"What happened? How did you get away?"

David sighed. "After they hit me a few times, I ran."

It wasn't the truth, but it was simple and didn't allow for more questions. Instead Gordon apologized some more, describing his own terror. David reminded him how they both had run that day at the mall, helping ease Gordon's guilty conscience. He was still shaken, though. When a tap came at the window, he jumped to his feet and spun around.

"It's just Connor," David said. Then he swore under his breath. The bed was covered with blood-soaked tissues, and David hadn't checked himself in the mirror. He glanced at the window, planning on slipping out to the bathroom while Gordon let Connor in, but it was too late. Connor had already seen, his eyes blazing with concern. David must have looked like hell for him to be able to tell that much through the dirty glass.

"What happened?"

Connor wasn't even halfway through the window when he asked. He hopped to the floor and looked David over, touching his face gently and wincing along with him. He appeared just as pale as Gordon did.

"Who did this? Chuck?"

David nodded, and the blood returned to Connor's face. "Where is he? Fuck it!" Connor turned to go. "I know where he lives."

"Just leave it!" David said.

"What? Why?"

"Because it's not going to make a difference!"

"It'll teach him to keep his hands off you!"

"I need to go home." Gordon's voice was a whisper.

David said goodbye, cutting short another of Gordon's apologies and waiting until he left before speaking again. This time his voice was soft, pleading.

"Just stay here with me, okay?"

"Tell me what happened."

David sighed but told the truth. He even painted Chuck as a victim of his own fear and stupidity. If he was trying to move Connor, he failed.

"I don't care if he's angry because he watched his entire family drown! It gives him no right to hit you."

"We're leaving," David reminded him. "None of this will matter next week."

Connor shook his head and paced the room. Then he strode to the open window.

"Where are you going?"

"Out. Alone."

David swallowed. "Promise me you aren't going after Chuck."

153

"Fine, but I'm too angry to stay here. You should look at yourself."

Why did David suddenly feel as if he had done something wrong? He struggled for the right words but gave up. He was tired. Connor slipped out the window and was gone. Feeling like he was back where he began, David shut the window, pulled down the blinds, and cranked up the music.

Red. Heat. The taste of copper. Drums pounding in his ears. Connor's hands were shaking so much that he could barely get the keys in the ignition. Fury flooded his veins like a drug. Of course he was going after Chuck. That David didn't want him to only proved what a good person he was, how wrong it was that he had been hurt. The engine growled, matching Connor's fury, and in minutes he was in front of Chuck's house. The Mazda was in the driveway.

Connor parked behind it and hopped out, walking to the front door. After pushing the doorbell, he retreated to the driveway. If Chuck saw him standing outside, he would never open the door—at least Connor didn't think so. Chuck had been gutsy when he dumped paint on Connor's car. Maybe he carried a gun now. If so, Connor wouldn't give him the chance to use it. As soon as he heard the front door open, he bumped against the Mazda. The alarm went off, wailing out a warning to stay away. A keychain jangled, the car beeping and falling silent. Connor held his breath, listening to the approaching footsteps. The second Chuck came around the corner, Connor grabbed him by the throat and shoved him against the garage's brick wall.

"This is your last warning," Connor snarled, his mouth so close to Chuck's face that he was tempted to bite off his pug nose. "I should break your fucking neck for what you did. As it stands, I'm still going to break something, but if you ever lay a finger on David again—if you even look at him—I'm going to kill you."

Then two things happened. First, Connor noticed Chuck fiddling with his keys. Attached to them was a bulky cylinder. Then Chuck's friend came around the corner. The newcomer wasn't a problem. He was licking his lips and backing up, but by the time Connor turned back to face Chuck, mace was spraying in his face.

Or maybe it was pepper spray. He didn't know, but it hurt

like hell. At the last second Connor turned his head away so that only his left eye was hit directly, but even the splash from it was enough to make the other eye cringe shut before it began to burn. He was blind, but he could still feel Chuck squirming in his grasp. The monster raging inside Connor came forward, and he let it take control. Only his left hand was free, but it was a start.

Blinded, he couldn't see where he was hitting Chuck, but he could guess. The first punch was half-hair, half-bone and skin—Chuck's temple. The nose came next, not dead on, but angled from the side. Pain or fear made Chuck struggle more, so Connor pulled him forward with his right hand and slammed him back again, the air wheezing from Chuck's lungs in a groan. Connor switched hands. Then his right hand hit hard bone, the fleshy fat of cheeks, then an eye. Connor lost track as he kept punching, his hand aching and his arm growing sore. Then he brought up his knee once, twice, and again. The sounds Chuck was making didn't even sound human anymore.

Connor forced open his good eye, even though it still burned, and saw blood coursing down Chuck's face, mingling with snot and tears. His eyes were spinning wildly; maybe he was convulsing. Maybe he would die. The thought made Connor release his grip and step back. Chuck slid to the ground, the brick against his back pulling his shirt up and exposing his flab.

"I'm calling the cops, man! I'm calling the fucking cops!" Chuck's friend had a cell phone in hand and was poised to run if Connor came near.

He had no intention of doing so. Chuck was a mess, and the burning had spread from Connor's eyes and into his lungs. He felt like puking as he stumbled to his car and slipped inside. The keys were still in the ignition, thank god, or he never would have been able to insert them.

Connor's good eye wouldn't stop tearing up, but he could drive. Barely. A car honked at him a block later, swerving to avoid him. Connor would never make it to the trailer park. David's place was only a couple of blocks away, but to get there would mean crossing a busy road. At the stop sign, Connor wiped his eyes, which just made them burn more. He could scarcely see the road, the cars blurs of color whizzing by. He waited until the world was mostly grey before he hit the accelerator.

Connor's stomach dropped, and his heart hit his throat. Other parts would surely end up in the wrong places too, if he didn't make it, but after a horrifying squeal of tires and angry honking, he arrived in David's neighborhood. He knew he should park the car out of sight, just in case the cops came, but the burning in his eyes was getting worse. Connor stumbled to the front door, not bothering to knock. Calling out David's name in a rasping voice, he let himself in, made it to the bathroom, and started splashing water in his eyes. He groaned in pain and spit into the sink. Rubbing his eyes only made them burn more, so Connor kept splashing, not that it did a damn thing to relieve the burning.

"What happened? Jesus!"

Connor felt David's hand on his shoulder and tried to tell him that everything was okay, that it was just a little pepper spray. Connor was sure of that now because it burned like a hot pepper. He had cooked with them enough to know that even a little chili oil on his fingers could burn like hell if he touched his eyes. This was the same sensation, expect a thousand times worse.

David disappeared, returning a few moments later. "Get over here to the tub. No, turn around, like when a hair stylist washes your hair. This will help, I promise."

That's all Connor needed to hear. He put the back of his neck against the tub's edge and cool liquid poured over his face. He licked his lips. Milk? David was pouring milk on his face? He was about to complain when the burning subsided somewhat.

"Oh god, keep doing that!"

David laughed nervously and poured more milk over him. "We'll have to use soap and water next. This is just to give you relief."

"It's working."

"Thank god for the Internet!"

They spent an eternity in the bathroom, David dabbing at Connor's face with a soapy washrag, rinsing and repeating countless times, but with each effort the burning ebbed away.

"One more time?" David asked, dipping the wash cloth in the sink.

"No. I think I'm okay."

"You don't look okay."

Connor checked the mirror. His eyes were red and puffy, like after a crying marathon, and his skin was irritated, but mostly he was fine. That was more than could be said for David. The cut on his cheek was starting to close, but the area around it was swelling. Dried blood crusted his nostrils. Connor lifted David's shirt. The places where he had been kicked already darkening. The future bruises began on his sides and grew in number on his back.

"I'm okay," David said softly, turning back around.

But he wasn't. He still had Florida sun on his face, remnants of the happy person he had been there. David looked like an angel rolled in mud. Somewhere beneath the grime that moment of perfection existed still. Connor only hoped he could return David there. He moved his fingers away from David's injuries, sliding his palm against the smooth skin of his stomach and up to his chest. Pulling David close as gently as possible, he held him for a moment, reassured at being so near.

"Let's go to my room," David murmured.

Connor nodded and followed him out of the bathroom, flipping the light switch at the same moment the doorbell rang. They both froze.

"Do you think it's Chuck?"

It would be a miracle if Chuck could do anything more than moan in pain right now. "No. Let me get it. You stay here."

"It's my house," David said, and headed for the door.

Why didn't he ever listen? Connor managed to push past him so he could be the one to open the door. He heard the crackle of a police radio and wasn't surprised. Of course they were here. Connor opened the door.

Two officers stood on the steps with their eyebrows raised, alert and ready in case Connor decided to run, attack, or do anything else unpredictable. Instead, he crossed his arms over his chest and waited. He had nothing to fear. Chuck had beaten up David first. Unless they were all going to end up in jail together, he was probably going to get a stern lecture and a warning.

"Connor Williams?" one of the officers asked.

"Yeah."

"Would you step outside, please?"

That wasn't a good sign. Connor thought they would come inside. One of the officers put a hand on his shoulder; the other walking close behind as they led him to the police car. Maybe he was going for a ride after all.

"Put your hands on the hood and spread your legs."

"Why?"

That was David. Connor knew better than to ask. He put his hands on the hood as instructed. One of the cops started patting him down, but the other was examining Connor's hands, making a grumbling noise when she noticed Connor's knuckles. Punching often injured a hand, and Connor had acted without discipline or care.

"Frank."

Her partner paused to look over Connor's shoulder before grasping Connor's wrist and pulling his arm behind his back. The cold kiss of metal touched his skin as the handcuffs locked into place.

"You are under arrest. You have the right to remain silent. Anything you say can and will be used against you in a court of law. You have the right to speak—"

The speech rambled on, and Connor had to stifle his laughter. He'd heard these words so many times in cheesy TV shows that they seemed too ludicrous to be real. But of course they were.

"You can't arrest him." David said. "He didn't do anything wrong!"

"Charles Bryl claims he did," the female officer said, "and we have probable cause to believe him."

"Chuck?" David was incredulous. "If anything, you should be arresting *him*. Who do you think did this?"

Connor couldn't turn to see, but he knew David was pointing at his injuries.

"If you want to make a statement, you need to call the police. Not send your friend over to start a fight."

"I want to make a statement right now!"

The officer sighed, but must have taken out a pad of paper because David started rattling off the whole story.

"Into the car, son."

The police cruiser door was opened and a hand placed on Connor's head to make sure it cleared the frame when David's voice rose.

"Aren't you listening? You need to arrest Chuck, not him!"

Connor was seated now and could see David's panicked face. His expression turned to horror when the officer spoke:

"Charles Bryl—Chuck—is in the hospital. We'll take a statement from him if he regains consciousness."

Then the car door slammed, shutting Connor off from the world of the free.

Chapter Fifteen

Arriving at the police station, Connor decided those television crime shows didn't seem as funny anymore. One of the officers, who introduced himself as Officer Doyle, stayed with Connor while his partner went elsewhere. Connor's fingerprints were taken, scanned into the system with the latest technology. Then he stood for mug shots, making him feel like judgment had already been passed. When Doyle sat him down to take a statement, Connor was eager to plead his case. He told him the truth, but made sure to mention all the times Chuck had threatened David.

"You saw him. David's not a big guy. I don't know if you've seen Chuck, but he's huge. At least he has weight on him. He also has a lot of friends, so it was never a fair fight. If I didn't stand up for David, no one would."

Doyle leaned back in his chair and shook his head. "You should have called the police. If you had, Charles Bryl would be in that seat instead of you."

Maybe, but only after David had been hurt. "What now?"

Doyle turned his attention to the computer screen on his desk and clicked the mouse a few times before he raised his eyebrows. "You're being charged with aggravated battery. It was battery when we brought you in, but the Bryl family lawyer is on top of this and wants to make it a felony."

"Battery? I thought that was when a husband beat his wife."

"In Kansas law, assault is threatening someone without bodily contact. Battery means there was physical contact. I'll let your lawyer explain the details, but aggravated battery is a felony." He clicked the mouse a few more times. "Your bail is set at $10,000."

Connor's stomach churned. "I don't have that kind of money."

"Who does? You'll have to call a bail bondsman. They charge ten percent. Can you get a thousand dollars together?"

He had a little more than that in savings, but that was for the move to Florida. "What happens if I don't pay bail?"

"Then you're stuck here until a judge can see you." Doyle checked the screen again. "You live at this address alone, or are you with your parents?"

"My parents."

Doyle must have been familiar with the neighborhood, because he didn't ask if Connor's parents could afford to spring him.

"Listen, I'll see if we can get you in front of a judge tomorrow. That way you'll only have to be here overnight. I don't suppose you have a lawyer in the family?"

"No." Strange how getting arrested could cost so much money.

"Well, if you don't want to hire one, we have some great public defenders," Doyle said without much enthusiasm. "Ready to see your room for the night?"

Connor didn't move. "What would you have done? Say it was your little brother, and he was getting beat up by someone bigger than him. Would you really just stand by and let it happen?"

Doyle considered him for a moment. "Did it happen right in front of you?"

"No. Not really."

"Then you didn't stop it by beating the guy up afterwards. Next time, call us. We'll take care of it. Speaking of which, is there anyone you want to call?"

Connor's parents couldn't do anything. If he didn't show up that night, they would assume he was at David's place. He could call David, but didn't know what to say, and the look of horror on David's face was still too fresh in his mind.

"Can I use my call later?"

"Sure. Let's go."

For the wealthiest county in Kansas, Connor expected more from the jail. Maybe it was as drab as possible on purpose. The furnishings—if they could be called that—consisted of a concrete slab just long enough to recline on and a heavily battered toilet and sink. That was all.

"I'll have some bedding and a pillow brought by," Doyle said.

Connor couldn't believe any of this was happening. These environments were surreal, something out of a movie or a child's game, but here he was, in jail. Three concrete walls and a fourth made of metal bars. Connor sat on the stone slab and leaned his head against the cold wall, wondering what the future held.

Rain pitter-pattered on the leaves outside, the air in the

bedroom cool and damp. David sat on his bed facing the open window, knees pulled up to his chin. There was no music playing to comfort him. For once, he needed silence. His ears strained over the sounds of wet tires driving by, hoping to hear a coughing engine pull into the neighborhood. Or a twig snapping along with the sound of footsteps on moist leaves.

Connor would come back to him, if he could. The second the police let him go, he would be at David's window, apologizing for having been away. David would laugh at his constant concern and welcome him with open arms. Connor would come back. And yet the day faded to dark, and the rain blew away, leaving only dim flashes of summer lightning in the distance.

His stomach grumbled, the frozen pizza untouched in the freezer upstairs. Normally David would consider it a welcome treat, enjoying the empty house while his father was out late at his seminar. But for once David wished he was home. Maybe his father could do something, like talk to the police. Anything but this constant waiting and not knowing.

David didn't move except to light a candle in the window, a beacon to guide Connor back to him. But he didn't come. David was listening so intently for sounds of his arrival that he flinched when the garage door rumbled open. Desperate hope drove him to his feet. He was at the kitchen door leading to the garage when his father opened it.

"David! My god!" His father dropped his leather satchel on the floor and rushed to him, holding him by the arms and examining his face in horror. "What happened?"

David told him in short truncated sentences reluctant to escape his throat. He wasn't sure if he was understood, but he fell into the hug his father gave him, whimpering and letting a few tears escape. Then he was brought into the bathroom and sat on the toilet seat, feeling like a little kid as he watched his father wet a washcloth with warm water.

"That boy won't get away with this!" His father squatted in front of him, dabbing at David's injuries with the cloth. With everything that had happened, David hadn't yet cleaned himself up. "This Chuck person is going to face charges!"

"I filed a report with the police," David said. "When they were taking Connor away."

"Good."

"Can't we do something to help him?"

His father leaned back to consider him before he stood and started rummaging in the medicine cabinet. "I'm sure the police have it all under control." He returned with a bottle of hydrogen peroxide, which he applied to a corner of the washcloth.

"Is that the stuff that stings?"

"A little. Connor shouldn't have gone after the other boy." His father concentrated on cleaning the cut on David's cheek. "Although at the moment, I don't I blame him."

"He loves me."

"I daresay that's obvious."

"*This* is why I need to get out of here," David said. He had his father's sympathy at the moment, and he felt bad for taking advantage of that, but his words were true. "I can't go to school here next year. It's just going to get worse."

"Leaving isn't the only solution."

"But it's the only one I want."

His father dabbed at his face a few more times before tossing the washcloth in the sink. Then he leaned against the wall, considering David and shaking his head at what he saw. "I talked to your mother."

"About Florida? What did she say?"

"That it was up to me."

David didn't feel liberated by this news. "She doesn't care about me."

"Don't be foolish! Of course she does." His father sighed. "You're too much alike."

"What's that supposed to mean?"

"Where do you think your wanderlust comes from? Whenever Sharon wanted something, she went after it, never looking back. She was never content with me, always restless. When she met Jeff, she somehow found the place she wanted to be."

That she had. David hadn't understood when he made his choice years ago that he was saying goodbye to her. Of course she was still there, but it had never been the same. Maybe she had been hurt by him wanting to stay with Dad, or maybe Jeff completed her in a way they couldn't. He didn't know.

"It's not like she went far," David said.

"No, but sometimes it doesn't feel that way, does it? Sometimes our hearts go on long journeys while our bodies stay in place."

That made sense. More than wanting to see exotic places, David had wanted to find where he belonged. That had never been here, not Kansas, not until he met Connor. Then he had been much more content, but Connor wanted to show him somewhere new, and David had found the best of both worlds. He loved Florida, and he loved Connor. As incomprehensible as it was, his mom must have felt the same way about Jeff. But to those left behind, there was a sense of loss, not discovery.

"I'd come back, Dad. I'd come visit on the holidays and call a lot. Or you could come down and see us. It won't be like Mom, I swear."

His father shook his head and stood. "This isn't the time to discuss it. Have you eaten?"

David didn't push his luck further that night. He didn't want to argue and couldn't stomach the idea of any more conflict. His father heated up the pizza for him, but by the time it was done, David's mind was on Connor again. He nibbled on a couple of slices with disinterest. When he went back downstairs to his bedroom, the candle had blown out. David relit it, curled up on far end of the bed facing the window, and waited.

The next morning dawned with a backache from hell and bland scrambled eggs with soggy toast for breakfast. Connor set his empty tray by the bars, but didn't see another living soul until past lunch time, if his grumbling stomach was any indication of the time.

The man who came to the cell didn't look much older than Connor. He was dressed in a pressed suit, had immaculate hair, and carried a small briefcase. Under ordinary circumstances, Connor would have thought he was peddling religion, but when an officer let him in the cell, the man pulled a file—not righteous pamphlets—out of his briefcase.

"The dreaded manila folder," he said with mock terror, tossing it on the bed and extending a hand. "Mark Zimm. I'm your public defender."

Connor shook his hand. "That means you're a lawyer, right?"

"That's right."

Mark sat on the bed as if they were now bunkmates. "Usually I'd talk to you in a conference room, but they're all booked up. It's a busy day for the court, which could be good or bad. Either way, the judge won't want to spend much time on you. How do you plan to plead?"

Connor's head was already spinning. "Can I get away with justifiable cause or something?"

Mark grinned at him. "Today the judge only wants to know if you plan to fight the charges or not. I understand this, uh—" The pages of the file were shuffled. "—Charles Bryl ended up in the hospital, so I'm thinking the answer is guilty."

"He was beating up my boyfriend."

Mark's smile faltered for a moment. "Okay. That's something better discussed in a trial. I wouldn't mention it today."

"David, the guy Chuck beat up, filed a statement with the police. Is Chuck in jail too, or is he still in the hospital?"

"I'm not sure where he is, but I'll tell you an ugly truth. In situations like these, the winner is often the one who calls the police first. When someone files a counter complaint after an arrest, the police usually see it as revenge and don't take it as seriously."

Connor exhaled. "That's fucking great."

"You didn't hear it from me," Mark murmured as he consulted some more papers, "but the law isn't always fair. I'm afraid the bad news doesn't end there. You're facing some serious charges. A felony in fact, which could mean more than three years in jail."

Connor stiffened. "Three years? Isn't there something you can do?"

Mark nodded. "Getting the charges lowered to plain battery would make a huge difference. That's just a misdemeanor and could get you a month or two in jail and some fines."

"Better, but I'd rather not do time at all. Is there another option?"

Mark set the file down. "Yes, but I'll tell you now that if this goes to trial, the judge is less likely to be lenient on you. Not taking up the court's time with cases like these usually earns some back-patting. It's up to you, but I would recommend pleading guilty."

Anger rose alongside Connor's despair. "Look, I know you probably don't get the whole gay thing, but I love David. Think of whoever is on the other end of that wedding ring you're wearing and imagine Chuck beating up that person. What I did might have been extreme, but who wouldn't do the same in my situation? Surely a jury would understand that, right?"

Mark studied him a moment. "Honestly, Connor, half that jury probably wouldn't see past your sexuality. Even if they did, the trial won't be about whether or not others would have done the same. The question would be whether or not you beat up Charles Bryl. Is there much room for doubt in that regard?"

Connor shook his head. Of course he did it. He wouldn't deny that. He didn't know much about legal matters, but he knew a misdemeanor was less serious than a felony. If he could just get through this, maybe it wasn't too late to salvage what he and David had together. A little time, some of his summer lost, and then they could still move to Florida. "If you can get me away from aggravated battery, I'll plead guilty."

Mark gave a curt nod and clapped him on the shoulder. "You're doing the right thing. You're due in court in two hours. I'll come get you shortly before then. Is there anyone you want to call? Your parents, maybe?"

Connor shook his head. "No. Not yet. I'll have a chance afterwards, right?"

"Absolutely. I'll see you soon."

At least Mark was kind enough to take the dirty food tray with him when he left. Connor lay back on the bunk and tried to remember everything he had been told. How much jail time for normal battery? Would anyone be willing to hire him with something like that on his record? Jesus, when his family found out! Or David's dad. The more Connor thought about it, the more hopelessly screwed it all seemed.

When Mark returned a couple of hours later, an officer was with him. Together they walked Connor through marbled halls to the courtroom, and for once, the situation looked nothing like TV. The judge presided over all the usual settings, but no jury or audience was held in rapt attention. Instead everyone seemed impatient or bored while they waited in rows of cheap chairs. Most of the time the judge's words were too quiet to hear, but those Connor picked up had to do with probation violations and traffic tickets. Few spoke to the judge for more than a minute or two, and those who left were soon replaced by newcomers. The entire business reminded Connor of a mall Santa.

Mark was right. The judge was busy, and to him, Connor

would soon be another forgotten face. How was he supposed to plead his case in a situation like this?

"Are you sure I shouldn't go to trial?" Connor whispered to his public defender.

Mark let his cheerful expression fall. "Trust me, you'd need a better lawyer than I am to avoid doing time. And more money."

Connor's name was called out and he flinched, thinking at first that he was being scolded for talking in court. He went up the aisle with Mark for his turn in front of the judge's bench. Another lawyer stood there, representing Chuck, who wasn't present. Connor understood about half the terms the lawyers spoke to each other before the judge addressed him directly.

Wiry eyebrows sat heavily over scowling eyes, the judge looking him over impatiently. Connor pictured him wearing hunting gear under his robes with a shotgun below his desk to grab as soon as the last case was heard.

"I understand you intend to plead guilty," the judge said.

"Yes, sir."

The judge grunted. "And are you repentant for what you've done?"

Damn. Connor hadn't counted on this, but now wasn't the time for pride. "I'm very sorry, sir. It's the stupidest thing I've done in my life." And yet he'd do it a hundred times over again to protect David. "I've never fought with anyone before and won't ever again."

The judge sniffed. "Do you have a job, young man?"

"No, sir," Connor said. "I did until just recently."

"And what happened?"

Connor swallowed more of his pride. At this rate, he wouldn't need to eat lunch or dinner. "I was fired, but I already have a new job lined up."

The judge didn't appear impressed. "When I was your age I was fighting in a war. I had a wife back home I was supporting with our first child on the way. Do you have a family?"

Of course he did. He had parents, Tommy, and Tracy, and if things kept going well, David. But he knew that wasn't what the judge was asking. "No, sir. I don't."

"Well, thank god for small favors." The judge shuffled the papers aside, already reaching for the next case. "A month in county jail should show you what your future holds if you keep acting like a fool. If not, the six months of probation will keep you in line."

"Yes, sir."

The judge had more to say, but Connor didn't hear. A month in jail. Away from David. After that, who knew? Connor reminded himself that it could have been worse, but he still felt like his entire life was ruined. Maybe David would still want to be seen with him, and maybe that job would still be waiting in Florida, but nothing was certain anymore.

"Your sentence was reduced to battery," Mark said in the courthouse hallway, looking victorious. The escorting officer had his hand on Connor's elbow. "The month in county will fly by, and your life will be back to normal before you know it. I promise. How about that call?"

Connor nodded. "Yeah. Thanks."

Mark left him with the officer, who took him to a small room with an old table, a couple of chairs, and a phone. Then the officer stood guard by the door, as if Connor would make a break for it. Ignoring this, he sat and started dialing home before he hung up again. Tommy usually answered, and for some reason, hearing his voice would be too hard right now. Instead he dialed another number.

"Connor?" David's voice sounded frantic. "Are you okay? I called the station, but they wouldn't tell me anything."

"I'm fine. I just got out of court. Look, I'm sorry."

"Sorry for what?"

"I don't know. I just am." Connor took a deep breath. "I'm going to jail, David."

The other line was silent a moment. "For how long?"

"A month."

"I'll wait for you."

Connor laughed. He couldn't help it. David sounded so sincere, so cheesy, but they were exactly the words that Connor needed to hear.

"Thanks. You stay away from Chuck, okay? When I get out, we're getting the hell out of Kansas. You were right. We never should have left Florida."

"Can I come see you?"

"I don't know. Listen, I need you to call my parents. Better yet, go by and explain things to them in person. I know I should tell them, but I can't handle it."

"Okay."

"And make sure Tommy doesn't know. Have them say you and I took another trip or something."

"I will. I love you, Connor."

He felt his lip tremble. The stupid cop at the door was staring at him with no intention of looking away. Fuck it. "I love you too. I'll make this up to you, David. I promise."

If David responded, Connor didn't hear it. He hung up the phone and steeled himself. Whatever the next month held, he knew he would have to be strong.

David was used to living in a state of panic. All the bullying he had suffered left him weathered to stress. He wasn't immune, by any means, but he had long since learned to cope, to shove anxiety aside so he could keep functioning like a normal human being.

All that training was failing him now. Getting beat up by Chuck was nothing. That unpleasant event took a backseat to Connor being arrested. Hell, it wasn't even in the car anymore! Riding shotgun next to David, screaming over the radio's music and distracting him from the road, was the knowledge that Connor was going to jail. And David could do nothing about it.

David's father came home early, as promised the day before. David was upstairs on the computer when he came into the office.

"Everything okay?" he asked.

"Not really." David quadruple clicked the stupid link he was waiting to open and shoved the mouse away with disgust. They needed a serious upgrade.

"What are you doing?" his father asked.

"Researching how jail works."

"Why?"

David turned around in the chair, and his father's chin dropped. He hadn't seen the injuries today that were now an ugly polluted purple. "Because Connor's going to jail for beating up the person who did this to me."

His father looked like he wouldn't mind taking a swing at Chuck himself. "Maybe we should go talk to the police today. Let them see what this other boy did."

Yes! "Okay. Maybe then they'll let Connor go."

His father's mouth snapped shut, jaw flexing before he spoke. "David, I understand why you sympathize with Connor's situation. You think he's a hero for what he's done, but real heroes work within the confines of the law. Chuck deserves to be punished, and I'm afraid Connor does too. It's just as well since I think you two should spend some time apart."

"What?" David stood. "Why?"

"Because a little time off will help you rethink your priorities, and because there's such a thing as feeling too passionate. Refocus on your goals, and you'll find Connor there waiting for you when you're back on track."

"Like Mom waited for you?" David shouted. "Are you completely heartless? You're like some insane computer that only thinks about my education. I don't care about any of that! Don't you get it? I'm not going to some stupid school! I'm waiting until Connor gets out of jail, then we're going to Florida, whether you like it or not!"

David shoved past him and ran down the stairs. The car keys were hanging on their hook, so he grabbed them and was out the door before his dad could stop him. David had promised to tell Connor's family what happened, and that's what he meant to do.

On the way, David passed the police station. Connor was there, waiting to be shipped off to some county jail, from what David had read. The county jail used to be across from the police station, but it had been cleared out and was being renovated. He didn't know where Connor would be taken, but once he did, he would be the first one there on visiting day.

If Connor went to jail at all. As David pulled into the trailer park, he began to hope. Once Connor's parents were told, they would go to the police and talk to them. Connor was legally an adult, but he was still a teenager who lived at home. That had to be worth something. Surely they could take him into custody, maybe putting him on house arrest instead.

Connor's father answered the door, greeting David like everything was normal despite his cuts and bruises. Past him, David could see Connor's mom cooking in the kitchen, her back to the door. They were oblivious to what had happened.

"Sorry, David, Connor's not home. We thought he was with you."

"I know," David said. "I need to talk to you and Mrs. Williams."

Connor's father eyed him for a moment before stepping aside and holding the door open. "Sure. Come on in."

Mrs. Williams greeted him, wooden spoon in one hand, looking puzzled. "Connor isn't with you?"

David asked them to sit, and their expressions made him realize how stupid this was. Now they probably thought their son had died or something, so he hurriedly told them the basics. Then it became serious. Mrs. Williams turned off the stove, and they both made him tell them every detail.

"We have to go up there, Steven."

Mr. Williams nodded at his wife and stood. "I'll get Tommy from the neighbors."

"Actually," David said, "Connor doesn't want him to know. I thought we could just say he's out of town or something. I don't know. Why don't you guys go talk to Connor. I'll stay here with Tommy."

Under the circumstances, David's suggestion was welcomed. In a daze, Mrs. Williams showed him how to finish the tacos she had been cooking. The meat was done. David was sure he could handle chopping lettuce and shredding cheese. He busied himself with the food until they were gone. Once he heard the car pull away, he went into Connor's room and sat on his bed, looking around at the side that housed Connor's life. It held even less than usual. Connor had been packing. Except for the battered old guitar on the wall and his tangled bed sheets, there wasn't much to see.

David lay down, breathing in Connor's scent and praying that something could be done for him. Mr. and Mrs. Williams would return with their son, and Connor would laugh at the clumsy job David had done in the kitchen. Then Connor would finish cooking for them and his whole family would gather around the table, celebrating his return.

The screen door slammed, jarring David from this fantasy, and he heard Tommy call out. David got off the bed, put on a brave face, and went to meet him. His puzzlement at finding David there turned into a hug as he ran to David and wrapped his arms around his waist. Then he looked up and·scrunched up his nose.

"What happened to your face?"

"Bike wreck," David lied.

"Is Connor in our room?"

"Nope. It's just you and me." David tried to make this sound like the best news possible. "Your parents had to run an errand and left me in charge. Do you like tacos?"

"Yeah!"

Food was a welcome distraction, but Tommy's inquisitive mind was working even as he was munching away. "If you're here, is Connor at your house eating dinner with Gordon?"

"No. Your brother is out of town. A friend of ours was in trouble, so Connor went to help him. Your brother is a hero, you know."

"A superhero?"

"Pretty much!"

"When's he coming home?"

David wished he knew. He shrugged and started talking about toys, which was enough to distract Tommy. After dinner they staged an epic battle with all of Tommy's action figures and were still playing when Connor's parents came home. Alone.

Mrs. Williams fussed over Tommy, her face strained, while Connor's dad motioned to David that they should step outside.

"Fucking pigs," is how he started the conversation. "You would think they couldn't charge a man's son without letting him know."

"Must be his age," David said as diplomatically as possible.

"I know." Mr. William lowered his head. With only a single weak bulb by the door to provide light, his features were lost in shadow. "They let us see him, at least."

"Is he okay?"

"Mm." He might have nodded. "There's no getting around it, though. A month in county jail. He'll be okay there. I'm not proud of it, but I served a stint in county myself. Boring as hell, but it's not dangerous like prison is."

David was eager to fill the awkward silence that followed. "I'm sorry. It's all my fault. Connor wouldn't be in trouble if I had stood up for myself."

"Two against one? There's no shame in backing down from that. It's the other boy who should be in jail, but of course he's at home right now, probably being tucked in bed by his mother."

"What?" A wind picked up, making the trees around them sway.

"Well, we asked after him, and they said the other boy was out of the hospital. I wanted to know if this person was being arrested and sent to jail for what he did, but they said he'd been sent home. Does that sound fair to you?"

David's heart started pounding and didn't stop until he was nearly deaf from the blood rushing in his ears. He said goodbye to Mr. Williams and drove home in a trance. How could Chuck get away with this? Was it money? The family lawyer? Or maybe Dr. Bryl bribed the judge with free dental work, sliding false teeth across the table like gold. The method they used to escape justice didn't matter. The idea that Chuck was free to make everyone's life miserable while Connor sat behind bars—that mattered.

David didn't remember driving home or walking through the front door.

"Where have you been? Young man, I'm speaking to you!"

He didn't bother responding to his dad. David went down to his room and threw himself on his bed. The next month was going to be hell. No doubt his father would pressure him every day and Chuck would find some cowardly way to get back at David, all while Connor's parents quietly went about their lives, knowing their son was in jail. And David would be alone, unable to see the person who mattered most to him. All of this infuriated him so much that he fantasized about finishing the job Connor started.

Of course, then David would end up in jail too.

He hopped off the bed before he could over-think the idea and opened his closet. There, in the back, was a never-used baseball bat given to him by a clueless uncle as a birthday present. The bat had been in the dark recesses of his closet for years, but now it was of the utmost importance. David wrapped his hand around the cool aluminum cylinder, lifted it, and stared at its brushed surface.

Then he left through the window that Connor had so often used. He feared his anger would ebb away as he walked to Chuck's house, that he wouldn't have the guts to go through with this, but instead his fury increased. Every time he had been picked on and every injustice he had suffered swam to the surface.

But chief among them all was the reason why. Chuck's motivation—the one thing they had in common. The part of David that had made him happier than anything else, had even given him a sort of strength since he would never compromise on it—was Chuck's greatest fear.

As soon as David could see the silver Mazda in the driveway, he ran toward it. A primal scream escaped from his throat as he raised the bat and swung it down for the first time. The car alarm shrieked, but this only fueled David's rage. The passenger-side mirror was batted to the concrete before David started on the windows, cracking three of them and breaking another. He was pounding the hood out of shape when a man's voice shouted at him.

David stopped long enough to look at an older, fatter version of Chuck with grey temples in his thinning hair. Then he noticed the monstrosity standing beside him. Both of Chuck's eyes were nearly swollen shut, his face more black and blue than any normal skin tone. Connor had indeed done a number on him.

David couldn't do the same, even now. The bat was meant only for the car, which David resumed striking while screaming. Chuck and his father had disappeared inside, no doubt calling the police. David grinned wildly before taking out another window. Then he hopped up on the rear of the car, and with the baseball bat across his legs, he waited.

When the police came, they didn't point their guns at him and demand he drop his weapon. They didn't need to. He tossed the bat aside and almost laughed with joy when they told him to turn around and put his hands on the car. A second police car pulled up while he was being patted down. Soon after, Chuck and his father came back outside again.

"All because you're a fag!" David shouted at him. "If you had the balls to come out or even live your life in secrecy, I'd call you gay, but you're the worst of us. People like you are the faggots, Chuck! That's why you feel so free to fling that word around, because it's what you call yourself every time you look in the mirror. It doesn't matter how much you hate me or anyone else who's gay. At the end of the day, you're still going to crawl into bed and hear that word echoing in your head. Faggot!"

The police handcuffed David and were dragging him toward the car. Chuck's eyes were as wide as they could manage, and his father looked on the verge of a heart attack. David stared at them for as long as possible, even turning in his seat as the police cruiser drove away. He wanted to memorize every detail of their miserable faces so he could describe them to Connor when they were together again. Tonight, David realized as he turned back around and tried to make himself comfortable. He and Connor would be together again tonight.

Chapter Sixteen

"Why are we here?"

The question may have sounded existential, but David meant it literally.

"This is your house, isn't it?"

Yes. It was. That was the problem. The other squad car had disappeared into the night, and the car David was in had driven him straight back home. The officer left the engine running and went to the front door alone. David swore when the door opened, framing his father in a rectangle of light. Did they need his permission before bringing David in?

No. It was much worse than that. The two adults spoke together, David's father signed something like he was accepting a package, and together they returned to the car. David had thought his rage purged, but it came back again as he was taken out of the vehicle and escorted to the front door.

"I'm going right back there and doing it again," David threatened as the handcuffs were removed.

The officer hesitated, but David's father quickly reassured him and shut the door, leaving them alone. It had been a long, long time since David had been spanked, and when he was grabbed by the arms and shaken, he feared his father was coming out of retirement.

"What the hell are you doing? Are you on drugs?"

David was so shocked he couldn't respond. Even during their recent arguments, he hadn't seen his father truly lose his temper. In fact, David hadn't seen him this angry since he was still together with Mom.

"Tell me you have a reason for acting so stupid. Please! Show me you're still capable of reason and that I shouldn't give up on you completely."

"I wanted to be with Connor."

His father's face turned a darker shade of red. "In jail?"

David nodded numbly.

"Go sit on the couch."

David did what he was told. His father stayed in the entryway with his back to David, trying to compose himself. Just how close had he come to getting hit? When his father finally came into the living room, he seemed calmer, but not much.

"Do you realize," he said, "that none of what you are doing is normal?"

David glared at him. "Like getting beat up is normal? What did you want me to do, write Chuck a thank-you letter?"

"Law breakers don't have the crimes they committed turned against them—we don't operate under 'an eye for an eye' rules. As a society, we don't steal from thieves or kill murderers."

"Unless they get the chair." David knew he shouldn't push back, but he did.

His father's response was cold. "Lethal injection, which is much more civilized, only occurs after a trial and no doubt many appeals. There is a system in place, and had you used it, neither you nor Connor would be in this situation right now."

David hated that this was true, but it wasn't the complete picture. His father was stripping away emotion as he always did, relying instead on logic. If a mother saw someone hurting her child, she wouldn't calmly call the police and wait for them to arrive. No, she would fight with teeth and claws to protect her baby. That's all David and Connor were doing.

"Instead of using your intelligence," his father continued, "you reacted. Stupidly. Did you really think they were going to put you in the same cell as Connor? You're a minor. He is an adult."

"They try people my age as an adult when the situation warrants it," David shot back.

"Yes, but not for a petty crime like vandalizing a car. My god, David, you need to get a grip! Your life hasn't even begun, and since you met that boy, you've been doing everything in your power to ruin it."

"It's not his fault!" David stood and pointed a finger toward the door. "You have no fucking idea what I go through out there. You want me to study and get good grades? Well, it's a little hard when some asshole is constantly trying to beat me up for being gay. And yeah, maybe I should have called the cops, but do you really think they would have done anything to stop him? Why do I have to get my ass kicked before anyone will help me?"

"You need to ask for help to get it, David."

"I tried telling you! You told me to keep my head down. Well, I did. Gordon and I were going for a walk, minding our own business, and look!" David lifted his shirt and turned around. The bruises were even darker now. He could only see the edges of them, but the shock on his father's face told them how bad they looked. "All you care about is me going to college. I'm sick of it! If you had bothered to talk to me about anything else, maybe none of this would have happened."

David doubtcd that was true, but throwing everything back at him felt good.

His father was quiet, staring at the bruises until David lowered his shirt. Only then did he speak. "We have to report to the police station tomorrow to deal with what happened tonight. While we're there, I'll make sure the boys who attacked you are properly punished. I'm going to show you that the system works, and I'm going to make sure this mistake doesn't haunt you the rest of your life. Do you understand?"

David blinked in surprise and nodded.

"Good. Now please go to your room and stay there. There's nothing you can do to get to Connor. He'll be in a county jail by now. Even if you get yourself arrested again, you'll be brought to a holding cell nowhere near him. The police can confirm that for you tomorrow if you don't believe me. Get some sleep. We'll deal with this in the morning."

His father stood and watched David until he went downstairs. David waited at the bottom of the steps, listening to his father click off living room lamps before he went up to his room. Or more likely to his office for a drink. David thought about sneaking out again, just to feel free from all of this, but he had nowhere to go and nothing he could do. Feeling powerless, he went to his room, got into bed, and stared at the ceiling until he fell asleep.

The next morning David and his father operated under truce. Breakfast started quietly, but his father reaffirmed his intention to take care of David while making sure Chuck and his friends were punished. He spent the rest of the morning on the phone as David washed the dishes and straightened up around the house. David was in enough trouble already, and he preferred his father remain an ally instead of an enemy.

In the afternoon they went together to the police station, David's stomach bubbling nervously. Once inside, he craned his neck at every opportunity, hoping to see Connor. Maybe he hadn't been moved to county jail yet. David might see him on his way out or sitting at a desk while an officer guided him through paperwork. This hope helped distract David from his anxiety, but he saw no sign of Connor as they were escorted to a conference room.

A man with a salt-and-pepper mustache joined them, dressed in a conservative suit. He shook their hands energetically and beamed at them as if they were welcome guests.

"Richard, David, it's nice to meet you. My name is Loren Corrigan, and I'm the district attorney. I believe you spoke with my assistant earlier today?"

David's father nodded. "Yes. Thank you for making the time to see us."

"My pleasure. I appreciate you being so proactive in the matter. Please, have a seat."

They sat at a generic table laminated with fake wood. David watched in fascination as Mr. Corrigan took a number of paperclipped documents from a briefcase and arranged them on the table. These papers held the power to change David's future, whether he liked it or not. When the district attorney spoke next, David was surprised to find himself being addressed instead of his father.

"Seeing as this is your first offense, David, we'd like to help you avoid going to court. Your father told me you've always kept your nose clean and that you're an intelligent young man. It would be a shame for you to have a criminal record before beginning life as an adult. Likewise, I think we can all agree that you entering a juvenile correctional facility would be less than ideal. Am I right?"

David nodded quickly. The idea of being with Connor in jail had made sense only when he was half-crazy with anger. Not only would Connor not be in juvenile hall, but people like Chuck probably would be. David wanted to avoid that at all costs.

"As I discussed with your father," Mr. Corrigan continued, "Johnson County does offer second chances to first-time offenders. The diversion program was created for situations like yours. Are you interested in that, David?"

He nodded again. "What would I have to do?"

Mr. Corrigan shuffled some papers. "Well, I suppose you could consider it a form of probation. You'll be signing a contract with the county, promising not to get into trouble in the next six months. You'll have to continue attending school, which I understand hasn't been a problem so far. You'll also be subject to drug screening if your diversion officer requests it. Usually there are extra classes covering topics such as anger management, but your father would prefer to attend therapy sessions with you."

David looked at his father.

"We both could use someone to talk to," he explained, "and a neutral perspective."

"Okay," David said. He still wasn't sure how he felt about the idea, but it sounded better than going to "anger management" classes.

"Aside from you staying out of trouble," Mr. Corrigan continued, "we need you to make amends with Charles Bryl. We don't expect you to interact with him directly, but you need to pay for the damages to his vehicle."

David expected as much, so this wasn't hard to swallow. If he took a summer job, he could probably earn enough money to pay it off and maybe even save a little for the move to Florida. If that was still possible. If diversion was like probation, the move might pose a problem, but now wasn't the time to ask about that.

"And finally, there are the charges against Charles Bryl."

"And Chuck's friend," David interjected.

Mr. Corrigan flipped through some papers. "From what I understand, the friend didn't attack you directly."

"He could have," David said. "It was hard to tell who was kicking me when I was balled up on the ground."

Mr. Corrigan raised his eyebrows, and David's father cleared his throat. They acted as if David was swearing in church when he was simply telling the truth. Chuck and his friend had committed a crime, so what was the big deal? David soon found out.

"There's one more stipulation to your diversion agreement. I've spoken with the lawyer representing the Bryls, and they are just as eager to put this whole incident behind them. My office is offering a diversion agreement to Charles as well. For him to qualify for diversion, he needs to drop all charges against you. By Kansas law, what you did is considered assault, possibly aggravated assault if the court considers a baseball bat a deadly weapon."

"But I didn't even touch him!"

"Putting him in fear of bodily harm is how our legal system defines assault."

In that case, Chuck had "assaulted" David countless times. Maybe his father was right. The laws were so screwed up that David should have called the police before now.

"Charles has already agreed to drop these charges against you. For you to qualify for diversion, you would need to do the same."

David's father cleared his throat. "There's a world of difference between damaging someone's car and being physically attacked. It seems to me that the crime you're asking us to forgive Charles for is much graver than the one my son committed. Show him your bruises, David."

He was glad to comply. He lifted his shirt and showed his back, and while Mr. Corrigan's reaction wasn't as shocked as his father's had been, he did appear sympathetic when David turned around.

"I wouldn't like seeing that happen to any of my children either," Mr. Corrigan said. "Have those injuries been photographed?"

David shook his head.

"We'll do that before you leave the station today." He turned to David's father. "I know what I'm asking isn't easy, but I need you to think of your son's future. Diversion is the only way to spare him from spending time in a detention center. The entire offense will also be stricken from his record." The district attorney made eye contact with David. "If you abide by the agreements set out, it will be like none of this ever happened."

The idea of forgiving Chuck nauseated David. Part of him was temped, purely out of spite, to refuse. Still, maybe there was a way he could turn this to his advantage.

"I'll agree if Chuck drops the charges against Connor."

"David," his father said warningly.

"What? It's only fair! Connor wouldn't have beat up Chuck if Chuck hadn't attacked me first. If we're going to sweep everything under the carpet, then Connor should be included."

Mr. Corrigan tensed. "The juvenile diversion program doesn't apply to Connor Williams. He is an adult and has already received his sentence. I understand your distress that your friend has to serve time, but there's no need for you to do the same."

"He's my boyfriend, not my friend," David muttered.

"I'm sorry, but there's nothing I can do for him."

David glared at him, not responding. Mr. Corrigan gathered up the papers on the table and put them back in the briefcase as if the deal were off. He stopped just before closing it and addressed David again. "I understand loyalty. Believe me, I do, but you getting into trouble over this isn't going to help Connor. You'll only be hurting yourself."

David's shoulders slumped. He didn't want to get locked up, and Chuck's family probably had a lawyer good enough to find some other way of keeping him out of trouble.

"Maybe I should give you two a moment to talk this over," Mr. Corrigan said.

"No," David said. "I'll agree."

The next half hour was taken up with filling out paperwork. Letting Chuck off the hook wasn't a happy experience, but the idea that he was betraying Connor was worse. Logically David knew Connor wouldn't want him to get into trouble, but the feeling was hard to shake.

When they were finished, the district attorney thanked them for their cooperation. Then a police officer took David to another room where his mug shot and fingerprints were taken. All a normal part of the diversion program, the officer assured him. David noticed his father's face was especially grim during this, as if his worst fears had been confirmed and David had begun his life as a career criminal. Then they photographed David's bruises, his father clenching his jaw through the whole process. David thought he was angry at him until they were in the car.

"I'm sorry."

"What?" David hadn't expected to hear these words.

His father scowled at the road ahead. "What they asked of you wasn't fair. You were attacked without provocation, and while I still don't agree with your reaction, the other boy deserved a lot worse."

"I agree," David said carefully.

"And I'm proud of you for doing the right thing and thinking of your future."

David covertly rolled his eyes. "So what's next? Ice cream?"

His father checked his watch. "We probably should have an early dinner before our therapy session."

"We're going *tonight*?"

His father ignored this outburst, so David turned and looked moodily out the window. Whoever the therapist was, if they dared asked how David was feeling, they were in for an earful.

"Have you ever considered, Richard, that by pressuring your son so much, you are ensuring he'll do the opposite of what you want?"

David stared. The psychologist was a tiny man with a bald head. He had a tidy dark goatee and was dressed in a business shirt and slacks that had quite possibly come from the children's department. Despite his small size, his intense blue eyes gave him presence—as did his last name, which was Wolf. If this had been a horror movie, the unassuming Dr. Wolf would of course turn out to be the werewolf terrorizing the village.

Except he wasn't devouring peasants. He was giving David's father a rather stern lecture. First he had spoken to David's father alone, then called David into the office. David had been sure he was going to get a telling off, but just the opposite was happening.

"When children are born, they are helpless. We have to guide their actions to keep them happy and healthy and safe, but as a child becomes independent, this habit can be difficult to break. It's normal for every parent to feel this way. But the child reaches an age, usually around puberty, where this heavy-handed guidance can work to your disadvantage."

David's father was at a loss for words, but only momentarily. "I don't think letting a teenager do whatever he wants is very wise."

"That's not what I'm suggesting," Dr. Wolf replied. "David, are you aware that your education is important to your father?"

"Are you kidding? That's all he talks about." David shifted on the leather couch. His father was seated beside him, which meant he didn't have to look at him directly. That made talking about him easier. "I'm doing the best I can, but I want to make my own choices."

"So you see," Dr. Wolf turned back to David's father, "there's little point in repeatedly telling him what he already knows. At this juncture, it can only do harm."

His father frowned. "Then what do you suggest?"

"That you let David decide when the topic of education is

important to him, or that you broach the subject by asking if he has any thoughts or questions. If he doesn't, let him be."

David couldn't imagine what dinner would be like without college or SATs dominating every conversation, but he was willing to find out.

His father wasn't quite ready to give up. "And I suppose I should let him live at home until he's thirty, not daring to mention that he needs to get a job, lest I scare him away from doing so."

Dr. Wolf remained tranquil. "Richard, why don't you take a break in the other room while I talk to David alone. How does that sound?"

His father didn't answer, but judging from the expression on his face, he was glad to leave. David waited until the door closed behind him before speaking.

"That was amazing! I've never heard anyone talk that way to him before. Besides Mom, of course."

Dr. Wolf smiled. "Well, Richard and I were colleagues before I decided to open my own practice. I suppose that makes it easier to be direct with him and tell him what he needs to hear. But enough about him. I'm interested in hearing more about you."

David squirmed. Therapy was a lot more fun when the questions were directed at someone else. "What do you want to know?"

"Well, why don't you tell me a little about Connor. What sort of person is he?"

Connor was normally his favorite subject, so David was surprised to find himself at a loss for words. At least, appropriate words. Dr. Wolf probably didn't want to hear how hot Connor was.

"Tell you what," Dr. Wolf said helpfully, "why don't you chose one word that describes him best."

"Misunderstood." David was proud of fishing this word out of the air because it told Dr. Wolf that Connor wasn't the bad person everyone made him out to be.

"Okay, he's misunderstood. And why do you think that is?"

"Because of the way he looks. He's sort of big and intimidating, and he has this scar that people have made up stories about."

"What sort of stories?"

184

"That he tried to kill his father and spent time in juvenile hall."

Dr. Wolf was quiet for a moment; David could guess what he was thinking. Connor *had* attacked someone and was now in jail. He would probably call it a self-fulfilling prophecy, but it wasn't. Connor knew he wasn't the person people made him out to be.

"And would you say your life has gotten better or worse since you met Connor?"

"Better."

Dr. Wolf tilted his head thoughtfully, the orange light from the nearby lamp reflecting off his bald head. "You answered that question very quickly."

David shrugged. "It's the truth. Everything's been better."

"Surely being on diversion isn't better."

"But that wasn't my fault."

Dr. Wolf raised an eyebrow.

"Yeah, okay. So it was my fault. I guess you could say everything was better until the day Chuck beat me up."

"Let's try something." Dr. Wolf leaned forward. "Pretend for a moment, that you had never met Connor. Do you think that fight would have happened?"

"It wasn't a fight because I didn't hit back. And yes, it still would have happened because Chuck was trying to beat me up before Connor was around."

"Fair enough. It still would have happened. But what do you think would have occurred after Chuck attacked you?"

David took a deep breath. "I would have gone home, just like I did."

"And then?"

"I guess I would have sat there feeling sorry for myself until Dad came home. Then we would have had dinner, I would have gone to my room, and my life would have kept on sucking."

"Your father would have reacted, though. He told me how upset he was when he saw the cuts and bruises. Do you think he would have called the police?"

"He wanted to, but I had already filed a complaint when the cops arrested Connor."

"Okay, but we're pretending you never met Connor. So when your father came home, he would have seen you and called the police. Then what?"

"I guess they would have arrested Chuck, and he would get diversion." Except David wouldn't have dropped the charges. Chuck wouldn't get diversion and would probably be sitting in juvenile hall right now.

Dr. Wolf must have seen the realization on his face because he nodded encouragingly. "So, in this particular example, you aren't better off for having met Connor."

"That's not true! For all we know, if I hadn't met Connor, Chuck would have attacked me sooner. Connor stopped him from doing so before. If I hadn't met Connor, maybe it would have been worse. Chuck only stopped kicking me because some guy came along. Under different circumstances, Chuck could have beaten me to death."

Dr. Wolf studied him for a moment, then smiled as if the conversation had been for their mutual entertainment and nothing more. "Your father says you don't have many friends except for Connor and a neighbor boy who is younger than you."

Connor wasn't his friend. David wished people would stop saying that. Connor was so much more than that, but instead of arguing the point he nodded.

"Do you ever feel like it would help to talk to other people your age in the same situation?"

"Why, is there a support group for guys who get revenge on bullies?"

"Possibly," Dr. Wolf said with good humor, "but I was thinking more of other people your age who don't see eye to eye with their parents, who also feel like they are under too much pressure."

David shrugged. "I never really considered the idea."

"Well, there's a facility I work with that has group sessions. I think such sessions could benefit you. What would you think about attending one—say, tomorrow?"

"Honestly, it doesn't sound like my kind of thing." In fact, David hated the idea.

Dr. Wolf wasn't discouraged. "Tell you what, just meet me there with your father. We can have a look around, maybe eavesdrop on the group instead of joining it. That way you can form a more educated opinion."

"Okay."

Dr. Wolf was wasting his time, but showing up and checking

out the group wouldn't do any harm. The session ended shortly after that. Dr. Wolf had a few more words alone with his father before they left. On the ride home, the car was surprisingly quiet without lectures about education or goals. Was it possible that Dr. Wolf had managed to muzzle his father? David leaned back in the seat and smiled. Who knew therapy could be so much fun?

Chapter Seventeen

New Century Adult Detention Center.

The name was ridiculous, trying much too hard to be anything but what it was—county jail. Maybe high school was too recent a memory, but Connor thought the word "detention" made the name sound childish. Regardless, this was to be his home for the next month. He felt a spurt of optimism as he was escorted to the building. The architecture was tastefully modern, appearing more like a cutting-edge university than a jail. But his hopes were dashed once he was inside. Everything—walls, ceiling, and floor—was painted concrete, which reminded him again of high school. Maybe the name was appropriate after all.

The receiving room had a counter to one side similar to a hospital nursing station. On the opposite wall were three barred cells. The officer patted down Connor once more—just in case any weapons had magically appeared on his person during the ride over—before taking him to one of the cells.

"They'll come get you when they're ready to process you," the officer said as the bars slid shut.

Connor turned around. The cell had benches on either wall, both occupied. Two men sat on one side, so Connor took a seat on the other. Eye contact between him and the other men was wary and fleeting. No one seemed interested in speaking, which was fine with him.

Connor waited. And waited. He didn't have a watch, but he was sure that three, maybe four hours passed before they came for the first man. Another hour sludged by until they came for the second. Shortly afterwards, a scrawny, unkempt man was brought in and left with them. Fumes poured from his nearly toothless mouth as he ranted and raved about god and, occasionally, his ex-wife. Thankfully the man and his stench chose the bench opposite Connor.

Half an hour later, Connor positively jumped off the bench when the officer said his name. The deputies, as they were called, wore uniforms similar to those of regular police officers, but the gun holsters on their utility belts were empty. Those working behind the counter were dressed more casually in black polo shirts with a badge and the county name stitched over their hearts.

One of the men behind the counter emptied a plastic bag that held Connor's wallet, phone, belt, keys, and a few intertwined paperclips he happened to have in his pocket. He was asked to sign an inventory of these items, including the clothes he was wearing, before they stood him against the wall for new mug shots. Before they took photos, they draped a robe over his front, much like the kind used by hair stylists.

"Any tattoos?" the guard asked in disinterested tones. The man was middle-aged, chubby, and had a mustache. Connor doubted he would be able to pick him out of a lineup of other randomly selected cops.

"No tattoos," he answered.

Next came fingerprints, followed by a visit to a small office where a woman waited behind a computer. Connor sat awkwardly in front of her desk, glancing over at the guard by the door. The woman didn't bother with introductions.

"I'm going to ask you a series of questions, and I need you to answer them honestly so we can get you placed in the correct housing area."

"Okay."

"Are you currently under the influence of any illegal substances?"

"No."

"Have you any time in the past six months used illegal substances?"

"No." Connor wasn't sure if drug tests happened here so he amended, "Well, I smoke a little pot now and then."

The woman clicked the mouse twice before moving on to the next question. "Do you have any medical conditions we need to be aware of?"

"Nope."

The questions rattled on and on. They wanted to know about his mental and physical health, if he was involved with gangs, and a bunch of other things that had him shaking his head in the negative. Until one came that he wasn't expecting. "Do you indentify as bisexual or homosexual?"

"No." Connor said after a pause. He had never before denied who he was, but he didn't want to attract the attention of other inmates or the deputies.

"You're here under a class B person misdemeanor, but I

understand your original charge was aggravated battery, which is a felony."

"Okay," Connor said, not sure if this was a question or not.

The woman looked away from the screen, her eyes lingering on Connor's scar. "I should probably put you in maximum security, but we don't have any beds left."

"Popular hotel," Connor joked, but the woman turned back to the screen without reacting. She clicked and typed some more before Connor's answers were printed out, so he could sign that they were accurate.

"All done here, Dave. You can get him showered."

The guard looked up from his cell phone and grunted. Connor had been wearing the same clothes for two days, some of it blood-stained. A shower sounded good, as long as Deputy Generic wouldn't be washing his back. The shower Connor was brought to was—surprise—a concrete stall with an industrial-sized bottle of shampoo and liquid soap.

"Get undressed," the deputy said, handing him a large plastic bag. "Fold your clothes and put them in this."

He seemed to have no intention of leaving or looking away. Connor started with his shirt, then his shoes and socks, but he still had an audience.

"All of it. You'll get your clothes back at the end of your sentence."

Connor knew he shouldn't press his luck, but it was worth a shot. "You aren't going to turn around?"

"Believe me, I wish I could. We need to make sure you aren't smuggling contraband into the facility."

Rubber gloves and KY Jelly sprang to mind as Connor kicked off his jeans and underwear, but thankfully the final search wasn't that intrusive. He had to lift a number of things—his arms, cock, balls, even his feet. Then he had to turn around and spread his cheeks, which easily qualified as the least sexy moment of his life.

"Okay. Get showered. The shampoo kills lice so you have to leave it in for three minutes before you rinse."

Connor tried to focus only on the shower, but Deputy Generic watched him the whole time. True to his word, he didn't seem to enjoy the experience. Once the ritual with the shampoo was complete, the guard's attention returned to his cell phone until Connor was done. Then he was led to the other side of the room and presented with his new clothes.

Connor laughed. He couldn't help it. The shapeless jumpsuit was striped, just like in all those cheesy comedy sketches and cartoons. These stripes were grey rather than black, but the suit still seemed too funny to be true. The shoes were less amusing—slippers molded from one solid piece of rubber.

In the shower room were several large plastic containers, like the kind Margie used in Florida to store some of her useless newspapers. Connor was given one of these to open, and even when the guard rattled off its contents, Connor needed a moment to realize these were all his possessions for the next month. Inside were some blankets, a towel, a bar of soap, a cheap toothbrush and toothpaste, a safety razor, and deodorant.

"—and here you have your rights and regulations, if you need something to read," Deputy Generic finished before putting the lid back on. "Pick that up and follow me."

This was the moment of truth. Connor was led down several hallways, each segmented by doors that had to be buzzed open. Their journey ended in a room with a triangular floor plan, the space filled with metal chairs connected in groups to the tables they surrounded. Apparently, everything in jail needed to be bolted to something bigger or the inmates would have things to throw or steal. The walls of this room were lined with doors, one of which Connor was led to.

Connor expected the room beyond to be a small cell with a toilet and bunk beds to one side. He was half-right. The room was slightly bigger than he expected, but it had three sets of bunk beds, all of them occupied by men who wasted no time in sizing him up. What little floor space existed was filled by two temporary beds—plastic frames with thin mattresses on top.

"Choose which bed you want before the next guy comes in," the deputy said. "Your new roommates can tell you anything else you need to know."

And that was it. The deputy shut the door, leaving Connor with six strangers. Already his tough-guy body language was in full effect. It came by instinct, as did his crazy eyes. Usually Connor let an outer layer of himself go a little insane while he watched, calm and detached, from inside. Now he hardly needed to pretend. This whole situation made him want to scream.

One of the two temporary beds on the floor was nearly up

against a wall. Connor went to it, kicking it until it was flush against the painted concrete bricks.

"Hey, you can't sleep there!"

He didn't see who said it, but Connor ignored them and the chorus of laughter that followed. Setting his storage container at the end of the bed, he slipped out of the strange rubber shoes and sat on the mattress, facing the room with his back to the wall.

Connor eyed his cellmates one by one. Three were Hispanic, two hanging out on their bunks while a third swung down from another bed to stand next to them. The fourth bed was occupied by a thin black man with glasses. After a brief glance in Connor's direction, he went back to reading his book. The fifth and sixth beds were home to two white guys, one old and dumpy who looked more suited to a stained wife-beater. The other was a man with skin so leathery that Connor imagined he had spent decades lost in a desert. His frame was lanky, his chest sunken, and his dark hair limp and much too long. His bangs reached down to his pointy rat nose. The desert rat leered at Connor, who saw in those eyes the same craziness that he sometimes summoned. But this man wasn't acting.

"What are you in for?" Desert Rat asked before rattling off a series of abbreviations. "PV? DUI? FTA? DV?"

"NOYFB."

Desert Rat blinked. "What the hell does that stand for?"

"None of your fucking business," Connor said with a straight face, making clear that he wasn't joking or looking to make friends.

A couple of the inmates laughed, but Desert Rat scowled. "Where did you get that scar?"

"Keep asking questions and you'll find out."

Connor stretched out on his mattress and stared at the ceiling, dismissing them as unimportant. After a few moments, conversation continued without him. The Hispanics chattered in Spanish and Desert Rat spewed a stream of ignorant thoughts and opinions at his bunkmate.

Time crawled by. Soon Connor was uncomfortable and bored. He considered unpacking his things, but where would he put them? Besides even making his bed sounded too feminine and vulnerable right now. Flipping through the rulebook would provide distraction, but that would also reveal his lack of experience. He wondered when the next meal was. The last thing he'd eaten was a sandwich just before being transported here. His internal clock said dinner time had come and gone.

The room smelled. Maybe a few of the guys here could use a shower, but mostly it was the lack of air flow. The far wall wasn't bars like Connor had imagined, but Plexiglas windows large enough for the guards to easily observe them. Being able to see the spacious main room beyond made the cell feel less claustrophobic, but no less stuffy.

A deputy in the main room shouted something Connor didn't understand, the inmates in his cell settling down in their beds. Then the lights clicked off, and Connor breathed out in relief. The darkness made him feel safer. He could move without feeling like everyone was watching and sizing him up.

In the dim light that remained, Connor considered the room. In addition to the three bunk beds was a stainless steel sink and toilet that were a little too close together for his comfort. The toilet, like everything else in jail, was one piece without even a seat that could be raised. There was no privacy. The toilet sat against the wall for all to see. Connor had heard someone using it before the lights were shut off. He wasn't pee-shy, so that wasn't a big deal, but what if he had to take a dump?

As his eyes darted around the room, Connor tried to come to terms with living here for the next thirty days. Eventually, he became tired enough for his body to sleep.

The sun came up the next morning, or at least the deputies switched on the lights. Without a clock, Connor had no idea of the time, but it sure as hell felt early. The door to their cell was opened by a deputy who briefly poked her head in to check the room. The faint smell of food reached Connor as she did, his stomach grumbling. The other men were soon on their feet and heading out the door. Connor waited until they were gone before he made quick use of the toilet and followed after them.

Most of the inmates were already sitting at the benches and eating. The large public room was crowded, but still felt spacious compared to their cramped quarters. Prisoners lined up for food at a rolling serving cart that had been brought into the room. Connor joined the line, cautiously eyeing everyone around him.

Maybe he was being paranoid. This wasn't maximum

security, after all. Most inmates were probably here for unpaid child support or for cheating on their taxes. Hardened criminals, the rapists and murders, were going to be in prison. But this reassuring thought hadn't kept Connor from jolting awake many times last night, certain that Desert Rat was creeping up on him. Connor wouldn't mind knowing what his cellmates were in for. Maybe he should ask them.

Connor reached the counter, took a plastic tray, and was given a disposable bowl of watery oatmeal and a paper plate with two slices of toast. Oh boy.

"How about a spoon?" Connor asked when the deputy motioned he should move out of the way.

"See your CO if your lost your utensil," the deputy snapped.

"I was never given one."

The deputy spared him a second glance. "You new? You should have been issued one during processing."

Connor took his tray back to his cell. He opened the storage container and dug through it, pulling out the blanket and pillow he had sorely missed last night. Toward the bottom was a spork slightly more durable than the disposable kind. Apparently he was supposed to take care of it. Maybe this rule stopped prisoners from shaping them into weapons if they didn't want to eat with their hands. Having breakfast in the cell was tempting, especially since it was now empty, but Connor knew that would make him appear weak.

Instead he took his tray back to the tables and sat down next to inmates he didn't recognize. They barely looked at him, so he focused on shoving food into his mouth. Once Connor was finished eating, he reevaluated the space he was in. The triangular room was two stories tall with another set of cells on the second floor.

All the cells were against one wall. The second wall was dedicated to a bank of payphones. The third wall was mostly blank, except for the exit, a shelf full of heavily battered paperbacks, and a billboard plastered with notices and information. At one of the triangular room's three points was a raised station where the deputies sat and observed everything.

Connor turned back to the other prisoners, watching them as covertly as possible. Most had finished eating and were socializing. Some of the prisoners returned to their rooms, but others headed toward stalls that interrupted the rows of cells. Connor heard showers running and toilets flushing, which meant private facilities were available. Well, sort of private. He could see the feet and heads of the men in each stall since the doors were very short. This allowed the guards to keep an eye on them, but it was still better than having to use the toilet in the cell.

Once the initial bathroom rush was over, Connor returned to his cell and took the essential items from his storage container. He made his way upstairs to the stalls on the second level that were less frequented since most people were in the common room downstairs.

The shower stall had the absolute basics, plus a hook on the back of the door that he hung his towel and jumpsuit on once he had stripped down. The door didn't lock, but Connor wasn't too worried. The stall door only came up to his chest. Everything above was exposed, as was everything below his knees. Turning on the mercifully hot water, a cloud of steam enveloped Connor. With his back to the rest of the room, he pretended he was at home and let his muscles relax.

By the second day in jail Connor felt more confident. Life on the inside had a simple system to follow and a unique vocabulary he was slowly picking up. The cells were called dorms, the main area outside the dayroom. Both sounded much too quaint for jail, but Connor overhead them enough that he began to think of them as such. Aside from three times a day—eight in the morning, one in the afternoon, and again at four—they had free access to the dayroom. During the three exceptions they were locked down for an hour, which meant they had to stay in their dorms. Of course they had little room to stand or do much of anything, so most inmates sat on their beds while the deputies changed shifts or rolled the food carts in and out.

The meals weren't inspiring. Lunch yesterday had been a hardboiled egg and a bologna sandwich. Dinner was beef stew with more toast. The stew wasn't too bad, as long as Connor didn't try to identify the chunky ingredients. The best part of this system was that Connor could easily avoid his cellmates. Not that any of them gave him trouble, but Desert Rat continued to leer at him and whisper jokes to his bunkmate.

Today Connor was feeling particularly hopeful. The

payphones were in constant use. There didn't seem to be restrictions to using them, meaning he could make daily calls if he wanted. Knowing that David liked to sleep in, he decided to wait until a little past ten in the morning. Then he had to wait another hour or so before a phone was free. He picked up the receiver, feeling as nervous as a schoolgirl about to call the handsomest guy in class. A yellowed note on the wall read "Collect calls only!" Connor didn't know if he could make a collect call to a cell phone, but it was worth a shot.

He dialed zero, waiting impatiently for the automated operator to stop repeating everything in English and Spanish. After punching a few more keys, he was able to dial David's number and record his name. When his name was parroted back to him, Connor thought it sounded shaky.

Riiing. Riiing. Riiing. Click!

A snippet of David's voicemail played before it went mute. Half a minute later and the automated operator told him that no one could take his call.

Well, maybe David was sleeping in extra late today.

After deciding to try again later, Connor wandered through the dayroom. He didn't have much to do besides socialize. With his combined total of four days in both jails, Connor was starting to feel desperate for conversation. He was walking the edge of the dayroom a few times for the exercise, when he spotted one of his cell mates—the black man who always had his nose in a book. He was seated at one of the tables, absorbed in a paperback with its cover torn off.

Connor sat across from him, nodding when the man looked up and made brief eye contact, then started drumming his fingers on the table while he tried to think of something to say to him.

"Good book?" Connor knew it was the most annoying question a reader could hear, but he couldn't think of anything else.

"Honestly?" The man answered without looking up. "It's terrible."

"Oh. Who wrote it?"

"Some hack." Now the book was moved aside as cautious brown eyes considered him. "Charles Dickens, actually."

Connor laughed, encouraging the man to continue.

"To be fair to Dickens, I've always despised *Great Expectations.*

I remember reading it in high school and hating it, but tastes change. I used to hate onions, for instance. As it turns out, my teenage self was right. It's a miserable book."

"I don't think I even tried," Connor said. "I used to always buy those little cheat guides. What are they called?"

"CliffsNotes." The man smiled and pushed his glasses up his nose before extending his hand. "I'm Wade."

"Connor. So, what are you in for?"

Wade shook his head. "That's one subject I don't talk about. I won't ask you, either."

"Fair enough." Connor could understand the need for privacy. "Although I'd sleep easier knowing what our cellmates did to end up here."

"Oh, they're not so bad," Wade said. "Mostly they keep to themselves, except for Leonard, who tried to scare me into giving him my Twix bars."

"You mean Desert Rat?"

Wade paused. "Now that you mention it, he does look like a rat."

"So what did you do?"

"I called the guard over to the door and asked him if I should give up my personal supply just because someone was threatening me." Wade smirked. "That put a stop to it. Leonard has done a lot of prison time. I think he's in on a parole violation, but he likes to pretend that prison rules apply here. For example, they don't tolerate snitches there, so he thought I would quietly take his abuse. As dull as this place is, it's nothing like prison. Thank god."

Connor wondered if Wade was speaking from experience but didn't pry. "Where'd you get the Twix bars?" Connor's stomach had been tight with hunger between dinner and lights out yesterday.

"From the commissary. It's a sort of store for prisoners. They come around every Wednesday with a list you can order from. No one has talked to you about any of this yet?"

Connor shook his head.

"Well, every inmate has an account here that you or your family can move money into. When you place your order with the commissary, they check the total against your available balance before processing the fee."

"Tax fraud," Connor said. "You must be in for that. You talk like an accountant."

Wade smiled. "My lips are sealed."

Whatever Wade was in for, Connor discovered he was a decent guy. That he knew the ropes was useful. Wade went over the basics and even helped him pick out a book from the limited selection, which gave Connor something to do during the next lockdown.

Later that evening, Connor called his family. Even though his mother's voice shook with emotion, he felt like he had been given an injection of pure sanity. He could still reach the outside world, if only with his voice. But one part of the world still seemed to be closed to Connor. When he tried calling David that night, half an hour before lockdown, he still wasn't answering his phone.

Chapter Eighteen

The name of the place was Gulfwood Hospital. David was sure a joke was in there somewhere. As he and his father walked across the parking lot, he played with the words. *Gulp wood.* Or maybe, *I want to engulf your wood.* Or *Wolfwood*, since they were meeting Dr. Wolf. When they entered the hospital, they found the doctor leaning over the admissions counter and talking with a young woman.

David wondered if Dr. Wolf was psychoanalyzing her. Maybe he did that to everyone he met, even the cashiers at the grocery store. When the doctor noticed them, he smiled and cast his arms wide as if he were meeting old friends whom he wanted to hug. One of his arms came around to shake first David's hand, then his father's.

"It's good to see you both. Come, this way."

They followed him to a double door with two vertical windows above the handles. As they approached, a man in pale blue scrubs came out the doors and held one open for them. Dr. Wolf thanked him, chattering about the hospital's good reputation as they followed. David wondered why they were getting a sales pitch when he heard the door shut behind him, the hard thunk of a lock slugging into the wall.

And he knew.

David nodded at what was being said, desperate to appear calm outside while inside he was going crazy. No, not crazy—that wasn't the best word to use right now. Maybe it wasn't too late. If David behaved himself, showed how well-balanced and polite he could be, maybe he wouldn't be forced to stay here.

Dr. Wolf led them to a door labeled *Admissions*.

David stopped. "Dad." He hated how the word came out, how his voice sounded pleading, but his father didn't look at him. He wore a determined expression that had "This is for your own good!" scribbled all over it in permanent marker.

"David, your father is very worried about you. We both think it would benefit you to spend some time away from the environment you've been struggling in." Dr. Wolf put a hand on his shoulder. "Think of this as a vacation, not just from Chuck and Connor, but from all the pressure you've been under lately."

David seriously considered punching Dr. Wolf. Instead he asked, "How long?"

"There's no set time here, no rush to get better."

"Better?" But David didn't hear the response. He was envisioning time slipping away, days and weeks that he wouldn't be writing Connor letters, going to visit him, or even answering his calls. He knew prisoners were allowed to make calls and had researched everything, even making sure his cell phone could accept collect charges. Would it be more than just weeks? Months? He pictured Connor getting out of jail, his hope of David meeting him there withering away as he stood on an empty street. If David was locked up for too long, maybe Connor would give up completely and head to Florida without him.

"Why are you crying?"

The woman inside the admissions office asked the question, but David had no idea how he had arrived there. Somehow they were inside the office and David was sitting. Maybe she could be reasoned with. Maybe they couldn't do this against his will.

"I don't want to be here," David said.

The woman, who looked like a plumper version of his mother, cocked her head and gave a sympathetic smile. "Oh, the same thing happened when I took my son to camp for the first time. He cried and clung to my leg when I had to leave, but you know what? When I went to pick him up two weeks later, *I* had to drag *him* away."

David stared at her. This wasn't a stupid camp he was being checked into! This was a mental hospital. He glanced over to see his father breezing through paperwork, equally desperate to leave, and went numb. They took the contents of his pockets, which were given to his father, and took a photo of him. Then his father and Dr. Wolf left the room to fetch his luggage. Apparently his dad had packed a bag without David knowing.

The woman attempted banal conversation with him, droning on about her kids. David felt infinitely sorry for them for having such a horrible mother. Dr. Wolf returned, but David's father did not, so David decided to feel sorry for himself as well. Dr. Wolf escorted him down more hallways with locked doors, each further reducing the possibility of escape. After walking through one final set of doors, they reached an area that looked like a giant living room. It was furnished with half a dozen couches and a handful of chairs. At one end was a television set. About twenty people his age were lounging around, like an airport populated solely by teenagers.

He wasn't allowed to stay there. Instead David was led down one of two side halls and into a room with two beds. The room wasn't quite as dire as most hospital rooms were—more like the cheap hotel room he and Conner had shared in Georgia. When David turned around, two nurses were standing behind Dr. Wolf, both in the same pale blue scrubs.

"This is David Henry, and he'll be staying for a while."

"Hi, David," the female nurse said. The male nurse only smiled.

When David didn't respond, Dr. Wolf turned to them. "He'll need to be on EP for the next couple of days. He's not a suicide risk, but could you go through his luggage to make sure there aren't any razors or anything?" Dr. Wolf turned back to David. "They'll get you settled in here. Just try to relax tonight. I'll be back tomorrow, and we'll attend your first group session together. How's that sound?"

"Like shit." The words surprised David, but if they were going to treat him as if he were insane, he might as well embrace it. He turned his back and walked to the window, ignoring anything said to him until the last adult had left the room. Then he looked up at the moon. Okay, so maybe it was just a streetlight, but it would have to do. David looked at the would-be-moon and swore he would be out of this place before Connor got out of jail.

"You must be my new roommate."

David sat up in bed and eyed the newcomer. He wasn't surprised that he was sharing the room, having noticed the bathroom supplies and clothes in one of the drawers. They were probably the same age. His hair was short and dark and a scattering of freckles covered his nose. His brawny build and the twang in his voice made David think of him as a country boy. Or one of the Beverly Hillbillies.

"Is this your bed?" David asked. "I wasn't sure which one was yours."

"You got the right one." He covered the distance between them in a few broad steps and shoved a large paw into his face. "I'm Elijah."

"David."

After shaking his hand, Elijah flopped onto the bed. "So, what are you in for?"

David hesitated.

"How about I go first," Elijah said. "Drugs. Dealing and taking. Mostly taking. I don't suppose you have anything on you? Any E or a hit of acid?"

David shook his head. "Sorry."

"Not a problem. I shouldn't do them anyway. You ever done acid?"

"No."

"Don't. I still get flashbacks, and believe me, they aren't fun."

"Uh, okay." David hesitated. "Didn't you just ask me for acid?"

Elijah grinned. "Well, yeah. If you already get the flashbacks, you might as well keep doing the drug. Tripping is still fun, you know?"

David didn't, and now he decided to never find out. "Have you been here long?"

"Yup. My time's almost up. End of the week and you'll have the room all to yourself. First time in a place like this?"

"Yeah. You?"

"Third." Elijah's expression became strained. "Parents can't seem to get me fixed right. What about you?"

David could either keep it all in or let it all out. Elijah reminded him a little of Chuck. Maybe it was just the hair, but he wasn't about to start hiding now. "Well, some guy beat me up, so my boyfriend beat *him* up. Then my boyfriend got arrested while the other guy didn't, so I freaked out and took a baseball bat to his car."

"Nice," Elijah said, but there was some hesitance. "So you're gay?"

"Yeah."

"You might want to keep that to yourself."

David glared at him.

"It's not me," Elijah said quickly. "I don't have a problem with anyone being gay. Listen, you should talk to Corey about it. Unless you think your parents already told the doctors."

David's dad rarely mentioned it to anyone. Even during the session with Dr. Wolf, he simply referred to Connor by name.

"I see you're on EP," Elijah said, nodding at David's hands.

David looked down at a plastic band on his wrist, neon green with the letters "EP" repeating over and over. He didn't remember anyone putting it on him during his admission, but he had been in a daze. "What's it mean?"

"Escape prevention. They think you're going to try to make a run for it. That means you're stuck in your room except for group, and they bring your meals to you instead of you going to the cafeteria. I was on EP when I got here. SP too."

"What's SP?"

"Suicide prevention." Elijah grinned. "Hey, check this out." He hopped off the bed and went into the bathroom. When he returned he had an electric shaver in his hand. Popping off its face, he turned it upside down to reveal the razors. "When you're on SP, they don't even let you have shoelaces—just in case you hang yourself with them."

"Seriously?"

"Seriously. No straight razors either, but they let me have this. I could have taken these razors out and cut myself." Elijah exposed his wrists. David saw pink scars, thin and faint but still visible. "Don't worry, though. Everyone is on EP the first day. You'll probably be mixing with the rest of us by this time tomorrow."

The door to their room opened, and an older man with white hair and a short beard poked his head into the room. His eyebrows were raised as he looked them over. Then, without a word, his head pulled back and the door closed.

"That's the third time that's happened," David said.

"Yeah. They do that to make sure no one is screwing, killing themselves, or running away. You'll get used to it."

Maybe so, but David didn't get used to it that night. He slept fitfully, startling awake every time the door opened. Sometimes, half asleep, he would mistake Elijah's breathing for Connor's until he remembered where he was. When he awoke the next morning, Elijah had already left the room. David took a shower and, coming out of the bathroom, found a tray of breakfast waiting on his bed. He ate the croissant and drank the orange juice but ignored the rest. Finally, a heavy-set woman came for him.

"Time for group," she said in a thick German accent.

Gulfwood had probably hired her for that alone. Who didn't love a shrink with a German accent?

David followed her, catching a glimpse of the huge sitting room before he was led to another hallway with evenly spaced doors—more rooms for more troubled teens, no doubt. When David entered the group room, he had to admit that they mostly did look troubled.

Just as he pictured, folding chairs had been arranged in a circle, each occupied by people whose body language marked them as either miserable or bored.

"This is David," the German woman said, making the *v* in his name sound like an *f*. "Please make him welcome now."

David heard a few mumbled greetings and stood there awkwardly until he noticed Elijah motioning to an empty chair. He walked over and sat, feeling two dozen pairs of eyes follow his every move. Finally, a man spoke. He appeared to be in his twenties, and had shaggy blonde hair and round John Lennon glasses.

"Hi, David," he said. "I'm Nick, the group leader."

David squirmed under so many gazes, but he managed to say, "Hey."

"Okay," Nick clapped his hands together, "everyone, let's begin today's session with an exercise. I'd like each of us to name one thing we did yesterday that we regret. I'll go first. Yesterday I didn't work as hard as I could have. I could have helped a lot more of you if I dug deeper to find the energy, and part of that comes from not taking care of myself. Okay. How about you, Michelle?"

The girl seated beside Nick looked weary. Now David understood why they all appeared so miserable—what a crappy way to start the morning! "Well, I didn't really eat much for dinner."

That was easy to believe. The girl was ramrod-thin with dark circles under her eyes. David realized she was probably here for an eating disorder. As each person struggled to name a regret, he tried to guess why they were here. If they looked especially sad, they were suicidal. If they dressed wildly, it was drugs. If they looked tough, violent crime. One he couldn't figure out. The guy was thin with foppish hair. When he spoke, he had a slight lisp and used effeminate gestures.

"I guess I shouldn't have argued with Bob," he said, a little involuntary shake of his head revealing he didn't mean this.

David watched him as the next person spoke. Was this Corey? Elijah said David should speak with him, but why? Because both of them were gay? Maybe Elijah thought gay people stuck together in droves, like some sort of dong-loving herd.

"What about you, David?" The group leader's voice jarred him back to reality. "What do you regret doing yesterday?"

"Coming here."

This comment caused a round of laughter, but Nick sighed in disappointment. "Maybe you don't understand why we're doing this exercise. Would you like me to explain it to you? By targeting the regret we feel, we can find where we need the most improvement. I'm going to work harder today, Michelle is going to try to eat more, and Steven will try to pay attention. So you see, we're turning something negative into something positive. Would you like to try again?"

David shrugged. "There's nothing *I* did that I regret, besides trusting my dad and Dr. Wolf."

"Try again."

Really? He was going to keep asking David until he got an answer he liked? Instead of playing this game, David examined his shoes. The silence in the room grew thicker and thicker until finally Nick sighed again, and the guy sitting next to him was asked about his regrets. David didn't pay attention to the rest of the session. Instead he kept wondering how he could convince his dad to get him out of here.

When the group session was over, everyone filed out of the room. David followed them, hoping to slip out in the crowd, but the German woman gently took his arm as he came out the door. "Come in here, please."

David was led to the next room, which was small and contained nothing but a chair and a desk.

"You meet with your psychiatrist in an hour, but you need to fill out these papers first."

The papers were already on the desk. David sat and pretended to be reading them while the door closed behind him. He stared at the paper until he felt enough time had gone by, then stood and tried the door. Locked.

So much for that. With nothing else to do, he returned to

the desk. The papers were a questionnaire—at first just general information, then probing health questions. David checked "no" over and over again, until the section that dealt with mental health. These questions were a little more interesting.

Do you often feel people are talking behind your back or laughing at you? Do you get angry when others disagree with your opinions or actions? Do you hear voices in your head? Are you attracted to members of the same sex?

David stopped and reread the question. Then he skipped to the next. *Do you ever have thoughts of suicide?* Then he reread most of the page.

"One of these things is not like the other," he sing-songed under his breath.

How could they sandwich in a question about being gay between one about hearing voices and another about killing yourself? Surely they didn't feel it was up there with talking to god or wanting to die, right? But there it was in black and white: A list of everything that could be wrong with a person, and loving someone of the same sex was included.

"You might want to keep that to yourself," David said, doing an admirable imitation of Elijah's accent. Now he understood Elijah's warning. Corey probably had the other half of the story and experienced what would happen if he was truthful.

David frowned at the words one more time. Then he checked "no" on all of the questions except his sexuality. That one he left blank.

Chapter Nineteen

Dr. Harland had a lot of energy for an older guy and looked like he belonged on a golf course. Maybe it was the polo shirt or the way he chose to walk down the hospital hallways with David instead of sitting across a desk from him. For the first ten minutes they strolled, David didn't have a clue who he was, except his name.

"Sorry," he interjected at one point. "Am I seeing you instead of Dr. Wolf from now on?"

"No, no. I'm your psychiatrist. Dr. Wolf is your psychologist. The easiest way to understand the difference is to think of me as a medical doctor. Must be nice to get out of your room. You could make a run for it right now, but I'm trusting you."

Dr. Harland changed topics like that a lot. David wondered if keeping up with his conversation was some sort of test. He did his best, nodding along to the different topics, even though most had nothing to do with David or his stay here. He kept his eyes on his surroundings too, reading signs on different doors and wondering what went on behind them. One room in particular, labeled *Electroconvulsive Therapy,* made him feel like bolting—no pun intended. But David was sure too many locked doors stood between him and freedom.

"We're going to make a couple of changes that will help you," Dr. Harland said, stopping in front of the electroconvulsive therapy door. David wondered if he did so on purpose. "I'm going to recommend they take you off escape prevention. How does that sound?"

"Good," David said.

"I'm also recommending protein shakes. You're below your ideal weight and could use some bulking up. That should help your confidence and scare those bullies away."

Right.

"I'd also like you to try a medication called Prozac. Are you familiar with it?"

David shook his head. "Not really. I mean, the name is familiar."

"I think it'll help you deal with some of the stress you're experiencing. Sound good?"

Nope. But David nodded anyway.

"Do you have any questions?"

He swallowed. "Electroconvulsive therapy. That means shock therapy, right?"

Dr. Harland nodded. "Are you curious about that sort of therapy?"

"No," David said quickly. "I just wondered if I understood the words right."

When he didn't have any other questions, Dr. Harland led him back to the hospital wing used for his age group. During their walk, David had seen areas for adults and another for children. He couldn't imagine what kind of parent would leave a little kid in a place like this, or what a child could do that was bad enough to justify it. Wanting someone else to deal with teenagers he could understand, but children? Dr. Harland led David to the nurses station overlooking the large living room and explained to the personnel there that David was now off escape prevention. The German nurse cut the band off his wrist, Dr. Harland said goodbye, and David was left to his own devices.

David was used to being the outcast, to walking by lunch tables and knowing he wasn't welcome there. First days of school were the worst because he still had hope of making a new friend or finding a place he fit in. He had that same feeling now, as he walked past reading chairs and around couches. Most seats were taken. Nearest David was a girl with more facial piercings than he could count, her thin legs draped over an armrest, feet encased in huge Frankenstein shoes.

He passed a hugely overweight guy who was thumbing through a magazine and humming to himself, one hand scratching the copious acne on his face. On the floor sat four girls, all as rail-thin as Michelle. Maybe she was one of them. He had a hard time telling them apart as they focused on their card game. Across the room at a foosball table, Elijah played animatedly against another guy who looked too handsome to be anything but perfect.

David should have fit in here among his fellow misfits, but he didn't see how to integrate himself, so he started toward the television. Then he noticed Corey standing by a window, looking glum. Just yesterday David was doing the same thing. Maybe all gay guys were prone to such dramatic poses. Regardless, David hoped he had looked half as cool yesterday as Corey did right now.

He decided to approach Corey, unsure what to say. *"Hey, I'm gay, too!"* seemed a little too direct. Corey turned to him as he neared, which didn't help matters. He was pretty: There was no other word for it. His skin was fair and free of blemishes, his blond hair was silky and perfectly styled, and even his lips were a shade of pink that normally only lipstick provided. Corey looked David up and down before turning back to the window.

"Hey. I'm David," he tried.

"I know. Group meeting, remember?"

Corey's tone was hardly friendly, but walking away now would be even more awkward. "You're Corey, right?"

This earned him another glance. "Have we met or something?"

"No. Elijah said I should talk to you. I was telling him about my boyfriend and—" David stopped. He didn't know the rest.

Corey smirked. "If you have a boyfriend, why are you talking to me?"

David felt his cheeks grow warm. "No, not like that. He said I shouldn't tell anyone that I'm gay. He acted like you would know why."

"Oh." Like a cloud passing over the sun, the arrogance disappeared from Corey's face. "So have you told anyone else?"

"No. They had this survey thing, but I didn't answer the question about it. I'm not in the closet or anything, but I saw this shock therapy room and—"

Corey laughed. "Well, don't worry. They aren't that bad here." He looked David over again. "How old are you?"

"Seventeen."

"And your boyfriend?"

"Nineteen."

Corey's smile was bitter. "You're a minor, like me. Your boyfriend isn't."

"So?"

"So, if your parents want your boyfriend out of the picture, they can do a lot of terrible things to him, all with the blessing of the law."

David shook his head. "The age of consent is sixteen in Kansas. I looked it up."

"Yes, but you're still a minor, meaning they can still drum up charges against him: corruption of a minor, transporting a minor over state lines, engaging in lewd behavior in front of a minor, contributing to the delinquency of a minor. I don't remember half of them."

David was quiet for a moment. "Did that really happen to you?"

"Yes." Corey scowled at the memory. "My parents have been in denial since they caught me kissing another boy when I was thirteen. They made me go to church, get extra blessings from the pastor, and attend some stupid Christian camp like they could cure me. Eventually I just stopped talking about it, but Paul and I were arrested for drinking a six-pack in his car. It didn't take long for my parents to figure out why a college guy was hanging out with a high school student."

"So they put you in here?"

"Yeah, and stupid me, I thought the doctors would recognize my parents as the crazy Bible-thumpers they are. But instead, they told my parents to take legal action. They hit Paul with so many lawsuits that it drove him away. That's the messed up part. It doesn't matter if the charges stick or not. They told him he was going to be registered as a sex offender and all kinds of crazy shit. Who's going to stick around when they're faced with threats like that?"

"I'm sorry."

"Yeah, honey, I'm sorry for you, too, because we have the same doctor. If Dr. Wolf thought it was a good idea for me, I don't see why he wouldn't do the same to you."

Connor wouldn't leave him, no matter what. David wanted to believe that more than anything, but Dr. Wolf was already hinting that Connor's influence had led to his current situation. What if they searched Connor's room and found the small stash of pot he kept there? They did sometimes smoke it together. Contributing to the delinquency of a minor, Dr. Wolf would surely call it.

"Are your parents rich?" Corey asked.

"No."

"Then you'll be out of here as soon as the insurance money runs out. Consider yourself lucky. My parents have enough money to keep me here until I'm eighteen. Paul won't even remember who I am by then."

Corey turned back to the window, and David was grateful for the excuse to leave. Corey was miserable but had reason to be. Elijah was right: David needed to hear this. Getting out was only half the problem. Keeping the blame away from Connor—that was the real challenge.

"Time for lunch, buddy!"

The country twang—along with a playful slug to his shoulder—brought David out of his daydream. He'd been staring unseeing at the television screen, but just the thought of food was enough to make his mouth water.

"You coming?" Elijah asked.

"Yeah!"

Down the never-ending maze of hallways was a lunchroom. Just like in school, everyone took a tray and walked down the serving aisle, but here the food options were plentiful. Better tasting too, if appearance was anything to go by. David loaded up his tray with a burger, fries, a side of macaroni and cheese, coleslaw, a brownie, and a Coke. Why were they pushing protein shakes on him when they had food like this?

And—completely opposite from his public school experiences—David found a seat waiting for him. Elijah was surrounded by people, but had one hand on the bench next to him until David got close.

"Take a seat, roommate!" He grinned. "You're about to get a crash course."

"Crash course?" David asked as he sat. He was surprised to see that the only things Elijah had on his tray were an apple, some toast, and a bottle of water.

"Well, you only have the benefit of my wisdom for the next week," Elijah said. "Someone's got to show you the ropes."

"He knows what he's talking about," Michelle said, sitting across from them. Her tray was overloaded with so much food that onion rings spilled onto the table. For an anorexic, she sure had an appetite.

"Rule number one," Elijah said, glancing around the room. "Always help your fellow man." In one smooth motion, he swapped his sparse tray for Michelle's miniature buffet. Then he passed a couple of desserts to the overweight guy with the acne.

David wasn't sure if this was the best idea, but who was he

to judge? Instead he stuffed half the burger into his mouth and waited for the next nugget of wisdom. Elijah was also eager to get some food down before continuing the conversation.

"They have you on any pills?" Michelle asked between nibbles on her toast.

"Yeah. Prozac."

"Take them the first three or four times they give them to you," Elijah said. "Say 'please' and 'thank you'. Don't worry. That kind of medicine won't mess with your head so quick. It has to get into your system. Once they stop watching you, just tongue the pill into your cheek until you're out of sight. Then pocket it and drop it in the toilet when you can."

Michelle pushed away her tray. "If they try putting you on anything else, always say yes. Worse comes to worse, you can sell it to James."

She pointed down the table to a punk with a multicolored mohawk who was staring into space with bloodshot eyes. He wouldn't be coming back into orbit anytime soon.

"Rule number two," Elijah said. "Or are we at number three? Eh, it doesn't matter. I don't really have a list. Rule number whatever, never disagree with them. Who's your shrink?"

"Dr. Wolf." David shrugged. "He seemed okay, but then he tricked me into coming here."

Elijah nodded. "Exactly. They're slippery devils, so you always have to make them think they're winning. Agree with them, but only after some resistance. Make them think they've won the fight. By the end of each session, you should be nodding at everything they say."

"You have to tell them a story," Michelle added. "Anything they say is wrong with you, think of a big reason why you do it. Don't act like you know that's why, either. Like me, I'm skinny because the idea of food makes me sick, and I don't want to look fat. That's not good enough for them, so I talk about how my stepdad always has *Playboy* magazines around the house and how insecure they made me feel. The bonus is that the psychologist made the bastard throw his porn stash away."

Elijah nodded. "Smart girl."

"Thanks. I think I've also come up with a way that'll force him to quit smoking."

"Always have a story ready," Elijah emphasized. "Don't make

it too obvious. Let them drag it out of you. Same thing for the group meetings. For those, you can make it up on the spot. As long as you say what they want to hear, they won't focus on you much."

"Okay," David said. "Doesn't sound too hard." Turning attention away from Connor might be, but the rest should be nothing more difficult than him agreeing to go to Stanford or whatever college his dad wanted.

"Last lesson of the day," Elijah said, mouth half-full of chicken. "Insurance is king." He chewed and swallowed. "The amount of treatment your insurance money will cover determines the length of your stay, not how well you are. Once the money runs out—boom!—you're out of here."

"How many days is that usually?"

"Just depends. A month or two. You can make it shorter by spending all the money you can."

"See these?" Michelle sat sideways and lifted one of her feet. "These slippers cost a hundred bucks."

David frowned. "They look sort of cheap."

"They are." Michelle shook her head. "The hospital charges out the wazoo for everything. That's why you shouldn't say no to any pills or anything else you can get."

"Kleenex, Q-tips, aspirin, mouthwash, sleeping masks—" Elijah counted off items on his fingers, which he soon ran out of. "Anything you can get will drain your insurance money. In the end, you might only cut a few days off your stay, but you're that much closer to freedom. Speaking of which, food is part of that bill. You coming?"

Elijah stood with his empty tray. David wasn't half done, but he could see grilled cheese sandwiches and ice cream ready for the taking. Maybe he would only have a bite of each, but who cared? He wasn't paying the bill.

"How are you getting along so far?" Dr. Wolf asked.

"It's not as bad as I thought it would be," David said. He wondered if this was too transparently false, so he added, "But I don't like that you tricked me into coming."

"Would you have agreed to come otherwise?"

"I guess not."

This battle of wits was taking place in a generic psychologist's office shared by the doctors that met their patients in the hospital. David was sitting up on the comfortable couch, and Dr. Wolf was in a higher chair with a tall, wide back. Like a medieval throne, it was designed to communicate power and authority.

"Have you given much thought to what we talked about last time?"

"A little."

"I believe we were discussing Connor's influence on you."

David pretended he was trying to remember. "I haven't thought about him much. I keep thinking about Chuck and how many times I came close to … I don't know."

Dr. Wolf leaned forward a fraction of an inch. "Came close to what?"

David looked away. "It doesn't matter anymore."

"It does to me."

"You're just going to think I'm crazy."

Dr. Wolf gave a comforting smile. "No one thinks you're crazy."

"Well, I was thinking about all the times I went by Chuck's house before. I figured out where he lived after he picked on me the first couple of times. I used to look at his car and think about how much I hated him."

"Was this with Connor?"

"Huh? No, this was before I met him. Sometimes I would even say things to the car. See, I told you this sounds crazy."

"I don't think so. You were reassigning your anger toward an object you associated with Chuck."

"I guess that makes sense. I used to swear at it, say the things I wanted to say to Chuck but couldn't. A few times I even walked by with the baseball bat, thinking about bashing it in. When Connor got in trouble, part of me was glad for the excuse to finally do it."

"Plus, you wanted to avenge your friend."

David shrugged as if that didn't matter. "I did pee on Chuck's car once."

Nothing like mixing a little truth into fiction. David was proud of the way he was weaving his story. By the end of the session, Connor's name was no longer being mentioned. Instead Dr. Wolf seemed fascinated in tracing back David's destructive impulses. Thank goodness their time ended before he ran out of material. David would have to dream up more before tomorrow, but for the moment, he felt more in control than he had in a long time.

Chapter Twenty

In routine, there is comfort. Connor knew what he was supposed to do and when it would happen. Short of using the toilet or shower, most decisions were made for him. He awoke at the same time every day, ate all three meals according to schedule, and went to sleep when the lights were turned off.

While this made for a very boring life, it also took the edge off his fear. Jail wasn't the hell he had expected. No corrupt warden, no gang of guys came after him with shanks. He even dropped the soap once, but in the solitary shower stall, no one could take advantage of Connor but himself. There was only routine here and slow-moving time.

Until the beginning of the second week.

"Time for you to go home!"

Connor wished the deputy's words were directed at him, but they weren't. Instead they were said to the Hispanic man sharing Wade's bunk. This didn't come as a surprise. Wade spoke a little Spanish and had tipped off Connor that the top bunk would be available soon, in case Connor wanted off the floor. The bunks didn't look much more comfortable, but had to be better than the plastic temporary beds.

At lockdown the guard came for their cellmate. The Hispanic man had barely crawled down from his bed before Connor stood and put his hand on the mattress.

"What do you think you're doing?" Leonard asked.

The guard paused in the doorway. Leonard peered up at him with his desert rat eyes before shrugging nonchalantly. Once the guard was gone, Connor started pulling himself up onto his new sleeping place. When he was sitting, a boney hand grabbed his ankle.

"Not so fast!" Leonard snarled. "In prison, only the bitches sleep on the bottom bunk. I've been here longer, and I ain't no bitch, so the bed belongs to me."

Connor yanked his leg free. "You're not in prison anymore, Leonard, and you already have a bed. Now get back in it and never touch me again or I'll show you who the bitch is."

Leonard glared but backed down. Connor felt pretty cool until he realized the others might think he was threatening rape.

He had meant that Leonard *was* a bitch, nothing else. Still, the threat had done the job. He stretched out and stared at the ceiling. Even this felt like a huge improvement. From the floor, staring upwards had meant seeing his cellmates in his peripheral vision. Now he could shut them out as much as possible. He could hear Wade turning pages on the bunk below and Leonard muttering to himself, but it didn't take much to pretend he was alone.

He slept like a baby that night. The next morning, Connor began his routine again. He woke up, ate breakfast with Wade, hit the shower, then walked circles around the dayroom. This was not only for exercise, but also to pass the time until he was sure David would be up so he could make his collect call. As he always did, he heard the very beginning of David's voice mail message before the line cut off. Sometimes he heard more than other days. Today he heard a hesitant "Hi, this is—" Once he had heard David say his full name before the robotic operator voice cut it off and asked unhearing ears for permission to accept the collect call.

Connor tried not to let this get him down. Hearing David's voice every day was better than nothing, but he was beginning to worry. More and more often, he imagined David's look of horror when the police had said Chuck was in the hospital. David had promised on the phone, before Connor came here, that he would wait for him. But now that David had time to think about it all, maybe he had changed his mind. Connor had sent him a postcard on his fourth day. Letters weren't allowed, only postcards, and David should have gotten it by now. If he had, he hadn't responded.

"Finish that book yet?" Wade asked Connor during one of his walking rounds.

Connor stopped by the table. "Are you kidding? It's the thickest book I've ever seen!"

Wade would have made a good librarian. He had an endless number of literary recommendations. The most recent was a horror novel about a killer clown. For such a crazy concept, it was full of a surprising amount of heart. The book was so fat it was a miracle the guards didn't categorize it as a potential weapon. Connor thought he would never finish it, but with nothing else to do, he made steady progress and was near the end.

"Today is Thursday," Wade reminded him with the hint of a

smile. "Anyone coming to see you?"

Connor nodded. "My mom or my dad. Not sure which. One of them has to watch my kid brother, so it's never both." Every Monday and Thursday felt like Christmas. Each prisoner was allowed one twenty-minute visit on these two days, a much-needed lifeline to the real world. "Anyone coming to see you?"

"Yes." That's all Wade said. He was still just as private as the first time they had spoken, but Connor was used to it. Wade was a good conversationalist as long as the topic wasn't himself. Being well-read made him an expert on just about any subject Connor broached.

Today the history of the prison system was on Wade's mind. Not a topic Connor cared much for but it helped pass the time until evening. To help the guards keep track of everyone, lockdown was in effect during the three hours visitors could arrive. This made the visits even more precious, since it allowed a brief escape from a very boring period of time. When the guards came for Connor, he noted with smugness that Leonard never had a visitor.

The guard brought Connor and three other men to a row of Plexiglas booths that were designed mostly to stop contraband from entering the prison, but also to prevent violent outbursts or escape attempts. Speaking through them took some getting used to, like having a cell phone conversation with a friend who was on the other side of a store window.

Connor saw that his mom was the visitor today and felt a lump rise in his throat. Conversations with her were always harder, since he couldn't hide his emotions from her. With his father, Connor could suck it up and act tough. His mother already had the red phone pressed to one ear.

Connor picked up the connecting receiver. "Hi, Mom."

"Are you okay?" She always asked this question first.

"I'm fine. It's like after-school detention—boring and harmless."

She gave him a probing look before she relaxed a little. "You look thin. Are they feeding you enough?"

"No, but I'll be all right. I stocked up on candy bars and chips from the commissary. How are you and Dad?"

"Fine. I think he's found a job."

"Really?"

"Well, he had an interview that went well."

Connor smiled. "Don't jinx it by talking about it. Is Tommy okay?"

His mom made an exasperated face. "He's losing teeth by the bucket load. I thought he was going to keep his baby teeth forever, but now he's spitting them out like watermelon seeds."

"Yuck!"

"Are you sure he can't come visit you?" His mom made big eyes. "He's missing you terribly."

"No! You haven't told him, have you?"

"No. He thinks you're off with David somewhere."

Connor exhaled. "Good. Uh, I don't suppose you've heard from him?"

"David? No. Why?"

"No reason." Connor licked his lips. "It's just I can't get hold of him. You know that last time you saw him, when he came by the house to tell you guys? Did he seem mad at me?"

His mother shook her head. "Not at all. He seemed sad. Maybe a little angry at the situation."

"Okay. Never mind. So Dad's keeping his nose clean?"

"He's fine. Well, we did have a setback. One of the neighbors gave him a bottle of painkillers. Your dad was complaining about his back, like he does, and the neighbor thought he was being helpful. Your dad tried to hide them from me, but I've spent years looking at those glassy eyes and knew right away."

"That sucks."

"Yes, and I was livid, but for once your father didn't walk away. We sat there and talked it out, and I told him everything I've been feeling over the years. He had a few things to say too, and we were up half the night. The next day—" His mother blushed. "Well, we're fine now, that's all that matters. *Really* fine."

The emphasis in her words gave Connor pause. "So that maintenance man at work, the one who had the hots for you—"

The corners of his mother's lips lifted ever so slightly before she shook her head. "I'm no longer interested."

"Well, well! Don't tell me I'll be getting a little sister soon."

His mom laughed. It sounded like music in the dire surroundings. The rest of their time together slipped away. The visits were terribly short, but Connor always walked away in high spirits. When he got back to his dorm, he headed for his storage container. Dinner on visitation days was even earlier than usual, meaning a huge stretch of time until breakfast. Connor removed the lid from the container and discovered three of his six candy bars and a bag of chips were missing. The thief hadn't even bothered removing the wrappers and crumbs, which Connor always threw away.

Leonard snickered behind him, but except for a tensing of his shoulders, Connor didn't reveal his agitation. He didn't even turn to look at him. A couple of candy bars weren't worth getting into trouble over, so he grabbed one of the remaining bars and his book and climbed up to his bunk, losing himself in a fictional world.

"I hope you're not hiding any deep, dark secrets."

The words seemed ironic coming from Wade, but Connor was too curious to come up with a snappy comeback. "What are they doing?"

A small platoon of guards walked beside the huge laundry cart that looked like a dumpster on wheels. Connor had seen them collecting dirty sheets and leaving fresh ones last week, but this time the cart was moving slowly, guards disappearing into each dorm for ten minutes at a time.

"Just a standard search," Wade said. "This place is so tight that they never find anything. Not much, anyway."

Connor was vaguely aware of the jail's drug trade, which mostly consisted of pills from the infirmary. Some of the guys farmed out from other jails and prisons, the way Leonard had been, brought stuff with them by wrapping it in plastic and shoving it up their ass or swallowing it before they transferred.

"You worried?" Wade asked when Connor kept watching.

"Well, there is that escape tunnel I've been digging with my spork."

They laughed and went back to reading. Later, when lockdown came again, Connor was putting the fresh sheets on his bed when the door buzzed open and a guard said his name. When he turned around, he found the guard backed by two others. One of them was holding handcuffs, the others had clubs.

"What's going on?"

"Turn around and put both hands on the bunk."

Connor complied, feeling like he was being arrested while

already in prison. They brought him to the dayroom, where a fourth guard waited with another handcuffed inmate. Then they were led out and down a short hallway to a door marked *Inmate Welfare*. The other inmate went in first, Connor sitting on a bench outside with guards on either side of him. He waited for what felt like an eternity, asking again what was happening, but the guards ignored him.

Then the other inmate reappeared, head low. He was sniffing like he was crying, but Connor didn't have sympathy to spare as he was brought into the room. Across a long table sat two male deputies and one female with an air of authority. On Connor's side of the table were a couple of chairs bolted to the floor. One of his wrists was freed so he could be handcuffed to the chair.

"Do you understand why you are here?" the woman asked.

Her blonde hair had streaks of grey. Crow's feet beside her eyes made her look tired. Or wise. Connor stopped staring long enough to shake his head.

"This is a disciplinary hearing because of the contraband found in your room."

Connor thought of the Twix bars in his storage bin and would have laughed if the faces across from him weren't so grim. "I don't understand."

"Contraband is the possession of forbidden items," the woman explained, as if he didn't know the word. "Things you hide from the staff working here. Would you like to tell us what you were hiding?"

"Nothing," Connor said, his face as earnest as possible. Suddenly he felt desperate that they believe him.

The woman sighed and nodded to one of the deputies beside her. He nodded in response, reached into a wooden box, and lifted out a small item and set it on the table. Connor stared at it, brow furrowed. It was a toothbrush and a broken pencil, bound together with a plastic wrapper of some sort. It looked like a bizarre homemade cross cobbled together by a desperate vampire hunter. Only when he saw the end of the toothbrush had been filed to a point did he understand, but pretended not to.

"What is that?" he asked.

The woman pursed her lips. "*That* is what we call a shank. Would you like to tell me who you planned on stabbing with it?"

Someone made of marshmallows, preferably. Even with the

pencil acting as a grip to allow more force, Connor doubted the flimsy plastic of the toothbrush was strong enough to break the skin. The would-be knife was the most pathetic construct he'd ever seen. "If there was one class I was good in, it was shop. I promise you, if I was going to make something like that, I would do a much better job."

One of the deputies snickered before hiding it with a cough. The woman didn't look amused. Connor wasn't trying to be funny. He really could have done better. Why not use the pencil as the blade? It had a much better chance of doing damage.

"Possessing a weapon, no matter the quality, has very serious ramifications," the woman said. "Your sentence can be extended, your commissary privileges taken away. You can be moved to a higher security level, or you can spend the rest of your time here in a disciplinary segregation module."

Connor swallowed. "I swear, that thing doesn't belong to me. I don't know where you found it, but if it was with any of my things, someone else put it there. I just want to keep my head down, do my time, and get out of here."

The woman sighed. "Every person through those doors says the same thing." She looked him over, eyes betraying a hint of sympathy until she strayed to his scar. Then he knew he was doomed. "Spend the weekend in disciplinary segregation," she said. "While there, think about the best way to stay out of trouble for the rest of your time here."

Connor thanked her in a last-ditch effort to show he was a decent person. Not that it helped. The guards led Connor to another part of the institution where a deputy manned a small station in a dark hallway of closed metal doors. They patted Connor down, as if he were bristling with shanks, before opening one of these doors and pushing him inside.

This was how he had pictured jail. The room was long and narrow and furnished by a slab with a thin mattress to sleep on. A toilet and sink were attached to the wall. Only a narrow slit near the ceiling allowed natural daylight in, too high to see out of. No matter what name they called it, this was solitary confinement.

Connor sat on the edge of the bed and thought. Leonard must have set him up. Like a good little inmate, Connor ignored the continued theft of his snacks, but now Leonard had upped the game. All because Connor had taken the upper bunk.

Connor clenched his jaw in anger and punched the mattress a few times. Then he paced the length of the room over and over. When he tired of this, he sat on the bed and waited.

Time always dragged in jail, but now it seemed a hundred times slower. Connor had no diversions, except for meals, which were delivered through a slit in the door. During the second day of his solitary confinement, Connor asked for a book. His request was ignored. He was left with only his imagination for company. At first his thoughts were preoccupied with revenge against Leonard. Most of the plans he envisioned were so violent they would earn him more time behind bars.

Then he tried to convince himself that he was better off here. He had his own room, giving him privacy at last. No Desert Rat, no smells from his roommates at night. But he was bored. He wanted to talk to Wade, lose hours in a book, or call someone in the real world.

And then he thought of David, tempted to give into despair, to once again worry about being left behind—trapped here forever while David moved on to someone with more potential. Connor resisted this melancholy, instead taking comfort in the memories they had made together. He worked backwards, mentally travelling into the past to relive every moment. When he reached their dance on the beach, Connor stopped and lingered there. In the silence, he could hear the waves, the song from the restaurant telling him not to dream it was over.

Connor sang the lyrics he could remember. His voice was no better than a rusty hinge, but in the small secluded world he inhabited, no one else could hear. He danced with David on that beach a dozen times before he let himself go further back to the freedom of their road trip. Even further into the past and he found himself in a moment of perfection.

Graduation day. David had laughed at Connor's silly joke of wearing nothing beneath his graduation gown. Then David had grown serious, and when they lay together, he had let Connor do whatever he wanted. He lost himself in the memory, reaching into his jumpsuit and touching himself, pretending it was David's hand he felt, but this pleasure paled in comparison to the words David had whispered to him that night. *I love you.*

And he did. Before David had ever uttered those words,

Connor asked him to promise never to leave him. Head resting on Connor's chest, David had said he never would, no matter what happened. The time for fear was over. David had made his promises, and Connor was ready to trust in them blindly. The failed calls, the unanswered letters—those meant nothing. Connor knew David would wait for him, would always love him. Eventually, he would be free and they would be together. And then Connor would never let anything come between them again.

Chapter Twenty-One

Routine. Group meetings in the morning and the afternoon, evenings spent hanging out with other "troubled teens." Three battles of wits with Dr. Wolf every week, and one pill hidden in his cheek every day to be spit into the toilet. More than routine, there was a comfort to all of this. David had no pressure from parents or school, no real threat from bullies. He was more social than ever before, since everyone at Gulfwood got along, more or less. The occasional argument between patients or shouting match with the staff broke out, but for the most part, life here was calmer than the outside world.

David found all of this useful. Someone should establish spas for teenagers where they could get away from their controlling parents or dysfunctional school life for a while. If they would ditch the ridiculous group meetings, drop the mind-warping medications, and—most of all—lose the therapists, then the hospital really would be helpful. Now he could understand why people joined cults, how a microcosm of acceptance in a huge confusing world could be such an irresistible comfort.

But David had no intention of growing complacent here. The more time that went by, the more desperate he was to contact Connor, to let him know what had happened and that he hadn't been abandoned. David had to be careful, though. Anything outside of the norm had to be cleared by Dr. Wolf. Already David had tested the waters regarding writing letters to people on the outside, feeling this might be the best way of getting news to Connor, and Dr. Wolf had agreed. All David had to do was give the letters to Dr. Wolf, and he would oh-so helpfully mail them off.

Fat chance.

"Looks like we've got a new recruit," Michelle said as she drifted by the chair where David was curled up.

It was evening. They were free to watch TV, read, or just hang out. David often stared at the TV screen while lost in thought. The hospital only had so many movies here—on glorious video cassette!—and he'd already watched most of them multiple times. David turned around and looked toward the entrance. Now that Elijah was gone, he might get a new roommate, but a girl walked through the door.

He started to turn back toward the TV, then did a double take. The girl's face was swollen from crying. David had already seen a few new arrivals. Crying or being pale and confused were the standards, so her tears weren't surprising, but she looked familiar. An elderly woman—probably her psychologist—said a few words to her before gesturing to the main room while speaking further with the staff. No EP for her, apparently.

Sabrina. That was her name. David recognized her from school. Back in freshman year, they'd been assigned to work together on a report for biology. David had biked over to her house and spent the evening making a cheesy video about mitosis. He remembered laughing a lot, but nothing came of their brief association.

Sabrina, clutching her overnight bag to her stomach, hesitantly walked into the lounge. David wondered if he had looked this scared on his first night here. Feeling sympathy for another newbie, he stood and gave her a little wave. Sabrina glanced in his direction before her face registered recognition. She practically ran to David, tossing the bag onto the couch.

"David! You're here too! Oh my gosh!" She held her hands in front her, as if she wasn't sure if she should hug him or not, so David extended one of his own. She took it and held onto it.

"I wasn't sure you'd remember me," he said with a grin.

"Are you kidding? I still have that video we made. *Double your luck with mitosis!*"

David laughed. "That's right! We did that corny commercial, like you could buy mitosis at the store or something. So lame!"

"Very." Sabrina beamed at him. "I watch that video sometimes when I'm drunk."

"Weird!"

They both laughed awkwardly. This was the extent of their history together, leaving them in uncharted territory.

"Well," David said, "let's sit, and you can tell me why you're here."

He led the way to a table and chairs on one side of the room. By the time they sat, Sabrina was on the verge of tears again. She was pretty, in her own way, and kind of a big girl. Not fat, but voluptuous. She had wavy blonde hair that belonged in a shampoo commercial, and her manner seemed elegant, like she came from money.

"Shawn Patterson," she said. "Do you know him?"

David racked his brain. "Really tall black guy?"

"Yes! He's my boyfriend."

"That's cool."

"I wish my parents felt that way."

David shook his head. "You're here because they don't like your boyfriend?"

Sabrina rolled her eyes. "I'm here 'because my grades dropped off.' I nearly failed last year, but I still passed. I used to be straight A's, so of course my parents flipped. But they didn't bring me here until they caught me and Shawn having sex in their bed."

"What?"

"They were supposed to be out of town," Sabrina said without a trace of shame. "They told me they were coming back a day later than they actually were. If they didn't want to see me getting it on, they shouldn't have lied. What about you?"

David shook his head. "I didn't have sex in your parents' bed."

Sabrina's laugh was a lady-like titter that ended in a snort. That alone was enough to make him fond of her. "No, I mean what are you doing here?"

"Ah. Well, similar reasons to your own, kind of, except the name of mine is Connor Williams."

"Connor?" Sabrina said with disbelief. "Like, scary eyes and scar Connor? You're dating him?"

David nodded.

"Oh my god! He is so fine!"

All right. David's feelings for Sabrina went from fondness to love. He spent the next few minutes telling her his story. She didn't bat one beautiful eyelash at him being gay, but did become disgusted at the injustice of Connor's arrest.

"Let me tell you something about Chuck," she said. "Carol Metzger dated him sophomore year, partly because she's completely clueless, and she said he's not even as big as this." Sabrina held up her pinky finger. "Couldn't keep it up either, so that might explain why he's so angry."

"Doesn't surprise me in the slightest," David said coolly, although he was secretly delighted at this news.

"So what about the other people here? Any mass murderers, or do all parents try to keep their kids from dating?"

"Oh, there's all sorts here. See the hot guy over there?" He pointed to Elijah's foosball-playing friend. "Obsessive-compulsive. Takes five showers a day and changes his clothes each time. Michelle over there is struggling with anorexia and hasn't put on a pound in the six weeks she's been here. Tyler tried killing himself after his girlfriend posted nude pictures of him online. Um, the nearly comatose guy on the couch is a junkie, the girl next to him wrote a love letter to her math teacher, and the guy with the acne is here because he's insecure."

"Insecure," Sabrina said in deadpan tones. "His parents put him in here because he's insecure."

"Yup. Welcome to Gulfwood!"

"Hit me. That's all. In the eye, hard enough to bruise."

Wade was unfazed, calmly considering Connor from behind lightly shaded lenses. Then he looked down at his hands, glanced over at the dayroom full of inmates, and back at Connor who was leaning against their bunk.

"Williams, you're crazy."

Connor nodded and grinned. "You get it though, right? Think it will work?"

"What I think is that the guards are going to see a black man punching a white boy, and that I'll be thrown in the hole you just got out of."

"Fair enough." Connor chewed his lip for a moment. "Tonight, then. After lights out when no one will see."

Wade dropped the smirk. "You're asking more of me than you know."

Connor wasn't sure what to make of that. Sometimes he thought Wade was in here for something he was ashamed to admit, like maybe he had touched somebody who was too young. He didn't seem the sort. He was smart and had an integrity that Connor admired, but then again, those people never seemed the type. If they did, no one would tolerate them being around kids. Now he wondered if Wade wasn't in here for reasons similar to his own.

"I'm going to ask you again," Connor said. "Tonight. If you don't want to, that's fine. I don't know how much longer you're going to be in here, but you have to admit that it would improve the atmosphere."

Wade looked over at Leonard's empty bed and shook his head ruefully. "Just don't drag me into this."

"I won't, I swear. Past this one thing, at least."

Wade left the cell, and Connor waited a few minutes before following and heading over to the pay phones. One was free. He called David's number, no longer expecting him to pick up. Once he had his fix, he called home and asked to talk to Tommy. He wouldn't know where the call was coming from, and hearing how his kid brother was idling away his summer made Connor feel like he was out there with him.

Once they were locked down for the night, Connor sat in bed and stared at a book, rereading the same lines over and over. He could feel Leonard's gaze on him and overheard more than one snide remark, but he ignored him as he had done since getting out of solitary confinement.

When the lights shut off, Connor remained as still as possible, listening to his cellmates breathing until he was sure all were sleeping—all except for Wade, he hoped. Connor stayed on his mattress but lowered his head and shoulders over the edge.

"Hey," he whispered.

There was silence, then a sigh, before long fingers touched his cheek, feeling his face like a blind person and stopping near his eye. An index finger remained just below his right eye, marking the point.

"Last chance," Wade whispered.

"Do it."

Connor closed his eyes just before a fist slammed into one. Wade packed a mean punch! It took all of Connor's will not to cry out. He held his breath, tears leaking from both eyes before he got himself under control.

"Thanks," he whispered before pulling himself up the rest of the way.

He was sure he heard Wade mutter "Crazy white boy" before the room returned to heavy breathing, snoring, and the occasional flatulence.

The next morning Connor awoke facing the wall. His cellmates stirred and drifted off to breakfast before he rolled over. Wade waited by the door. He took one look at Connor, his calm eyes growing wide before he shook his head and left.

The cell had a sort of mirror made from the same polished steel as the toilet and sink. Previous inmates had scratched it to hell, but Connor could still see that his eye was black and puffy. He was glad Wade had made him wait. The bruise was much more impressive now after eight hours sleep.

The next part of the plan required subtlety. Connor wouldn't run crying to the guards; that would be too obvious. Instead he kept his head down as if he were ashamed and went for breakfast. None of the food servers took more than passing notice, but as he was carrying his tray to the table, one of the female deputies stopped him. He was in luck. Her name was Deputy Houston, and very little escaped her notice.

"What happened to you, Williams?" she said.

"Nothing." He turned his head so she couldn't see.

"Have you reported this?"

He shook his head, knowing he was waving the bruise back and forth. "I don't want any trouble."

"Eat your breakfast," she said, moving toward the control station. She wasn't the sort to let this go unreported.

Connor sat down across from Wade, risked a smile, and enjoyed his breakfast for the first time since coming here.

Nothing happened for the next couple of hours. Connor was beginning to worry that nothing would. When the next lockdown came and they were crammed back into their dorms, Leonard took particular delight in Connor's black eye.

"What happened? Tried sharing a shower with someone bigger and straighter than you?"

Connor kept quiet, which was good because the cell door buzzed open. Deputy Houston was there with one of her colleagues. They handcuffed Connor and led him out into the hallway. His heart sank when they took him to the inmate welfare room again.

The room was empty, but a door to the right led to a small office. The same waspish woman who had sent him to solitary confinement sat behind a desk. She nodded at him as the handcuffs were removed and he was allowed to sit, this time without being cuffed to the chair.

"Would you like to tell me about that black eye?"

Connor showed reluctance, and for once it wasn't an act. Then he sighed and looked at his hands in his lap. "It was just a misunderstanding."

"Between you and whom?"

He hesitated a moment longer. Then he said, almost too quiet to hear, "Leonard. A guy in my cell."

"And why would he hit you?"

Connor had a few stories prepared, but they suddenly seemed too hokey or transparent. Instead he kept it simple. "I don't know. He just hit me."

"When did this happen?"

"Yesterday. After dinner."

The woman scribbled across a pad of yellow paper. "And is there anyone who can substantiate your claim?"

"Sorry?"

The woman sighed impatiently. "Anyone else who saw this happen. If you don't report these things when they occur, you can't expect us to do much about it. Attacking another inmate is a serious offense that can result in an extended sentence. I can't just charge anyone you point at without corroborative evidence."

Connor's palms were sweating. He had promised not to get Wade involved, but the ante had just been upped. Getting Leonard in trouble had been his goal, but Connor never thought Desert Rat would get more time. He'd hit revenge jackpot! But only if he had a witness.

"Wade," he blurted.

Ten minutes later Wade was brought into the room. He didn't look happy.

"Mr. Williams says that he was attacked, and that you saw what happened."

Wade shrugged, and Connor feared he would say that he hadn't. "I was reading at the time. Didn't see or hear much, really. Just noticed when Leonard punched him."

"Do you have any idea why Leonard would do such a thing?"

Wade was quiet for a moment. "I think he hates the Irish."

Connor almost laughed. It wasn't a bad explanation, really — just crazy enough to be true.

After a few more dead-end questions, they were both taken back to the dayroom. The guards didn't lead them to their dorm. Instead they were led to the side. They watched as their dorm was opened by two other deputies and Leonard was brought out in cuffs. He didn't notice them until he was almost to the halls. His eyes locked with Connor's and burned with rage. Unfortunately for Leonard, Deputy Houston was also watching him. As corroborative evidence went, nothing was better than a guard's observations.

Who knew that having a girlfriend could be such fun? That's what David called Sabrina, even though he had to be careful. Another couple had fallen in love, and once the staff caught on, they were put on restriction. This meant that they couldn't come within so many yards of each other without getting in trouble.

Not that David's relationship with Sabrina was romantic. They were strictly friends. Calling her his girlfriend was only a term of endearment. Most of the time they were together, they talked about their boyfriends. Sabrina was one naughty girl, not hesitating to dish out details of her sex life with Shawn. After some prompting, David began sharing details about Connor too.

"I *love* the idea of two guys hooking up!" Sabrina told him. "Guys are always going on about lesbians, and it used to irritate the hell out of me until I saw my first gay porn. I keep pressuring Shawn to let one of his guy friends go down on him while I watch."

"Poor guy is sexually abused," David said, shaking his head in pity.

Sabrina grinned. "Hell yeah, he is!"

When she wasn't all hormones, she was going on about hip-hop, even rapping shamelessly. Seeing ladylike Sabrina busting rhymes was surreal, but eventually David joined her. Their impromptu performances got a lot of laughs and the occasional cheer. They were even working on some amateur lines about the hospital they were in:

> *Life ain't easy in the old Gulfwood,*
> *Living our lives in the head-shrinker hood.*
> *Keep popping those pills like they say you should,*
> *But take too many and you can't get wood!*

The days flew by with Sabrina around, even though Gulfwood did its best to trip them up.

"It's that time of year again!" said Nick, the group therapy leader with the shaggy blond hair and hippy glasses. At first David thought they were doing some sort of Christmas in July thing, but he groaned along with the rest of the group when Nick continued. "It's back-to-school time at Gulfwood."

"School doesn't start until the end of August," Michelle said.

"Yes, and we want to help you prepare for it," Nick responded. "We have three different classrooms, and in a moment, I'll give each of you your schedules."

Sabrina and David ended up in the same class, which helped lighten their spirits. The next day they were escorted in groups to each classroom. Bizarrely, in addition to three other people from their wing of the hospital, their class also included six kids who couldn't be much older than Tommy.

School was a joke. The teacher mostly focused on the younger kids because they were harder to control. The students David's age were given assignments. Each was told to pick a book from the limited library and do a report on it in a week. He chose Bram Stoker's *Dracula*, but two days later, he still hadn't cracked the cover. Instead he and Sabrina joked and talked each time one of the younger kids misbehaved and created a diversion.

"The whole jailbird thing is hot," Sabrina said during one such moment.

David paused. "You think so?"

"A guy behind bars? It's so James Dean."

"Did he ever go to jail?"

"You know what I mean. Connor is a rebel without a cause. Well, besides you."

David doodled hearts on his pad of paper. "I guess the fantasy is kind of hot, but it's not like there are conjugal visits or anything." He started covering the hearts with bars of ink. "The worst part is that he doesn't know what happened to me. I haven't visited. I'm sure he's called, but obviously I can't answer my phone. He probably thinks I dumped him."

"Sorry," Sabrina said. "I didn't think of that."

"It's okay. I just wish I could send him a sign that I still love him."

The exasperated teacher walked down their aisle, checking on their progress. Today they were supposed to be filling out a math worksheet. They acted busy until one of the younger kids rushed to the chalkboard and started banging erasers against it. The teacher sighed and headed toward the clouds of chalk.

Sabrina leaned toward him and whispered. "They have phones here, don't they?"

"Barely. Even the nurses aren't allowed to bring their cell phones in, but there's an old-fashioned one at their station."

"Well? Why don't you call Connor?"

David scoffed. "I can't just march up and ask to use it."

"No," Sabrina said, "but if there was a big enough distraction—"

They needed another two days to come up with a satisfactory plan and another week before David became desperate enough to enact it. He kept picturing Connor, alone in his cell, waiting endlessly for any sign of support. This made David's relative freedom feel like a betrayal. He couldn't leave Gulfwood, but he could lounge around on couches and watch TV or hang out with his new friends.

Of course placing a quick call to Connor in his cell wasn't possible, which is why David needed so much time to figure out what to do. The answer was much less direct than calling Connor. Finally ready, he worried that Sabrina would no longer be willing to go through with it. When he asked her, putting on his best puppy dog eyes, she just grinned and said, "Tonight, I'm going to win an Emmy!"

David lay in bed, staring at the shadows on the ceiling. The sheets were down to his belly button because he wanted the nurse doing the rounds to see he was in bed. From the waist down he was fully dressed, but they would never notice that from the door. They checked in on him not once but twice, his eyes closing each time he heard the door opening. The second time they checked he even let his mouth fall open so he would look totally conked out. Then he started watching the clock.

When the time was finally right, he crept to the door, opened it a crack, and listened.

"I want to go hoooome!" a voice wailed.

"What's wrong?"

"What are you doing out of your room?"

The nurses' voices grew quieter as they moved away. David risked sticking his head out the door. His room was nearest the nurses station in the boys' wing. The girls' wing was on the other side of this station. David couldn't see down that hall, but he could hear Sabrina making a fuss.

"Leave me alone!" she sobbed. "I just want to go home to my own bed. I'm sick of sleeping he-ee-ee-errrrrrr."

Okay, maybe she was overdoing it a little bit, but she had the staff's full attention. David dashed to the nurses station, diving behind it like he was under fire. He listened to make sure Sabrina was still wailing before he raised his head over the counter and snatched the phone. The cord attached to the wall was long enough to take the phone with him under the desk. Then he lifted the receiver and held it to his ear.

Nothing.

No dial tone. Just a clicking noise. The university where his father worked was the same. Punching "nine" got an outside line. David mentally crossed his fingers and pushed nine. There it was! A droning dial tone. David tapped in a cell phone number and held his breath. After three rings, each lasting an eternity, someone picked up.

"Hello," Gordon said, his voice sleepy.

"Hey! It's me."

"David?" Gordon sounded much more awake. "Are you out of the hospital?"

"No. I'm still there. Listen, I need a favor."

"Wait! I need to apologize first. I keep thinking about what happened and how different it would have been if I hadn't run."

David didn't have time for this, but Gordon's voice was shaking. He risked a peek over the counter and saw he was still in the clear.

"I should have stayed by your side," Gordon continued. "I should have fought like a brother in arms. Then Connor wouldn't have had to go after that guy and neither of you would be in trouble."

David grinned despite the situation. Good old Gordon. David missed him, but now wasn't the time for sentiment. "You're still my brother in arms," he said. "In fact, I need a favor that only you can grant."

"Name it!" Gordon breathed, desperate for redemption.

"I need you to get in touch with Connor and tell him what happened to me. When my dad is at work, go into the house through my bedroom window and look for my cell phone. It might not be in my room, so you may need to search the house. That way you can see if Connor called or anything. Even if he hasn't, maybe you can write him a note or go up there and visit him. Tell him—" David hesitated. Any kind of lovey-dovey message would be awkward to say to Gordon, but he thought of something appropriate enough and relayed it to him.

"I'll tell Connor, don't worry!" Gordon said. "I won't fail you again."

"I know you won't." A fat foot stuffed into a dainty shoe came into David's field of vision. When he raised his head, he looked into the eyes of a very angry German woman. "Uh. Gotta go."

David hung up the phone and smiled sheepishly. The nurse said something in her native tongue. David didn't understand a word, but he could tell that he was in big trouble.

Dr. Wolf thumped his pencil rhythmically on the pad of paper in his lap. He gazed down his nose at David, sizing him up. "Who were you trying to call?"

"No one," David said, relieved that he was being asked. He had worried they could check the phone records and find out. Then again, maybe they had and this was a test of his honesty. "Just a friend," he added to be on the safe side.

"Was it Connor?"

David felt the blood leave his face. He had succeeded in steering the conversation away from Connor, his name not being mentioned at all in recent sessions. Until now. "How could I call him? He's in jail, isn't he?"

"That doesn't mean you couldn't have tried. The nurse wasn't sure if you reached anyone, but I think you did."

Time for a little truthful misdirection. "I called my best friend Gordon and got his voicemail. I left him a message telling him that I'm doing all right."

Dr. Wolf nodded, but then said, "I thought you might have called home. It's not unusual for a patient to get homesick."

No, it wasn't. That's why Sabrina had decided on that role, which had earned her a day on EP. No one suspected that what she had done was related to David's call. They simply thought he had taken advantage of the situation.

"You didn't call your father," Dr. Wolf continued. "I know, because I spoke to him. Then I asked who he thought you might have tried calling. He suggested Connor. This surprised me since you don't speak of him much."

David shrugged and did his best to look bored.

Dr. Wolf pursed his lips. Then he leaned forward. "David, are you a homosexual?"

"Are you?" David's reaction was defensive, and he regretted it instantly.

"No, I'm not," Dr. Wolf replied easily, "but I wouldn't have anything to hide if I were. I'm just concerned that you haven't been completely honest with me. We've been dealing with your issues of anxiety and difficulties with integrating into society. I think your alternative sexuality has a lot of bearing on that."

"Yeah, I'm gay," David said. Obviously his father had already let it slip or Dr. Wolf wouldn't be asking. No point in denying it now. He just hoped his father hadn't said much else.

"And Connor is your boyfriend?"

"I didn't call him," David said.

Dr. Wolf smiled. "That's not what I asked you."

"Well, that's what you wanted to know. I called Gordon. He's my best friend. I missed him, but not in a gay way. Is that all right with you?"

"You seem upset."

"Yes, I'm upset!" David said, his voice louder than he meant. "Do you ask other patients if they're straight? Do they have to fill out some crappy questionnaire that asks if they like the opposite sex—right alongside a list of mental illnesses? No, of course not! I called my best friend last night, and you're trying to make this about me being gay. Well, it isn't!"

Except it was, since David was trying to contact his big gay boyfriend, but he was tired of playing cat and mouse with Dr. Wolf and he was sick of being here.

Dr. Wolf wasn't perturbed by his angry outburst. Instead he wrote something on his notepad and set it aside. He smiled serenely at David and allowed him some time to calm down before he asked his next question.

"David, you're seventeen years old. How old is Connor?"

"Fuck you." David stood up. He wasn't having any part of this. "Take me back to my room. I'm done talking to you."

Dr. Wolf raised his eyebrows, then his hands. "Very well. We'll have plenty of time to discuss your relationship with Connor during your father's next visit."

David glared at him. He would tear the hospital apart brick by brick before he let them file fake charges against Connor. But when he got to his room and shut the door, his anger turned to despair. He could do nothing to escape, no matter how much he wanted to. As the day wore on, he began to wonder if letting go of Connor was the only way of keeping him safe.

Chapter Twenty-Two

Connor wasn't happy. He should be, considering the circumstances. Leonard wasn't just transferred to a different dorm, but to a completely different cell block. This meant not having to see him at all, even in the dayroom. His replacement was an old black man who soon made friends with Leonard's former bunkmate. Together, the two old timers talked about television shows and politicians the rest of them had never heard of. They might as well have been from a different world.

For a while, Connor was content. His conviction that he and David could still be together hadn't faded. But when he last called to hear that snippet of David's voice, a generic message informed him that the voicemail was full. No doubt this was due to the countless times Connor had tried, the collect call request being recorded but never heard. This was practically good news. It meant that David wasn't ignoring Connor. But it also meant that he couldn't answer his phone.

Since then, Connor had done nothing but wonder why. What had happened to him? Maybe it was something small, like he was grounded from his phone. But what if Chuck had rallied and put David in the hospital? Or worse, maybe David had done something drastic.

No longer able to hear David's voice, Connor hadn't tried calling him for the last three days. Instead he called his sister. She had sent word through their mom that she wanted him to.

"Get your butt back down to Florida," she said. "Kansas is too ass-backwards. And bring David with you."

He had laughed and promised he would, but now he wondered if that dream was even possible. Would Connor feel it if David took his own life or been hurt? Would he shoot upright in the middle of the night, a pain in his heart, or hear the ghost of David's voice? He needed to hear that voice now, more than anything.

Deciding it was worth another shot, Connor waited his turn for a payphone. Then he dialed the number so familiar to him that his fingers worked on their own.

Riiiing. Riiiing. Click.

"Uh, hello?"

The line went mute as the collect call service sought permission. That wasn't the voicemail message! But was it David? It didn't sound like him. Connor waited, the phone in his palm slick with sweat.

"Connor?"

"Yeah! Who is this?"

"It's Gordon. I was just writing you a letter!"

"What?" Connor decided it didn't matter. "Where's David?"

"That's a long story."

And it was. Connor listened as Gordon filled him in on everything that had happened. At the end of the tale, Connor struggled with too many questions, all competing to come first. One eventually won out over the others.

"Is David okay? I mean, when he called you, did he sound all right?"

Gordon thought about it. "I guess so. He was kind of in a hurry. He just said I should tell you what happened to him. Oh, and one other thing."

"What?"

"He said no matter how much time goes by, that he'll always be your Sweet Sixteen."

"Okay. Thanks." It was all Connor could manage to say around the lump in his throat.

"Is it some kind of code?" Gordon asked.

"No." Connor laughed, throat muscles loosening as he wiped at his eyes. "Not really."

"Oh. Well, when do you get out?"

"A little under a week. Do you know when David will be out of the hospital?"

"His dad said he might be in there for a long time. Maybe even a couple of months." There was a heavy sigh. "I miss him."

"Yeah. So do I."

They didn't have much left to talk about, so after an awkward silence, they said their goodbyes.

"One more thing!" Gordon said as Connor was about to hang up.

"What?"

"Watch out for stool pigeons."

Connor shook his head. "I'll do that, Gordon. Thanks."

He hung up the phone and took a minute to collect himself.

Then he turned and, with a dopey smile, faced the dayroom full of inmates.

Dr. Harland strolled into David's room, pushing buttons on his cell phone before tucking it in the inner pocket of his suit jacket. David, stretched out on his bed, eyed him suspiciously. Sometimes he thought Dr. Harland and Dr. Wolf were some sort of Jekyll and Hyde duo, one old and direct, the other friendly and accommodating. Both were deceptive.

"Hey, sport!" Dr. Harland gave David a swat on one of his shoes. It seemed friendly enough, but could have been a sign that David shouldn't have his feet on the bed. "Heard you had a rough time the other day."

"Yeah." Which rough time? Getting caught using the phone or his argument with Dr. Wolf? The latter was what David really regretted. He'd kept his cool for weeks only to blow it now. He positively dreaded his father's next visit.

"Everything else going okay? Hey, did you hear about the game yesterday? The Royals got slaughtered!"

Dr. Harland rattled on about sports. Like all of his visits, he seemed to be reading from an internal script. He spoke about David's issues only in passing, which was just as well. He probably only showed up so he could bill the insurance company. It wouldn't be a bad job, really. Maybe David could become a psychiatrist. Then he could get paid for shooting the shit, although he would probably be fired for helping all the kids escape.

"Well, it's good to see you," Dr. Harland said, starting for the door. "Oh, yeah, is the Prozac treating you well?"

"Yup."

"Good. Good. We're going to start you on something else. Dr. Wolf feels it will help your stress levels. No biggie. Just don't be surprised when the nurse hands you two pills next time."

"All right."

When David next reported to the nurses station, two pills waited in the little paper cup they handed him. The male nurse there was giving David the eye, so he did what Elijah told him and swallowed them without question. Hopefully the new pill, like Prozac, would take several days of doses to affect his system.

Boy, was he wrong.

An hour later he was sitting in one of the lounge chairs. His arms and legs felt heavy, his mind muddled as if he had slept too long and couldn't quite wake up. Not that he cared. Nothing seemed to matter at the moment, which was a welcome relief. His father's visit, Connor facing trumped-up charges, or even being stuck in here when Connor got out of jail. None of it was important.

"Hey, you sexy thing!"

David turned his head, feeling like he was underwater. Sabrina's grin faded in slow motion.

"What happened?" she asked. "Are you okay?"

David smacked his mouth. "Yeah. Fine."

"Okay. Well, guess what Michelle just told me? You know how the new guy was put into Brandon's room? Well, apparently Brandon walked in on him beating off to a *Highlights* magazine." She laughed, and David did his best to smile. "It's a kid's magazine! How can you jerk off to that? There aren't even photos in there. Just drawings of hedgehogs and stuff."

Her words blended together, so David nodded while embracing the empty haze in his mind. When he came around again, Sabrina was no longer sitting across from him. David closed his eyes. He wasn't tired, but he didn't really need to see anymore than he needed anything else.

"Hey!"

That was Sabrina's voice again, and she seemed to be shaking him, so he opened one eye reluctantly. There she was, sharing his frame of vision with a punk. The mohawk had once been red and orange, but had faded to pale hues that reminded David of strawberry and orange sherbet.

"Yum," he said.

Sabrina turned to James. "Well?"

"Hm." James's face became a mask of terror. "David!" he shouted. "The hospital is on fire and the flames are spreading this way! Didn't you hear the alarm? We gotta go, man! We're going to die!"

David shrugged.

James's features relaxed. "Tranquilizers," he said. "Strong ones. What was the pill they gave you, man? A little blue diamond? Or was it a circle with a V in the middle?"

"No, no," David said. "It was like an A in the middle, but

without the little connecting bar."

James chuckled. "Or an upside-down V. Valium's not my favorite, but they must have you on a high dose to get you this messed up. You pocket them next time, and I'll slip you some cash."

"Whatever."

James and Sabrina exchanged more words that David didn't hear. His concentration came and went, but whenever he came back, Sabrina was with him. She looked concerned, but he saw her hide it when someone else approached. Then she pretended they were deep in conversation—a private one, she would say if the other person didn't go away.

Later she walked David to the cafeteria for dinner. He ate because she said he should. And she made him drink cup after cup of coffee. David hated coffee, but arguing with her was too much effort. Besides, she stirred in plenty of milk and sugar for him. By the time they walked back to the main room, his synapses were starting to spark again. David even mustered up some fleeting concern for the state he was in.

"When it's time for the evening pills," Sabrina said, "pop them in your mouth, but put them on your tongue and press it to the roof of your mouth before you swallow. Then come back over to me."

She must have given him these instructions a million times in the next hour, enough that David didn't forget. By the time he came back to her, his mouth was full of a bitter taste that made him retch.

"Here." Sabrina held out a tissue. "Quick. Spit them into this."

David did so gladly, but it didn't help much. The foul taste was even more sobering than the coffee.

"Better go rinse out your mouth," Sabrina said, shoving him toward his room. "Spit for once, don't swallow. I'll flush these."

Once in his bathroom, David swirled water in his mouth and spit a few times before brushing his tongue with his toothbrush. The world was starting to come back into focus, but he still felt tired, so he got into bed. All the caffeine coursing through his system wouldn't let him sleep, so he lay there, the cotton balls receding from his mind. Eventually he was sober enough to recognize just how wasted he had been. One thing was for sure:

He was never taking those pills again.

Sabrina grinned at David over her pancakes. "I'm getting out of here!"

"What?" He hadn't meant to sound so panicked, but the idea of Sabrina leaving didn't make him happy.

"Just for the day," she said. "Don't worry. There's a family reunion tomorrow and my parents are pulling me out so I can be part of it."

"Ah, the old 'be around your annoying relatives' punishment," David said sagely.

"That, or they don't want to explain to everyone that their daughter is in the loony bin for having a black boyfriend."

They laughed, but Sabrina seemed distracted for the rest of the day. During class, she ripped a page from her notebook, carefully tore it in half and handed it to David.

"Here."

The page had her cell phone number and email address written on it. He stared at them dumbly, amazed by how foreign such things had become. "What's this?" he managed finally.

"My digits, sweet cheeks."

"I know, but I can't exactly call you from my room."

"I know you know," Sabrina said. "I thought we should exchange contact info. Just in case."

"Just in case of what?"

"I don't know. You'll probably be out of here before I am, right?"

But she didn't sound convinced.

Sabrina went from distant to clingy in the evening. David decided she was probably nervous about being out in the real world again. Or maybe she hoped her parents would keep her out permanently. He tried not to think about it. They had found an ancient version of Trivial Pursuit in the classroom that day and brought it back to the lounge to play in the evening, trying their best to make every question obscene. *What's the fastest swimming marine animal?* became *What's the fastest urinating animal?* And *How many furlongs to a mile?* was transformed into *How many dongs to a mouth?* They had so much fun that David didn't think about her leaving until the next day, when he missed her at breakfast.

Saturday was never a good day at the hospital. Visitors were more likely to come then, and more often than not, these visits brought memories of lost friends and freedoms. This particular Saturday was especially depressing because Sabrina wasn't there.

David's mom came to visit him, but Jeff was with her, which made conversation stilted and awkward. Jeff, for once, seemed happy, like David was finally where he belonged. Jeff gave a lecture about growing up and taking responsibility, which David tuned out early on. He was glad to see them go.

David's father wouldn't come until Monday. He had an optional workshop with his students this weekend—one of the downtown tours he enjoyed so much. David wished his father had come today instead of his mom. The suspense was unbearable, waiting to see what Dr. Wolf had up his sleeve, if he would do to Connor what they had done to Corey's boyfriend. He worried that Dr. Wolf was working on his father in the meantime, convincing him to cut Connor out of David's life one way or another.

The slow Sunday wore on, and as night fell, David began to wonder how long family reunions lasted. He had only been to a few, each one in a public park where everyone ate grilled burgers, homemade potato salad, and devilled eggs. It was nearly bedtime when Nick called him into the room used for his group meetings, the circle of chairs empty.

Nick polished his Lennon glasses, peering at David as if deciding how to proceed. "We need you to be honest," he began. "Think about your friend's safety. That's the important thing. No one is in trouble, so you won't be telling on anyone, really."

"What are you talking about?"

Nick cleared his throat. "Sabrina."

Then David knew. He didn't need Nick to go on, though he did.

"She stole her parents' car. The police are trying to find her, but she'll be in a lot less trouble if her parents can find her first. We need you to tell us where she went or at least where she's likely to go. She's not in trouble."

But she would be, no matter how much Nick repeated that lie, and Sabrina was much too clever to tell David her plan. That way he couldn't rat her out even if he wanted to. Not that he ever would have. He didn't take it personally that she hadn't confided in him. Maybe her escape had been spontaneous. But she must have suspected, because she gave him her contact information.

"I don't know," David said. "She talked about Branson, Missouri, a lot. Her boyfriend kept promising to take her there. That's all I can say."

Nick's eyes lit up like he had a lead. David waited until he was back in his own room before he laughed. David had lied, of course. The police would probably call every hotel in a ten-mile radius of Branson, but David couldn't imagine a lady like Sabrina ever going there. She was much too classy.

David was going to miss her charm, her contagious laugh, and the way she spoke a little too loud when excited. He would never forget the way she took care of him when he was doped up. He hoped, somewhere down the road when he and Connor were together again, that they would run into Sabrina and her boyfriend. Hell, maybe they would start their own commune, a sanctuary for forbidden loves. They could build a fortress circled by walls, and shun society the way they had been shunned. Mostly, though, he was glad she was free.

Chapter Twenty-Three

"Not much longer for you, is it?" Wade set down his book, finished with another one already. His question was odd, since he usually preferred to discuss the author's style, the plot's pacing, or other literary matters. "Two days left, right?"

"Three," Connor corrected.

"Somebody waiting for you out there?"

"Yeah." So far their personal lives hadn't been a subject they shared. Wade was never forthcoming or interested when Connor talked about his own.

"That's good. Nice girl?"

"Guy, actually."

Wade mulled this over. Then he nodded. "Okay."

Connor wasn't sure where to take the conversation from there, so he nodded toward the book Wade had set down. "Any good?"

"It was the first time I read it. The second, third, and fourth as well." Wade pushed it away. "Now I'm getting a little tired of it."

"Don't they ever bring in new books?" Connor asked. "I mean, how did these books get here?"

"Brought in by visitors and left behind by inmates. Maybe a few were donated."

"All right, well, I still owe you a favor for backing me up with Leonard. I could bring some books in for you. How about that?"

"Not a bad idea," Wade said.

"Any requests?"

"Now that you mention it …"

Wade took out a folded piece of paper he'd been using to mark his place. He handed it to Connor, who unfolded it. In tidy handwriting were ten titles and the corresponding authors.

"Do you always carry this around?" Connor asked.

Wade appeared embarrassed. "Actually, I was planning to ask you for some books once you're out. You mentioned it before I had a chance."

They both laughed. Too bad they hadn't met in the outside world. Connor liked to think they would have been friends. Maybe that would be possible in the future.

"Do you have much time left?" Connor asked.

"A couple of months."

"Not bad." He wanted to know more but held back.

"I hurt someone I love," Wade said, answering the unasked question. "I didn't mean to. It was the first and the last time, and it was very wrong of me. This guy that's waiting for you out there. You love him?"

"Yeah," Connor said. "I do."

"Just be careful. Passion is a bridge that connects love and hate. When you're standing in the middle of that bridge, don't let yourself get turned around. You've got to make sure you know which direction you're heading. Watch yourself."

"I will," Connor said.

"You know the problem with this book," Wade said, tapping the paperback, "is the way the author sets up each chapter."

Wade launched into his usual book analysis, Connor nodding along, but really he was still thinking about what Wade had said. Passion hadn't led him to hurt David, but it had driven him to hurt Chuck. And while he still didn't feel sorry about that, he did regret that it separated him and David. When he got out of jail and David got out of the hospital, Connor would run across that bridge straight back to love and never look back.

A gentle knock came on the door. David sat up, stomach filling with dread when he saw his father's head poking around the door. Since Sabrina had gone AWOL, David had done little except fear today's meeting. He stood and opened the door the rest of the way, grabbing onto his dad tightly when he opened his arms for a hug.

"Good to see you, David."

"Yeah, you too. Dr. Wolf's not with you?"

"Stuck in traffic. He called me on my way here."

"Oh. Well, come in."

David's room wasn't much, but his father made his usual cursory inspection, looking at everything with polite interest as if this were David's first apartment. Then, without prompting, he started making the bed. David hadn't bothered because they changed the sheets on Mondays.

He watched his father work. David had been making his own bed since he was twelve, so this didn't happen often. He wasn't huffing and getting it done as if David should have done it himself. Instead there was something loving about the gesture. Once he was finished, his father sat on the bed's edge and looked up at him.

"Dr. Wolf has some strange ideas about Connor," he said.

David swallowed. "Like what?"

"He thinks I should … Well, he seems to feel your association with him isn't healthy."

During the past few days, David had imagined leaping to his feet when this topic was broached, declaring his undying love for Connor, and shouting that no one would ever tear them apart. Instead he sat down on the bed next to his father and asked, "What do you think?"

His father sighed. "I kept thinking of how he called the house before your birthday, and how excited he was about taking you to Florida. He didn't ask for a penny. Just my permission. And he promised to take care of you. I don't think he meant only the trip. What he did to Chuck, well—" He cleared his throat. "Your mother and I went to a bar once, after one of those dinner theaters she was so fond of. I came back from the restroom and found a man talking to her. I heard her tell him to go away. Then the man said something lewd and put his hand on her arm. It was bare, because of the dress she was wearing, which made it even more upsetting."

"What did you do?"

"I marched over there and pushed him aside."

"You did?"

His father laughed nervously. "Yes. Thankfully I'd already had a few drinks. This man was about twice my size, but he must have felt sorry for me because he backed down. Thank god he did. I wouldn't have lasted long in a fight."

"But you took the risk anyway."

"I was a lot younger then," his father said dismissively.

A silence fell between them until David decided to take advantage of it. "This isn't working," he said. "Me being here, it's not helping. I'm not turning my back on Connor, and I still want to move to Florida. I don't know if I want to go to college, but if I do, it's got to be on my terms. You can go bankrupt keeping me in here, but it won't make a difference. I don't think it does for anybody."

At least not that he had seen. Michelle hadn't gained any

weight, James still spent every waking moment high, and Sabrina had run off with the guy she loved. Many similar stories filled these halls, and David couldn't honestly say any of those people had benefitted from being here. At best, the hospital was a rest stop, a small repose from the world that had damaged them in the first place.

"I miss seeing you around the house," his father said. "The silence reminds me of when your mother left. You didn't say a word to me for weeks. Do you remember?"

David nodded.

"I think you blamed me for driving her away. I blamed myself. Sometimes I still do." His father took a deep breath. "But usually I understand that she fell in love with another man and that such things can't be helped, just like your feelings for Connor. I don't want to drive you away. You can go to Florida if you want, and I'll call you every day to make sure you're in school and heading toward college. I can't help loving the things I do either. But promise me, David, that you'll always come back to see me."

David's throat was painfully tight in his effort to hold back tears. "I promise," he managed.

"Okay." His father clapped a hand on his back and stood. "Pack your things. It's time for you to come home."

David couldn't believe his luck, but he didn't hesitate. He got his things together while his father went to the nurses station to let them know David was leaving. Ten minutes later, David walked into the hall, luggage dangling from one arm. Just as his father turned away from the desk and nodded at him, the door buzzed open so they could leave—but Dr. Wolf walked through from the other side.

Stomach sinking, David stopped and watched Dr. Wolf speak with his father. They became animated, gesturing in an effort to make their points. Then Dr. Wolf shook his head and walked around his father, heading down the hall toward him.

"David," he said, "you're making a very bad mistake."

That was all he managed before his father's hand clamped down on Dr. Wolf's shoulder, stopping him from coming nearer.

"Gerald, you no longer have permission to talk to my son."

David saw then, that the man at the bar hadn't felt sorry for his father. There was a fire in his eyes like nothing David had seen before. Even Connor's crazy eyes couldn't compete. Dr. Wolf turned and saw it too, and didn't dare speak another word as David and his father walked out the door.

Prisoners were released during lockdown periods. Otherwise the deputies would have to pluck them from the dayroom, risking escape attempts from some of the less satisfied guests. Connor was prepared. He had given his leftover commissary goods to Wade. When the guard came, he hopped off the top bunk. They told him to pick up his plastic storage bin and carry it with him. On the way out the door, Connor nodded at Wade.

"Thanks," he said.

He wasn't sure that made sense as a parting word, but he really was grateful. The time would have passed a lot slower without Wade's conversation and book recommendations. Wade nodded at him, as if he understood.

Connor's mother had visited him the day before. She was coming today to pick him up, but something about her smile—or the one she tried to hide—he didn't trust. No doubt this had to do with Tommy. He made her promise not to bring his little brother, and his mother had argued that the jail didn't look like one from the outside. Regardless, Tommy could be disarmingly perceptive. At the very least, he would notice all the police cars and start asking questions.

Paperwork was the last obstacle between Connor and freedom. He filled it out impatiently—most of it concerning the six months of probation he still faced. Then they gave him his possessions, including his clothes. When the deputy saw that his shirt was stained with blood, she offered to throw it away and get Connor a new one. Then he was brought to one of the shower rooms to change. The plain white shirt he had been given was a size too large, and his jeans still had a few specks of blood on them, but already Connor felt more like a real person again.

At first the clothes felt odd against his skin, just like winter clothes did after wearing shorts and T-shirts all summer. Once his shoes were tied, Connor stayed seated and tried checking his cell phone for messages but the battery was dead. He supposed no one really called him besides David, who was stuck in the hospital. How lonely life had been before they met!

Connor planned on making an appearance at home and

getting cleaned up. Then he would go by David's house to speak with his father. He wasn't sure what that would accomplish. Maybe he could at least get a message to David. Connor stood, left the shower room, and waited for someone to tell him what to do. Being unsupervised felt strange.

Finally one of the deputies noticed him and asked if he was ready. Connor nodded and was escorted to a public area where other families were waiting. None of them were his.

"Don't come back now, ya hear?" The deputy escorting him guffawed at his own joke. He probably did every time he made it.

Then Connor was left alone. For a moment it seemed too good to be true. He could go anywhere and do anything he wanted. He considered sitting on one of the lobby chairs and waiting for his mom, but the sun was shining through the double glass doors outside. That's where he wanted to be.

Connor strode through the lobby to the door. The light pouring in from outside had warmed the metal handle. He left his hand there a moment, enjoying the sensation, before he pulled the door open and stepped out into a warm summer day.

The parking lot was full of cars. He expected to see his parents there, Tommy exploding from between them and rushing him for a hug. His mom would shrug an apology, and Connor would laugh and forgive her. Except he didn't find a friendly face in sight.

"I baked you a cake with a file inside, but the guards wouldn't let me give it to you."

He swung around. There, leaning against the brick next to the entrance, was his heart's desire. Connor wasted no time in picking David up and kissing him long enough to leave them both breathless.

"I thought you were in the hospital," Connor panted.

"I got out." David looked him over. "I like your hair."

Connor reached up and ran a hand through it self-consciously. It had grown out quite a bit over the last month, especially since he was about to get it buzzed again before all this had happened. But still, if David liked it longer, maybe he would leave it that way.

Connor wasn't the only one who had changed. There was something different about David too. He stood taller, held his head higher. The self-confidence that made brief appearances in Florida had made its way to Kansas. If it was here to stay, Connor would have more trouble than usual keeping his hands to himself. Then again, maybe David wouldn't need him anymore.

David's face softened. "I missed you so much!" he said and threw himself into Connor's arms.

Of course David still needed him, but maybe now, all he would need was love and not protection. They stood and held each other until an officer asked them to move along. Connor was happy to oblige. He kept his arm around David as they walked to the car, only separating so they could climb inside.

"Tell me everything," Connor said. "Gordon told me you were in the hospital. He said something about you bashing the hell out of Chuck's car with a baseball bat!"

"Don't worry. I drove by the other day, and he already has a new car."

Connor laughed. "Then I'll buy you a new bat. Hey, how did you know when I was getting out?"

"I called your family. Then I begged and pleaded with them to let me pick you up alone." David flashed him an insecure smile, proving he hadn't completely changed. "I thought it would be romantic. Just like in the movies."

"That it is," Connor agreed.

"So should we head over there so you can see everyone?"

"No!" Connor said. "I mean, later, but right now … Is your dad home?"

"Ah," David said knowingly. "That's the part they *don't* put in the movies."

"Well, I've been locked in a cell with five other dudes, and there wasn't a lot of privacy. Aside from a couple days in solitary confinement, I haven't had a chance to deal with those carnal urges."

"Solitary confinement?" David stared at him before laughing. "Sabrina was right. Jailbirds are hot!"

As soon as they were back at David's place, Connor was happy to prove just how hot he was. He couldn't get enough of David's lips, their kisses stopping only a fraction of a second so they could strip off their shirts. Then they pressed their skin together, their bodies so hungry for each other that even this simple sensation was pure bliss. Their long separation made it feel like the first time all over again—but with the benefit of experience. Now Connor knew how David liked him to gently run his teeth along his neck, gently nibbling him there before tonguing his ear.

And David knew how sensitive Connor's back was, how brushing fingertips along his muscles would send tingles up and down his spine. Connor pulled David close, hanging on to him as they fell backwards onto the bed. He let David remain on top, his weight a welcome reminder that all this was real and not some prison fantasy. They tasted each other's lips over and over, their crotches grinding together. Connor could feel the head of his cock poking out from his jeans, so he rolled over on top of David before grabbing one of his hands and guiding it down.

Connor raised his hips so David could get to the button and zipper. Once his jeans were pulled down far enough, he kicked his legs free of them. Then he climbed upward, writhing as David's hand stroked him, and continuing up until he reached David's mouth. The tip of his dick brushed against David's lips before they parted. Then Connor began thrusting, the sensation sending him on a high that he never wanted to end.

Soon Connor missed their bodies being close together and scooted back down. David had undone his own jeans and was playing with himself, which wouldn't do at all. He'd had all month to do that. Now that they were together again, there was no need. Connor helped David out of his jeans, then took one of David's feet, tickling the underside before kissing his big toe. He smiled as David laughed, then added another kiss on top of his foot. Then his ankle, his calf, his knee, and a couple on the inside of his thigh. Connor let David squirm in anticipation before taking him into his mouth, the familiar taste and scent spurring him on. He worked single-mindedly until David placed his hands on his shoulders and pushed him away.

"I want all of you," he said.

Connor looked into those tender brown eyes and would have given him anything in that moment. Luckily, he and David wanted the exact same thing. He grabbed the lube from the side of the bed and squirted some on both of them, spreading it with tight strokes. They moaned and exchanged half-lidded gazes of pleasure before Connor placed himself between David's legs.

He was gentle, as he always was. They were both out of practice, but soon found their rhythm. Usually Connor would hold himself up and look down at David's face. That got him off just as much as the physical sensations did. This time, David had his own needs. He pulled Connor close, squeezing their bodies together. Even when Connor's full weight was relaxed on him, it didn't seem to be enough. David tangled his legs around Connor, desperate for them to become one, now and forever.

Connor's face was buried in David's hair when he felt him tense and come between their stomachs. Connor only lasted another minute after that, feeling like he was gushing an ocean. Then, worried that he was crushing David, he rolled them both over on their sides. He pulled away just enough to clearly see David's face and caressed his cheek with a thumb.

"I love you," Connor said.

David laughed, as if this were the most obvious thing in the world. Connor supposed it was.

"It wouldn't have been so bad if they had locked us up together," David said.

They were still in bed, the covers pulled up to their armpits, having spent the last hour talking and trying different positions. Sometimes David had his head on Connor's chest. Other times they spooned. Right now they faced each other, heads propped up on elbows.

"I would have preferred the hospital," Connor said. "At least you had movies to watch. And a buffet for every meal would have been killer."

"The movies were all old," David said. "Besides, they didn't try doping you up in jail."

"You would have hated it there."

"We could have been bunkmates!"

Connor chuckled. "Well, next time we get into trouble, hopefully you'll be old enough to do time with me. Won't that be nice?"

"I call top bunk."

"Fine, but that's the only time you get to be on top!"

David grinned. "I wouldn't have it any other way."

Connor stretched, flopping onto his back. "We should probably get showered and dressed. I want to hit a toy store before we see my family, find something for Tommy that looks like it's from out of state."

"Like what?"

"No clue."

"Speaking of which," David said, "what are we going to do?"

"Do?"

"Well, we *were* on the verge of moving to Florida."

Connor gave him an incredulous look. "I'm on probation."

"And I'm on diversion," David said.

"What's that?"

"It's like probation for kids. Isn't that cute?"

"No, but it's even more reason for us to stay. We're grounded in Kansas—at least for a while. After all we've just been through, do you really want to break the law by crossing state lines?"

David thought about it for a moment. He could look like such an angel at moments like these. Then he nodded, a devilish grin destroying the illusion.

"Yes," he said. "That's exactly what I want to do."

Epilogue

David was graduating and wished he wasn't. Well, sort of. He was ecstatic that high school was just moments away from being over. Forever. He just wished he was graduating from Seabreeze High School in Florida. He imagined the students there had to surf across the waves to collect their diplomas from a parasailing principal. Then they probably rode dolphins into the sunset while sipping banana daiquiris.

Instead, David was in the same dingy Olathe South gymnasium that Connor had graduated from. They did return to Florida, but not until Connor's probation was over six months after his release. That had been in late January, David skipping a few days of class to make a long weekend, which they used to escape the Kansas winter. They celebrated Connor's birthday there with his sister. The locals thought the weather was cold—the beaches all but abandoned—but David still managed to get a sunburn in the middle of winter.

Being in the Sunshine State again reminded David of how much he wanted to get away, but he had to consider his father's feelings. David couldn't live with his dad forever, but he could give him one final year. Of course it didn't help that his father and Connor had teamed up. Connor became Mr. You-Have-to-Finish-High-School, while David's father remained Mr. Oh-Look-Another-Letter-From-An-Interested-College. Helpless against this twin barrage of wills, David had buckled down and decided to get through one more year.

"David Henry!"

He hopped out of the cold metal seat, which hadn't had time to get warm. At least his last name came relatively early in the alphabet. He heard a respectable amount of cheering too. As he made his way down the aisle, he glanced over at his miniature fan club. His father was there, high on education and cheering his head off. He wasn't quite as loud as Tommy, who was riding on Connor's shoulders and screaming like a banshee. Next to them was Gordon, yelling with the mad passion of a brainwashed cultist and decked out in one of the school's letter jackets.

Last year's crazy summer had the most dramatic effect on Gordon. While Connor was locked up in jail and David was matching wits with Dr. Wolf, Gordon was in the midst of his own rebellion. Gordon had argued all summer with his parents to let him go to public school. David never understood why. He would have thought that nearly getting beaten up by Chuck would have scarred him for life, but instead Gordon seemed to have something to prove.

After enough pressure from their son, Gordon's parents finally agreed. David had entered his senior year with a very nervous junior clinging to him. In a way, that made facing another year of institutional hell much easier. David was so concerned for Gordon's safety that he barely had time to consider his own. Not that he needed to worry. After the first month, Gordon had adjusted fairly well. He never really understood when people were making fun of him, which gave him the reputation of having thick skin. Unable to get a rise out of him, most quit trying.

Now Gordon behaved as if he had found the greatest video game of all time. He navigated the hallways like they were a dungeon map, collected good grades like experience points, and had even found treasure in the form of a girlfriend. She was only a freshman and wore glasses that made her eyes appear huge, but it had been love at first scoff. Gordon had asked if she played the Dragon Death games, and she had scoffed when learning that he didn't play the original Japanese versions.

And of course Chuck was still there and just as miserable as before, but he stayed away from David. The only time they ever spoke was when David caught him giving Gordon a hard time.

"I gave him my old baseball bat," David said to Chuck in the hall shortly afterwards. "Not that he'll need it. He's on the school newspaper and working on an article about bullies who compensate for personal issues. Things like wetting the bed, fear of abandonment … or hiding something they feel ashamed about. It's up to you if he publishes it or not." Chuck hadn't exactly cowered at David's words, but he did back off.

And now it was graduation day. David danced up the steps to the principal, winked at the man, grabbed his diploma, and headed for the doors. His family and friends would follow. David wasn't staying for any sentimental speech. Meeting Connor was the only good thing that had happened to him here.

Walking into the evening air, he let out a sigh of relief. He was free. Really and truly free. For the next year at least. David would go to college, but only because he had some good scholarships and wasn't sure what else he wanted to do. The University of Florida had accepted him, which meant that he could finally live where he wanted. His father had made peace with that, although he still left the occasional Stanford brochure for David to find.

But all that was the future. He and Connor were moving to Florida, and by this time next year, David would qualify for in-state tuition. In the meantime, David would enjoy a blissful, directionless year of doing nothing but living in sin with his boyfriend. Speaking of which—

He spun around just as the double doors banged open. Connor came first with Tommy still on his shoulders, his younger brother wearing a jack-o-lantern smile.

"You sure hightailed it out of there," Connor said.

"I told you I didn't want to go."

"Funny," Connor said. "I remember not wanting to go last year, but someone made me."

David smirked. "I didn't *make* you. I just encouraged you with my puppy dog eyes."

"You have a puppy?" Tommy asked.

"No. I'm just good at imitating one." David barked and pawed at the air for his amusement. His father and Gordon came through the doors next, looking puzzled at this behavior.

"Well, at least we beat the crowds," his father said. "Who's hungry? It's on me tonight!"

There was a chorus of agreement.

"We can't stay out too late," David said. "Connor and I have an early start tomorrow."

"You aren't driving to Florida," his father said sternly.

David's jaw dropped open. "What? Of course we are! You've known about this for months!"

His father shook his head. "It isn't safe. With all due respect, Connor, your car isn't likely to make it to Missouri without breaking down."

"My car *is* on its last legs, so to speak." Connor said sadly. "It overheated twice on the way over here. I guess we're screwed."

"What?" David's head whipped back and forth between them. What new conspiracy was this?

"It isn't safe," his father repeated. "I forbid you to ride in Connor's car again. *But*, I suppose you could make it to Florida in record time with this." He held up the key to the family car before tossing it to David.

He should have caught it, but hand-eye coordination was never David's strong suit. He fumbled it and bent to pick the key up off the ground.

"You're giving me your car?" he asked in disbelief.

"Well, it is getting old. I could use a new one."

David laughed. "It's only a few years old."

"And it's paid off," his father said wistfully, but then he smiled. "This means you're coming back here on holidays. Understood, young man?"

"Understood. Thanks, Dad."

"So what did we decide for dinner?"

Gordon was at David's elbow. "Joe's Crab Shack," he whispered, sounding desperate.

David pursed his lips. "That would be the seafood restaurant where the poor waiters have to sing and dance every twenty minutes?" It also just happened to be where Gordon's girlfriend worked. "Sounds ideal!"

"Then it's a date!" Gordon said with a little too much enthusiasm.

"When Connor and David get married," Tommy chimed in, "will that mean that David's dad and my dad are married too?"

"Not quite," David's father said, before trying to explain to him the concept of in-laws. Gordon was checking his hair in a pocket mirror, smoothing it back with a little spit, and Connor looked exasperated as Tommy interrupted to ask how two boys could have a baby. Then Connor caught David's eye and smiled. In that moment, David couldn't be happier with his perfectly dysfunctional family.

David awoke to the roar of the ocean and the scent of salt water in the air. When he woke up a little more, he realized the waves were the sound of an ancient vacuum cleaner and that the salty air smelled more like pancakes. Still, as mornings went, it had promise. The sun was already burning bright, as it did most days in Florida. Just when David grew sick of the sunshine, a wild storm would roll into Daytona to mix things up. He knew these weather events didn't happen just for him, but Florida felt like his own little paradise regardless.

David's contentment didn't come solely from the weather. High school and all of its hard lessons were behind him. Gordon had a new life and wouldn't be lonely. David's father was coping too, sending daily emails that mostly dealt with college curriculum strategy. In one email, his father joked about getting a job transfer to the University of Florida, just to keep an eye on him. At least David thought it was a joke.

Connor had taken a job cooking at the restaurant where Tracy worked. The chef there was a nightmare, and Connor often came home tired and swearing he would never cook again. But by the next morning he was usually at the stove, helping the grannies with breakfast. His passion for cooking couldn't be extinguished completely. David expected he'd keep at it until one day he became a chef himself.

A career sounded like an appealing prospect to David. He wanted to get a job and earn a little cash, but Connor insisted that he enjoy this one year off. It was hard to argue against sleeping in late and lounging around the house.

How far they had come! Almost a year ago, they had both been locked up, their future uncertain. But now they were building a life together. The world still brought problems and no doubt would try to shake them up, but David didn't believe they could ever be separated again. They had grown too strong together.

David lay in bed and thought over the crazy times they had been through, his thoughts lingering on Sabrina. He had called her once things had settled down, but her cell phone had been disconnected. He wrote her an email too but had never heard back—until last week. Funny how the past could catch up so unexpectedly. David reached for the laptop next to the bed. It belonged to Tracy, but he was always stealing it away from her. Bringing the machine out of sleep mode, he reread the email.

David,

I'm sooooo sorry I never wrote you back. I wanted to, believe me. Shawn and I were laying low until we were both eighteen. Not that I didn't trust you, but you never know who is reading your mail. Anyway, in case you never heard, when I went to the family reunion with my parents, I played it cool for about an hour before I jacked their car. Can you believe it? I wish there had been a wild police chase or something, but there wasn't. I ditched the car close to Shawn's place, and the rest is history. We've been in Chicago ever since. For a while it was rough, but Shawn landed a great job a few months ago so we're doing better. As for me, brace yourself! I'm pregnant! If it's a boy, maybe we'll name him David. Or Connor. Ha ha! I hope you and your jailbird managed to fly away together. I'm dying to hear from you!

Your girlfriend,

Sabrina

David still hadn't answered her email, so he started to now. But then the door opened and Connor came in, already showered and dressed. David tensed and waited for the inevitable.

Connor saw his reaction and laughed. "Don't worry, I'm not going to say it."

"Good."

"Do you have any wishes, though?"

David mulled it over. "Birthday sex?"

"Ha! Maybe later. The grannies expect you to eat cake for breakfast, and my sister is climbing the walls to give you your present."

"I need a shower."

"Better hurry!"

Once David was downstairs, he was assaulted by hug-hungry women. Well, Margie gave him a playful slug to the shoulder, and while it hurt, he knew she meant well.

Breakfast was everything but cake. Eggs, toast, pancakes, hash browns, sausages, even a fruit salad. Anna had probably started cooking as soon as he went to sleep the night before. Halfway through his meal his plate was shoved aside by a present.

"Happy birthday!" Tracy crooned.

"I thought we weren't allowed to say it," Margie grumped.

"Well, she has now," Anna said, "so happy birthday, David!"

"Sorry." Connor grinned from across the table. "I coached them as best I could."

"It's okay," David said. Anything was forgivable when presents were involved.

"That's from all three of us," Tracy said.

"Thanks." David sheepishly unwrapped the present, feeling a little confused when he saw it was a GPS unit. "Nice," he said. "I love gadgets. Thanks!"

"You don't even know what it's for," Tracey teased.

"Speaking of which—" Anna hopped to her feet and rushed out of the room. When she came back, she was carrying the promised cake, candles ablaze. Tracy started singing first, her voice not much better than her brother's. Then the others joined in. Only after David made a wish and blew out the candles did he notice the number written in frosting.

"But I'm eighteen," he said.

"Nope." Connor came over and stole a quick kiss. "You said you'd always be my Sweet Sixteen."

"Aaaaw," Tracy said, doing her best impression of a studio audience.

"Which piece do you want, dear?" Anna asked. "This one? Okay! I'll get it packed up so you can take it with you."

The puzzle pieces clicked together. The GPS and cake on the move. Connor was taking him on another trip!

David looked at Connor, his sly expression all the answer he needed. "Where are we going?"

"To work," Connor answered, throwing him for a loop. "Come outside. I'll show you my present."

Outside? It's not like they needed a new car, so it couldn't be that. A pony? What else would need to be outside? As a group, they stumbled out of the house, Tracy trying to squeeze through the door at the same time David did. Outside was a huge eighteen-wheeler parked along the curb. Connor was standing next to the semi truck, like he owned it.

"Come see the world with me," he said. "Or at least the United States."

"That's yours?" David asked in disbelief.

Connor laughed. "I wish. No, this is my job, at least for the next year. You once told me that you wished we could always be on the road together."

"Now you can be!" Tracy said, slapping him on the back. "I'm so envious. If only I could find someone so romantic … who wasn't my brother. Or a dude."

"You're all packed up and ready to go," Margie said, dropping a suitcase next to David and nearly crushing his foot.

"Come here!" Anna gave him a hug and a Tupperware container full of cake before she and Margie disappeared indoors.

Then Tracy assaulted David, getting him in a headlock, but after a gentle noogie she let go and hugged him. "I always wanted a little brother," she said dramatically.

"You have two," David reminded her.

"Yeah, but a little brother I actually like." She looked him over and shrugged. "Maybe someday I'll find one." She winked and went back inside the house.

Connor watched him for a moment, David meeting his gaze, not shying away from its intensity. Then Connor strolled toward him. He was sure they were going to head back upstairs to the bedroom, but Connor stopped in front of him and took his hand. "What do you think?"

"I'm completely lost," David said. "What about your cooking job?"

"More of an internship. I'll have time enough for that later. You have the next year off, and I wanted to show you more of the country. Of course that's expensive, so I thought this way it would be paid for, *and* we'll earn money on the way. Uh, is this the dumbest idea ever?"

David, tears rising, did the manly thing and forced them back. "Not at all!"

Connor smiled. "Come check it out! It's an older truck, but it has a bed, lots of storage room, even a little refrigerator. Tracy loaned me her old portable TV too."

After a grand tour and a little preliminary groping on the small bed, David crawled into the cab's passenger seat, bouncing up and down to test the springs. The seats were much more comfortable than those of a car, designed for hours and hours of butt-numbing sitting. The only thing he didn't like about them was the space between him and the driver's seat, but David could imagine sitting on the floor with his head in Connor's lap for an on the road nap. Or other things.

"You ready?" Connor asked.

"Yeah!"

The engine came to life with a rumble of thunder. David held his breath as Connor put the truck into gear. Slowly, they cruised out of the neighborhood and onto one of the larger roads.

"Where are we going?"

"All sorts of places," Connor said. "The first route takes us through Texas and over to California."

"What about Chicago?" David asked. "I have friends there."

Connor nodded. "We're hitting Chicago, but not before we pass through Kansas."

"Wait until my dad sees. He'll flip!"

"In a good way, I hope."

David grinned. "And to think what shameless criminals we were last year—trashing McDonald's and assaulting bullies. Now look at us! Playing by the rules and living a respectable life."

Connor cleared his throat. "Almost."

David stared at him. "What do you mean *almost*?"

"Well, I did lie about my age. You have to be twenty-one to haul across state lines."

"You lied to the company that hired you?"

"No!" Connor said, as if this were unthinkable. "I lied to the DMV when I got my commercial driver's license. And it wasn't a lie, really. Just a little forgery on my birth certificate."

They looked at each other and laughed as the truck turned onto the highway. Then Connor reached over, bridging the gap between them, and took his hand. David looked at him as if for the first time—at the muscles of his neck decorated by the scar of his past, the broad shoulders that would bear any burden for him, and the wild green eyes that always searched his soul. But beneath all of this was the gentlest heart that David had ever known. Right now Connor appeared hopeful, maybe a little uncertain. He looked at David, grinned sheepishly, and said:

"David and Connor conquer America. Are you ready for this?"

David was quiet a moment, considering the endless road ahead and all the adventures that awaited them. Then he leapt out of his seat and answered Connor with a kiss.

Also by Jay Bell:

Something Like Summer

Love, like everything in the universe, cannot be destroyed. But over time it can change.

The hot Texas nights were lonely for Ben before his heart began beating to the rhythm of two words; Tim Wyman. By all appearances, Tim had the perfect body and ideal life, but when a not-so-accidental collision brings them together, Ben discovers that the truth is rarely so simple. If winning Tim's heart was an impossible quest, keeping it would prove even harder as family, society, and emotion threaten to tear them apart.

Something Like Summer is a love story spanning a decade and beyond as two boys discover what it means to be friends, lovers, and sometimes even enemies. This full-length, gay romance novel is available in paperback, Kindle, Nook, and other eBook formats.

For more information, please see:
www.jaybellbooks.com

Also by Jay Bell:

The Cat in the Cradle

To set out into the world, to be surrounded by the unknown and become a stranger. Only then would he be free to reinvent himself. Or fall in love.

Dylan wanted one last adventure before the burden of adulthood was thrust upon him. And to confront the man he hadn't spoken to since their intimate night together. Stealing a boat with his faithful companion Kio, their journey is cut short when they witness a brutal murder. A killer is loose in the Five Lands and attacking the most powerful families. Dylan--a potential target--seeks sanctuary from an unpredictable bodyguard named Tyjinn. Together they decide to turn the tables by hunting the killer down. Along the way, everything Dylan thought he knew about himself will be challenged, but if he survives, he stands to win the love he never dreamed possible.

The Cat in the Cradle is the first book in the Loka Legends series and features twenty-five original illustrations created by Andreas Bell, the author's husband.

For more information, please visit:
www.jaybellbooks.com

CPSIA information can be obtained
at www.ICGtesting.com
Printed in the USA
LVOW12s2012271017

554039LV00005B/547/P